Dear Friends,

When I wrote my very first published novel—*Restoring Love*—back in 1981, it was set in Charleston, South Carolina, one of my all-time favorite cities. It seems fitting somehow that I'm returning to Charleston for *The Backup Plan*, my 100th book. And since, in the intervening years, I've grown fond of writing series, it seems even more appropriate that this is the start of a trilogy set in this wonderful Southern locale.

Many of you will be reading *The Backup Plan* in winter, when there's snow on the ground and a definite chill in the air, but trust me when I tell you that Dinah Davis and Cordell Beaufort will stir up some heat for you. From the moment I "met" them, they were steaming up my reading glasses as I sat in front of the computer.

Dinah's a woman at a crossroads in her life, an intrepid foreign correspondent who's been through too much and is very close to coming unglued. Cord is one of those laid-back bad boys we all dream about, but at his core he's one of the genuine good guys. For Dinah he may turn out to be her greatest risk ever, but he definitely promises to offer the greatest reward.

I hope you'll enjoy visiting South Carolina's Low Country so much that you'll be anxiously awaiting Maggie's story—*Flirting with Disaster*—in December 2005, just in time to warm up to your holiday season.

All good wishes,

Sherryl

the Backup Plan

Sherryl Woods

MIRA

ISBN 0-7783-2149-5

THE BACKUP PLAN

www.MIRABooks.com

Printed in U.S.A.

1

Her producer was tiptoeing around bad news. Dinah could see it in his eyes, hear it in his voice. After a decade of working in TV journalism with basically the same news team, she'd learned to recognize the signs.

Ray Mitchell was an outstanding producer, but he was lousy at subtle communication. Barking out directives was more his style. In fact, he belonged in another era, one of hard-drinking, cigar-smoking journalists and legendary war correspondents such as Ernie Pyle, Edward R. Murrow, Walter Cronkite and Dan Rather. They had brought battle coverage to new heights through shrewd performances. Watching Ray try to sheepishly soft-pedal whatever was on his mind was painful.

"What is it you're trying so hard not to tell me?" she finally asked. "Is there something wrong with the piece I just turned in? It was a great interview."

The pictures had been good, too, even if they weren't as great as her previous cameraman's would have been. But they were better than adequate.

Ray looked even more uncomfortable. "For somebody else, maybe," he said with the familiar bluntness Dinah had always respected. "Not for you."

On some level Dinah had been anticipating that comment. Still, she stared at him in shock. She wasn't used to being even gently criticized for her work. The many years of accolades from her colleagues in the field and her superiors in their lofty New York towers made her expect praise. "What are you saying, Ray? Just spit it out."

It was hot as blazes without air-conditioning in their makeshift newsroom, but Dinah knew that wasn't the reason Ray needed to mop his round face with a handkerchief. He was so nervous that he looked miserable.

"Okay," he said eventually. "You want the truth, here it is. You've lost your edge, Dinah. It's understandable, given what happened a few months ago, but—"

Dinah tuned him out. Nobody ever mentioned the incident in front of her anymore. Not being able to talk about what had happened had been difficult for Dinah. Whenever she brought up the subject of that tragic nightmare, everyone's eyes filled with pity as they murmured soothing nonsense and then cut off any further discussion.

That was partly because for weeks after the episode, Dinah had listened dry-eyed to everyone's sympathy or made the kind of impersonal, caustic comments that all reporters made to keep their fears and grief at bay. They'd all taken their cues from her and had stopped discussing it. Now that she was finally able and eager to talk, their grieving was over and they didn't want to be reminded that only through the grace of God had they not been on that deadly roadside. They no longer wanted to face their own mortality, or consider the risks inherent in this hellish assignment.

War correspondents were a special breed of journalists. The burnout rate was high for those who favored ambition over self-preservation.

"They're asking questions in New York," Ray continued.

That got her attention. "What kind of questions?" she asked testily. She'd grown complacent about the network's hands-off approach to most of her pieces.

"They want to know whether you shouldn't be taking a break, you know, just until you've had time to deal with what happened," Ray said carefully. "You're due some time off, anyway. More than a little, in fact. No one can remember the last time you took a vacation."

Her stomach sank. A break was the last thing she needed. Work defined her. It motivated her to get out of bed in the morning. Turning in one supposedly subpar interview when she'd given them dozens of prizewinners and nearly single-handedly earned the upstart cable news operation industry-wide respect deserved better than this treatment.

"I don't need time off," she said flatly. "I need to keep working."

"How about a different assignment then?" Ray suggested. "Go to the London bureau for a while. Or Paris. Maybe even Miami. Now there's a cushy one. Sunshine, palm trees and beaches."

The image didn't impress her. In the days immediately following what she still thought of as the "incident," she'd considered quitting. But then she had realized that this was the only work she truly wanted to do. If it was harder, if she was scared every minute of every day, she was determined to overcome her fears. Now when she walked out of the hotel and into uncertainty every single day she considered her actions a personal tribute to the bravery of every correspondent who'd died while making sure that the world had a close-up view of the action.

"Come on, Ray. I'd be wasted in London or Paris. And you can forget about Miami," she said with a shudder. "Covering war is what I do. And I do it better than ninety percent of the other reporters around."

He looked at her with concern. "Until recently you were better than all of them."

"And I will be again," she insisted. "I just need a little time to…" What? Adjust? Not possible. Go on? Maybe. That's what she was aiming for, one day at a time.

"Wouldn't it be better to take that time someplace else?" he asked, trying one more time. "You've paid your dues, Dinah. You were due for a break before any of this happened. We talked about it, remember? I thought you were planning to go home, see your folks. Why not do it now? People rotate in and out of here all the time because nobody can live like this without getting their heads all screwed up. You're not Superman. Why should you be any different?"

Because if she left now, everyone would see it as a sign of weakness, she thought. They would think she'd folded in a crisis and she wouldn't allow anyone to see her that way. She was used to commanding respect.

Ray went right on. "I'd think you'd want a chance to see your family, do something normal for a while. Weren't you looking forward to that?"

She had been, but not any longer. Things had changed too drastically. Working was what she needed to do if she were to remain sane and maintain her self-respect. She wasn't sure she wanted to go home until everyone there had forgotten whatever they'd heard about her. She didn't want to face all the questions back home just yet.

"Not now, dammit!" she said more sharply than she'd intended. "Forget it, Ray! I'm not going anywhere."

Alarm flared in Ray's eyes. "This is what I'm talking about. You never used to snap, no matter how tense things got. You're not yourself, Dinah, and I'm worried about you. I don't want you coming unglued on air one of these days."

She stared at him with sudden understanding. "That's why I've done so few live shots lately, isn't it? You're afraid I'll lose it."

He regarded her with obvious discomfort. "It's a chance I'd rather not take," he admitted. "For your sake, not the network's. I don't give a damn what they think."

She suspected that much was true. Ray had always been an ardent advocate for his team. He babied his reporters and cameramen as if they were his own kids. He'd go to bat for them with the powers-that-be in New York whether it was in his own best interests or not.

Because she had faith in his motives, she deliberately forced herself to calm down before she replied. "You're being an old fussbudget," she accused lightly. "I'm fine. If that changes, if I think I can't do the job anymore, I swear I'll let you know."

Ray looked doubtful. "You've never known your own limits, because you never had to set any for yourself. You did whatever it took."

Listening to him, she felt guilty. If Ray knew what a struggle it was for her to walk out of the hotel on every assignment, he'd be even more adamant about sending her away.

"I still do whatever it takes," she told him, knowing that much was true. It just cost her more. "Come on, Ray. Cut me some slack here."

"That's just it. I have been cutting you a whole lot of slack."

This was another shock, and it was more humiliating than the first. She regarded him with dismay. "What are you talking about? Are you saying I'm not carrying my weight?"

He regarded her with discomfort. "Okay, here's the plain, unvarnished truth. And listen up, because you need to hear this. We've missed some stories, Dinah. Things that never should have gotten past us. Everyone up top has been ignoring it, because of the circumstances, but they're getting impatient back home. It's been a few months now. I'm not going to be able to hold them off much longer. The decision of whether you stay or go could be taken out of my hands...and yours."

Dinah tried to think of stories they'd missed. She hadn't paid that much attention to the competition and what they were reporting. With her contacts, she'd always been so far out in front, she hadn't needed to. Was it possible that the other journalists were taking advantage of her distraction? Maybe so, she admitted truthfully.

"Okay, that stops now," she promised Ray, filled with a renewed sense of determination. "I'll be back on top of things from here on out. If I'm not..."

He met her gaze. "If you're not, you're going home, Dinah," he said flatly. "Whether it's what you want or not."

The unflinching warning shook her as nothing had in weeks. "It won't come to that," she said grimly.

All she had to do was push those godawful images out of her head and focus on the here and now. She'd put aside horror in order to do her job a thousand times through the years.

She could do it again, she told herself staunchly. She was going to get it together and come back better than ever. She owed it to the viewers who counted on her to tell an honest, objective story on the nightly news. She owed it to the network that had given her a chance when she was barely out of journalism school.

Most of all, though, she owed it to herself. Without this job, who the hell was she?

Two weeks after her conversation with Ray, the sound of her cell phone ringing at 4:00 a.m. sent Dinah diving under her hotel bed. It wasn't the first time she'd become skittish over nothing, but the incidents were becoming more frequent and more dramatic.

So were the nightmares that woke her in a cold sweat. She hadn't had a decent night's sleep in weeks. It didn't take a genius to tell her she was suffering from post-traumatic stress syndrome, but she'd been convinced she could weather it on her own through sheer will. It wasn't working.

Eventually, she crawled out from under the bed, still shaking, and sat on the floor in the dark with her knees pulled up to her chest, waiting for the worst of the panic to ease.

Maybe Ray was right. Maybe she couldn't continue working right now. But what could she do instead?

Home. When Ray had mentioned it, she'd been dismissive, but now she recognized a surprising hint of longing whenever she thought of that simple word. She had always thought of home with a sort of detached nostalgia. Home was where she came from, not where she wanted to be. Just a couple of weeks ago, she'd hated the idea of returning.

Suddenly, though, the images of South Carolina Low Country were appealing. Trees draped with Spanish moss, and the sultry summer air thick with the scent of honeysuckle seemed idyllic. It was certainly as far removed from the tumultuous, horrific world of Afghanistan as she could possibly imagine.

Not that she'd appreciated it all that much when she'd been growing up on the outskirts of Charleston in what she'd considered little better than a mosquito-infested swamp. She'd hated the slow pace, the unhurried speech, the steamy nights when it was almost impossible to catch a decent breath of air. She hadn't been able to leave her overprotective parents quickly enough.

Being the debutante daughter of Dorothy Rawlings Davis, a woman able to trace her roots back to the first ship to dock in Charleston, and Marshall Davis, a man whose granddaddy had amassed a fortune in South Carolina banking, gave Dinah a skewed view of her own importance. She'd been wise enough to recognize that and to rebel against it. Her brother hadn't been so lucky. He'd drifted along, not only in his daddy's shadow, but that of all their proud ancestors. Tommy Lee had nothing he could point to with pride and call his own.

Dinah hadn't been content to inherit her place in the world. She'd wanted to make one for herself. She'd needed to prove that she was as capable, as independent and as fiercely strong as the toughest of her ancestors. She wanted to be a successful woman first, a Southern woman second. Anyone who'd grown up in the South knew there was a difference.

She'd chosen television journalism for a career because it was a profession with noble ideals, and she'd taken assignments that had placed her in the line of danger just to prove that she could stand tall next to the brightest and best in her field. It wasn't enough to be good. She was determined to be outstanding, the correspondent viewers relied on for learning the truth behind the headlines.

For ten years Dinah had accomplished exactly that by covering unfolding events in Chechnya, the Middle East, and lately Pakistan and Afghanistan. Whenever or wherever news was being made, Dinah was there.

Her last assignments had been the most challenging. It had been impossible to calculate the risks, impossible to find trustworthy sources, impossible to predict whether she would live long enough to get the story on the air. Many said it took a danger junkie to accept such assignments, but she'd never seen herself that way. She simply had a job to do. The risks were worth it because events that unfolded without the glare of news cameras often led to untold horrors and chilling secrecy.

Yet in all of her thirty-one years she'd never had such terrifying dreams. She figured she'd come too close to the edge and seen too much. She'd lost friends this time, some of the best and brightest in the business. That had sucked the life right out of her.

Maybe Ray had been right. Maybe it was time—past time—for her to go home. There was nothing left to prove here.

As she crouched beside her hotel room bed after being frightened by the unexpected ring of a phone, her heart finally slowed to a more normal rhythm. In that instant she realized that she couldn't get home fast enough. If she stayed here any longer, she'd come completely unglued.

* * *

Later that morning when Dinah told Ray what she'd decided, she was hurt to see relief and not regret in his eyes.

"It's for the best," he assured her.

"It's not forever," she replied because she needed to believe it. "A few weeks, a couple of months at most."

Ray got up and closed the door, then gestured for her to sit down. "Listen to me, Dinah. You get back to South Carolina and make a place for yourself. Get a job at the local station. Be their superstar. Find yourself a good man. Settle down and raise a family. This is no life."

"It's *my* life," she protested, horrified by what he was suggesting. It was too damn close to anonymity and suffocation.

"Not anymore," Ray insisted. "I've seen it happen before. An excellent reporter goes through a close call, sees someone they know die right in front of them, whatever, and they start cutting back on the risks. They're a little more hesitant, they play it a little safer. Or they do the opposite and turn into some sort of rogue I can't control. Either way, a reporter like that is no good to me."

Anger filled her at the grim picture he presented. "Are you saying I'll never be able to do this job again?"

"Never as well," he said bluntly. "You're beautiful and smart and talented. Put all of that to work for you back home. If not in South Carolina, then at the network in New York or Washington. I can get a transfer authorized anytime you say the word. Find yourself a real life and live it. What we do over here, it's necessary, but it's not living. It's courting death."

"Are you telling me this just because I'm a woman?" she asked heatedly. "That's a little sexist even for you."

"Maybe so," he admitted candidly. "Mostly, though, I'm telling you this stuff because I like you. I want to know you're out there somewhere safe and happy. I don't ever want to have to make the same call to your folks that I've had to make to other reporters' relatives."

Dinah drew in a deep breath and asked him the question that was burning in her gut. "Spell it out for me, Ray. Are you telling me I can't come back, that you don't want me here?"

Ray hesitated before replying. "No," he said with obvious reluctance. "The network would have my head for saying this, but I'm telling you I hope like hell you won't."

He regarded her with a worried frown. "Listen to me, okay? Think about what I'm saying. You've done the heroics, proved whatever you set out to prove to yourself. You're a top-notch journalist, one of the best, but maybe it's time to stop and figure out who Dinah Davis really is."

Her stomach sank. She thought she had figured that out the day she turned in her first television news report. Now this man she trusted was telling her she'd gotten it wrong.

"Then you think I should quit?" she asked, hating the fact that her respect for him ran so deep that she was actually considering doing as he asked.

"Yes," he said firmly. "Get a real life, Dinah."

She tried to picture the peaceful, ordinary life he was describing. The image eluded her. "You actually think I'm destined to be somebody's wife and mother?" she asked.

"Why the hell not?"

"And if I decide that what I am is a foreign correspondent, that it's all I was ever meant to be?"

He gave her a sad look. "Then I pity you."

"It's what you've done all your life," she reminded him.

"And look at me. No wife. No family. No one who gives a damn whether I come home or not. That's not a fate I'd wish on you. Isn't there someone back home you think about from time to time, some man who got away?"

Dinah started to shake her head, but then an image of Bobby Beaufort appeared in her mind. She couldn't stop the smile that spread across her face. It had been ages since she'd thought about Bobby. He'd been in her life almost as far back as she could remember. He'd wanted to marry her, but she'd turned him down to chase after her dream.

"There," Ray said triumphantly. "I knew it!"

"He was no one special," Dinah insisted. "Just a friend."

A good friend who'd promised to be around if she ever got tired of roaming the globe. If she was ready for love, she was supposed to turn to Bobby. She would always own a piece of his heart, at least that's what he'd claimed. All she had to do was come home, say the word and they'd be married before she could say Las Vegas. That was what they'd agreed when she left town. He was her safety net, her backup plan. She'd never expected to need him.

She didn't need him now, she asserted silently. All this stuff Ray was saying meant nothing. She'd straighten herself out and come back here...eventually.

In the meantime, though, she met Ray's worried gaze. "Okay, then," she said at last. "I quit. I suppose there's no point in doing this by half measures."

She said it halfheartedly, but Ray gave her an encouraging smile.

"Good for you, Dinah! It's the right thing to do."

Maybe so, she thought despondently, but just in case she'd made a huge mistake, maybe the first thing she ought to do when she got back to South Carolina was look up Bobby Beaufort. Maybe he was meant to save her from the kind of lonely life Ray was describing. She'd know when she saw him.

Bobby had never made her palms sweat or her pulse race, but he was a good guy. Soothing and dependable, he'd never, ever let her down. In fact, his sweet attentiveness had nearly suffocated her, but maybe she'd changed. Maybe she was ready for someone to lavish her with love and attention.

She thought of that and her lips curved once more. Yes, indeed, a woman who'd just impulsively quit her dream job needed to keep her options open.

2

After four dinner parties in a row to welcome her home, Dinah called a halt.

"Mother, that's enough! I'm pretty sure there's not a soul in Charleston, at least in certain social circles, who doesn't know I'm back in town."

Dorothy Davis regarded her with dismay. "Just one more," she coaxed. "A few people from the committee to save Covington Plantation." Her eyes suddenly lit up. "In fact, Dinah, if you'd give a little talk, we could turn it into an impromptu fund-raiser. I'm sure people would be fascinated with all your adventures. And these renovations are going to cost a fortune. Wouldn't it be wonderful if we could work together to raise some additional funds?"

Dinah glanced at her mother. Her adventures were precisely what she was trying to forget. If Dinah tried to explain that to Dorothy it would heighten her mother's overprotectiveness. It had taken her several unnerving calls months ago to convince her mother that she was fine and that there was nothing for her to worry about. Apparently she'd been successful in downplaying what had happened because her mother hadn't mentioned a word about it. Dinah didn't want anything to kick those maternal antennae back onto alert now.

She tried another tactic.

"Haven't your friends pumped me for every bit of information they'd care to hear, Mother? No one wants to know what it's really like over there." Dinah was a hundred percent certain of that. "It's not great dinner table conversation," she added. "They're content knowing it's happening on the other side of the world."

"Not everyone here is shallow, darling," her mother scolded. "You've always sold us short."

Dinah sighed. It was true. She had. But she'd heard nothing since coming back to change her impression of her parents' friends. They lived in their monied, insulated world and were happy enough if it didn't rain on their golf games.

"Forget the fund-raiser, Mother. I've never been any good at that sort of thing. And please don't plan another dinner party. I came home for some peace and quiet. As it is, I've barely had a minute alone with you or Dad or Tommy Lee and his family." Not that she was all that unhappy about missing out on the questionable joy of being around her brother's children. From what little bit she had seen, they were holy terrors.

Still, there had been precious little of the quiet she'd anticipated. Aside from the dinner parties her mother had held at their house, she'd been trotted out to lunch with her father's business cronies half a dozen times. She had yet to see a single one of her own friends, not that she'd kept in touch with that many of them since she'd left for college.

She wasn't exactly excited about seeing anyone at

all. Every chance she got, she stole off to the solitude of her room or sat in the back garden with an unopened book in her hands. She'd told herself the inertia was only temporary, that she'd snap out of it in a few days, but she was beginning to wonder if it wouldn't be easier just to give in to it.

Judging from the worried frown that creased her mother's otherwise unlined face, Dorothy had taken note of Dinah's reluctance to leave the house.

"Is something going on that you haven't told me?" her mother asked. "Sitting around in this house all day is not like you."

"I don't just sit in the house. Sometimes I sit in the garden."

Her comment drew another chiding look. Dorothy Rawlings Davis had never known what to make of her only daughter. Dinah had scoffed at tradition. Though she'd reluctantly agreed to go through with it for her mother's sake, Dinah had made a mockery of her debutante ball. She'd attended private school under protest and, worse, had chosen to go to college out of state, to New York, no less. It had grated on her father, who'd attended the Citadel and then Clemson, and her mother who'd graduated from the University of Charleston without ever leaving home.

Her brother had thankfully followed tradition or her parents would most likely have died of shame. Dinah's celebrity had allowed them to hold their heads up just a bit higher these last few years. She wondered what they would think if she told them she was thinking of giving it all up forever.

Even at eight o'clock in the morning the vast differences between Dinah and her mother were apparent.

Her mother was wearing an expensive, tailored suit, antique gold jewelry that winked with diamonds, Italian designer pumps, a perfect French manicure and had every strand of her perfectly highlighted hair in place. Dinah wore a favorite pair of old shorts, a halter top and she was barefooted. She hadn't had a manicure or pedicure in years and her hair was cut in a haphazard style that could best be described as wash-and-wear. In less than a week she'd fought off six attempts by her mother to change that with a spa day. When it came to style Dinah was still a bitter disappointment to her socialite mother.

Even so, her mother did seem to be touchingly happy to have her home. Dinah could even understand her desire to cash in on Dinah's reflected celebrity. She wasn't a bit surprised that her mother wasn't taking no for an answer.

"Darling, it's just that you're so rarely here," her mother said. "I want to be sure that everyone gets a chance to see you before you go gallivanting off on your next assignment."

Dinah told herself she should admit that she wasn't going anywhere anytime soon, but she wasn't ready to do that. Silence allowed her to go on pretending that this was a temporary sabbatical. It would be another few weeks before she started to wear on her mother's nerves. Then her parents would start asking the really tough, unanswerable questions about how such a fabulous career had wound up in the toilet. Right now they were proud of her and it was nice to bask in that, at least in small doses.

She forced a smile. "I know, Mother, but let's put it off a few days, okay? Let me catch my breath. I haven't even seen Maggie yet or any of my other friends."

Maggie Forsythe was the one person Dinah truly was anxious to see aside from Bobby. She was the only one Dinah dared to mention. If she uttered a peep about tracking down Bobby Beaufort, her mother would draw the wrong conclusions. The prospect of a wedding was just about the only thing that might distract Dorothy from her daughter's news about being all but kicked out of Afghanistan by her worried boss.

"Okay, if you insist, I'll reschedule for the week after next," her mother finally relented. "You will still be here, right?"

"I'll be here," Dinah assured her.

Satisfied, her mother rounded the dining room table and pressed a kiss to Dinah's cheek. "I'm so glad you're home. Your father and I have missed you."

Dinah's eyes stung at the sentimental tone in her mother's voice. She had always shunned her mother's overt displays of affection, but all of a sudden the little impromptu hugs and kisses made her weepy.

"I have to run. I have a meeting about the renovations at the plantation this morning. It's likely to drag on all day," her mother said. "What will you do today? If you don't have anything in mind, you could come with me and take a look around. We're making excellent progress. I think you'd find it fascinating."

Dinah knew her eyes had probably glazed over at the suggestion, so she tried to feign enthusiasm for her mother's latest pet project. "If you're involved, I know it's bound to be amazing," she said. "I promise to get there, just not today."

Her mother hid her disappointment well, but Dinah

knew she'd hurt her. It had always driven her crazy that Dinah showed no interest in any of her favorite civic or historical preservation projects.

"Okay, then, I'm off," her mother said. "Will you be here for dinner?"

"Of course," Dinah said. "If that changes, I'll call or leave word with Maybelle."

"I'll see you later, then."

When her mother left, the sound of her heels tapping on the hardwood floors, the scent of Chanel lingered in her wake. Dinah felt the tension in her shoulders ease the minute she was finally alone.

Coming home had been harder—and easier—than she'd expected. She'd been welcomed like the prodigal daughter, pampered by their longtime housekeeper, and treated like a celebrity by her family's friends.

The hard part was lying and keeping the pretense that she was just fine, that her career was perfect, her life amazing. She kept it up because she wasn't ready to admit the truth, not to them, not even to herself.

Some days she could convince herself that she *was* fine. As if her body sensed that she was in a safe haven at last, she hadn't had a major panic attack since she'd arrived. The nightmares had even diminished. She'd only awakened a couple of times in a cold sweat with her heart hammering so hard she'd felt it might burst from her chest.

She'd managed to accommodate her parents' meet-and-greet dinners as well as the thankfully brief lunches at her father's club. Increasingly, though, the mere prospect of leaving the house had made her palms turn damp. Although she'd been able to face the possibility of a roadside ambush or a car bomb a mere week ago, she now could barely stand the thought of walking down the comparatively safe, familiar streets of Charleston. She knew that hiding out wasn't smart, or healthy. Nor was it one bit like her. Always full of energy, Dinah was determined to recapture some of her old spirit.

She decided to start by looking for Bobby. It would be good to see him, catch up a little, figure out if there was a single spark that could be fanned into a conflagration that might help her forget what she would have to give up to stay here.

She gathered up her dishes and took them to the kitchen.

Maybelle Jenkins, who'd run the Davis household Dinah's entire life and her mother's family's before that, immediately rushed to take them from her. "What do you think you're doing?" she scolded. "You trying to get me fired? Tidying up is what I do around here."

Dinah grinned at her. "We both know you do a whole lot more than that. You keep this place running. You hold this family together."

Maybelle swept her into a hug, one of many she'd readily dispensed since Dinah's homecoming. "Lordy, but I've missed you. You've been away too long, girl. It's about time you came back to see us. Some of us, we ain't getting any younger, you know."

Though she looked ageless with her smooth brown complexion, Maybelle had to be at least seventy-five. She'd been almost twenty when she'd gone to work for Adelaide Rawlings when Dinah's mother was born. That was fifty-five years ago.

Dinah grinned at her now. "Who're you kidding, Maybelle? You'll outlive all of us."

"Especially if you keep getting in the way of them guns and bombs," the housekeeper chided. "That close call you had 'bout gave me a heart attack. Never saw the sense of you doing such a thing. Thought we raised you to be smarter."

Dinah met the dark brown eyes of the woman who'd been such a constant in her life. A sudden need to unburden herself nearly overwhelmed her. Maybelle had always patiently listened to every one of her childhood hopes, dreams and heartaches.

"Can I tell you something you can't repeat to anyone?" Dinah asked.

"You askin' if I can keep a secret? I've kept enough for you and that brother of yours, don't you think?"

Dinah laughed. "Yes, I suppose you have."

"So what's one more?"

"I might not go back," Dinah said, testing the words.

"Well, praise the Lord and hallelujah!" Maybelle said exuberantly. "That's the best news I've had in years. Why you want to keep such a thing a secret?"

Dinah regarded her sadly. "Is it good news?"

"If it means my baby's gonna be safe, then it's good news to me." She gave Dinah a penetrating look. "You don't seem too happy about it, though. You quit or get yourself fired?"

"I quit, but no one around here's to know that. I don't expect you to lie for me, but hem and haw if anyone asks, at least for now." She gave Maybelle a stern look. "Promise?"

"I gave you my word, didn't I?" She hugged Dinah again. "Whatever's going on with you, you'll work it out. I know how you like to mull things over in that head of yours. But if there comes a time when you need someone to talk to, I'm here, same as always."

"Thank you. I love you."

"And I love you, same as all those children I gave birth to, and those grandbabies and great-grandbabies that are coming along," Maybelle told her. "You're family to me."

Tears welled up in Dinah's eyes. She swiped at them impatiently. "Now you've gone and made me cry," she teased. "I'll have to redo my makeup before I go out in public or Mother will be totally humiliated."

"Since when you put on makeup?" Maybelle asked wryly. "Your mama cares way too much about stuff that don't matter a hoot to anybody but her and those social-climbing women she spends her days with." At Dinah's amused look, Maybelle added, "And don't think I wouldn't say the same thing right to her face. I knew her when she was in diapers, too."

"Ah, Maybelle, you keep telling us like it is. Maybe one of these days we'll all get our priorities sorted out."

Maybelle laughed. "You, maybe, but I think it's too late for that brother of yours. He's fallen into the same pattern as your daddy. They're both so full of themselves it's little wonder they can never see eye to eye on anything." She shooed Dinah toward the door. "Now get along out of here, girl. You might be unemployed, but I'm not. This old house doesn't clean itself and it takes me a mite longer to get around than it used to."

Dinah wandered upstairs, intending to freshen up and change her clothes before heading out in search of Bobby, but she found an old high-school yearbook and got distracted.

By the time she'd closed the book, it was past lunchtime. Still wearing the same old shorts and halter top, she added a pair of sandals, ran a brush through her hair, then begged a sandwich from Maybelle. It was nearly four o'clock when she finally set off to look for Bobby. Maybe once she saw him, some magical something would click and she'd know whether or not she was home to stay. In her experience, though, life was rarely that clear-cut.

All during the tedious meetings at Covington Plantation, Dorothy had been distracted. She couldn't seem to shake the feeling that something was going on with her daughter. Dinah hadn't been herself since she'd arrived home.

Her gentle resistance to all the dinner parties was to be expected. She'd always hated that sort of fuss. But isolating herself in the house and only reluctantly talking about her work made Dorothy think that the close call Dinah had minimized months ago might have taken more of a toll than she'd led them to believe.

Since there was never a chance to talk to Marshall about any of this—or anything else—at home, Dorothy made a detour to his office at the bank. Based on the stunned reactions of everyone she greeted there, she concluded it had been far too long since she'd paid her husband an impulsive visit. In fact, there had been little spontaneity in their lives for a very long time. It was just one worrisome aspect of their marriage lately.

When she entered his office, Marshall was on the phone. He gave her a distracted wave and kept right on talking. She gazed around at the room she'd helped him to decorate years ago when he'd first taken over the presidency and was shocked to discover that many of her carefully selected furnishings had been replaced. The color scheme was bolder and, to her eye, far more modern and jarring than suited a sedate banking establishment. Nothing in the room spoke of the bank's conservative tradition.

She doubted the change had been Marshall's idea. Her husband cared little for that sort of thing. He must have given carte blanche to someone to redecorate. She found that oddly disturbing. There had been a time when they discussed everything going on at the bank, when he relied on her opinion and taste. When had that stopped? Months ago? Years?

Were the bright artworks and sleek leather and chrome furnishings symptomatic of the problems she'd been ignoring in their marriage? Had they grown so far apart, communicated so little, that something like this could happen without her even knowing about it? It was a minor thing, but it forced her to face the fact that she hardly knew what was going on in her husband's life anymore.

She looked at her husband with dismay and wondered where they'd gone wrong. They were only in their early fifties, too young to have drifted so completely apart.

When Marshall finally hung up, he regarded her not with the delight he once would have shown, but with a trace of impatience.

"I didn't know you were coming by," he said. "I have a meeting in less than ten minutes."

She swallowed the first bitter retort that came to mind and said briskly, "Then I'll finish what I have to say in nine minutes. I want to talk to you about Dinah."

He looked startled by that. "What about her?"

"Something's wrong, Marshall. Haven't you seen it?"

He shook his head, his expression still blank. "She seems fine to me."

"You don't find it odd that she's barely left the house?"

"What are you talking about, Dorothy? She's left the house. She's had lunch with me three or four times in the last week."

"Because you made the arrangements and told her where to go," she said impatiently. "And she turns up for dinner because I tell her what time to be downstairs. But there's no life in her, no spark. She stays in her room or sits in the garden and broods. It's not like her."

He looked bemused. "She's rarely home, so you can't say if it's like her or not these days. Hell, after all she's been through, she's entitled to some peace and quiet. All this commotion we've stirred up has probably been too much for her. After all, this entertaining we've been doing is a far cry from the kind of life she's been used to the past few years. Maybe we've crammed in too much of it at once."

"That's pretty much what she said," Dorothy acknowledged.

"Well, there you have it," he said, clearly satisfied that the problem was solved. "Now, if you'll excuse me, I need to get ready for this meeting."

His dismissal was annoying. Dorothy stood and started for the door, but then she turned back. "When did you redecorate in here?"

Marshall looked up from his papers, clearly disconcerted by the question. "A few months ago. Why?"

"I'm just surprised you didn't ask for my help."

"You've been tied up with your own projects," he replied. "I had my secretary hire a decorator."

"And you like what they did?" she asked, not sure why any of it mattered so much.

He looked around the room as if seeing it for the first time. He shrugged. "It's a change."

"It certainly is," she said tartly. "And not for the better."

Feeling thoroughly disgruntled by the whole exchange, Dorothy stalked out of his office, her back rigid, her temper barely in check. She'd started the day with one worry on her mind—her daughter. Now she had two.

Her marriage, which she'd always accepted as faintly staid, but solid, was anything but secure. She'd been around long enough to know that enough tiny little fissures could seriously undermine the foundation of the most fortified structure. Discovering that her marriage was riddled with such fissures was a shock.

Unfortunately, for the moment Dinah had to be her priority. She simply had to hope that when she got around to focusing on her own life, it wouldn't be too late.

Cord Beaufort lazily swatted at the fly circling his bottle of now-lukewarm beer. It was the end of a steamy, grueling day, a day that had tested his patience and sent his nerves into more of an uproar than the last time he'd engaged in far more pleasurable, rambunctious sex.

He'd met with the board of directors for Covington Plantation and to a man—and woman—they were the most impossible, exasperating group of self-important human beings he'd ever had the misfortune to work for. They wanted to micromanage everything and not one of them had the expertise for it.

Worse, he'd had to wear a suit and tie, even though the temperature was pushing ninety. If there was one thing he hated more than placating a bunch of wealthy, egotistical bosses, it was wearing a suit and pretending not to be bored to tears while they yammered on and on. Things that should have been decided in less than an hour had taken the whole damn day.

Stretched out in a well-used Pawleys Island hammock strung between two ancient live oaks, he now wore comfortable jeans and nothing else. He was trying his best not to move a muscle until a breeze stirred, which probably wouldn't happen until November. He was not feeling especially optimistic at the moment.

The sound of a car bouncing along the dirt lane leading to his house did nothing to improve his mood. He wasn't feeling any more sociable than he was optimistic. He'd left all the ruts in the damn road as a way of discouraging visitors. Most people had long since gotten the message.

When the car finally came into view, he tried to place it and couldn't. The sight of a pair of long, shapely, bare legs emerging from the front seat, however, did improve his outlook marginally. Only one woman in all of South Carolina had legs like that. And she pretty much hated his guts. He couldn't say he blamed her.

If all the rumors he'd been hearing were right and Dinah Davis had decided to come home and appear on his doorstep it could only mean one thing. She was here to redeem the idiotic offer his brother Bobby had made to her years ago. Bobby, much as Cord loved him, was a damned fool. Who'd want a woman whenever she felt like it, even if that woman was as drop-dead gorgeous as Dinah Davis?

Cord watched her as she exited her car, wondering if her uppity mama knew she was going around town in a pair of shorts that left little to the imagination, and a halter top that wasn't exactly on the approved fashion list for a one-time Charleston debutante who never strayed from the straight and narrow. Right now she looked more like somebody he wouldn't mind taking a tumble with, which would flat-out horrify her mama.

Then again, maybe Dinah's choice of attire explained why Mrs. Davis had been on such a royal tear at the board meeting today. A rebellious daughter, even one who was thirty-one or so and internationally famous, could unsettle an uptight woman.

"Well, well," he murmured as Dinah lifted her chin with a familiar touch of defiance and started in his direction. "Just look at what the cat dragged in."

Bright patches of color immediately flooded her cheeks and her devastating, dark blue eyes flashed with irritation, but her good breeding quickly kicked in. She was, after all, on his turf. An uninvited guest with manners, Cord thought with amusement as he awaited her response.

"Good evening, Cordell," she said, her voice as sweet as syrup, yet unmistakably insincere. "I see your manners haven't improved with age."

"Not much," he agreed, refusing to take offense. "Time's been kind to you, though. You're as pretty as

Miss Scarlett and twice as tough, judging from what I've seen of you on TV."

"I'm amazed you watch network news," she said. "I thought the cartoon channel would be more to your liking."

"Sugar, I'm a man. Surfing channels is in my nature. Even I slow down when I see a hometown girl lighting up the screen in my living room, while bombs blow things up behind her."

"Yes, I imagine it gives you something to fantasize about on one of your lonely nights," she said, her voice cool with disdain.

"I am never lonely except by choice." Lately, though, he was making that choice more and more. Women, gorgeous and fascinating though they could surely be, were proving to be more trouble than they were worth.

Dinah gave him a withering look signaling that she found his claim laughable.

"As pleasant as it is chatting with you," she said in that same syrupy voice that was all about properly-bred, South Carolina manners, "I'm here to see Bobby. Is he around?"

Cord took a long, slow sip of beer and an insolent, long, slow head-to-toe survey of her before replying. "Nope."

She regarded him with unmistakable impatience. "Expected back?"

Cord saw no reason to help her out when he disapproved so heartily of her apparent mission. "Eventually."

"Which means exactly what?"

He grinned. Riling Dinah had always been a snap. It was a pure pleasure to see that hadn't changed. "I thought I was clear enough. He'll be back when he gets back. You know how it goes with us lazy, good-for-nothing Beauforts. We're not much on timetables."

Dinah sighed heavily, which had a fascinating effect on the rise and fall of her barely clad breasts. Cord wondered if she had any notion of the raw sensuality she projected or just how close he was to summoning the energy to drag her straight into his arms and give her the kiss she was half-begging for. Probably not or she'd have hightailed it out of here, instead of pestering him for answers he would not give her. He intended to protect Bobby from his own foolishness.

"Is Bobby due back tonight? Tomorrow? Next week?" she asked, her tone impatient.

"Could be next week," he said, then shrugged. "Maybe not."

"Has anyone ever told you how impossible you are?"

"Before you?" he asked.

She scowled.

Cord grinned. "Now that you mention it, I believe your mama said something very similar to me just this afternoon."

Her eyes widened, pleasing Cord with the fact that he could still surprise her. Shocking Dinah had been one of his primary delights back when she and Bobby had been dating. It had been a long time since he'd taken such pleasure in stirring a woman's temper or her dismay.

"Where on earth did you see my mother?" she inquired.

Her tone suggested he surely must have done something illegal to have such an encounter with an upper-crust paragon. If Dinah weren't so cute up there on her high horse, he might be insulted that she couldn't imagine any circumstance under which he and Dorothy Rawlings Davis would cross paths.

"Out and about," he replied mildly. "Charleston is, after all, a small town in many ways. In fact, I do believe that was why you were so anxious to leave."

"I left to attend college and pursue a career," she said, her voice tight as her cool gaze raked over him. "Maybe that's something you should consider doing."

He held up his beer and gestured around him. "Why leave? If you ask me, it doesn't get much better than this—a roof over my head, a little money in the bank, a cool drink and up until a few minutes ago plenty of peace and quiet."

"Thank heaven your brother doesn't share your total lack of ambition," she said.

Her uppity little tone of voice was starting to get on his nerves. He frowned at the comparison in which he came out wanting. He could have told her a few things about what he'd been up to, but why bother? She enjoyed thinking of him as a low-life. Why take that pleasure away from her when she'd just gotten back to town? It would be so much more fun for him watching her eat those words later.

"Please tell Bobby I'm home and looking forward to seeing him," she said. "You can remember a simple message, can't you?"

"If I put my mind to it," Cord agreed. Not that he intended to. Dinah Davis would eat his brother alive. Bobby didn't need the aggravation. Of course, the last time he'd tried thinking for his brother and interfering in his so-called romance with Dinah, there had been hell to pay.

"Well, try real hard," she said.

Then she sashayed back to her car, providing him with a fantastic view of her very fine derriere. Cord shook his head. Too bad she was so aggravating. Otherwise, he might enjoy tangling with her himself. Instead, he'd just content himself with keeping Bobby out of her clutches.

3

"I don't know how Bobby and Cordell could possibly come from the same gene pool," Dinah told her friend Maggie as they sipped iced tea on the veranda of Maggie's converted gatehouse a few blocks from the harbor in the historic downtown section of Charleston. "Bobby is sweet and kind and smart and ambitious. Cordell is…" For a woman who made her living with words, she couldn't find any to describe just what a low-down scoundrel she thought he was.

"Handsome, smart, sexy as sin," Maggie supplied.

Dinah regarded her with amazement. "Are you crazy?"

"Don't tell me you didn't notice," Maggie teased. "That's why you're all tongue-tied and pink-cheeked. What was he wearing? Jeans and nothing else, am I right?" She fanned herself in an exaggerated gesture designed to make a point. "He's the only man I know who can turn denim into a proper fashion statement." Her grin spread. "Or should I say improper?"

"I didn't notice," Dinah claimed piously.

"Like hell, you didn't. You're a female, aren't you? All women notice Cordell's…" She paused significantly, then added, "Attributes."

"Magnolia Forsythe! A lady does not utter such a comment about a gentleman."

Maggie grinned at the direct quotation uttered all too frequently by their prim principal throughout their grammar school days. "According to you, Cordell is no gentleman. Give it up, girl. You've been gone a long time and probably hiding out in caves for much of it. The only reason you're so upset with Cord is because he made you sit up and take notice of what a real man looks like."

"Don't be ridiculous," Dinah declared emphatically. Seeing Cord had reinforced just what an ill-mannered lowlife he was. He'd always taken an inordinate amount of pleasure in aggravating her. Nor would she ever forget or forgive what he'd once done to try to drive a wedge between her and Bobby. "I wouldn't give him a second look if he were the last man on earth. Bobby overcame those unfortunate Beaufort genes, but Cord certainly hasn't. He's pond scum. Always was. Always will be."

Maggie's knowing smile spread.

"Well, he is," Dinah insisted.

"Whatever you say, though you were far less judgmental when we were in grammar school. Weren't you the one who insisted that both Cord and Bobby needed to be included in our birthday parties, even when our folks cringed at the very idea of it?"

"I was thinking of Bobby," Dinah insisted. "I didn't want his feelings to be hurt. After all, he was our classmate. He's the one who insisted on dragging Cord along. He worshipped his big brother, though Lord knows why."

"And you didn't give two figs about Cord's feelings?" Maggie asked, her skepticism plain.

Dinah frowned. "Okay, yes. Maybe a little. It would have been rude to leave him out. Neither one of them could help that they were poor. Bobby took the opportunities they were given and made something of himself. Cord's apparently as lazy as ever."

Maggie merely raised a brow at that. "And I thought journalists were supposed to gather facts, not leap to conclusions."

There was something in her friend's tone as well as her words that suggested Dinah had gotten it all wrong. "Why have you turned into some big defender of Cord Beaufort all of a sudden?"

"I'm not. I'm just encouraging you to do your research before you rip apart a man you haven't seen in years," Maggie said defensively.

"Are you telling me I'm mistaken?"

"I'm telling you to do a little of that investigative reporting you're so famous for."

The chiding note in Maggie's voice silenced Dinah. She took a long swallow of her sweet tea and sighed. It was a little like drinking ice-cold syrup. "This is heaven. I haven't had tea like this since I left home."

"It's about time you remembered some of the good things about living here," Maggie said lightly. "Maybe you'll come home more often."

Dinah hesitated before responding. She'd known Maggie since they'd made mud pies together in preschool. Of all the girls at their fancy private school, they'd been the only two who hadn't been afraid to get their pretty little school dresses dirty. They'd become best friends growing up together, sharing confidences, talking about boys and sex, hopes and dreams.

Maggie was the first one Dinah had told when she'd

decided to defy parental expectations by going after a job as a foreign correspondent rather than marrying well. Maybe it was only fitting that she be the first one Dinah told that she quitting her dream job.

"Actually, I'm about eighty percent sure I'm here to stay," Dinah said quietly. Despite the fact that she'd said the words to herself before leaving Afghanistan, she hadn't entirely believed them. Now that she was home she knew the chances of her returning to her network career were decreasing daily. She wasn't getting any happier about it, just more resigned to the fact that Ray Mitchell had been right. If she could sit around for an entire afternoon sipping sweet tea without getting antsy and bored, then she couldn't ignore the probability that she had lost the hunger, drive and insight required of a top-notch reporter. Maybe quitting had been the smart thing to do, after all. Maybe it hadn't been the colossal mistake she'd assumed it was the minute the words had left her mouth.

Maggie let out an exuberant whoop not unlike Maybelle's, then sobered at once. "Why?" she demanded, her gaze raking over Dinah. "You didn't go and get yourself shot or something, did you? Not after that close call you had a few months back. That must have been awful, by the way. I told your mama to give you my love."

"She did," Dinah confirmed. "And no, nothing's happened since then."

"Then you're not recuperating? You didn't catch some fatal disease?"

"No, I wasn't shot and I'm not sick," Dinah said. Her soul had broken and it couldn't be mended in any hospital or even by a long rest at home. "I'm just tired."

"Well, why on earth wouldn't you be? Sometimes

when I see you on the air and realize where you are and what you've seen, my heart just aches for you. Your mama and daddy must be over the moon knowing you're safe and back for good."

"Actually I haven't told them yet. You're the only one who knows. Well, besides Maybelle, and I've sworn her to secrecy. I'm asking you to keep this quiet, too. I'm not ready to explain it to anyone." She gave Maggie a pointed look. "Not even you, okay?"

"No, it most definitely is not okay," Maggie said. "What is wrong with you? What's to explain? Tell them, Di. They'll be ecstatic." She regarded Dinah with concern. "If it's something you can't tell your parents, surely you can tell me. You know I'll be discreet. I never told a living soul that you spent the night with Bobby after prom, instead of with me, did I? I won't say a word about whatever you tell me now."

"I know you wouldn't, but my mind's still reeling. I need to work this out before I talk about it. As for my parents being ecstatic, I'm not so sure about that," Dinah said. "It's true that they weren't that happy when I left. Mother thinks anything outside South Carolina's borders is Satan's turf, but they've come to enjoy bragging about their little girl being a foreign correspondent. I think they're going to be disappointed that I'm giving it up."

"Don't you believe that for one single second," Maggie scoffed. "I can't tell you how often your mama has said how much she misses you and wishes you'd come back here and settle down and give her some grandbabies." She grinned impudently. "Those brats of your brother's can't be much fun," she said, then amended politely, "No disrespect intended."

Dinah laughed. "They are out of control, aren't they? They were at the house for dinner night before last and it was all I could do not to suggest we hogtie 'em and leave 'em in the backyard till the rest of us had finished having a civilized meal. If my children turn out like that, please take me out and shoot me."

"You couldn't possibly have children like that," Maggie said loyally. "You were raised by a Rawlings."

"So was Tommy Lee," Dinah noted, thinking about how oblivious her brother had seemed to his children's bad behavior during the family dinner. He and their father had been at odds, too. She supposed she ought to sit down with Tommy Lee and figure out what was bugging him, but she knew she needed to get her own life straightened out before she could be a help to anyone else, even her own brother.

Maggie gave her a disbelieving look. "Maybe your mama influenced Tommy Lee, but men aren't the ones who teach their children good manners. It's left up to women. And your sister-in-law's as sweet as can be, but she wasn't exactly raised by a woman familiar with Emily Post's rules on etiquette."

Lord knows, that was true enough, Dinah thought. Her brother's wife had narrowly escaped a troubled past and an uncertain future when she'd met Tommy Lee under circumstances no one ever dared ask about. That the two were head over heels in love had been enough for everyone to look the other way, with the possible exception of Dorothy Davis who made repeated attempts to bring her daughter-in-law up to her own high standards of conduct.

Unfortunately, all the lessons in the world weren't going to turn Laurinda into anybody's notion of a genteel Southern belle. Dinah almost admired the stubborn way she'd clung to her own identity. Standing up to Dorothy Davis took more courage than Dinah had ever had. In fact, her tendency to let her mother push her into doing things was one of the very many reasons she'd been so anxious to escape Charleston. It was bad enough that she'd undergone the torment of a debutante ball, but the prospect of having a lavish wedding to a suitable, hand-chosen man had been more than she could bear. She'd just about literally run for her life.

Now she was back and within the scope of all her mother's plans. It didn't bear thinking about.

"Let's not talk about Laurie and Tommy Lee," Dinah begged since thinking about those two had sent her off down memory lane.

"Then let's get back to you," Maggie agreed readily. "Why were you over at the Beauforts' last night, anyway?"

"I went looking for Bobby."

Maggie's gaze narrowed with suspicion. "Because?"

"He's an old friend, just like you. What other reason do I need?" Dinah asked, aware that a defensive note had crept into her voice.

Maggie regarded her blandly. "I don't suppose it had anything at all to do with that ridiculous backup plan you two devised when you graduated from college and turned down his proposal."

Dinah winced. That was the problem with sharing confidences with a woman who never forgot anything. Still, she feigned ignorance. "Backup plan?"

"You know, the one where the two of you get married if no one better comes along. I believe it was to kick in when your biological clock started ticking too loudly.

I'm certain it was all on your terms. To this day I have no idea what Bobby got out of it, other than some dim hope that you'd eventually come to your senses."

Dinah cringed at the suggestion that she'd manipulated that agreement out of Bobby and that she was taking advantage of him even now. "You make it sound as if Bobby's nothing more than a last resort."

"Isn't he?"

"Of course not. I just want to get together with him and catch up."

"Is that some euphemism for getting him into your bed?"

"You're being crass again," Dinah accused. "It's not about sex."

"Then you've given up fame and fortune and rushed home because you suddenly had an epiphany in the middle of Afghanistan and realized that you're wildly in love with him?" Maggie asked skeptically. "Because that's the only reason that would justify you getting that poor man's hopes all stirred up again after all these years."

"I've always loved Bobby," Dinah replied carefully. Not that he'd crossed her mind more than a half-dozen times in recent years and always with more fondness than passion. Good marriages had been built on a whole lot less, she told herself.

"Not the same thing as being in love with him," Maggie replied. "Does your heart go pitter-pat when you see him?"

"I haven't seen him in ten years," she retorted irritably. The truth was her pulse had never skipped so much as a single beat at the sight of Bobby. He'd been comfortable and back then that's all she'd wanted, a man who wouldn't tangle her emotions into knots. That had left her free to pursue her own dreams.

Deep down Dinah recognized that Cord had seen her intentions and had set out in his own way to protect his brother, but Bobby hadn't wanted his protection and she'd been shocked and angry that Cord would betray his brother's trust the way he had.

"How would I know if Bobby turns me on?" she grumbled defensively.

"My point precisely," Maggie said, clearly satisfied. She gave Dinah a knowing look. "I'll bet Bobby has never once gotten you all worked up the way Cordell did just last night. Now there is a man worth throwing away a career just so you can have him climbing into your bed."

Dinah thought of the way her blood had sizzled through her veins within ten seconds of trying to carry on a sensible conversation with Cord Beaufort. That was irritation, plain and simple. He'd been annoying her like that since they were toddlers.

"Bobby is sweet and kind and smart," she repeated emphatically.

"And dull as dishwater," Maggie countered. "You'll be bored stiff in a week."

"And you think Cord would be an improvement?"

"Definitely."

"You're out of your mind." The very last thing she needed in her life was a man who made her feel prickly and restless, the kind of man who prided himself on taking women on some sort of emotional roller-coaster ride. She'd given up danger when she'd left Afghanistan.

Maggie grinned. "We'll see," she said with smug confidence.

Dinah decided it was past time to turn the tables on her friend. "What about you, Magnolia?" she inquired, deliberately using her friend's hated real name. "Anyone special in your life? Since you seem so fascinated by Cordell, perhaps you should be encouraging him to give you a tumble."

"I tried, to be perfectly honest," Maggie admitted. "He wouldn't give me a second look. I'm far too tame for the likes of Cordell."

"And I'm not?"

"You play a form of roulette with car bombs and rebel gunmen," Maggie replied. "I'd say that qualifies you for a man who likes living on the edge."

Dinah sighed. Though no one here knew it, she'd fallen for a man like that, a man who courted real danger every day. She'd wound up with a broken heart. Of course, there was a vast difference between physical danger and the emotional minefield a woman would have to tiptoe through with Cord. Even so, Dinah wanted no part of it.

"I've had it with risk-taking," she told her friend emphatically. "I think Bobby's definitely the way to go."

"But you haven't caught up with him yet?"

"No. I asked Cord to have him call me, but so far I haven't heard a word."

"And you haven't gone chasing after him?"

"Not yet."

"Maybe that should tell you something," Maggie suggested gently.

"What? That Cord didn't pass on the message?"

"That, or maybe you don't care enough to make the effort. Then, again, maybe it means that Bobby's moved on with his life. It has been ten years. Even an eternal optimist can get tired of waiting around after that long."

Dinah studied Maggie. "What do you know that I don't?"

"Just that I don't want you to be setting yourself up for disappointment if Bobby doesn't fall right in with your plans."

That was definitely something Dinah hadn't considered. Maybe she really was a self-absorbed idiot to think he'd been waiting for her all this time. Their deal had merely been that they'd get together, if they happened to be available.

"You think he won't?" she asked Maggie.

"I can't say. That's up to him."

Dinah had a feeling there was something that Maggie was deliberately keeping from her. She usually wasn't so circumspect. "If you know something you think I should know, tell me," she commanded.

Maggie shook her head. "Not a chance. This is between you and Bobby." She grinned. "And maybe Cordell. Something tells me he's going to figure in this before all is said and done."

"You are turning out to be almost as exasperating as he was," Dinah accused lightly. "Doesn't mean I'm not happy to see you, though. Can we have dinner soon?"

"My calendar's disgustingly open. Just tell me when," Maggie said. "Now I'd better get back to work before my employees stage a rebellion. The last time I took a long lunch they sold a valuable painting at half price. Said they couldn't find a sticker on it, so they negotiated. They claimed their blood sugar had dropped so low, they forgot about the price list we keep in the file."

Dinah chuckled at what was most likely no exaggeration. "I promise I'll come by to see this gallery of yours in a day or two and we'll schedule dinner."

"Don't wait too long," Maggie ordered. "Or I'll come looking for you."

"It's good to see you, Maggie. I've missed you," Dinah said, giving her friend a fierce hug.

"Missed you more."

Dinah stood on the sidewalk in front of Maggie's place and watched her friend head off down the street to her successful gallery. She looked purposeful and confident, two traits Dinah wondered if she'd ever feel again.

Covington Plantation was a labor of love for Cord. Putting up with the board members and fighting for every penny to do the job right took more patience than waiting for the first cool breeze of fall, but it was going to be worth it to see this grand old house restored to its former glory.

For a kid who'd grown up in a place that was little more than a run-down shack, a house like this represented everything his home hadn't been. It was solid and spoke of proud ancestors. His own ancestors had been unremarkable and there had been nothing dependable about the two people who'd raised him and Bobby. They'd contributed genes and not much else. It was the charity of others that had given him and Bobby a chance at a better life. As much as it had grated to accept the private school tuition, the church handouts, the free lunches, they'd swallowed their pride and done it.

Bobby had fit in better than Cord. Even as a kid, he'd

had an ingratiating way about him, while Cord had radiated little better than grudging tolerance for those who'd extended a helping hand. He'd seethed with ungracious resentment and unwarranted pride, but he had managed to keep it under wraps for Bobby's sake and ultimately for his own.

He felt a whole lot better about it now, knowing that he had the respect of some of those same people who'd seen helping him and Bobby as their ticket into heaven. With the wisdom of age, Cord was just realizing that some of those folks were simply being generous because they'd seen two kids in trouble. They had honestly wanted to help put them on the right track.

It was a matter of pride, though, that he'd earned their respect, that they'd turned to him when they were ready to proceed with the Covington Plantation renovation. He hadn't had to beg for the chance to bid, though he might have done it just for the opportunity to be a part of saving the house. As a kid he'd liked riding his bike out here.

He liked the stately old plantation house best early in the morning with the sun just starting to filter through the ancient trees and the sound of the birds breaking the silence. Sometimes as a boy, he'd sat on the front steps with a cold Coke in his hand and imagined he could hear the squabbles coming from the family inside or the distant singing of slaves working in the rice fields. Being here spoke to him of the past more clearly than any history teacher ever had.

He'd never want to go back to that sad time period, but now that he was all grown up, he liked knowing that he could preserve a little piece of it as a reminder of another era. More than that, he liked saving structures that

had been meant to last, restoring their beauty and craftsmanship for future generations to enjoy.

Usually this half hour before his crew arrived was a
tranquil time, but ever since Dinah Davis had come by
the house in search of Bobby, there hadn't been a peaceful moment in his life. That woman had gotten under
his skin, just as she had years ago. A part of him wanted
to put her in her place. Another part—the very male part
of him—wanted to kiss that uppity expression off her
face. He'd struggled with the same dilemma as far back
as he could remember.

Okay, maybe not quite as far back as elementary
school, but it had definitely crossed his mind starting
with puberty. Even then he'd somehow known he would
be better for her than Bobby, who'd followed her
around like an adoring puppy. When he couldn't stand
his brother's attitude a minute longer, he'd done something about it, something that had almost caused a permanent rift with his brother and had left Dinah hating
his guts.

When his cell phone rang, he glanced at the caller
ID and suffered a pang of remorse.

"Hey, Bobby," he said, stuffing down the faint trace
of guilt he felt over keeping his mouth shut about Dinah's return. What was a little guilty silence, when the
end result would be his brother's happiness? "How's it
going in Atlanta?"

"We're on schedule and under budget," Bobby announced. "Which you would know if you read the reports I fax over there every damn day."

Cord grinned. He enjoyed keeping up the pretense
that he ignored all Bobby's carefully detailed paper-
work. It drove his brother nuts. "I believe I swept up a

whole bagful of those reports just the other day. Summarize for me."

Bobby did just that in tedious detail.

"Sounds like everything's under control, then. You're doing great work," Cord praised. "That project's going to be a real showcase for us and you deserve all the credit."

The truth was that they made a great team. Bobby knew the construction trade almost as well as Cord did, but while Cord loved working with his hands and considered himself a skilled craftsman, Bobby excelled at staying on top of the details, working out cost projections and smooth-talking their backers. He was a natural for the Atlanta renovation project.

The Atlanta development was the most ambitious they'd done so far, encompassing an entire section of old buildings that had been destined for a wrecker's ball until Bobby and Cord had put together a proposal and bid on the property. When it was finished, there would be shops, restaurants and apartments in high-ceilinged old buildings with glowing hardwood floors, beautiful crown molding and a dozen other historic touches rarely found in this day and age. They and their backers stood to triple their investment, to say nothing of what the finished project would do to move them into the ranks of the elite historical preservationists in the country.

Suddenly Cord recalled one of the first things Bobby had said. "Just how far ahead of schedule are you?"

"A few weeks. I'll be back home before you know it, bro. I've got to tell you, I can't wait. Living in a hotel room is getting on my nerves. I was thinking I might drive over this weekend. It would give us a chance to go over those other projects we've got lined up. We need to think about assigning someone to oversee them. There's too much work for us to do it ourselves."

Cord flinched. "No rush on that," he said at once. "Just concentrate on wrapping things up in Atlanta. I've got everything here under control."

"You still on speaking terms with the board at Covington?" Bobby asked worriedly.

Cord laughed. "Haven't insulted anybody in a couple of days now, as a matter of fact." Unless he took into account Dinah, but that was definitely not something he cared to share.

"You sure about that?" Bobby asked, his skepticism plain. "I know there was a big meeting this week and I know how you hate that kind of thing."

"We all survived it."

"Any ruffled feathers need smoothing over?"

"None," Cord assured him. "I was on my best behavior. I swear it."

"Why don't I find that nearly as reassuring as you evidently want me to?"

"Because you're a suspicious kind of guy?" Cord suggested. Because he feared that sooner or later he'd slip up and mention Dinah, Cord balled up a piece of paper beside the mouthpiece of the phone. "Hey, Bobby, the connection's going. We'll talk again soon, okay?"

"Don't you dare hang up on me. I know that trick," he declared just as Cord hit the disconnect button.

Cord sighed, thanking his lucky stars that Bobby wasn't the kind of man who asked about the latest gossip. When his phone immediately rang again, he ignored it.

The last thing Cord wanted to do was utter an outright lie. It was better for Bobby to keep right on working his tail off in Atlanta in blissful ignorance. Since Bobby also happened to have a fiancée, Cord could even tell himself he was being noble and protecting her interests as well.

Just then another fleeting image of Dinah Davis with her endless legs and lush curves popped into his head and made a liar out of him. That didn't mean he intended to do anything about the attraction, he assured himself. He surely wasn't going to go chasing after her.

But the best part of having known a female since childhood was the long-standing awareness of her weaknesses. Sooner or later frustration and indignation were going to kick in and Dinah was going to come to him.

Cord lifted his cup of coffee in a silent toast to predictability. God bless it! He'd gotten more women just by waiting them out than most men had with flowers and candy. Patience was a gift, no question about it. Luckily, he'd been born with an abundance of it.

4

Two weeks passed without a word from Bobby. Dinah was disappointed that he didn't seem nearly as eager to renew their old relationship as she was. Or as she *might be,* she corrected. She wasn't exactly sure what to expect. Was she just trying to find something to replace her career if she couldn't conquer her post-traumatic stress issues and eventually go back to the network?

Acknowledging that possibility gave her a momentary twinge of guilt. Maybe Maggie was right. What right did Dinah have to disrupt Bobby's life after ten years when she merely *might* be ready for marriage? Sure, at thirty-one her biological clock was probably ticking loudly, but she hadn't even been listening to it until recently, not like a lot of women would be.

No, a relationship with Bobby was all about her desire to fill up her days with something that wouldn't get her killed, to be around people who weren't in danger of dying on a daily basis, to get her own equilibrium back.

Suddenly her reasons sounded damn selfish, but that didn't stop her from wanting to meet Bobby and see how she would react. What was the point of having a backup plan if she wasn't going to use it? If Bobby wasn't interested in sticking to their deal then she'd have her answer. But how was she supposed to know how he felt without talking to him? Surely, after all they'd once meant to each other, he would at least tell her face-to-face that she was too late. He wouldn't leave her twisting in the wind like this. It wasn't one bit like him.

It was, however, a lot like Cord. There was always the very real possibility that Cord hadn't gotten around to mentioning her visit to Bobby. It would be just like him to deliberately keep her message from his brother just to annoy her. It wouldn't be the first time he'd done something totally underhanded to the two of them.

Another woman might have waited longer for Bobby to call on the off chance that he had made a conscious decision not to see her. Another woman might have feared being totally humiliated by the prospect of laying her heart bare and risking rejection, but Dinah wasn't most women. She'd braved far greater risks than rejection.

Besides, she was growing restless and increasingly tired of trying to evade her mother's worried interrogations. She'd come home on a mission. Perhaps it was a misguided one, but it was time she made something happen. Sitting around idle or being evasive wasn't her style.

She intended to take Ray's well-meant advice to heart. She was going to seriously consider getting married and having babies and put her dangerous, nomadic life behind her. She was beginning to wonder if she wouldn't prefer being shot at, rather than bored to death but the instant that thought crossed her mind, she knew that she needed to find Bobby immediately. She couldn't leave her fate in some other person's hands, especially when that person was Cordell.

With that in mind, Dinah went shopping, found herself the prettiest little sundress in all of Charleston, then drove right back out to the Beauforts'. She planned on busting right past Cord if he was guarding the threshold again. This time she would see Bobby or find evidence that would point her in the direction of wherever he was.

As she made the trip, she realized what a wonder it was that she'd ever gotten to know Bobby and Cordell. They weren't exactly poor, but they definitely hadn't run in the same social circles as the Davises. They had been befriended by someone who did travel in the same circles and so Dinah had met them at an early age. Only much, much later had she realized the enormity of the gift that someone had given them by enrolling them in the best private schools in Charleston.

Cord had been a pain in the neck even then. Two years older and precocious, he'd seemed to sense that he and his brother were tolerated rather than accepted. He understood that they were in that fancy private school because of someone's charity and he'd resented it. He'd set out to stir things up in a way that pretty much guaranteed that he wouldn't even be tolerated by the time he hit his teens. Whoever their benefactor had been, he or she had let Cord's ungrateful behavior pass. Maybe the person had even understood the cause of it. Dinah certainly hadn't, not back then, anyway.

Of course, as time went by, that dangerous, rebellious streak had only made Cord more attractive to a certain group of risk-taking debutantes intent on giving their mothers the vapors. Dinah had most definitely not been one of them. If she'd held a secret fascination for the black sheep Beaufort brother, she'd been far too sensible to act on it. Even-tempered Bobby had suited her then and he suited her now. She'd come home in search of someone comforting, not a man who exasperated her at every turn, no matter what Maggie thought to the contrary.

Unfortunately, after she'd jarred her teeth driving over the rutted road that supposedly passed for a driveway, she found only Cordell. He was again sprawled in that shaded hammock, beer at his side, jeans riding low on his hips, his amazing abs now in full view. Her impression that he hadn't changed from being a lazy, good-for-nothing jerk was correct. But for the first time Dinah couldn't help but admire his body. Maggie had been right. God had given this man a real gift and he was wasting it out here in the middle of nowhere. He ought to pose for his own calendar, so women everywhere could ogle him in the privacy of their own homes. Dinah realized that even that would be too enterprising for Cord Beaufort.

When Cord didn't immediately call out some insult, she concluded with relief that he was asleep. She decided to creep past him and go in search of Bobby.

She'd almost made it, when Cord's hand snaked out and grabbed hers, hauling her to a stop. She couldn't help noticing that despite his annoying, powerful grip, there was something amazingly sensual about the way her hand fit into his, the way his thumb rubbed a lazy little circle over her pulse. She swore to herself that the heat suddenly sizzling through her blood was due to the steamy afternoon temperature and had nothing at all to do with his almost hypnotic touch.

"I thought you were sleeping," she accused, struggling to free herself.

"That's not the first mistake you've made about me," Cord said, his mouth curving into a grin. "I imagine you're still prowling around looking for my brother."

She saw no reason to deny it. "Yes."

"He's still out of town."

Something in his overly-pleased tone told her that he most likely had something to do with that. "How much longer is he going to be gone?" she asked.

His gaze caught hers and held. "How long are you going to stick around Charleston?"

His words all but confirmed her suspicion. She scowled at him. "Why don't you want me to see Bobby?"

Cord gave her a stunned look that was all innocence, or would have been if he were the sort to be constitutionally capable of maintaining an innocent act. Dinah acknowledged that it was a fairly decent attempt, though. Lord knew, he'd had enough practice perfecting it.

"Hey, my brother's a grown man," Cord told her. "He can see anyone he wants to see."

"Then you've told him I'm here?"

He considered the question with a thoughtful expression. "Could be that it slipped my mind," he finally admitted.

"Why?"

"I have a lot going on these days," he said with a shrug. "I can't remember everything."

"Yeah, right. I can see for myself just how busy you are. It must be purely exhausting walking clear across the lawn to get your next beer."

"Sugar, surely you're not suggesting that I'm lying to you," he said with a trace of feigned indignation.

"That's exactly what I'm suggesting," she retorted.

"Why would I want to keep you and Bobby apart?" he asked, feigning innocence once more.

"I was wondering that very thing myself. I don't understand it today any better than I did ten years ago when you made up a whole passel of lies to try to come between us. What is it, Cord? Can't you bear the thought of your brother being happy?"

"With you?" he asked with such blatant skepticism that Dinah winced.

"He loves me," she retorted.

"Is that so?"

"He proposed to me."

"When exactly was that?"

"A while back," she said, unwilling to admit just how long ago it had been.

"Ten years," Cord said, proving he knew more than Dinah had suspected. "And you assume he's been sitting around here pining for you all this time? How insulting is that? Bobby and I may not be a bit alike, but saint that he is, he's still a man with needs, if you know what I mean."

As smart and intuitive as Dinah had always thought herself to be, she was forced to concede that she'd never seriously taken into account the possibility that Bobby might have moved on. She assumed he'd dated, but she'd only considered then dismissed the possibility he'd found a new love of his life. But maybe Cord was right. Maybe she *was* taking Bobby's affections for granted. In light of the deep feelings she'd developed for someone else during the past ten years, she had to acknowledge the possibility Bobby had indeed found someone else.

Studying Cord, she asked, "Is your brother involved with someone else?"

Cord seemed to be debating the answer to that one, but he finally said, "You'll need to ask him that yourself. I got in the middle of your business once. I won't make that mistake again."

"Meaning he isn't, but you wish he were," she concluded with a little sense of triumph. Or was it relief she felt?

"No, meaning this is between the two of you," Cord responded flatly.

His careful dance around the question echoed what Maggie had told her, which was more disconcerting than Dinah cared to admit. They both implied that they were leaving out an important truth that they thought only Bobby had a right to share with Dinah. She decided to try to get to the bottom of it, though she'd probably have better luck with Maggie than with Cord. He had a stubborn streak that Maggie didn't share. Still, Cord was here and her best friend wasn't. She might as well push him a little and see what happened.

"It would be between Bobby and me if you'd given him my message," she said. "As it is, you're right in the thick of it, Cordell. Why is that? Surely you're not jealous."

His low chuckle grated on her nerves. It spoke volumes about what he thought of that explanation.

"It's not as if I'm a bad catch," she grumbled.

"You'd be a challenge, no question about it," he replied, his smirk still firmly in place. "In fact, if I had to comment, I'd say you're too much woman for my brother."

"Now who's being insulting to Bobby?" she retorted. "Bobby can handle me."

"Is that so? Then this ridiculous backup plan the two of you hatched was his idea? He talked you into it?"

She frowned at that. "No."

Cord cupped his ear. "What was that? Did you say no?"

"It would never have worked if Bobby and I had gotten married ten years ago. He knew that," she said defensively.

"But it will work now?"

"Yes."

"Because you've gone round the world sowing all your wild oats, so to speak?"

"I didn't sow any oats, dammit. It wasn't about that," she said, feeling her temper kick in.

"Oh, that's right. You had to go and make a name for yourself. You wanted to be somebody special. And now what? You're ready to settle down and be my brother's wife and let him count his lucky stars every night that you deigned to come back to him?"

"Why are you so determined to put an ugly spin on this? I don't have to listen to you question my motives," she declared, whipping around to go.

"Maybe you should listen," he said, a quiet command in his voice that compelled her to turn back. "This is all about you, Dinah. I'd wager you haven't spent more than a minute or two thinking about what might be best for Bobby. You probably sat over there in Afghanistan and got some bee in your bonnet about your own mortality and decided it was time to come home and play it safe. Bobby's not the love of your life. He's just convenient."

Because there was an undeniable element of truth to his stinging words, Dinah flinched. She searched for a ready comeback to put him in his place, but there wasn't one.

Just then the wind kicked up. Black clouds rolled in the sky above them. Dinah could all but feel the stir of electricity in the air.

"Looks like we're in for a storm," Cord noted without moving a muscle. "Run along, Dinah, before you get drenched. There's nothing for you here."

She hated the patronizing tone in his voice as much as she hated his dismissal. She would have said so, too, then taken off, if a bolt of lightning hadn't split the sky just then, immediately followed by a crack of thunder.

Her brain told her this was nothing more than a good old-fashioned summer storm, the kind that hit hard, turned the hard-dried ground into rivers of mud, then passed on, leaving the air steamier than ever.

But her heart and her nerves took over her rational thought and she felt immediately transported back to Afghanistan where car bombs exploded and gunfire prevailed all around. She dropped to the ground, lay on her stomach, and heard her heart pounding so hard she thought it might explode, before the first drop of rain even fell from the sky. Humiliating whimpers escaped before she could stop them.

Two seconds later Cord was beside her, gathering her into his arms, holding her tight against all his solid strength and bare skin, murmuring soothing nonsense words as the storm raged around them. Dinah clung to him, no longer caring that he was the bane of her existence. She could hear the steady beat of his heart and her own pulse finally slowed to match it. Her terror eased, but still she clung, his skin warm and slick beneath her fingers.

"Sugar, I'm going to take you inside now, okay?" Cord said, his tone surprisingly gentle. All traces of animosity and disdain had vanished. "We need to get you dried off and cleaned up, okay?"

Dinah shivered uncontrollably, but managed to nod. She prayed he couldn't distinguish between the rain and the tears spilling down her cheeks. Given that he'd seen her take a nosedive into the dirt at the sound of thunder, it seemed absurd to worry about having him see her cry, but she still had a tiny shred of pride left.

Of all people, why had it been Cordell who witnessed her coming unglued? It was just going to give him one more thing to gloat about, one more reason to say she wasn't good enough for his brother. He'd probably tell Bobby that he'd have to be insane to take her on.

Inside the house, Cord started to set her down in an easy chair, but Dinah couldn't let go of him. When he realized she wasn't going to release him, he sat in the chair himself and held her cradled against his chest.

With surprisingly gentle fingers, he brushed damp curls away from her face. When she finally risked a glance at his expression, she saw not the contempt she'd expected but a combination of understanding and tenderness. It brought more salty tears to her eyes. Cordell Beaufort's compassion was the last thing she'd expected, the very last thing she wanted.

They sat like that for an eternity, neither of them speaking. Dinah slowly lost the sensation that she was spinning out of control. When she finally relaxed and sighed, she caught a glimpse of the satisfaction on

Cord's face. Some of the tension in his body eased, as well.

In the back of her mind, she noted with more than a little surprise that he didn't seem interested in taking advantage of the situation. Based on his reputation, the Cord of old would have turned this into a seduction, or at least an attempt at one. He'd have considered it his duty.

"You've been through a rough time, huh?" he said, breaking the silence.

The note of sympathy in his voice made her eyes sting with more tears. "I can't talk about it," she said. She didn't even want to think about the last year and she certainly didn't want to discuss it with him. Of course, not talking about it hadn't worked all that well.

"Maybe you should. It usually helps with this sort of thing. Brings the demons out of the closet, so to speak."

"You have no idea what you're talking about," she said disdainfully.

"You think not? The Gulf War wasn't much of a picnic, Dinah. There were..." He hesitated, seeming to search for a word. "After-effects," he said eventually. "There were after-effects for a lot of us."

She blinked at that. "You were there? You had post-traumatic stress syndrome?"

He nodded, his face empty of expression. "Still do, I suppose."

"And?"

"I survived."

She gave him a wry look. "Apparently you don't think what's good for the goose is good for the gander. You could be a little more forthcoming than that."

"It's been more than ten years, Dinah. I've done my talking. I've put most of it behind me, at least as well as anyone ever can."

"How?" she asked, unable to keep the plaintive note out of her voice. She hated sounding vulnerable, especially in front of Cord, but she needed to know that the dreams, the panic attacks would eventually end.

"Time, mostly."

Dinah sighed. "I'm not sure there's enough of that left in my lifetime."

He gave her a faint grin. "You're not that far over the hill, Dinah. You've probably got at least one or two good years left."

"Sometimes I feel ancient," she responded wearily.

A whisper of a breeze stirred over them and Dinah shivered, then realized that they were both sitting under a ceiling fan soaking wet. Though she hated leaving the unexpected comfort of his embrace, she pushed away and stood.

"I should go."

"Not when it's pouring like it is out there. The driveway will be a sea of mud. You'll just get stuck and then I'll have to tow you out of a ditch."

As much as she wanted to go now that the panic had faded, she knew he was right. "Why don't you pave the stupid driveway?" she grumbled.

He chuckled. "Because keeping it like it is generally keeps away unwanted visitors." He gave her an insolent once-over that heated her blood. "Lately it's not working half as well as it's meant to. Some people apparently can't take a hint."

He stood up slowly and tucked a finger under her chin. "Stay put, okay? I'm going to get you one of my shirts and a towel, then you can take a warm shower and dry off while I throw your clothes in the washer."

His sudden kindness was confusing her. She wasn't sure how to react to it. It was easier to deal with Cord when he was being exasperating. "Why are you being so damn nice to me?"

"Maybe I don't want you suing me for letting you catch pneumonia on my property."

She gave him a disbelieving look. "I don't think you can file lawsuits for something like that."

"You have no idea what people will sue over these days. The world's a crazy place. Now, are you going to stay put like I asked, or are you going to be stubborn and try to set out in this weather?"

"I'm stubborn, not stupid. I'll stay, at least till the storm's over."

Something told Dinah there was a distinct possibility she was going to live to regret it.

Cord listened to the shower running in his bathroom and thanked his lucky stars that he'd gotten Dinah out of that sexy, soaking wet sundress and sent her off to change before she'd noticed that he was completely and totally aroused by the sight and feel of her. She'd fit a little too snugly in his arms, smelled a little too provocative. Her dress, respectable enough when dry, had been way too revealing when wet.

Sweet heaven, what was he thinking? Him and Dinah Davis? No chance in hell. She might be grateful to him right this second, but she'd come to her senses before the night was out and remember that she hated him, that she had good reason to. Add in that he was just too low class for her and any relationship between the two of them was doomed.

What grated was that he was certain now that she'd never dismissed Bobby as low class. Hell, she was all set to marry his brother, or thought she was. Cord figured it would be a cold day in hell before that happened.

By the time he heard the shower cut off, Cord had poured a couple of beers into glasses, mostly to prove he could be civilized when it suited him. He'd put a couple of chicken breasts topped with mushroom gravy into the oven to bake. He was in the process of making a salad when Dinah came into the kitchen.

She didn't make a sound when she entered, but he knew she was there just the same.

"What's all this?" she asked.

"Dinner. I figure even people who watch their waistlines for the camera have to eat something. Besides, the adrenaline rush from one of those attacks always left me starved."

"What's in the oven?"

"Chicken."

"It smells…good," she said hesitantly, with yet another note of surprise in her voice.

Cord grinned, though he was glad she couldn't see his face. He doubted she would appreciate knowing how much she amused him with her faltering attempts to be polite. "You keep dishing out those lavish compliments, sugar, you're going to turn my head."

"I was trying to be polite," she said crossly.

"I get that, but there's no need to try so hard. Us low-lifes don't expect much. A simple please and thank-you now and then will do."

He turned to set the salad on the table and got his first

good look at her in one of his old light-blue dress shirts. He damn near swallowed his tongue. He should have remembered how those long, bare legs of hers affected him. If he had, he would have come up with something else for her to put on…maybe baggy sweatpants, even if it was still eighty-eight degrees, despite the storm passing overhead.

"Why don't you have a seat?" he suggested when he could speak without stammering. He needed to get those legs of hers out of sight before he started to imagine them wrapped around his waist while he buried himself inside her.

He yanked open the freezer door and stuck his head in, wishing it could be another part of his overheated anatomy.

"What are you looking for?" she asked, sounding puzzled.

"Ice," he said.

"Isn't that an ice dispenser on the door?" she inquired, amusement in her voice.

Cord cursed the oversize, stainless steel refrigerator Bobby had insisted they buy. "Broken," he lied tersely. He turned back to the table with a handful of ice, almost regretting that he couldn't shove it down the front of his jeans.

"I see," Dinah said, though she still looked skeptical. "And what was it you needed the ice for?"

"Water," he said at once, dumping the handful of cubes into a glass, then running tap water over them and drinking every drop of the cold water straight down. It slaked his thirst, but did nothing for the hunger that had been gnawing at him since he'd gotten a good look at Dinah in his shirt.

He busied himself with getting the rest of their dinner on the table, grateful that Dinah had finally gone silent. Maybe she'd realized just how close he was to hauling her into his arms and kissing her senseless.

When he finally sat down at the table, she studied him quizzically. It was the kind of curious, penetrating look that he imagined her using on some reluctant interview subject. No wonder she'd won so many awards. All but squirming under that gaze, he'd have told her just about anything she wanted to know.

"What have you been doing with yourself all these years?" she asked eventually.

Cord was a little surprised her mother hadn't told her, maybe not about the company, but at least about his role in the restoration of Covington Plantation. Then, again, maybe he wasn't a hot topic for the Davis women.

"This 'n that," he said, not sure why he didn't want to tell her the truth and disprove once and for all the apparently low impression she had of him. In the end he figured he wasn't the bragging type.

She frowned at his response. "Don't you think you should have found steady work by now?"

"Oh, I do well enough," he said.

"You can't rely on Bobby to support you," she said.

Her assumption that he was dependent on Bobby's largess stuck in his craw. "Oh? How do you know it's not the other way around? Maybe I've been carrying Bobby all these years."

She gave him a look filled with undisguised skepticism. "Please, Cordell. We both know that Bobby would never depend on you. He got an excellent college education, which I'm sure he's put to good use."

Cord could barely suppress a grin at her uppity tone. "Is that so? And just how much do you _know_ about what Bobby's been doing since you took off? Maybe he's gotten friendly with Jack Daniels and hasn't done a·lick of work. Wouldn't be the first time one of the Beaufort men couldn't hold his liquor."

She looked a bit flustered by the question. "Are you telling me that your brother is an alcoholic?"

"Nope. Just saying you can't possibly know one way or the other. You've made a lot of assumptions in the last couple of weeks or am I wrong? Have folks been filling your head with tales, Dinah?"

"No, I haven't heard anything specific," she admitted. "But I do know you."

He shook his head at her confident tone. "Oh, sugar, I wouldn't be too sure of that. The truth is you don't have a clue about either one of us. Never have. Never will."

She regarded him with a huffy expression. "I've known you since grade school, Cordell. Bobby was always thoughtful, generous and hardworking. You were an arrogant, smart-alecky kid without a lick of ambition and I don't see any evidence that you've changed a bit."

He laughed at that. "Then you must not be half the journalist you're cracked up to be."

"Meaning what?" she asked, her cheeks pink with indignation.

"That you must have missed all those lessons on objectivity and fact-gathering. You're making assumptions right and left here."

"Then set me straight," she retorted at once.

"Why should I?" he asked. "I think it's going to be a whole lot more entertaining to let you make a few discoveries all on your own."

5

Twenty-four hours after humiliating herself in front of Cord and with his indictment of her fact-finding skills still ringing in her ears, Dinah went in search of Maggie for information. If Cord wasn't going to tell her anything about Bobby or himself, then she was just going to have to drag it out of her best friend. Besides, it had already been a couple of weeks since she'd promised to go by the gallery and set up a date for dinner. Surely once she was there she could lull Maggie into revealing something helpful about Bobby's whereabouts.

She found Images on a narrow alley in downtown Charleston, only a few blocks from the Battery. It had a lovely wrought-iron fence, climbing rosebushes in full and fragrant bloom in the tiny courtyard, and old brick that had faded to a lovely shade of pink. Everything about it spoke of charm and class. Knowing her friend as she did, Dinah hadn't expected anything less than the classiest of businesses. Maggie had always had excellent taste, even though she'd occasionally rebelled against it.

A bell rang when Dinah opened the door and Maggie emerged from the back, a smile spreading across her face when she saw her friend.

"It's about time you came by," she declared.

"I know," Dinah said readily. "I'm sorry it's taken me so long."

"I'm sure you've been busy. Knowing your folks, they're probably still showing you off every evening."

"Not really. I called a halt to that after the first few days. The last thing I want is to be trotted out like some visiting celebrity. It'll just make it that much harder to explain to everyone when I don't go back overseas on another assignment."

Maggie's gaze immediately narrowed. "What's up, then? Is everything okay? Come on in the back and I'll pour us both some tea and we can talk."

"Not till I've had a look around," Dinah said, mostly out of genuine interest, but also to put off Maggie's inevitable questions.

She made a slow turn in the main room, admiring the watercolors that hung on the walls and the sculptures and art glass displayed on an assortment of antiques that Maggie had obviously brought from her family's home. It was an eclectic mix set against a backdrop of warm wood furniture, gleaming oak floors and creamy walls. The effect was inviting, not intimidating, though the price tags certainly put the inventory several steps above most people's pocketbooks. She imagined that Images had a very wealthy clientele, mostly from Charleston's oldest families and the recently rich who needed to add the look of family heirlooms to their homes.

"Very, very elegant," she said at last. "You have a good eye, not just for the art, but for how to showcase it. I'm impressed." She gestured toward a familiar desk that had once been in the Forsythes' living room. "You're not selling off the family treasures, are you?"

"Hardly. My mother's horrified enough that I insisted on bringing some of Great-grandmother's prized pieces to a shop. If she thought they might wind up in someone else's home, she'd probably disown me. As it is, I've convinced her to think of this as an unofficial museum." She grinned. "It helped that it gave her an excuse to go shopping for some new furniture for the house."

"You have a great talent for display, though," Dinah said, truly impressed. "I imagine everyone who comes in wants to take the entire package—art and presentation."

Maggie beamed at the compliment. "Does that mean I can sell you something before you leave? It's been a slow morning."

"You could if I had someplace to put it. Unfortunately our house is packed to the rafters, as you well know."

"I remember," Maggie said. "Isn't it time you started to look for a place of your own, if you're going to stick around? Just think how beautifully you'll be able to furnish it with all those antiques your folks have hidden away in the attic. I could help you sort through them." Her expression brightened. "And I know the perfect place for you. There's a wonderful carriage house on the market just a few blocks from here. The owner's anxious to sell because she's relocating to California, so I imagine you can get a good deal if you act quickly."

Dinah automatically shook her head. "No, thanks. I'm not ready for that."

"But you just said…" Maggie regarded her with confusion. "Surely you don't want to go on living at home."

"It's not forever," Dinah said. "Just till I get my bearings."

"Get your bearings? Are you sure you're not afraid that you'll change your mind about staying?"

"That's one reason," Dinah admitted. Not even to herself had she contemplated what she would do if Bobby didn't fall right in with her plans for the two of them.

"And the other? I hope you're not counting on moving into someplace with Bobby," Maggie said, frowning.

"You say that as if it's a totally ridiculous notion," Dinah said, grateful that her friend had given her the perfect opening for her interrogation. She used her very real annoyance to lay out the questions she wanted answered. "Why is that, Maggie? What do you know about Bobby that you're not telling me?"

Maggie didn't look the slightest bit intimidated by her accusatory tone. She held up her hands. "Not my place to say another word."

"You and Cord," Dinah muttered in disgust. "You're both tossing out all these maddening hints and innuendoes, but neither one of you has the guts to just say what's on your mind. I never thought I'd live to see the day when I'd be lumping you in with Cordell Beaufort. You're supposed to be my friend."

"I am your friend, which is why I have no intention of getting caught in the middle of this. I've already told you my opinion and you've rejected it, so I'm staying out of it from now on," Maggie replied. "And when did you see Cord again, by the way?"

"What makes you think I've seen him again?"

"Because it's obvious you're still exasperated. Since

you rarely hold a grudge for long, I figure he must have done something recent to get you all stirred up again. Am I right? Have you seen him?"

Dinah saw no real point in hiding it beyond depriving Maggie of a chance to gloat. "Last night, if you must know."

Maggie's eyes brightened. "Oh, really? How utterly fascinating."

"It wasn't fascinating. It was exasperating." And maybe just a little surprising, when she thought about how gently he'd held her when she'd suffered another one of those disconcerting panic attacks. "Stop trying to make something out of me running into Cordell."

If anything, Maggie only looked more amused. "Where did the two of you cross paths? The grocery store, perhaps? On the street?"

"Back out at his place," Dinah admitted defensively. "And don't even go there. I can see that you want to make something out of that, but I went back to look for Bobby. Period."

"I was merely going to comment that you seem to be making yourself at home out there," Maggie teased.

"I've been there twice," Dinah replied impatiently. Then, since Maggie didn't seem to be buying it, she added emphatically, "Both times looking for Bobby."

"Has it occurred to you yet that you're looking for him in the wrong place?"

Dinah stared at her in sudden confusion. "What do you mean? He lives there, doesn't he?"

"Usually," Maggie said.

Dinah bit back a groan. "What does that mean? Please don't tell me he's living right here in town."

"Actually you might have better luck finding him in Atlanta," Maggie admitted with apparent reluctance.

"Atlanta? What on earth is he doing in Atlanta?" She frowned at Maggie. "And don't tell me you don't know because I can tell that you do. It's time to start spilling some information, Maggie, or I'm going to have to wonder if you're not as anxious as Cord is to keep the two of us apart. He has a history of it. You don't."

Maggie sighed. "You're really not going to drop this whole ridiculous notion you have about getting together with Bobby, are you?"

"No. At least not till I've spoken to him and he tells me that he wants no part of what we used to have."

"That's what I was afraid of. Okay, he's over in Atlanta working."

"Permanently?"

"No. He's been handling a project over there for a while now, a few months at least."

"Why the hell didn't Cord just tell me that?" Dinah grumbled, the scowled at Maggie. "Why didn't you?"

"I just did."

"You could have mentioned it the other day. I could have seen him in Atlanta by now."

"What would have been the fun in that?" Maggie asked. "I've already told you that I think you're wasting your time on Bobby. Personally, I like the idea of you and Cord butting up against each other and setting off sparks for a while. I think it's just what you need."

"I don't," Dinah replied emphatically. "So just tell me what you know. How can I reach Bobby in Atlanta? Do you suppose he's renting someplace? Or is he staying in a hotel?"

Maggie shrugged. "I have no idea. You could ask Cord."

Dinah frowned at the suggestion. "I am done asking Cordell anything at all."

Maggie's lips twitched. "Is that because you don't like the answers he's giving you or because you're starting to like the fireworks a little too much?"

Dinah regarded her friend impatiently. "You really need to get a life."

"Probably so," Maggie agreed readily. "But until I do, I'm happy to meddle in yours."

"Stop it," Dinah pleaded. "Especially if you have some insane notion that Cord and I are the perfect match."

"Maybe not perfect," Maggie said thoughtfully. "But darn close, and definitely hot."

Dinah gave her a helpless look. "You've never even seen us together. What makes you think there is anything hot between us?"

"Oh, sweetie," Maggie said, laughter in her eyes, "even if a woman would have to be dead not to react to Cord, it's written all over your face every time you mention his name. The man ties you up in knots."

"Don't be ridiculous," Dinah scoffed, then hesitated. Much as she hated to admit it, Maggie did know her well. "What do you think you see when I mention Bobby?"

"Comfortable," Maggie said at once.

"Perfect," Dinah said happily. "Comfortable is exactly what I'm after."

"Maybe so, but it's not what's best for you and it is definitely not what will make you happy, not for the long haul."

"And you know that because?"

"Because I've known you all your life and I know your deepest, darkest secrets. Cordell Beaufort was always the one who made your heart pound."

"Only because he infuriated me," Dinah snapped. "Which you are starting to do, as well."

Maggie merely laughed. "Because you know I'm right. Now that we've established that, let's talk about dinner. Are you free tonight?"

So she could listen to more of Maggie's absurd theories? Not a chance, Dinah thought. "I'm busy tonight," she said.

"Doing what? Trying to track down Bobby?"

"Yes, as a matter of fact. If he doesn't have a number listed with information, I will call every hotel in Atlanta till I find him," she said with grim determination. Maggie and Cord might be totally opposed to this, but she knew what she needed and it was Bobby Beaufort. "If there's one thing I know how to do, it's how to work the phones to find someone who doesn't want to be found."

"Wouldn't it be easier just to ask Cord?" Maggie repeated.

"Been there, done that," Dinah reminded her. "Whatever his reasons, Cord doesn't seem inclined to share what he knows."

Besides, if there was any chance at all that Maggie might have it exactly right about her attraction to Cordell, Dinah needed to keep the contact between them to a minimum. She couldn't afford to be distracted by something that didn't have a chance of turning into anything more than a wild, no doubt self-destructive fling.

* * *

The minute Dinah got home she headed straight for her father's den. He kept all sorts of phone books around. There was bound to be one for Atlanta. The bank probably did a lot of business there.

She was sitting on the antique Aubusson carpet, pulling phone books out of a credenza and piling them haphazardly on the floor, when Maybelle came in.

"What on earth are you doing in here?" the housekeeper demanded, looking dismayed. "Besides making a mess of your daddy's stuff, that is. You know how he likes everything in order. Never known a man to be so set in his ways."

Dinah grimaced. Maybelle was right about that. When he noticed them at all, Marshall Davis liked his life and his surroundings to be orderly.

"I'll put it all back," Dinah promised, then grinned. "How many times do you suppose you came in here and had to set things to rights before Daddy came home and pitched a fit?"

"Once a day from the time you could walk," Maybelle responded at once, a tolerant smile on her face at the memory.

"And how many times did he find me out, anyway?"

"Most every one," Maybelle said, grinning. "That daddy of yours surely did dote on you, though. If your mother or me got so much as a paper clip out of place in here, he'd raise the roof. If it was Tommy Lee, he'd paddle his behind. But if it was you who turned things upside down, he'd just smile and say one day that curiosity of yours was going to pay off big-time. Turned out he was right about that."

Even so, Maybelle frowned at the chaos Dinah had

created. "You're too big for me to be following around
after you and cleaning up your messes, young lady.
You put those things back before your daddy gets home,
you hear. He might not be so tolerant these days. You're
a grown-up woman who ought to know better than to
mess with someone else's things."

"It's a few phone books, Maybelle. Not top secret
files."

"In his mind, there's not much difference."

Dinah laughed. "Stop fussing. I can handle Daddy."

After the housekeeper left, Dinah finally found the
current Atlanta phone directory and flipped through
the pages. She found two Robert Beauforts and one
Bobby, but after calling all three numbers, it was evident none was the right man. She called information to
see if there happened to be a more recent listing that
hadn't made the directory, but she struck out there, too.

That left hotels and motels, she concluded with a
sigh. She dragged over the Yellow Pages and started
with the downtown hotels. It was a mindless, tedious
task, but that was just about all she could cope with.

She'd made at least a dozen fruitless calls, when she
heard her father's voice escalating in the foyer. It was
countered by her mother's equally exasperated response. Dinah sat there in shock. She'd never heard either of them raise their voices. It wasn't that they hadn't
had disagreements. It was just that her mother especially had been brought up to believe that a raised voice
was unseemly. She soothed and placated when it was
called for. She certainly didn't shout.

Listening to them now, but unable to discern what
the argument was about, Dinah sat frozen in place.
She'd always assumed that her parents' marriage was

calm, if not passionate. She'd seen nothing since coming home to change that view. So, what had she missed? Was this heated discussion an anomaly or was it a significant symptom of a problem they'd been hiding from her? Did they feel free to argue now because they thought she was out of the house? Or were they so furious that they simply didn't care if she overheard? Whatever the explanation was, hearing them was an unwelcome shock.

She was tempted to open the door and step into the hallway, but concluded that would only embarrass all of them. She stayed where she was and hoped that her father would go upstairs to change clothes, rather than stepping directly into his den as he usually did.

Luck wasn't with her. The door to the den opened and he stalked into the room, slamming the door shut behind him. When he spotted Dinah, he stopped short. Embarrassment sent a tide of red flooding his handsome, patrician face.

"You heard, I suppose," he said, looking chagrined.

"Just that you were arguing," she said. "Not what it was about."

He nodded slowly. "That's good, then."

"Can I help?"

His lips curved slightly. "Your mother and I have been working out our own problems for a lot of years now. I don't think we need counseling from you."

He said it without rancor, but somehow it stung. Dinah busied herself with putting away the phone directories to avoid having him see the hurt that was in her eyes. Maybe she hadn't been around for years now, but she still considered herself to be a part of this family, not some intrusive outsider. Her father finally muttered a curse under his breath, then hunkered down beside her. "I didn't mean to hurt your feelings, Dinah. I was just trying to say that there's no need for you to get all worked up over this. Your mother and I have been doing this a long time now. We've survived so far."

Dinah regarded him with disbelief. "I never once heard the two of you argue."

"Because we didn't want you to," he said reasonably. "Sounds as if we did one thing right."

She studied him curiously. "You did a lot of things right. You were great parents."

"Thanks for saying that, though it seems like you're revising history a bit," he said, his eyes suddenly sparkling with amusement. "Didn't you tell us we were smothering you right before you left for New York and college?"

"Of course I did," she said, nudging him with her elbow. "How else do you think I'd have gotten out of here without drowning the two of you in tears? There was a part of me that wanted to stay right here in my safe little cocoon."

His expression sobered and he gave her a penetrating look. "Is that what you're doing now, hunkering down someplace safe?"

Apparently Dinah had always sold her father short. It seemed he had more intuition than she'd ever given him credit for. "Maybe just a little," she admitted.

"Did something happen over there?" he asked. "I mean something worse than the obvious mayhem you must have seen on a daily basis?" He searched her face, a worried crease in his forehead. "Dammit, Dinah, did someone hurt you?" he demanded angrily.

She winced at his sharp tone. "A lot of things happened over there," she said a little too lightly, hoping to change the entire tenor of the conversation. She knew the kind of things he must be imagining and she didn't want to go there.

"You know what I mean, Dinah," he chided. "If there's something on your mind, if you were hurt in some way—*any* way—you surely know that you can talk to me or your mother about it. Does it have anything to do with what happened a few months ago? Were you just covering up when you said you were fine so we wouldn't worry?"

"I am fine and I do know I can always talk to you."

He lifted his brows at her quick response. "Of course, you should know that, but just in case you'd rather talk to someone else, I do know a few people who are good listeners and more impartial than your mother and I."

She gave him a startled look. "You mean a shrink?" It was the very last thing she'd ever expected to hear her father suggest.

He seemed amused by her surprise. "Yes, a shrink. There's no shame in asking for help, Dinah. I imagine a lot of folks coming home from that war over there could use professional counseling to deal with what they've been through. When I came back from Vietnam, I wish I'd done that, rather than wrestling with all those demons on my own."

His admission barely registered, though she knew it was something she would ponder later. It wasn't the same for her. She wasn't a troubled soldier.

"I don't need a psychiatrist," she said sharply. "I'm just a little tired. A couple more weeks of rest and I'll be good as new."

Her father didn't look as if he believed her, but he nodded finally. "So what were you looking for in here? Can I help?"

She realized that he might very well know exactly how she could get in touch with Bobby, but she didn't want to ask. She wasn't entirely sure why, either. Maybe it was because she didn't want to have to explain to her very traditional father why she wanted to find a man she hadn't seen in more than a decade. Or maybe it was because she was afraid he, like Cord and Maggie, would not agree hers was a good idea and then withhold some crucial piece of information.

"I'd just like to borrow one of your phone books, if you don't mind," she said.

"Of course," he said at once. "Just put it back when you're finished."

"Believe me, I will," she said fervently, taking the Atlanta directory and giving her father a quick kiss before heading back up to her room.

She assured herself it was better to finish this search the way she'd started…on her own.

After all, she thought a little ruefully, she'd been independent and proud of it for a number of years now. Somehow, though, in recent months independence had lost its allure.

6

Dorothy was still seething over her argument with Marshall. He refused to attend an important function Dorothy had arranged for them to attend together.

"Go on your own," he'd told her when he'd arrived home from work just as she'd walked in the door after a rather tedious meeting. "You love that sort of thing, but you know I hate it."

She'd stared at him incredulously. "Since when?"

"Since forever."

"You were always eager enough to go in the past, when it suited your business interests," she'd reminded him, her voice ringing with impatience.

"No, I've been accommodating long enough," he corrected. "Tonight I'm tired and I have no intention of going out again. If you don't want to go alone, call Tommy Lee. I'm sure he'd be happy enough to escort you. Our son needs to spend a little time cultivating those people, if he expects to take over at the bank someday."

She'd stared at him in shock. "What do you mean *if?*" she'd demanded, her voice rising to a level she'd never in her life resorted to before. Then again, Marshall had never been more exasperating than he was being right at this moment.

"I don't mean anything," he said in the tone that indicated just the opposite. It merely meant he was tired of the whole subject. To prove it, he'd walked away from her, gone into his office and slammed the door.

Now she sat in front of her dressing table mirror and stared at her reflection. What on earth was happening to them? It was as if she was suddenly married to a stranger.

Their marriage had never been the passionate love match that some of their friends claimed to have, but they'd been well-suited in many ways. They'd found a rhythm for their lives that worked, especially after their children were born. Her role had been to support Marshall's busy career, raise their children and to be socially active in a way befitting their standing in the community. She'd always accepted that she and a small cadre of her friends were the style-setters in town.

Charleston was, in many ways, still a small town with a well-defined hierarchy. With their combined family backgrounds, it had been a foregone conclusion that they'd be accepted as a part of the crème de la crème of Charleston society, but maintaining that lofty position required real effort. It wasn't enough to send the occasional check to charity or to be seen at the right galas. They'd had to serve as chairmen of key events, which meant that she did the work and Marshall reaped the rewards. For a time she'd done it gladly.

It was only in recent years that it had all begun to bother her. She'd found her own worthwhile causes and put her time and energy into those. Maybe that was where the gulf now evident between them had started.

Tonight she'd been forced to face the fact that it would take a sturdy bridge to cross that deepening chasm.

When someone tapped on the bedroom door, she assumed it was Dinah, but it was Marshall who entered. She regarded him with dismay. She wasn't up to another angry exchange.

"Unless you've come to say you've changed your mind about tonight, you can leave," she said coolly.

Instead of doing as she asked, he sank down on the edge of the bed. "I came to talk about Dinah."

"Now?" she asked incredulously.

"Yes, now, dammit! I came to tell you that I just had a very disturbing conversation with her. I saw for the first time what you meant when you came by the office to discuss your concern, Dorothy. She's obviously distraught over something. I think we need to get to the bottom of it."

Dorothy put aside her annoyance and turned to face him. The encounter must have been troubling indeed if it had put such a worried frown on his face. "What do you suggest we do?"

He regarded her with a helpless expression. "I have no idea. This is your area of expertise."

She smiled at that. "At least I still have one skill that you admire."

He frowned at her bitter comment. "What the hell do you mean by that? Can't you put aside whatever differences you have with me for one minute and concentrate on our daughter?"

She bit back a sharp retort and held up her hand. "I agree that now's not the time, Marshall. Let's concentrate on Dinah. Did she tell you anything?"

"Nothing," he admitted. "But something happened

to her over there. Something bad. I'd stake my life on it. She says it wasn't that incident she was involved in a few months ago, but I'm not convinced she's being entirely truthful."

Alarm spread through her. "You don't think she was...?" She couldn't even bring herself to say the word.

"Raped?" he said with a visible shudder. "To tell you the truth, I don't think we can rule it out. I don't think we can rule out any sort of atrocity at this point."

"Oh, dear God."

He took her hand in his. "Come now, Dorothy. Don't fall apart on me. We don't know it was anything like that, but she's been living in an uncivilized atmosphere. Anything's possible. Since she refused to tell me anything, I tried to get her to agree to talk to a psychologist I know, but she refused. Do you think she's talking to her friends?"

"No. I don't even think she's seen anyone outside of Maggie."

"Maybe Maggie knows something, then," he suggested.

"I'll call her," Dorothy said at once. "First thing in the morning. For now, though, I'd better finish dressing. I'm running late."

Marshall hesitated, then regarded her with a faintly sheepish expression. "Perhaps I will go with you tonight, after all, unless you've made other arrangements."

"No. I did speak to Tommy Lee, but he and Laurie already had other plans."

"They're probably line-dancing at some country-western bar," he suggested, his tone scathing. "That seems to be the kind of entertainment they go for these days."

She frowned at him. "This isn't the first time you've hinted that you're unhappy with Tommy Lee. Would you care to explain?"

"It would take too long and you said we're already running late."

"I won't let you put me off forever," she warned. She wasn't about to let her entire family unravel right in front of her eyes.

"Fine," Marshall said. "Meantime, I'll meet you downstairs in what? Ten minutes?"

She nodded.

He stood up and started for the door, then turned back. "I'm sorry about earlier."

She glanced up in the mirror and met his reflected gaze. "Me, too."

Sadly, though, she knew that neither the apology, nor the last-minute decision to join her were going to solve the real problems between them. In fact, she had literally no idea what might end the sad stand-off they seemed to have reached in their marriage. They were drifting, not connecting, and not communicating. If there was a quick fix for any of that, she couldn't see it.

With a feeling of utter relief, Dinah heard her parents leave, presumably for the evening. Once the front door closed, she went back downstairs in search of something to snack on for dinner.

In the refrigerator she found a covered plate of fried chicken and potato salad that Maybelle had left for her. *Eat every bite,* a note left on top commanded.

Grinning, Dinah took the ridiculously huge meal and sat at the kitchen table. As a kid she'd always preferred to eat in here with Maybelle, rather than in the stiff, formal atmosphere of the dining room. She'd barely taken a bite of the chicken when the back door opened and Tommy Lee came in.

"Coast clear?" he asked, looking harried.

Tommy Lee was two years younger than Dinah, still in his twenties, in fact, but he looked older. Maybe it was from too much sun, but she suspected some of the lines on his face came from hard living and stresses she couldn't even begin to imagine. Trying to walk in his father's footsteps couldn't be easy.

"You trying to avoid Mother or Dad?" she asked as he plucked a chicken leg off the plate and sat down opposite her.

"Both, as a matter of fact."

"Then you came to see me?" she asked, surprised.

"Actually I came to beg some food from Maybelle," he said with a grin. "Finding you in here is just a bonus."

"Laurie's not cooking tonight?"

"Laurie can't cook worth a lick," he said without rancor. "If it doesn't come in takeout, we don't have it at our house."

"You really were rebelling when you picked her, weren't you?"

"You have no idea," he said, though without the slightest trace of self-pity. "So, what's up with you? I thought you'd be bored to tears and heading out of here by now."

"Already anxious to be rid of me?"

"Hardly. With you underfoot, it's taking the pressure off me."

"What pressure?"

"To live up to Dad's high expectations." He stood up and reached in the refrigerator and pulled out a beer. He popped the top and swallowed a long gulp.

Since no one else in the house drank beer, Dinah had to assume that these food forays of Tommy Lee's were frequent enough that Maybelle had started stocking the beer for him.

"What's going on between you and Dad?" she asked him.

"Nothing new," he insisted. "He wants me to be somebody I'm not. He's just now waking up to the fact that I'm never going to change."

"Out of spite?"

"No, darlin' sister, out of self-awareness. I'm not the least bit suited to a nine-to-five job hustling money. I know the banking business. I just don't want to do it."

"And you've told him that?"

"In every language I know." He grinned. "Which is pretty much limited to plain old Southern. You'd think a man like our daddy would grasp that one."

"Want me to talk to him?" Dinah asked.

"Lord, no," he said with a shudder. "If you start fighting my battles for me, he really will think I don't have any gumption at all. No, this will all come to a head soon enough." He finished the piece of chicken he'd stolen from Dinah's plate, snagged a couple of forkfuls of potato salad, then drank down the rest of his beer. He sat back with a satisfied sigh. "Damn, I miss Maybelle's cooking."

"Me, too," Dinah said. "I used to wake up nights thinking about her corn bread and her mashed potatoes and gravy."

"Not a lot of that on the menu where you've been, I imagine."

"Not even close," she said.

He studied her intently. "You really okay, Dinah?"

She groaned. "Don't you start, too. Everybody thinks I'm cracking up. It's getting tiresome."

He held up his hands. "Since nobody knows how that feels better than I do, I'll quit poking around in your life right this second. You change your mind, though, I've still got a big ole shoulder you can cry on anytime you need it."

Dinah reached over and tucked her hand into his. "When did you turn into my *big* brother? You always were this puny little thing pestering me to set you up on dates with my friends."

His expression suddenly turned unbearably sad. "I grew up while you weren't even looking, Dinah."

The momentary melancholy in his eyes disappeared so quickly Dinah wasn't even certain she'd seen it. He stood up with his more typical jovial expression firmly in place.

"Better get my butt home with the Chinese takeout." He leaned down and dropped a kiss on her forehead. "I'll see you around. You need anything, you call me, okay?"

"Love you," she said as he walked out the door.

"Love you," Tommy Lee echoed, but only after he was far enough away that she couldn't see his face.

He'd always been that way. He'd never wanted anyone to see his sentimental side. In fact, after spending just this small amount of time with him, she couldn't help wondering if he even knew he still had it in him or if the pressures of battling their father's expectations had driven that little bit of self-awareness right out of him.

It had been days now and Cord hadn't been able to shake the image of normally confident, wisecracking, steady-as-a-rock Dinah Davis flat on her stomach in the dirt in a pretty little sundress, shivering so hard he'd wondered if he'd ever get her to stop. There was no question about how messed up she was, since she'd let him tend to her without uttering a single protest.

As if that memory weren't disturbing enough, he couldn't seem to forget the way she'd felt in his arms, the way her body curved toward him, hanging on for dear life. He knew she'd been embarrassed by what she would consider a display of weakness. She'd never have done such a thing if she hadn't been having a panic attack, but he couldn't help wishing that she'd been in his arms for another reason entirely.

Maybe that was why he lied to his brother.

"Bobby, I need you to stay in Atlanta for another week," he said right after Bobby had told him he was coming home. "Maybe longer."

"What!" his brother exclaimed. "Are you crazy?"

Cord held the phone away from his ear at the expected explosion. He couldn't very well blame Bobby for being anxious to get back to Charleston. Living in a hotel room wasn't the same as being at home and he'd been doing just that for months now. Worse, he'd been separated from his fiancée for most of that time. They'd already had this conversation once, so Cord knew pretty much what to expect. He wasn't looking forward to it.

"I've been over here for months now," Bobby reminded him. "All of the leases are signed. There are only so many nails left to be pounded and so much paint left to be applied. The crew is perfectly capable of finishing up."

Cord bit back an impatient sigh. How the hell was he supposed to argue with that logic? He desperately grasped at one last straw. "What about the old hotel we've been looking into restoring? Is that a done deal?"

"I've greased every wheel there is to be greased," his brother insisted, then added with a touch of defensiveness, "If we don't get the job restoring that hotel, it won't be for lack of trying on my part."

Cord could see that Bobby was about to misinterpret his words and jump to the conclusion that Cord was dissatisfied with his work. He needed to do some mighty fast tap-dancing to keep Bobby where he was with his morale intact. The success of their partnership depended on mutual respect for their very divergent talents. He was treading on Bobby's toes right now, no question about it.

"I know that," he said hurriedly. "You've done a fantastic job, Bobby. I just think it'll pay off if you're right there and accessible if any questions come up. I want the other investors to know we're as committed to that project as we have been to the one we're finishing up. In fact, it might make sense for you to think about buying someplace permanent there."

"You want me to move here? No way in hell, Cord. If you think one of us needs to be here twenty-four/seven, it'll have to be you. You can move over here and prove how committed we are," Bobby retorted. "You're not the one who hasn't seen his fiancée in four freaking months, except on weekends."

Unfortunately, Bobby had a point, Cord conceded.

Rianna was sweet and smart and totally in love with his brother. She was also the primary thing standing between Bobby and that crazy agreement he'd made years ago with Dinah. Cord definitely wanted to keep Rianna happy and his brother otherwise occupied.

"Have her come on over to Atlanta for a week or so," Cord encouraged. "The company will spring for a luxury suite and all the champagne you can drink. You can talk wedding plans, maybe even write out your engagement announcement for the paper. That ought to make her happy." And it would finally put Dinah on notice that she was too late to make her play for Bobby.

"Can we afford even a few days in some fancy hotel?" Bobby asked doubtfully, his mind immediately going to the bottom line. "I thought we were doing all this stuff on a no-frills expenses budget, so every penny would show up in the work."

If the money had to come out of his own pocket, Cord would see that there was enough. "Absolutely. We'll find the money. You deserve some R & R after all the time you've put in."

"You're right about that. Thanks," Bobby said, appeased for now. "Maybe I can convince Rianna to get married while she's here and skip the fancy shindig," he added wistfully. "Just the thought of it is beginning to give me hives."

"Great idea," Cord said with more enthusiasm than the idea normally would have merited. It probably was best not to stir up questions about exactly why he was suddenly so eager for his brother to get a wedding ring on Rianna's finger, when he'd expressed doubts about the big rush in the past. Still, since Bobby had given him an opening, he asked, "You two ever think about running off to Vegas?"

"I think about it all the time," Bobby said with a laugh. "Rianna's a tough sell, though. She wants tradition and an impressive guest list. Much as I would like to skip all the hoopla and elope, I know I'll never hear the end of it if I talk her out of having the wedding of her dreams."

Cord chuckled, despite his dismay. "Yep, sooner or later, we always pay when women don't get exactly what they want."

In fact, something told him if he continued to be the roadblock between Dinah and his brother, all those other visions he was entertaining about getting her into his own bed were going to go right up into smoke. Last time he'd tried it, not only had Dinah ripped him apart with language totally unbefitting a lady, but it had almost cost him his relationship with Bobby. Best not to carry round two too far.

Dinah had no luck in tracking down Bobby. It was as if he'd fallen off the face of the earth. She'd tried every hotel in the Atlanta directory and was debating starting on the outlying suburbs.

In one last desperate attempt to locate him without going back out to tangle with Cord, she got on the Internet and did a search of the Atlanta newspapers to see if there had been any mention of whatever business he had over there. Unless he was a lot more high-profile than she imagined, it was a long shot, but it was all she had short of going to Atlanta and doing a whole lot of tedious legwork. Of course, that might be preferable to sitting around the house much longer while her parents watched her with their increasingly worried expressions.

She typed in Bobby's name, hit the search button and was stunned to see three stories listed, all with glowing headlines about the work of Beaufort Construction in Atlanta. The most recent feature, which had appeared just last Sunday, had pictures of the detailed craftsmanship in their new project. The architecture critic who'd written the piece had given it a raving review. There was even a picture of Bobby, wearing a very expensive navy blue suit, crisp white shirt and silk tie. There was no question that Bobby was a success.

When she read on her mouth dropped open.

"Good grief," she muttered as she scanned the rest of the article and realized that not only Bobby, but Cord had assembled impressive credentials during the years she'd been away. Their firm was considered one of the most well-respected around in their line of restoration work.

When she came to the part about their work at Covington Plantation, her jaw dropped yet again. *That* was where Cord and her mother were crossing paths? Not only that, he had publicly acknowledged her mother's role in him landing that particular job.

"Well, I'll be damned," she muttered. It seemed she was going to have to swallow a whole lot of crow next time she saw Cord. Now she had some idea why he had been so amused by her conclusions about him. He could afford to sit back and wait patiently for her eventual comeuppance.

Of course, he could have simply told her the truth and saved her the embarrassment. But that would have spoiled his enjoyment of the moment when she'd be forced to admit her mistake.

Dinah recalled his comment about her mother giving him grief and realized that it must have had to do with Covington Plantation business. It was all her mother could talk about lately.

Irritated with herself for not heeding Maggie's disparaging remarks about her investigative skills—to say nothing of Cord's similar criticism—and not putting the pieces together sooner, she turned off the computer, grabbed her purse and headed for the door. It was time she paid a visit to her mother's pet project, so she could see for herself just what was going on over there.

It was only after she was on her way that she realized that she'd let checking out Covington Plantation and Cord's work take precedence over getting to Atlanta in search of Bobby. She didn't want to think about why that might be, because the one reason that immediately popped into her head was simply intolerable. Cord Beaufort, she assured herself staunchly, was not that damned fascinating.

7

Cord was about at his wit's end. He'd expected to make excellent headway on restoring the molding in one of the upstairs bedrooms this afternoon, but instead he'd spent the whole blasted day placating Dorothy Davis. He saw now exactly where Dinah got her most exasperating qualities. They were two peas in a pod when it came to issuing ultimatums and assuming they knew everything about everything.

Still, he couldn't help but admire Mrs. Davis. For all of her designer clothes and society ways, she wasn't afraid to get her hands dirty or to challenge his expertise every step of the way. Even more impressive, she really did know a lot about the work and the way it should be done. She wasn't just opinionated. She was knowledgeable, which made their confrontations challenging and lively. She won the debates about as often as he did, not out of some desire on his part to placate her, but because her ideas were good ones.

When he eliminated the nuisance factor, he was forced to concede he was actually learning quite a bit from her. Not that he would ever in a million years admit that, especially not on a day like today when she was proving to be particularly exasperating.

"You know if you keep poking around out here, I'm going to have to buy you your own hard hat," he told her.

"I'd like one in pink, if possible," she retorted. "And you might as well buy it now, because I'm not nearly done poking around."

He frowned at her, even though they'd been over this ground before and he was confident of her faith in his work. "Don't you trust me?" he asked one more time. It never hurt to make sure nothing had changed. With her connections, Dorothy Davis could enhance his reputation or destroy it, depending on how satisfied she was with the end results at Covington Plantation.

She regarded him impatiently. "Of course I do, Cordell, or you wouldn't have gotten this job in the first place. But you know perfectly well that I didn't take on this project so I could sit on the sidelines. I have just as much at stake as you do."

He looked at her with disbelief. "Such as?"

"My credibility," she said at once.

"You mean because you recommended me?" he asked, that niggling hint of self-doubt back despite all the years he'd struggled to rid himself of it, despite the growing collection of clippings from prestigious publications about the work he and Bobby were doing all over the South.

"Oh, for heaven's sakes. Haven't we dispensed with that?" she asked irritably. "You're very talented and everyone around here knows it. No, I'm talking about the fact that I recommended we take this on in the first place. Maybe the time is past when people will want to visit a plantation that only brings back memories of a shameful part of the South's history."

Cord shook his head. "No, that's exactly why it needs to be restored. The South was about more than slavery. We had a fine culture and deep-rooted traditions. There's a lot worth remembering. These old rice plantations gave this region a valuable industry and economic base."

Her expression brightened. "That's it exactly," she said excitedly. "And it was a gracious lifestyle, when people worked hard, but spent time entertaining their friends. I sometimes wish we hadn't lost sight of those ways. Everyone's so rushed now. I read those articles about the so-called 'new' South and they make me cringe. We'll just turn into crowded cities filled with hurried, rude people that won't be one bit different from New York, if we're not careful."

Cord laughed. "I doubt anyone will ever confuse Charleston with New York, least of all your daughter."

Her expression registered surprise. "You've seen Dinah?"

"A time or two," he admitted, ready to kick himself for the slip.

She gave him a penetrating look that he'd learned to interpret as a warning to get his guard up.

"How did she seem to you?" she asked.

Cord wasn't about to get into his impressions of Dinah. They were a tangled mess of contradictions, anyway. "Okay, I suppose," he equivocated. "Why? Are you worried about her for some reason?"

"For a lot of reasons," she said. "To be perfectly honest, I think she's holding something back. So does her father. She's just not herself. Marshall tried to talk to her about it, but she claimed there was absolutely nothing wrong."

"Then I suppose all you can do is take her word for that," he said, unwilling to admit that he'd seen the evidence first-hand of just how troubled Dinah was. And while he didn't know the precise incident that had caused her post-traumatic stress problems, he knew that was the label to pin on it.

Mrs. Davis didn't seem convinced by his suggestion that they take a wait-and-see position. "You know," she said, her expression turning thoughtful. "You could do me a huge favor, Cordell."

"Oh?" he said warily. Dorothy Davis's requests tended to be huge. The last time she'd asked in that sweet, persuasive tone he'd wound up in a tuxedo at some fancy society dinner where she wanted him to charm some of the plantation's prospective benefactors. And the time before that he'd been front and center in some absurd bachelor auction. He still shuddered at the embarrassment he'd felt parading down that ridiculous runway while women in the audience hooted and shouted out their bids.

"Spend a little time with Dinah," she requested. "See if you can find out what's really going on with her."

His jaw dropped. "You want *me* to hang out with your daughter?"

She gave him an impatient look. "You say that as if you're shocked. You're a perfectly respectable man. You've long since overcome your difficult beginnings. You can hold your head high around anyone in this town and don't you dare let anybody suggest otherwise."

"Yes, ma'am," he said meekly.

She chuckled. "Oh, can that humble act, Cordell. We both know your ego is solid enough. Now, tell me, will you spend some time with Dinah?"

He worked hard to hide his pleasure. "I'll do what I can," he said, still feigning reluctance. "But Dinah may not go along with it. She and I haven't always seen eye to eye."

"Water under the bridge, I'm sure," Dorothy Davis said with a dismissive wave of her hand. "Besides, didn't you just tell me you'd already seen her a couple of times?"

"In passing," Cord said, since she obviously didn't know about Dinah's efforts to track down his brother. "Besides, what makes you think she'll say anything to me, when she won't talk to you?"

"You're a very handsome, charming man," she replied at once. "I'm sure you can think of some way to get a woman to open up."

Cord nearly choked at that. "You want me to seduce the truth out of her?"

She laughed. "Perhaps something short of that would be preferable," she said, then winked at him. "Then again, do whatever you feel is necessary. Now, if you'll excuse me, I never did finish going through the downstairs rooms this morning."

Still trying to recover from her outrageous suggestion, Cord merely nodded. She was almost out the door, when he thought to ask, "Did you want me to come downstairs with you?"

"No need. I'll call for you if something's not to my liking."

Cord didn't doubt that for a minute. He shuddered to think what she would do to him if he took her daughter to bed then wound up breaking her heart. The woman was perfectly comfortable handling some frighteningly sharp tools.

Still reeling from her discovery about Cord's connection to her mother's work at Covington Plantation, Dinah drove straight to the outskirts of Charleston. Only when she was on the once-familiar country road to the plantation did she finally start to calm down.

It was peaceful out here on the road shaded by towering oaks draped in Spanish moss. Sun filtered through the trees and an occasional snowy egret or white ibis could be spotted on the side of the road. The Low Country was called that because of the prevalent swampland that made much of the area useless for building. As much as she'd hated it, Dinah thought now that there was something to be said for the pristine, natural beauty that no developer would ever destroy except at great expense. The low-lying area which was prone to flooding had been ideal for the rice that had been grown there centuries ago.

There was no sign marking the driveway to Covington Plantation, but she'd been there so often she knew her way. Twenty years ago and more, when they'd lived not far from the plantation, rather than in their current home in town, her mother had been fascinated with the old, deserted house. She'd taken Tommy Lee and Dinah there for picnics on the sweeping veranda, then made up stories about the place until they fell asleep for their naps.

The once-graceful old house had fallen into disrepair decades ago. Still, the long, winding driveway was lined with towering magnolias and colorful azaleas in shades of pink, magenta and purple. It was evident that change was underway. The lawn was neatly trimmed now and the veranda looked almost as if mint juleps could be served there at any second. Only the sound of saws and hammers and shouts disturbed the tranquility of the setting and suggested that the plantation was under siege by workmen.

She found her mother in what was once the formal dining room downstairs. She had a hard hat on her head, dust on her cheek and an irritated expression on her patrician features. She was standing practically nose to nose with Cord.

"Cordell Beaufort, I thought I had made it clear that these old floors were to be preserved at all costs. Why are you ripping this one up?"

Several workmen stood around, obviously waiting for further instructions. Judging from their amused expressions, these battles were not uncommon. In fact, even Cord looked more amused than intimidated, which no doubt riled Dinah's mother no end.

Hands shoved in the pockets of his jeans, he rocked back on his heels and said, "And I told you if we leave this rotted wood in here, we'll be courting a lawsuit. Of course, we could always offer a prize to the first tourist who falls through and breaks a leg."

Dorothy Davis scowled. "But the historic integrity of the plantation—"

"Will be perfectly intact," Cord assured her in a placating tone.

Her mother's gaze narrowed. "How?"

"I've found a supply of wood that matches this exactly in an old house that's being torn down in Savannah," Cord said. "It's in excellent condition, given its age. I researched it very carefully. It can be dated to the same period."

Dorothy seemed slightly mollified. "I suppose that would work."

"Of course it will. When the board gave me this job, I assumed it was because y'all knew I'd do it right." He caught sight of Dinah just then and winked. "Hey, sugar, I hope you came to take your mama on home. She's had a long day."

Despite her annoyance with him only a short time earlier, Dinah barely contained a chuckle. "I imagine it was a lot longer for you than it was for her."

His lips twitched. "I never said such a thing, now did I?"

"Only because you're too polite," Dinah said, admiring his restraint. "Which is something I never thought I'd say about you."

His grin spread. "Stick around. You may discover a whole lot of things about me you never expected to learn."

Dinah caught the speculative look in her mother's eyes and decided the exchange had gone on long enough. "Mother, could I see you outside?"

"Of course, darling. Cord and I were just finishing up. This room was the last one on my inspection tour."

"Is that right?" Cord said. "Are you certain there's not some nook or cranny that you've missed? I believe I actually managed to put in a whole fifteen minutes of work upstairs today."

"Don't be a smart-aleck with me, young man," Dinah's mother responded with unmistakable affection. "And don't forget any of the instructions I gave you, either." She cast a pointed look in Dinah's direction, then beamed at her. "Okay, darling, let's go outside where we'll be able to hear ourselves think. There's too much racket in here."

"Hasn't stopped you from making conversation with me," Cord said. "I'll be upstairs again, if either of you need me for anything."

"Maybe you can give Dinah a tour of the place, after she and I finish up," her mother suggested.

"Glad to," Cord responded, then met Dinah's gaze. "Just come and get me when you're ready."

Dinah couldn't seem to tear her gaze away when he left the room. Those blasted jeans fit his behind and his thighs like a particularly snug glove. Sadly, his black T-shirt covered up the stomach she knew for a fact was hard as a rock.

She didn't realize she'd sighed until she caught a glimpse of her mother's amused expression.

"Let's go outside," she said hurriedly, her cheeks flaming.

But once there, Dinah couldn't decide which question she wanted to ask first.

It was her mother who broke the silence. "Cordell has turned into an amazing young man, hasn't he?"

"I wouldn't know," Dinah said. "I'm surprised you never mentioned that he was working on Covington Plantation."

Her mother gave her a wry look. "Be honest, Dinah. This sort of thing always bored you to tears. You never had much interest in the preservation of our Southern heritage. When I suggested you drive out here with me the other day, you practically yawned in my face."

That was true enough.

"Unless, of course, your real interest isn't the house, but Cord," her mother remarked slyly.

"Don't be ridiculous," Dinah said. Hearing the words, she realized she'd had a few too many occasions lately to use them in connection with her feelings for Cord. "Actually, since his company is doing this project, I was hoping you'd be able to tell me how to get in touch with Bobby."

Her mother looked vaguely disappointed. "I'm almost certain that Bobby is in Atlanta. They're finishing up a rather large restoration project there and bidding on something else, I believe."

"Can you get a number for me?"

"Well, of course, but why? I wasn't aware that you and Bobby had been in touch recently. I thought you two ended your relationship years ago."

"We did," Dinah admitted, then added with what she hoped was just the right casual note, "But seeing him is one of the reasons I decided to come home. I thought we could catch up, as long as I'm in town."

Dinah was not about to go into detail on that subject. Her mother would be horrified by the thought that her daughter actually had some sort of coolly calculated backup plan for getting married and having babies. She might want Dinah settled, but she was romantic enough to want it to be a love match or at least some mutually agreeable social arrangement.

"Why didn't you just ask Cordell?" her mother asked. "He mentioned that you two had run into each other recently. I was rather hoping… Well, never mind. You've always insisted on doing things your own way."

"I have asked Cord to give a message to Bobby. Apparently he hasn't seen fit to do it. I decided to track Bobby down myself."

"Don't lay the blame on Cordell. Perhaps Bobby's been too busy to get back to you," her mother said gently. "He works very hard and he does have a fiancée, after all. She might not want him spending time with an old flame."

Dinah felt as if all the wind had been sucked right out of her. "Bobby's engaged?" She could hardly get the words past the boulder in her throat.

"Why yes, to a lovely girl," her mother replied, as if it were common knowledge. She clearly had no idea that her casual remark was shocking to Dinah. "He brought her to the house for dinner when we were finalizing the deal for this restoration. She's absolutely crazy about him. I think they're about to set a wedding date."

"But they haven't yet?" Dinah asked with one last crazy hope of salvaging her own plan despite the very clear evidence that it was too late.

"Only because he's been away on this business trip," her mother assured her.

Thankfully, she was oblivious to the fact that she was quietly turning Dinah's world completely upside down. What the hell sort of backup plan was Dinah supposed to come up with now?

To Cord's disappointment, Dinah had never come looking for him. But when he finally quit for the day and walked outside, he found her sitting on the front steps looking like a kid whose puppy had just run off. He dropped down beside her, then gave her a curious look.

"When you never came looking for me for that tour, I thought you must be long gone," he said. "Have you been waiting out here for me?"

"Not really."

"I see," he said, trying to hide his reaction to yet another blow to his ego. "Car break down?"

"No." She gave him a bleak look. "Bobby's engaged."

Ah, so that was it. Her mother had spilled the beans. He studied Dinah's face and concluded she looked more dejected than brokenhearted. That was encouraging.

"Yes," he agreed.

She poked an elbow in his ribs. "Why didn't you tell me? I asked if he was involved with anyone and you told me to ask him. You could have saved me the trouble. Or did you want me to feel like a total idiot? Were you looking forward to that?"

"Making you feel like an idiot definitely didn't enter into it. I figured it was his news to share." He shrugged. "Or not. I've said all along this was between the two of you. I did enough damage last time I got involved."

She gave him an odd look. "You think if he finds out I'm back it will make a difference?"

Cord didn't like the sudden glint of hope in her eyes. "No," he said flatly, determined to discourage her from rocking that particular boat. He didn't care to analyze his reasons for that, either. He was keeping his head in the sand on a lot of his own motivations lately, especially where Dinah was concerned.

"Then you think this woman is better for Bobby than I am?"

Cord sighed. Obviously she wasn't going to be satisfied until she'd analyzed this whole thing to death. Going out with a woman just to listen to her mope around about the man who'd gotten away wasn't his idea of a good time, but in this case he decided to make an exception.

He met her gaze. "Have dinner with me."

She stared at him as if he'd suggested they run naked along Charleston harbor. "Why?"

He grinned at her baffled reaction. "Because it's been a long day, I'm starved, and you look as if you could use a good meal. You're too skinny."

"I am not skinny," she said, immediately rising to the bait.

"Matter of opinion," he said easily. "Come on. I know a place where we can get shrimp and the best onion rings in the South."

She regarded him with a faint glimmer of interest. The meal seemed to intrigue her far more than spending time with him. He could live with that, at least for now.

"Murrells Inlet?" she asked.

"Maybe. You'll have to come with me to find out."

"That's a long way to go for dinner."

"A couple of hours at most. You have someplace else you need to be? Or is it all that time alone with me in a car that has you turning skittish?"

She rose to her feet in a fluid motion, then gave him one of those cool, considering looks that oddly made him want to kiss her senseless. "For a meal like that, I'll even spend an evening with you."

"What a gracious acceptance," he said, lips twitching. "I'm surely honored."

She gave him a grin that made his heart skip a beat.

"You should be," she said. "And then once you've fed me, you can tell me everything you know about Bobby's fiancée."

"So you can plot a strategy to break them up?" he asked, feeling vaguely uncomfortable about getting any further involved in her whole scheme than he already was. "I don't think so, Dinah."

"If they're in love, there won't be a thing I can do, will there?"

"You can cause trouble, the same way I did between you and Bobby," he said direly. "Bobby's my brother. I don't want to see him hurt."

She gave him a weary look. "Neither do I, Cordell. I just need to figure out where the hell I belong these days."

Cord could understand that kind of need. He'd struggled with it for a long time himself. He just didn't know why a woman who'd made an international reputation for herself would sound so sad and desperate.

"That's a mighty tall order for one evening," he told her lightly. "But with enough shrimp and beer under our belts, I'm sure we can tackle it."

She gave him another one of her wistful looks that made his insides twist.

"I surely do hope you're right," she murmured.

He tucked a finger under her chin and met her gaze, keeping his expression serious. "I'm warning you, though. It sounds like we might have to save devising a plan for world peace for another night."

Her lips curved slightly into the beginnings of a smile. "Is that what you want to talk about?"

"Indeed, I do. I want to hear some solutions from a woman who's been in the thick of the trouble spots."

"Then maybe you ought to try Madeleine Albright or Margaret Thatcher. I'm sure they have a much better grasp of the issues than I do."

"But you're prettier," he said, then winked. "Nothing turns me on more than listening to a beautiful woman with a clever mind talk about war and peace."

She laughed finally. "You're demented, you know that, don't you?"

"Quite likely. Now why don't you run along home and freshen up. I'll be by to pick you up in an hour, unless you think you ought to sneak out of the house because your mama and daddy won't approve of you running around with the likes of me."

"Don't pull that with me," she said. "I saw you with my mother not two hours ago, Cordell. It's plain she adores you."

"She admires my skill with a hammer," he corrected. "And there are some days when she's not too certain of that."

"I don't believe that for a second. I know my mother. You wouldn't be doing this project if she didn't trust you completely."

"Does that mean you might consider trusting me, too?"

"Enough to let you take me to dinner," she retorted. "We'll see after that. There's a lot of history between the two of us that makes the whole trust thing tricky."

"I only did what I did because I was worried about Bobby," he said in his own defense.

"You told him I was sleeping with another man. You lied to him to break us up."

He gave her an unflinching look. "It was the wrong tactic to use," he admitted. "But I was desperate."

"Why?"

"Because you and Bobby were all wrong for each other back then. You still are."

"I don't see how you can say that. It's not as if you know me that well."

"Sure I do, darlin'. And you proved me right in the end, didn't you? You went off and broke his heart."

"We agreed—" she began.

Cord cut her off. "Only because you gave him no choice. He had too much pride to fight you."

Dinah sighed. "I never meant to hurt him."

"You wouldn't mean to hurt him now, either, but you would. I can see the train wreck coming."

"So you're going to jump on the tracks?" she asked a little too hopefully.

Cord chuckled. "You wish. No, I'm sitting this one out," he said, considering it only a small fib. "You do what you have to do."

"Maybe you can give me some ideas over dinner," she suggested.

Fat chance in hell, Cord thought, but he nodded solemnly nonetheless.

"Maybe," he agreed.

Of course, if he had his way, they'd get off the subject of Bobby and onto more fascinating topics before they finished the first round of beer.

8

Still shaken by the news of Bobby's engagement, Dinah decided to make a call to Afghanistan to speak to Ray before Cord came to pick her up for dinner. Maybe it wasn't too late to rethink this whole career change thing. It was possible that this unexpected news about Bobby was a sign that she shouldn't have given up so easily, that she needed to get back to work, if only to prove to herself that she was strong enough to do it.

Being at home had not proven to be the panacea she thought it might be. Perhaps it was time to get back into action, back to what she knew and loved.

Marriage and babies? What had she been thinking? That wasn't who she was. She was a journalist and a damn good one, despite everything that had happened. She was beginning to think her backup plan never would have worked, even if Bobby had gone along with it, because of who she was and all she had seen.

When Ray answered the phone he sounded harried. Dinah belatedly realized she'd caught him just as he was preparing for the live satellite feed for the cable outlet's primetime broadcasts.

"I'm so sorry, Ray," she apologized at once. "I

wasn't thinking. This is a terrible time for me to be calling. I'll call you tomorrow."

"Don't be crazy. I can always spare five minutes for you," Ray said. "Talk to me. How's it going at home?"

The gruff concern in his voice filled her with a longing to see him again, to be back in the thick of things polishing a news segment about to be aired.

"Good," she lied, though without much conviction. "It's been great to see my family." That much, at least, was true, though it was getting increasingly uncomfortable knowing she wasn't disclosing the whole reason for her lengthy visit.

"And that man you left behind?" Ray asked. "How's that working out? Should I be expecting a wedding invitation one of these days?"

"Afraid not. It seems he's engaged."

Ray fell silent.

Dinah sighed. "Sort of throws a new wrinkle into things, doesn't it?"

"There are other men, Dinah. You don't have to settle down tomorrow, just open yourself up to the possibility."

She knew Ray was right, but she'd wanted to kick-start the plan so she wouldn't feel quite so lost. She'd always been the kind of woman who set goals for herself then worked like crazy to achieve them. Now that she had no real sense of direction or purpose, she was scared without quite knowing what it was that terrified her. Maybe it was the possibility that she *would* grab the first man or job that came along.

"Talk to me, Dinah," Ray commanded. "This hasn't given you some crazy idea about coming back over here, has it?"

She heard the dismay in his voice and knew he would fight her, at least until she could demonstrate complete conviction about her choice.

"No," she said at last, fighting to keep the resignation out of her voice. "I suppose not." When the time came to go back—*if* that time came—she needed to be emotionally strong and ready to fight for the right she'd earned to be there. Right now she couldn't think of a single argument in her own favor except her desperate need to do *something*.

"Going home was a sound decision, Dinah," Ray assured her. "You still having nightmares?"

"Once in a while," she admitted.

"And the panic attacks?"

"Better." The last one had been that humiliating scene at Cord's.

"But not gone?"

"No."

"Have you talked to anyone?"

"No. I'll be fine. I'm sure it's just going to take a little more time."

"That's exactly right," he said encouragingly. "Give yourself all the time you need, okay? Don't be too hard on yourself. I know you hate sitting around, twiddling your thumbs, but healing takes time, kiddo. Be patient."

"Sure, Ray," she said, trying to keep a defeated note from her voice. The last thing she wanted was his pity.

"You hang in there, kid. I've got to run. Five crises have landed on my desk while I've been on the phone with you. We'll talk again soon."

"Take care, Ray. Stay safe."

She hung up feeling more depressed than ever. Almost before she realized what was happening, she felt her palms turn damp. Her breath snagged in her throat.

"Breathe, dammit!" she murmured, gasping as the all-too-familiar sense of panic swept over her. All she had to do was talk herself down. She just needed to remind herself that everything was going to be okay and take nice even breaths.

Think about Cord, she thought. There was a man who epitomized laid-back relaxation. Maybe he could teach her his technique for sprawling out in a hammock and letting the world and his troubles slip away.

Or maybe he was trying to figure out a solution for world peace, after all, she thought, and suddenly there was a smile on her lips. Her pulse eventually slowed and the tension that had seized her eased.

If she couldn't have Bobby and she couldn't go back to an overseas assignment, at least not in a war zone, she would figure out what she could do. Cord could probably help with that. He certainly wouldn't hesitate to give her an honest opinion. The man didn't know the meaning of sugarcoating the truth. Right now she'd welcome any impartial sounding board around.

If it just so happened to be a man who was easy on the eyes, so much the better.

When Cord arrived he was surprised to find Dinah waiting on the front steps, looking even more distressed than she had when he'd left her earlier. She was still wearing the exact same clothes and it didn't appear to him that she'd so much as run a comb through her hair.

Not that he gave a darn about appearance. She'd look incredible after a two-day hike through a sandstorm in the desert. He knew because he'd seen her looking just like that during a news report one night. She'd still made his pulse race.

He just found it worrisome that her apparent dejection had made her oblivious to what he knew she expected of herself. Looking presentable, even stylish, was as ingrained in a Southern-bred socialite like Dinah as saying please and thank you. Ten years in war zones couldn't strip her entirely of that sensibility.

"Everything okay?" he asked cautiously.

She forced a blatantly phony smile as she crossed the yard to meet him. "Of course. Let's go. I'm starved."

"Anything you say," he said, watching appreciatively as she hauled herself up into the front seat of his truck. She might be too skinny, but she still had the most attractive derriere he'd seen in a long time.

He closed her door, then went around to get in on the driver's side. Noting that she was staring straight ahead, looking miserable, he quietly said her name.

When she turned toward him, Cord leaned over impulsively and touched his lips to hers. It could hardly even be counted as a kiss, but it was enough to put some color in her cheeks and some fire in her eyes. He nodded with satisfaction.

"That's better," he said.

She scowled at him. "Why the hell did you do that, Cordell?"

"Because you were looking mighty pale," he said, then grinned. "And now you don't. Worked like a charm."

"Kiss me again and I'll demonstrate what I learned in all those self-defense lessons I took before I went on assignment overseas," she said sourly.

He laughed. "Oh, sugar, now you've gone and made it interesting."

"Don't even think about turning that into some sort of a dare," she retorted.

"Hard to think of it as anything else," he said as he pulled away from the curb. "But I surely will try, at least till I get someplace a whole lot more convenient. Wish now I'd brought my convertible. That backseat's a whole lot more comfortable than tussling around a gearshift."

Her frown deepened. "Forget tussling with me. This is not a date, if that's what you're thinking."

"Of course not," he agreed readily. "Just two old friends going out for dinner."

"We're not old friends."

Amused by her stubborn insistence on labeling the evening, their relationship and most likely everything else that occurred between the two of them, he gave her an alternative. "Acquaintances, then. Surely you can agree to that."

"Whatever." Her gaze narrowed. "As long as you understand the ground rules."

"There are rules?" he asked innocently. "Maybe you'd better run through those for me. I don't seem to have gotten my copy. Must have been in with all those memos your mama tosses at me on a regular basis."

Exasperation flashed in her eyes. "Why am I even going to dinner with you?" she muttered. "You are impossible."

"Now that's where you're wrong," he chided. "I am very possible, though I think in your case I'll play hard to get a little longer. Seems to me your feminine wiles could use a good workout. You're clearly out of practice, darlin', or you'd be chasing over to Atlanta right this second, instead of sitting here beside me."

Her stern expression wavered, then dissolved entirely as she chuckled. "I must have been crazy to think I could spend an entire evening with you. You're still the same exasperating man you always were. And I'm not going to Atlanta because I don't chase after men who are committed to other women."

"You would if you truly thought the two of you were in love," he suggested.

"Are you telling me I should go?" she asked.

"Absolutely not. I'm just telling you my interpretation of why you're not. You don't want my brother bad enough to fight for him. You're content just to mope around. You'll probably do it for a few days, then move on to someone else." He winked at her. "I'm available."

"As if I'd ever get involved with a man I can't trust from here to that SUV in front of us. For all your newfound professional respectability, Cordell, something tells me you're the same sneaky, conniving man you were ten years ago."

He laughed. "Most people like knowing that some things never change. It gives them comfort."

"Believe me, I would take a lot more comfort in knowing that your brother was still available and still in love with me."

Trying not to feel wounded by that, he turned to her. "Why is that exactly? When it comes to love, isn't it usually the first instinct that's right? You walked away from Bobby ten years ago because you knew in your heart he wasn't the right man for you."

"No, I knew it wasn't the right time for us," she corrected. "That's entirely different."

"I'm no romantic, but I'm pretty sure timing isn't supposed to come into play when you're talking about true love. Aren't you supposed to get swept away by passion?"

"And leave common sense aside? You don't know what you're talking about," Dinah said. "How many times have you been in love, anyway?"

"Never," Cord said immediately, then thought about it. "I take that back. Once."

Unfortunately, it had been with Dinah Davis and she hadn't been any more enamored of him then than she was now. A wise man would have gotten the message.

Then again, none of the other lessons in his life had come easily, either. Looked as if this was just one more he was going to have to wrestle with and see if he couldn't make things come right in the end.

Over dinner Dinah spent a lot of time reassessing her opinion of Cord. He was surprisingly good company, smarter than she'd ever imagined and more insightful. Of course, there also seemed to be very little he took seriously, so she was stunned when over dessert he finally got around to calling her on her decision to come home.

He took a long, slow swallow of his beer, tipping up the longneck bottle, his gaze locked on her face. She was prepared for another impudent question, but definitely not for the topic he chose.

"You gonna get around to telling me what you're doing here?" he inquired in the lazy tone that teased her nerves.

"You mean here with you tonight?" she asked, deliberately misreading the question. "I've been trying to figure that one out since I climbed into that truck of yours."

He gave her an impatient look. "Come on, sugar, you know what I'm asking. It's one thing for you to breeze back into Charleston like the prodigal daughter, say hi to your folks and then breeze right out again. It's another thing entirely for you to stick around for weeks. You don't even seem that restless, not even now that you know Bobby's not available."

"Believe me, I'm restless," she replied.

"You made any plane reservations to go back yet?"

"No."

"How come?"

"I just haven't, okay? Could we drop this, please?"

"I don't think so," he said, his gaze unrelenting. "Something tells me we're finally getting to the good stuff."

"Good stuff?"

"You know, the intimate little secrets about what makes Dinah Davis tick."

She shuddered at the thought of this man poking into her psyche. "I didn't come with you tonight so you could analyze me or the decisions I'm making. You're hardly qualified."

"I thought we established the other night that I do have some qualifications for this particular conversation," he told her. "Come on, Dinah. Talk to me. I'm not asking you what happened over there to make you so skittish, because I can imagine." He studied her intently. "But are you gonna let it change the course of your life?"

"That's not what I'm doing," she said defensively. At his blatantly skeptical look, she sighed. "Okay, maybe that is what I'm doing, but it's my choice, Cordell. It has nothing whatsoever to do with you."

"It does if you still intend to use my brother to soothe whatever itch you're suddenly feeling."

"It's not like that," she said emphatically. "Besides, that's a nonissue now that I know he's engaged. I get it. You can stop worrying."

"Now I know you're messed up," he said. "If you came back here because you woke up one morning and realized you were madly in love with Bobby, you wouldn't let a little thing like an engagement stand in your way. I said it before, you'd fight like crazy to get him back."

She gave him a scandalized look. "I most certainly would not. I do have some scruples."

"It's not about scruples," Cord declared. "It's about fighting for something you want with everything in you. I know you'd probably never set out to wreck a marriage, but an engagement would be nothing more than a minor inconvenience to a woman who's convinced that some other woman is with her soul mate."

"Which just shows how little you know about honor and integrity," she snapped, then regarded Cord curiously. "Have you done a one-eighty here? I thought you were doing everything you could to keep me away from Bobby. Now it almost sounds as if you want me to break up his engagement."

"No, I just want to see some evidence that you've got that same old spunk I remember."

"I have plenty of spunk."

"Not that I can see," he said, then added with a sad shake of his head, "It's a sorry thing, too. I never pegged you for a quitter, Dinah, yet here you are. You've run away from your career. You've given up on Bobby in a split second. What's next? You gonna start spending your days lolling around beside your daddy's backyard pool and wait for some rich man to come along and marry you? That might please your mama, but it doesn't seem to suit you unless times have changed more than I realized."

Dinah didn't like the label of quitter or any of the rest of his assessment one little bit. "I wasn't running away from anything," she said heatedly. "I was running to something better."

"My brother?"

"Yes."

"And now you've dropped that idea, right?"

"I certainly have and you know perfectly well why. Do we have to keep going over and over this?"

"Yes, we do. Are you in love with him?" he pressed.

"Yes, dammit!"

He studied her for what seemed to be an eternity, then shook his head. "I'm not buying it."

She regarded him incredulously. The man had more nerve than anyone she'd ever met, and she did not mean that as a compliment. "I don't give two figs whether you buy it or not," she snapped.

"Why not at least try to convince me?" he prodded. "Let's start with the fact that you and Bobby haven't seen each other for the better part of ten years, haven't even kept in contact really. How am I doing so far?"

Dinah didn't much like the sarcasm in his voice. He was right to be so skeptical, but she wasn't anywhere near ready to give him the satisfaction of admitting that.

"What makes you think we haven't been in touch?" she inquired irritably.

He lifted one brow. "Did you know about our business?"

"No," she conceded grudgingly.

"I didn't think so," he said, his expression smug. "May I continue?"

She sighed. He would whether she wanted him to or not. "Please do."

"So you thought you'd just come on home and dive right back into his life and what? Get married? Have a few kids? Live happily ever after?"

"You make it sound like I was hoping for something bizarre. Aren't marriage, kids and happily-ever-after something most people want?"

"Nothing wrong with the dream," he agreed. "Not that I believe much in it, but let's say it worked out that way and you got what you wanted. What was supposed to happen when you got a little bored and restless?"

"You're not giving Bobby much credit. Being married to him and having a family wouldn't be boring."

"Not for someone like Rianna, who adores him and is perfectly content with the prospect of staying at home, raising his babies. She doesn't aspire to anything more than being a great wife and a fantastic mother. Can you say the same?"

Of course, he knew she couldn't, Dinah acknowledged. Practically everyone in Charleston knew that when it came to ambition, Dinah had more than anyone else in her graduating class. She'd been openly disdainful of the traditional wife and mother path.

"Maybe I've been everywhere I wanted to go and accomplished everything I set out to accomplish," she told him.

"Is that so?"

"Yes," she said emphatically. And it was true, up to a point. She could always tackle a new assignment, one more challenging, more fascinating than the last. And more dangerous, she reminded herself. That's what had scared her in the end. She saw no need to admit any of that to Cordell.

Cord regarded her with obvious disbelief. "Face it, Dinah. You can lie through your teeth to me and even to yourself, but we both know boredom would eventually set in. Then what? You'd abandon your family and go back to work?"

"Of course not," she insisted. "I would never do that."

"Then you'd just stick it out and be totally miserable? Now that would be a picnic for everyone concerned, wouldn't it?"

"You're just being cynical, because you don't understand the first thing about the power of love."

"Love's a great thing," Cord replied. "Powerful, even, but it's not a miracle worker. It can't change human nature."

"You're wrong," she said flatly. "Haven't you heard? Love can move mountains."

Cord laughed. "You show me one example of that happening and I will gladly tell you exactly where Bobby is and drive you there myself."

"I don't even know why I'm having this conversation with you," she said. "You just keep twisting everything I say."

"Do I? Or am I simply making you see how ridiculous it was to think you could come home and recapture the past?"

"It wasn't ridiculous. Bobby and I made a deal."

Cord's gaze bore into her. "Just out of curiosity, did this deal include remaining true and celibate?" he asked.

She frowned at the question. "No, though I'm not sure I see why that's any of your business."

"Just checking on the rules. For all I know Bobby's been violating them by getting all mixed up with Rianna. If that were so, I might be willing to sit him down and have a brother-to-brother chat with him on your behalf."

She gave him a withering look. "There weren't any rules," she repeated. "We had an understanding. If the time came when we were ready to get married and we were both available, then that's what we'd do."

"Then you can hardly blame my brother for deciding at some point to get on with his life."

"Of course, I don't blame him."

"And you, did you get on with your life?"

She frowned at the far too personal question. "Are you asking me if I slept with any men?"

His gaze filled with a surprising heat. "Yes, Dinah, that is exactly what I'm asking."

"I don't see how that's any of your business."

"Then you did," he said flatly, obviously drawing his own conclusion from her reticence.

"Okay, yes," she snapped. Even though she owed Cord absolutely nothing, she felt the need to defend herself and her actions. "I was in a lot of dangerous situations. It was natural to reach out to someone."

"But no one special?"

She thought of the one man who'd really mattered, then deliberately blocked him from her mind. The memories were still too raw, still too painful, even after all these months. She couldn't think about any of that, not without losing it completely. One meltdown in front of Cord was enough to last her a lifetime. He obviously thought it had given him the right to delve into her psyche.

"No one," she lied.

Cord's gaze remained steady and disbelieving. "Really?"

"Why are you pushing this?" she asked.

"Because it's obviously important. You're avoiding a straight answer, Dinah. Who was he? What happened to him? Why aren't you with him, instead of chasing after my brother?"

Dinah flinched at his persistence. If she let him—or anyone—rip the scab off the still-fresh wound of her tragic loss, she was almost certain that she'd start screaming and never stop.

"Tell me, Dinah," Cord commanded, his hand covering hers.

Images of Peter filled Dinah's head and her pulse began to race. And then she was back there…back in hell.

Afghanistan, six months earlier

"Go! Go! Go!"

Frozen in place, Dinah heard the urgency in Peter's voice, knew in her gut that she should follow the softly-spoken, but unmistakably frantic command, but how could she? He was asking her to run, to leave him to face the terrible uncertainty of armed rebels who'd stopped their car on a deserted stretch of highway. The driver had already moved away from the car toward the guerillas, possibly negotiating, but more likely joining their ranks. The men hired by foreign journalists as drivers and translators often had divided loyalties. And American journalists were good targets these days. Al Qaeda incidents garnered worldwide attention.

"I can't," she whispered, hating the unexpected taste of fear and cowardice. It didn't matter that she'd wriggled out of more hot spots in the past than some of the military's most impressive operatives. All that counted was here and now. Fast talk wasn't going to cut it. The situation called for immediate action and she simply couldn't move.

Worse, she knew she'd gotten them into this mess. She'd insisted on going out alone with Peter to get this interview, despite all the recent protocol that journalists should travel in at least two separate cars on all excursions. If one was stopped or broke down, the other might have at least a chance of getting away.

"I can't," she repeated.

"Yes, you can," Peter said forcefully. "I mean it, Dinah! When I get out of this car, I'm going to get out shooting. All the attention will be on me. Open your door, crouch down and move. Then as soon as you're clear, run like hell. That's why we've been training. You've built up speed and endurance the last few months. You *can* do it."

When she didn't respond, he shook her. "Dammit, are you listening to me, Dinah?"

"I can't," she whispered again, her stomach churning. She was going to be sick. "We always agreed we'd stick together. I can't leave you." That was the worst of it, abandoning Peter, leaving him to almost certain death while she at least had a chance to live. None of their planning had prepared her for that.

Working with the same cameraman for so many years had given Dinah an intuitive ability to understand the way Peter's mind worked and vice versa. They were an award-winning team. They took risks together. More than that, she loved him. How could she possibly forget all that and go off on her own?

"You have to," he insisted, refusing to cut her a moment's slack for indecisiveness. "Would you rather we both die here? Because we will, Dinah. Look at them. They're not kidding around. They'll kill you or, worse, take you hostage."

Those words, more than any others, shocked her back to the grim reality they faced. She swallowed the bile that crept up the back of her throat. They both knew what happened to hostages, especially women. They'd interviewed too many victims, read the cold forensics reports on those who could no longer speak for themselves. She'd rather die in a hailstorm of bullets, no question about it.

"You know I'm right," he coaxed. "At least if I know you're safe, I might have half a chance to get away. Or you might have time to get help. We're only a couple of miles from town. You can make it and alert the authorities. You'll come back and save my butt."

But it wouldn't happen that way, she thought, gulping back an hysterical sob. This man she'd fallen in love with, this brave cameraman who'd been through multiple wars in godforsaken places with her, was going to die here and now on a deserted road, and he was giving her a slim chance to save herself.

That was Peter, brave and noble to the end. His courage—not hers—was the trait that had gotten them stories no one else could get. She got all the attention because her face was on-screen, but it was Peter's images that captivated the audience and had made her into a network superstar.

Peter reached for her face and cupped her chin, his brilliant blue eyes that saw so much through the lens of a camera filled now with selfless love and determination. "Do it, Dinah! No fooling around, okay? Just do it! Understand? I can't sit here arguing with you."

Accepting that there really was no choice, she finally nodded, unable to speak.

"On the count of three, then," Peter said with astonishing calm. His gaze unwavering, he added, "I love you. Don't forget that, okay? Never forget that."

Dinah's eyes welled with tears. She'd always known something like this could happen. The risks came with the job. These days being a television journalist, a war correspondent, wasn't glamorous. It was dangerous and often deadly. Terrorists didn't play by the rules. Reporters who got in their way were just as likely to be killed as soldiers or local civilians. And stories didn't take place in nice, mostly secure hotel lobbies.

Somehow, though, she'd never thought it would happen to her. She was careful. She calculated the odds every time she set out to do an interview. Tonight, eager for a sought-after exclusive interview, she'd made a dreadful miscalculation.

She'd always had Peter by her side. His solidity lent her strength, no matter what atrocities they faced in the hellholes they'd been assigned to cover by the network. They were known back home for being an intrepid twosome, who always came back with Peter's incredible images of people and places others weren't daring enough to find. His amazing videotaped pictures with her powerful words had won every one of journalism's top honors.

They were recognized everywhere except the most remote villages, respected by some, reviled by others. She had a feeling that recognition was behind their current predicament, that it wasn't mere anti-American sentiment that had set them up for this ambush. They would be used as examples of what could happen to anyone who dared shine a light on terror.

She looked at the deadly gun in Peter's hand and shuddered. The fact that Peter was carrying a gun at all was testament to the unpredictable turn the war on terror had taken since 9/11. Rarely had journalists armed themselves in the past, and even now the practice was debated frequently over dinner and drinks wherever correspondents gathered.

Dinah had had her doubts, but right now she was glad for that gun Peter had insisted on carrying whenever they went on assignment, happier still that he was trained and unafraid to use it. It gave them an edge—a chance—albeit a very slight one.

"One!"

Peter's steady voice jarred her. They had minutes, maybe only seconds, to make decisions that could change whether they lived or died.

"I love you," she whispered, wanting to believe that she would have a million other opportunities, but needing to say the words now, just in case she didn't.

She fisted a handful of his shirt in her hand, pulled him toward her and kissed him hard, knowing it could be for the last time. In that couple of seconds, she tried to memorize the taste and texture of his mouth, then released him.

He winked at her. "Two," he said and gave her hand a reassuring squeeze.

This was it, then. Dinah turned and reached for the handle on the door.

"Three!"

Never looking back, Peter stepped from the car, already firing his gun, the flimsy door his only protection. Dinah fought the temptation to watch. Instead she rolled out the open door on her side, staying low, praying that Peter had the full attention of the insurgents. She was behind the car, out of view in an instant, the uneven firefight raging around her.

And then she sucked in a deep, cleansing breath and ran, away from the battle toward town, just as she and Peter had agreed, anticipating at any second the sharp pain of a bullet hitting her in the back.

She'd gone only a hundred yards or so when the world exploded around her. She was lifted into the air by the force of it, then came down face-first on the dusty road, rocks cutting into her painfully.

The sky rained more rocks down on her. She covered her head from the worst of it, knowing her arms would be bloodied, if not broken, then waited as the noise echoed for what seemed like an eternity before finally dying.

Only when it was quiet, the air oddly still, did she finally struggle to sit up, then dare to look back. The earth where the car had been was scorched. The metal of the car—or at least the part that was still identifiable—was blackened. Acrid smoke billowed in the air. Bodies littered the road.

"Oh God, no!" The cry tore from her throat. She made herself get up and make the frantic dash back to the last place she'd seen Peter.

In that split second before she reached the scene, she told herself she'd find him wounded, but alive. She promised herself that.

But as she drew closer, she saw that there was no hope. She'd seen this kind of car bombing horror before, but never with anyone she knew at the center of it, never when she'd escaped it herself by a matter of seconds.

At first she couldn't make sense of it. Why detonate a car bomb here? Had it been accidentally set off in the flurry of gunfire? That was the only explanation that made sense.

Shaking, she examined every piece of debris. When at last she found a shred of the flak jacket Peter had worn, she clutched it in her hand, looking desperately for more, terrified she would find it, terrified she wouldn't.

When she finally found him, barely recognizable amid the rubble and scattered remains, she knelt by the side of the road and retched, her stomach heaving for what seemed like an eternity.

Her heart, always full when Peter was around, emptied of all feeling. The drive and ambition that motivated her to take risks died right there on that deserted road. In that instant she knew she had nothing left to give, not to her profession, not to herself. Icy with shock, she sat beside what was left of the man she'd loved, and shivered, clutching his broken and bloodied hand in hers.

It was hours later when a convoy of American soldiers found her, dazed and incoherent. She wasn't surprised when they insisted on taking her for medical treatment for the cuts and scrapes she'd suffered when she'd been thrown to the ground and pelted by flying debris. She didn't think anything would ever surprise her again.

"Dinah!"

Cord's voice finally snapped her out of the horror of that scene. Only when he touched her cheek did she realized she'd been crying.

"Tell me," he pleaded, his gaze filled with worry and compassion.

She shook her head. "I can't talk about it."

"Then there is something to talk about, something specific?"

"Leave it alone, Cord, please."

He regarded her with obvious reluctance, but he finally nodded. "Okay, darlin'," he said softly. "I'll leave it alone for now, but not forever."

Dinah wasn't worried about forever. She didn't much believe in it anymore, anyway.

9

"Dinah, honey, is that you?" Dorothy Davis called out when Dinah returned home.

Dinah bit back a groan. The last thing she needed after spending several hours defending herself to Cord was to tap-dance around her mother's questions about how she'd spent her evening. Nor was she anxious for her mother to get a good look at her eyes which were probably still puffy from crying and even if they weren't, Dorothy Davis had radar when it came to her daughter's state of emotions. Still, she concluded with resignation, there was no ignoring her.

She walked into the living room, where her mother was seated at an antique Queen Anne desk strewn with papers. She had a surprising pair of drugstore reading glasses on the tip of her nose. For a woman who'd never held an actual job in her life, she seemed to have the knack for bringing home more work than her banker husband.

"You look busy," Dinah said.

"Budget figures and cost projections for Covington Plantation," her mother said. "I like to be sure they're in order before the rest of the board gets their hands on them."

"Isn't that something Daddy could help you with? Where is he, by the way? I didn't see his car outside."

Her mother shrugged. "He's at a business meeting of some sort, I suppose."

"You don't know?" she asked.

"He doesn't check in, Dinah," her mother responded irritably. "As for Covington, he doesn't like to get involved in what he refers to as my little projects."

Dinah had never realized that. She'd always assumed that they'd been a team. "Why on earth not?" she asked, wondering what else she'd gotten wrong about her parents' marriage. Added to the argument she'd overheard, she was beginning to wonder if they were having real problems. Surely the upright, pillar-of-the-community Marshall Davis wasn't sneaking around behind her mother's back having an affair. Not that she intended to ask her mother that question. Dorothy would probably slap her silly for such impertinence.

"He claims it's smarter that way," her mother replied, then added with an unmistakable edge of sarcasm, "No one will ever be able to accuse us of conspiring to cook the books, I suppose."

Dinah stuck to the one fissure in the relationship that seemed safe enough. "Are you serious? Dad has never backed any of your projects?"

"Not a one," her mother confirmed.

"And the bank? Surely it's involved."

"No. I deal with another one."

"But that doesn't make any sense," Dinah protested, indignant on her mother's behalf. "Daddy's bank has always prided itself on its civic projects."

"As long as they're not mine," her mother explained. "That would be a conflict of interest for board members," she added, then forced a smile. "Now tell me where you've been. Maybelle said you left here with a very handsome young man. It's wonderful to know you're seeing someone here."

Dinah reluctantly changed the subject. "Cord took me to dinner at Murrells Inlet," she said. "No big deal."

"How perfectly lovely!" her mother exclaimed. "Shrimp and onion rings, I imagine."

Dinah laughed. "Am I that predictable?"

"Only when it comes to that one thing, I'm sure," her mother soothed. "The fact that you went with Cord definitely wasn't predictable. I thought you two didn't get along that well. You certainly didn't as children. Bobby was always the one for you."

"Times change," Dinah said lightly. "But don't go making anything out of this. It was just a casual dinner. We got to talking after you left Covington. He mentioned Murrells Inlet and I couldn't resist the chance to see if the food was as delicious as I remembered."

"Was it?"

"Even better," she said.

"And the company?"

Dinah searched for a word that wouldn't stir up even more questions. "Acceptable."

Her mother regarded her with amusement. "I saw the way you looked at him earlier this afternoon, Dinah. There was something there, a little spark. You could do worse, you know. There are a lot of women in Charleston who'd be thrilled to have Cord ask them on a date. He made a fortune for the plantation project last year when we held a bachelor auction."

Dinah nearly choked. The image boggled the mind. "Cord let himself be auctioned off for charity?"

"To the tune of five thousand dollars, as I recall. It was the high bid of the night."

"Who on earth paid that much to spend an evening with him?" she demanded, her tone incredulous. It had to have been some bored widow or divorcée.

Her mother grinned. "As a matter of fact, it was Maggie."

Dinah couldn't have been more shocked if her mother had announced that she was the one who'd paid big bucks for a few hours of Cord's company. "That doesn't make any sense. I can't imagine Maggie being that desperate."

"Oh, sweetie, I don't think desperation had anything to do with it," her mother chided. "The man is a certifiable hunk and one of Charleston's most sought-after single men. Maggie has the money. And it's a very worthwhile cause. It was a win-win situation for everyone."

"But Cord is infuriating, impossible and impertinent. Why on earth would Maggie spend a single dime to waste an evening with him?" she asked before she recalled that Maggie had actually informed her that she thought Cord was hot. So she'd paid to see just how hot? Dinah was appalled at the apparently sorry state of her friend's social life if she was reduced to such a level.

Her mother's eyebrows rose at the description. "Why on earth would you say Cord is impertinent? In what way?"

"Surely you've seen it, Mother. He was certainly in your face at the plantation this afternoon. I can't imagine you tolerating that from anyone else. I was stunned that you didn't bring him down a peg or two, especially with all those workmen looking on."

Her mother waved off the comment. "That's just the way Cord and I communicate." Her gaze turned speculative. "Please tell me, though, that he didn't do anything out of line with you tonight."

Dinah didn't want to travel down that path. Not only would it be untrue, but she didn't want to cause a rift between her mother and Cord when they obviously enjoyed working together. "Of course not, at least not the way you mean. He was just poking his nose into things that are none of his business."

"Such as?"

"Things I didn't want to talk about."

Her mother's gaze narrowed. "Used to be you didn't hide anything. You had the sunniest, most open disposition of any child I've ever seen. Your life was an open book. Being a journalist has changed that. Is your own life now off the record, the way some of your sources probably insist on being?"

"It's got nothing to do with that. I've grown up," Dinah said defensively. "There are some things that are supposed to be private. It will be a cold day in hell before I let Cordell Beaufort pick apart the choices I've made."

"That's up to you, of course," her mother said, her tone suddenly more placating. "But something's troubling you, Dinah. We can all see it. If you won't talk to your family, then open up to someone else. Maggie, perhaps. You two have always been best friends. I can't imagine that all these years apart have changed that."

"No, of course not," Dinah said, mostly to satisfy her mother.

But Maggie had kept Bobby's engagement from Dinah, so how good a friend was she really? She'd let

Dinah be blindsided by the news. And she'd humiliated herself by paying to go out on a date with Cord. Maybe Maggie was more messed up than Dinah was. She was too tired to try to figure any of that out tonight.

"Mother, I'm exhausted. I'm going up to bed, unless you'd like me to keep you company until Dad gets home."

"No telling when that will be. You go on." Her mother looked as if she wanted to say something more, but then she merely sighed. "Good night, darling. Sleep well."

"You, too."

But as she plodded wearily up the stairs, Dinah doubted she would ever sleep well again. Her best friend had withheld an important fact from her, something she never would have suspected, and now Dinah had the nagging sense that her parents' marriage was not all she'd believed it to be. She wondered what other beliefs were about to crumble around her.

Dinah set out for Maggie's house the next morning.

She found Maggie on the tiny brick patio in back of her carriage house, sipping a cup of tea and eating what looked to be a fresh orange-cranberry scone with real clotted cream.

"Is there another one of those?" she asked, startling Maggie so badly she spilled tea all over the table.

"What on earth?" Maggie said as she mopped up the mess. She stared hard at Dinah. "You're out and about awfully early. Is something wrong?"

"I wanted to catch you before you went to the gallery."

"Any particular reason?"

"We need to talk and it's not something I think we should get into when anyone could come wandering in and overhear us."

Maggie regarded her warily. "Oh? Is this about you? Do you finally want to talk about your real reason for coming home?"

"No, it's about you, and I absolutely refuse to get into it until you tell me where I can find another one of those scones."

Maggie grinned. "Nice to know your priorities haven't changed as much as I feared they had. You always did put food first, at least until you started to panic that every pound would show up on camera. The scones are on the kitchen counter. Help yourself. Tea's in the pot right next to them."

"I guess the novelty of having me home has worn off. A couple of weeks ago, you would have gotten them for me."

"And now I need the time to brace myself for whatever it is that brought you over here not much past the crack of dawn. You know your way around my kitchen."

Dinah went inside and found the scones, still warm from the oven. She poured a cup of tea, then brought the entire plate of scones back with her. It was likely to be a stressful conversation.

She sat down at the wrought-iron table, put a dollop of the heavy cream on the scone and bit into it. "Oh, my God, where did you get these?"

"I baked them."

Dinah stared at her in amazement. "You're kidding."

Amusement spread across Maggie's face. "Sweetie, while you were learning to ask all those tough interview questions, I was learning to be a proper wife. There's not a recipe that I can't follow when pressed."

"If you bake like this all the time, why aren't you the size of a house?"

"Because I only bake when I'm stressed out."

There was the opening Dinah had hoped for. "Why are you stressed out? Isn't the gallery working out the way you'd hoped?"

"The gallery is an amazing success."

"And you enjoy it?"

"Of course I do." Maggie peered at her curiously. "Why do you ask?"

"You said you were stressed. I'm just trying to get to the bottom of that rather cryptic remark. Is it about a man? Cordell, perhaps?"

Maggie burst out laughing. "Is that what brought you scurrying over here this morning? You want to know if I have the hots for Cord?"

Dinah saw little point in denying it. "Something like that. Do you?"

"I think he's gorgeous and definitely hot, but I told you that the other day. It's hardly a deep, dark secret. Why are you bringing it up again?"

"Because I just found out last night that you paid five thousand dollars to go out with him. I'd say that implies more than a casual interest in the man."

Maggie shrugged. "A moment of temporary insanity for a good cause."

"I hope so," Dinah said worriedly. "I can't think what possessed you to bid on any man at an auction, much less Cordell. You're this totally fantastic, successful woman. You don't need to buy a date."

"You make it sound as if I called some tacky escort

service. This was a charity auction. There were a lot of other women paying for dates that night. It was all in good fun. It was a chance to buy into a fantasy."

Dinah didn't find that explanation nearly as reassuring as Maggie evidently intended her to. "And you've been fantasizing about Cord? For how long?" And why the hell had she been trying to push Dinah together with him, if she wanted him for herself?

"Most of my adult life," Maggie said. "But before you go too far down this road you're on, let's do a reality check here. The man is not the least bit interested in me. He never has been."

"Well, he should be!" Dinah said with only the slightest twinge of regret. "What can I do to help? If you want him, then let's get him for you. We were certainly well-schooled in every feminine trick in the book."

Maggie regarded her with evident dismay. "God, it's no wonder you thought you could snap your fingers and Bobby would come running," she said. "You really do have absolutely no idea how relationships work. It's all about the chemistry, sweetie. Cord and I don't have it, much as I might wish otherwise. Neither do you and Bobby, if you don't mind me saying so for the umpteenth time. Now Cord and you..." She fanned herself dramatically. "That's chemistry."

Dinah just stared at her. "But you're crazy about him."

"And some people love peanuts, but get sick eating them. It's just a fact of life. I've gotten over it. So should you."

Dinah thought about what Cord had said to her the night before about fighting for a dream. "You can't just give up," she advised Maggie. "Tell me about the date. What did you do?"

"You're not dropping this, are you?" Maggie looked at her with a resigned expression. "We went to the movies, then had dinner."

"Someplace romantic?"

"When did you turn into some sort of voyeur?" Maggie inquired impatiently.

"I'm not looking. I'm asking for pertinent details so I can help. Was it romantic?"

"There was candlelight, if that's what you mean. And fancy silverware on the table. It wasn't romantic, because when I looked into Cord's eyes, all I saw was friendly interest. Not one single spark I could interpret in any other way."

"The man's an idiot," Dinah declared. It wasn't the first time she'd come to that conclusion.

Maggie smiled at her fierce tone. "No, he just has a single-track mind. He always has."

"Meaning?"

"You're the one he wants, Dinah. Why you haven't figured that out by now is beyond me. And, frankly, if you don't do something about it now, then you're the idiot."

"Cordell is not in love with me," Dinah said dismissively, but suddenly the memory of the heat in his eyes when he'd asked about the other men in her life came flooding back. Was it possible that jealousy had put that trace of anger in his voice?

It didn't matter, she told herself staunchly. She wasn't interested in anything with Cordell Beaufort, especially not with her best friend pining for him.

"Have you seen him again?" Maggie asked.

"We had dinner last night," Dinah admitted. As she'd said to her mother, she also assured Maggie, "It was no big deal. I'd just found out about Bobby's engagement, which you should have mentioned. I was a little down. He drove me along the coast to Murrells Inlet to cheer me up."

"Did it work?"

"Actually he spent most of the evening infuriating me."

Maggie grinned. "There's that chemistry thing again."

Dinah scowled at her. "Go suck an egg. If you want Cordell, you're more than welcome to him."

Maggie shook her head. "If only that were true. Nope, I'm afraid he's yours, unless you turn out to be too stupid to grab him."

"And what about you?"

"Oh, I have a few irons in the fire, romantically speaking. Don't you worry about me."

"Seriously?"

"Would I lie to you?"

"If you thought it was the only way to give me permission to be with Cord, yes."

"Well, I'm not lying. And you don't need my permission to do whatever you want to with Cord. That's between the two of you."

Dinah was oddly relieved to hear that, even though she adamantly believed that she would never agree to spend another evening with Cord and his steady harangue of uncomfortable questions. That was not what she'd come home expecting.

But, she thought ruefully as she got in her car, she of all people should know that life had a way of taking surprising twists.

Maybe Cord had been right. Maybe she'd been wrong to dismiss the idea of going to Atlanta after

Bobby. She should at least give him the chance to tell her himself that it was over between them, that this Rianna person was the woman he wanted.

Pushing aside that nagging voice in her head that was shouting about scruples and good sense, she impulsively whipped her car around in the middle of downtown Charleston and headed for Atlanta.

A few hours later she was pulling up in front of an impressive restoration project that was clearly nearing completion. A tasteful sign on the side of the building announced that it was the work of Beaufort Construction. Below that was an Atlanta contact number for leasing information. She jotted that down and picked up her cell phone, then decided the call could wait until after she'd poked around inside to see for herself what Bobby and Cordell had been up to.

The inside of the old brick building had been carved up for shops of varying sizes. Judging from the painted signs on the windows and doors that opened onto an airy central corridor, most of the spaces had already been leased to some very upscale boutiques. Restaurants and a large independent bookstore would serve as anchors, taking up huge square footage at each end and in the middle. With a new multiplex movie theater going up just down the block, Dinah knew that this would quickly become a hot new Atlanta destination.

Just as she was about to head back outside to call the office, a man in blue jeans, a tight T-shirt and tool belt headed her way.

"You need some help, sugar?" he inquired with an impudent smile that reminded her just a little too much of Cord's.

"I was looking for Mr. Beaufort. Is he around?"

"Would that be Bobby or Cordell?"

"Bobby."

"Now what would a spunky woman like you be doing looking for an old stick-in-the-mud like Bobby?"

"Excuse me?"

"You are Dinah Davis, aren't you? I've seen you on the news. You've got gumption, I'll give you that. Wouldn't let a woman of mine do what you do."

Dinah forced a smile. "Then aren't I lucky I'm not one of your women? Is Bobby around or not?"

"Not. I believe he's gone over to Charleston to meet with his brother. I'm Josh Parker. I'm the foreman around here. Anything I can help you with?"

Dinah groaned. So much for being impulsive. "No. I need to speak to Bobby. How long is he going to be over there?"

"Hard to tell. He might be spending some time with his fiancée while he's there. If so, then he won't be back before tomorrow. You want me to tell him you came by?"

Dinah debated that and decided to let well enough alone. She'd made one impetuous move to see Bobby and missed him. Maybe that was the final sign that she ought to give up on this ridiculous quest of hers.

"No. I'm sure I'll catch up with him sooner or later," she told the man. "Thanks for your help, Mr. Parker. The building's lovely, by the way. You and your crew should be proud."

"The credit goes to Cordell. The man's a stickler for getting every detail just right. I've learned more from him than I have on any job I've ever done and, believe me, I've worked on some of the best restoration projects around."

"And you think Cord knows his stuff?"

"Best in the business, no question about it. This company's going to do great things, thanks to his expertise and Bobby's salesmanship. Me, I'm just going along for the ride."

Dinah was very much afraid she was going to have to change her opinion of Cord, if accolades like this kept piling up.

Wearing goggles, Cord concentrated on cutting the new crown molding that would match the original when he felt a tap on his shoulder. He jerked the power saw upright and very nearly severed his arm.

When he whirled around he saw his brother, which was an even worse shock. He stripped off his goggles and threw them at him. "Jesus, Bobby, scare me to death, why don't you?" he snapped.

"Sorry. I was trying to let you know I was in the room."

"Then try walking around and standing in front of me, instead of sneaking up behind me. What the hell are you doing here, anyway? You're supposed to be in Atlanta."

Bobby kept his expression neutral and merely stared him down. "You're in a piss-poor mood this morning," he accused eventually. "You get up on the wrong side of the bed or have you been sleeping alone too long?"

Cord bit back a sigh. "Maybe both."

"I'm sure you could remedy that, if you wanted to. Half the women in this town would trade their fancy BMW convertibles for a roll in the hay with you."

"I think you're overestimating my appeal," Cord said dryly. There was at least one woman who wasn't impressed with him and unfortunately, she seemed to be the only one he wanted. "Come on downstairs. I could use something to drink. You can tell me what you're doing here."

In the kitchen, which already had a large, professional-grade refrigerator installed, Cord reached for a couple of cans of Coke and tossed one to Bobby. He popped the top on his, then took a long sip.

"Damn, it's hot," he muttered. "I never thought I'd say this, but I'll be glad when we finally get the central air-conditioning installed in here."

"I thought you'd been fighting that," Bobby said. "Something about maintaining the historical integrity."

Cord grinned. "I lost that battle, and for once, I'm damn glad of it. Now tell me what brought you home in the middle of the week."

"Rianna has some fancy party she wants to attend tonight," Bobby explained. "I couldn't say no. I've said it way too often lately. I figured I'd come by here, get a look at the progress. Then tonight I'll suit up in my tux and do the party scene, then scoot back to Atlanta tomorrow." He studied Cord with a narrowed gaze. "You have a problem with that?"

"No," Cord said. How could he? It was a perfectly reasonable plan. He just prayed that Dinah wouldn't show up at whatever party the two of them were attending. As vulnerable as she was, he doubted she was ready to face the sight of another woman on Bobby's arm, even though she would now be prepared for it. Thanks to Cord's silence, however, Bobby wasn't prepared at all to bump into Dinah.

"Whose party is this?" he asked.

"Some friend of Rianna's from college is hosting a

fancy black-tie dinner in some hotel ballroom downtown to celebrate something or other." He grinned. "You know me. I don't give a rat's ass about that kind of thing. Other than making sure I got the date right, I didn't pay much attention to the rest of the details."

Cord laughed. He completely agreed with his brother. He might be welcome—or even expected—at all the city's society balls and black-tie functions now that he was considered a respectable businessman, but he got out of about twice as many as he actually attended. He showed up just often enough to stay in the good graces of the people with whom he was doing business at any given moment.

At any rate, it didn't sound as if wherever Bobby was going tonight was likely to be such a big deal that Dinah would be included. She and Rianna had never traveled in the same circles. Rianna had gone to the Charleston public schools. Ironically, Bobby was her ticket into the upper echelons of Charleston society.

Still, even though it seemed unlikely that Bobby and Dinah would cross paths at this particular event, maybe it would be a smart idea to make sure she was otherwise occupied.

"Listen, bro, there's something I need to do. Wander around and get a good look at the place. It's coming along great. Give Rianna my best when you see her tonight, okay?"

Bobby regarded him with a puzzled expression. "You're suddenly in an awfully big hurry to take off. Where are you going?"

"Just some business I need to take care of."

"Oh?"

"Nothing for you to worry about. Will I see you before you go back in the morning?"

"Yeah, I think so. Something tells me there's something going on in your life I should know about. I'll come by the house before I take off. Make sure the coffee's on." He gave Cord a speculative look. "Or will I be interrupting something?"

Cord chuckled at his display of discretion. "Sadly, no."

Bobby shook his head. "What's happened to you, man? You used to be my idol. You had a date every night."

"It got old," Cord said. After he realized that he could sleep with every woman in Charleston and it still wouldn't help him forget the one he really wanted in his bed, he didn't enjoy the dating thing.

And now that Dinah was back in town and driving him flat-out crazy all over again, he wasn't about to waste his time on also-rans. As unlikely as a lasting match-up between him and Dinah was, he intended to give it his best shot.

Bobby gave him a long, penetrating look, then asked quietly, "Who is she, Cord?"

He stared at his brother, keeping his expression blank. "Who's who?"

"The woman who's got you tied up in knots."

"You're imagining things," he lied. He removed his hard hat and clamped it down on his brother's head. "Keep it on while you're here, okay? I know you've got a thick skull, but accidents happen."

He strolled out of the kitchen, aware that his brother's worried gaze was on him the whole way.

Once he was out of earshot, he uttered a curse that rarely crossed his lips. It was the first time in his life that he'd kept anything from his brother and he didn't like the feeling one bit. Maybe when Bobby showed up at home in the morning, he'd just tell him everything about Dinah's return, her hopes for reigniting something with Bobby and his own fantasies about stepping into Bobby's place in her life. Then he'd let the chips fall where they would.

He considered such honesty, then sighed. He knew when he faced Bobby in the morning, he wouldn't say one single word. There was too much at stake for all of them...Bobby, Rianna, Dinah and maybe for him, most of all.

10

While Cord drove home, he formulated a plan for getting Dinah to agree to spend the evening with him. He had a hunch she was going to be a tough sell, because he knew she'd been unnerved by all of his questions during their dinner at Murrells Inlet. She wouldn't want to subject herself to that again, even if a good shaking up was exactly what she needed to get herself to think things through and get back on track with her life.

That meant that calling her and inviting her on a date was out of the question. She'd just turn him down, assuming he could even get her to accept his call in the first place. His only choice, then, was to show up uninvited and make the invitation so irresistible she'd simply have to accept. As confident of his charms as he was, he wasn't entirely certain what Dinah would find irresistible. He hoped her mother was around to give her a little nudge in his direction.

He pulled his cell phone out of his pocket and called the Davis number, which he now knew by memory thanks to the frequency of the messages he received on any given day from Dorothy Davis. Dinah's mother answered on the first ring. He liked the fact that answering the phone wasn't a task she relegated to the housekeeper.

"Hey, Mrs. Davis," he said, knowing his refusal to call her Dorothy annoyed her.

"Cordell," she said, her exasperation plain. "What can I do for you?"

"Is Dinah around?"

"She just got home a few minutes ago. I believe she's upstairs. Hold on and I'll check."

"No," he said urgently. "I don't want to speak to her. I just wanted to make sure she was home."

"If you don't mind me saying so, you're not making a lot of sense."

He laughed. "Nothing new about that. Actually I was hoping to persuade Dinah to go out dancing tonight, but I may need you to help me coax her into it. What do you say? Do you know if she has other plans?"

"I'm sure she doesn't," Mrs. Davis said. "And if you can get her to budge out of this house, more power to you. When she came in just now, she looked even more glum than she did when she got back here last night. I'll help in any way I can, especially if it means you can finally figure out what's going on with her. I suspect you didn't have a bit of luck last night."

"Not much," he admitted.

"Well, I know you tried, because she was quite annoyed with you."

"I figured as much."

"Okay, then," she said briskly. "Let's concentrate on tonight. What do you want me to do?"

"I honestly don't know. I was hoping you'd have some ideas. You usually do about everything else."

"Thank you, I think," she said, chuckling. "Let me give it some thought. I'm sure I can come up with something. What time will you be by?"

"Around seven," Cord said. "Will that work?"

"Perfect. I'll encourage her to dress for dinner tonight, so she won't be able to claim she has nothing to wear or have any excuses about holding you up while she changes."

"Have I mentioned that I love how your mind works?" he teased her.

She laughed. "No, you're usually too busy telling me what a nuisance I am, so thank you again."

"You're welcome. See you soon."

"Cordell?"

"Yes."

"Thank you for spending time with Dinah, too. She needs friends, whether she realizes it or not. Something tells me you're going to be a good one."

Cord was more touched by her confidence in him than he cared to reveal. "Thanks."

"She won't make it easy, you know."

He laughed. "Oh, trust me, I've gotten that message. But you know me, Mrs. Davis. I never walk away from a challenge."

"Yes," she said quietly. "That's one of your most attractive traits, Cordell. You haven't even let me scare you."

"You?" he teased. "You're just a woman who knows her own mind. I admire that."

She chuckled. "Stop wasting all that flattery on me. You'll need it with Dinah."

"Don't worry. I have more than enough for both of you. See you soon."

He hung up, smiling. A lot of men would shy away from getting tangled up with either of the Davis women. They were too strong-willed and cantankerous. But Cord figured all that practice he'd had battling wits with the mother was just a good warm-up for holding his own with the daughter. Besides, what was the fun of chasing after a woman if she made it too easy?

After her fruitless trip to Atlanta, Dinah watched three straight hours of television talk shows. Her mind had been going numb and she had changed channels in search of a cable newscast, but each time she'd started to watch a report from anywhere in Iraq, Israel or Afghanistan, her stomach had knotted up and she'd gone back to the discussions of obesity or abuse or teenage rebellion. The world was clearly a mixed-up place, even thousands of miles away from a war zone.

"Dinah, dear, are you in there?" her mother asked, rapping on the door, then entering without waiting for an invitation.

Dinah clicked off the TV, almost relieved by the distraction, though her mother rarely sought her out without some ulterior motive. "Did you need something, Mother?"

"I just wanted to let you know that I thought we'd dress for dinner tonight."

They hadn't adhered to the old formality in years. "Why?" Dinah asked suspiciously.

"Because we don't do it nearly often enough anymore." Her expression turned nostalgic as she sat on the edge of the bed. "When I was growing up, my parents insisted on dressing up every single night. I guarantee you none of us ever showed up at the table in jeans and

T-shirts. Your father and I started out following the old tradition, but we lost the habit somewhere along the way."

Dinah regarded her mother with increased suspicion. She didn't believe for a second that this was some whim to recapture the glory of the old days. "Are we having company? You promised me there would be no more dinner parties."

"No," her mother insisted. "I just thought it would be nice for all of us to come to the table looking our best for a change."

Dinah had a hunch this was her mother's polite way of pointing out that she'd gotten in the habit of dressing like a careless slob. "Maybe I'll just have dinner in my room," she suggested, trying out the idea to see if she could get away with it.

Her mother looked genuinely scandalized. "Absolutely not. I will not have Maybelle trudging up these stairs with a tray at her age, when you're perfectly able to come down to dinner. I'm ashamed that you would suggest such a thing."

"I could come down and get my own tray," Dinah replied defensively.

"That's not the point. Dinner's at seven. I expect you to be there," her mother said emphatically, then walked out and shut the door firmly behind her.

Dinah stared after her in shock. What on earth had that been about? Maybe her mother wanted Dinah downstairs as a buffer between her and Dinah's father. If that was it, she could hardly say no. She resigned herself to dressing up. Heck, maybe she would even feel marginally less depressed if she went to the effort to put on something pretty and added a little lipstick and mascara.

It had been days since she'd felt the need to do anything more than change into her swimsuit and sit by the pool, then come inside and stare at the TV. In her room she didn't have to deal with anything at all, and the atmosphere was such a far cry from the spartan hotel rooms in which she'd been living that she could almost pretend that the past ten years had never happened.

The pattern of pretense was so unlike her, even she was beginning to wonder if she didn't need help. Her spur-of-the-moment trip in search of Bobby had been an anomaly. Given how badly it had gone, she doubted she'd do anything impulsive again anytime soon.

She searched her closet till she found the perfect little black dress that had been her all-purpose date dress overseas. It was wrinkle-proof and fit like a dream. Peter's eyes had bugged out the first time he'd seen her in it.

"You look like a girl," he'd exclaimed in what had to be the most awkward compliment ever delivered.

Recalling that moment, Dinah sat on the edge of the bed and let the memories of that night flood over her. It had been their first real date after months of working together. He'd invited her to dinner and, unlike all the other meals they'd shared, they weren't surrounded by other correspondents. He'd even found a restaurant that still used real tablecloths and added the romantic ambiance of candlelight.

For the first time ever talk of work gave way to a sharing of more personal details. It had been the most comfortable first date Dinah had ever had because they were already colleagues who had a deep respect for each other's work. Yet she had known without question from the very first moment that they would become something more that night.

She remembered Peter's first kiss as if it had happened only yesterday. It had been gentle and had made her suddenly see all the possibilities of what could be between them.

In all the months that had followed, however, one thing had been missing. Never once had they talked about the future, because in the places where they worked, the only guarantee was the present. At the time, she'd understood completely, but now it made her unbearably sad to think that neither of them had ever believed they would have a happily-ever-after ending.

A tear tracked down her cheek, but she brushed it away impatiently. She knew as well as anyone how impossible it was to change the past.

Hurrying now, she splashed cold water on her face, fixed her makeup, then went downstairs just in time to hear the doorbell ring.

"I'll get it," she called out, wondering if there was company coming for dinner after all. When she opened the door and found Cord on the threshold wearing a suit, her mouth gaped. "You!"

He grinned, clearly not the least bit insulted by her undisguised dismay.

"Definitely me the last time I checked," he confirmed cheerfully.

She studied him with a narrowed gaze. "Did my mother invite you for dinner?"

"No."

"Then why are you here?" she asked ungraciously. "Are you dropping off some papers or something?"

He held up his empty hands. "No. Want to check my pockets, too?" he inquired, a wicked gleam in his eyes.

"You wish," she muttered, then asked again, "What are you doing here?"

"I came to get you. You look fabulous, by the way. I love that dress."

"Excuse me? I'm confused. Did we have plans that I forgot about?" She knew perfectly well they didn't. Her resolution to avoid Cord wasn't that old. She hadn't broken it yet.

"Nope. I just got to thinking about going dancing and I couldn't think of anyone I'd rather go with than you."

"So you just showed up without even calling? How rude is that?"

"I called," he protested. "I know something about manners, sugar."

Alice in Wonderland had nothing on Dinah. She felt as if she'd tumbled straight down that rabbit's hole, too. "I know with absolute certainty that you and I never spoke on the phone, Cordell."

"Actually, it was your mother I spoke to. She said you didn't have plans for tonight."

Dinah was finally beginning to get the picture. "So, you made these plans with my mother," she said. "And that's why she insisted I dress for dinner."

She wasn't sure which one of them she should be more furious with, her mother for tricking her or Cord for assuming that she would just go along with this crazy scheme of his.

"Well, since you and my mother seem to be getting along so well, I suggest you take her dancing," Dinah said. "I do not want to go out with you, Cordell."

"Your daddy might not appreciate me stealing his

woman, even for an evening, and while I'm quite sure your mother could keep up with me, you're the one I want to take out."

She frowned at him. "As flattering as that is, I'm not interested."

"In dancing or in me?"

"Either one," she assured him.

"Really?" He regarded her with blatant skepticism.

Without another word, he reached for her and before she realized his intention, he swept her around and into his arms, did a quick couple of dance steps, then dipped her. Her head was already spinning, when he leaned down and kissed her. His lips never left hers as he set her back upright. His mouth was a masterful thing, persuasive and demanding all at once.

Dinah let herself melt into the heat and tenderness she felt in him. Her hands clung to his shoulders, then moved to his cheeks that were rough under her fingers, even though she had no doubt at all that he'd shaved before leaving home. He was simply one of those men who'd always look just a bit disreputable and unkempt in the most masculine way possible. There were movie stars who probably had to spend hours in makeup to achieve that look.

Maybe Maggie was right. Maybe she was nuts for turning her back on Cord.

"Gotcha," he murmured. "Now let's talk about dancing."

"I don't want to talk about dancing. I don't want to go dancing. In fact, I do not want to go anywhere with you," she repeated, though with slightly less conviction than she had before. She couldn't deny that in five seconds he had made her feel alive again, but she wasn't entirely sure she appreciated it. "I don't appreciate you and my mother conspiring behind my back as if I'm some kid who doesn't know her own mind."

Cord nodded slowly. "I suppose we could go to your room and finish what we just started, since that did seem to interest you, but I think that might be pressing my luck with your mama's tolerance."

She could tell he was partly serious. "You are outrageous, you know that, don't you?"

He grinned. "Something tells me that you need to get stirred up, Dinah. You're used to taking chances. Take this one. It's just dancing and a good meal."

Maybe it was what she needed. It was certainly better than sitting in her room watching one of the nightly reality TV shows where people actually had fun doing disgusting things like eating worms. Even dancing with Cord had to be preferable to that.

Before she could utter her decision, her mother swept in, looking innocent as a lamb. "Why Cord," she said, surprise written all over her face. "I had no idea you were here."

Dinah rolled her eyes. "Can the act, Mother, though I must admit if you'd ever decided to go on stage, I'm sure you would have excelled. The secret's out. I know you two plotted this."

"Plotted what?" her mother asked, still maintaining the charade.

"To get me down here in a dress so I'd be all ready when Cord showed up."

Her mother beamed. "You do look lovely. The dress is very flattering. Where are you two going?"

"We were just about to decide," Cord said. "Ballroom dancing, disco night, or line dancing, Dinah?"

"Let me see," she said thoughtfully. "Which one will give me more opportunities to step all over your feet?"

Cord grinned impudently. "You're selling me short, sugar. I've been dodging women's feet for a good long time now."

"Yes, I imagine you have. Perhaps if you weren't so pushy, it wouldn't happen nearly so often."

Dinah heard a strangled laugh and turned to see her mother trying unsuccessfully to hide a smile. "What?" Dinah demanded.

"It's just that it's so wonderful to see those sparks back in your eyes," she said. "I think Cord is good for you."

Dinah didn't like the gleam in her mother's eyes one bit. "Don't get any ideas, Mother. The only thing Cord is good for is infuriating me."

He gave her a bland look. "Is that so? I thought I'd just proved otherwise."

Dinah avoided her mother's fascinated gaze. "If we're going, let's go before I come to my senses."

"Anything you say, sugar," Cord said meekly, then ruined the effect by winking at her mother.

Dinah turned to her mother. "If I come home driving his car and all alone, you'll know I've dumped his body in a ditch. Call a lawyer for me."

"Happily," her mother said. "But something tells me it won't come to that."

That had gone well, Cord thought as he drove toward the club that had eventually been Dinah's choice. He was pretty sure her threats had been idle ones, especially after she'd responded to his kiss with so much passion.

Then again, passion tended to make women unpredictable creatures. Just to be safe, he wouldn't turn his back on her for a minute. Not that he wanted to. She looked hot in that dress with most of her long legs exposed. Thinking about those legs had kept him awake more nights than he could count.

"You really do think you're something, don't you?" Dinah muttered as they neared their destination.

"In what way?"

"Because you talked me into this."

"I consider myself lucky, that's all," he assured her.

She scowled at him. "Just don't get any ideas."

"Such as?"

"That this is a date. That the kiss meant anything. That I'm going to sleep with you." She gave him a meaningful look. "Ever."

He swallowed a chuckle. "I'll keep all of that in mind."

"Good."

"Am I allowed to have a few fantasies?"

Her lips twitched. "Okay, fine. You can have all the fantasies you want as long as you don't give one second's thought to acting on them."

"And what if you go crazy and try to seduce me? Am I supposed to resist?"

"It'll never happen," she retorted.

"You seducing or me resisting?"

"The seducing part, so your resistance will never be tested."

"Too bad," he said sorrowfully. "I have excellent willpower."

Her expression suddenly sobered. "Why are you doing this, Cordell?"

"What? Teasing you? Because it's so easy and it's so much fun."

"No, I meant why have you turned me into some sort of project all of a sudden. You don't even like me."

As he cut the car's engine, he stared at her with genuine surprise. "Why would you say a thing like that?"

"The way you've been acting ever since I turned up out at your place. You made no attempt to hide your disdain for me or the fact that you think I'm all wrong for Bobby."

"You've got things all wrong. As for me not liking the idea of you with my brother that doesn't mean there's anything wrong with *you*," he said emphatically. "In fact, there are a lot of things right about you."

She regarded him wistfully. "Such as?"

"You really don't know?" he asked, thoroughly bemused.

She shook her head.

"Now that really is pitiful," he said sincerely. "Okay, let me lay it all out for you, Dinah, and I'm being sincere about this. This isn't just flattery so I can lure you into my bed."

"I think we've already established that would be a wasted effort," she said wryly. "What do you see as my good qualities?"

To Cord's surprise, she looked as if she were truly hanging on his words. Because of that, he chose his words carefully.

"You're beautiful and smart and brave. You have legs that could drive a man wild." He slanted a look at her. "Me included, in case you were wondering."

Her lips curved slightly.

"Now, what else?" he said thoughtfully. "You're

confident…or at least you used to be. I have a hunch that will come back to you once you put whatever happened in Afghanistan behind you. You always knew what you wanted and you went after it without letting anybody stand in your way. Who would have believed that a sheltered debutante would wind up being an internationally famous war correspondent? With your looks and brains, you could have been an anchorwoman in some nice safe studio, but you chose something a lot of men don't even have the guts to do. I admire that."

"You do?"

"Well, of course I do. I can't say I didn't find it worrisome when I'd flick on the TV and see you five feet from where some car bomb had been detonated, but I was as proud to know you as I imagine your mama and daddy were."

She seemed stunned by that. "What about now that I'm home? Are you disappointed in me?"

Cord turned the question right around. "Are you disappointed in yourself?"

"Yes," she admitted in a small voice.

"Why?"

"I don't know if I'm brave enough to go back."

"Is that something you have to decide today or tomorrow?"

"No."

"Then don't worry about it until you have to. Concentrate on healing."

She regarded him with puzzlement. "I'm not injured."

"Sure you are," he said. "There's more than one way to be wounded in a war, Dinah, and stitches don't tidy up all kinds of wounds. And in case you still have doubts, neither will marrying the wrong man."

He thought the conversation had gotten way too serious, even if she had needed to hear what he had to say. He deliberately winked at her. "Now, since you obviously have two perfectly good feet under you, let's go inside and dance up a storm and forget all this, just for tonight. Let's just be a couple of old..." He deliberately hesitated as his gaze locked with hers. "Acquaintances," he said at last. "We'll be a couple of old acquaintances having ourselves a good old time."

She nodded slowly, looking relieved. "Think you can keep up with me, Cordell?"

"I'm going to give it my all, sugar. I am definitely going to give it my all."

And, though it was too soon to say it, he was looking way beyond whatever tricks she could come up with on the dance floor, too. He wanted Dinah to start thinking of the two of them in terms of possibilities.

11

Dinah hadn't danced—or laughed—so much since her debutante ball. In fact, this was better. Back then, she'd been filled with so much cynicism about the whole event that she'd hardly enjoyed the evening. The boy she'd taken had been awkward and as immature as most eighteen-year-old boys were. He'd had sweaty palms and pimples, as she recalled.

She glanced across the table and saw that Cord was studying her curiously.

"Taking a trip down memory lane?" he asked.

"How did you know?"

"For a woman who's trained to keep her expression neutral on the air, you really don't hide your emotions all that well. You looked a little sad."

"Not sad," she assured him. "Just thinking about my debutante ball debacle."

"I thought that was the highlight of every little Southern girl's life?"

"Not mine. I thought it was an absurd waste of money, but my mother insisted it was an important tra-dition, so I went along with it. Maggie and I were determined not to have a good time, so we invited the most inappropriate boys we could find."

Cord grinned at that. "You didn't invite me."

Dinah laughed. "On the inappropriate scale, you were way out of my league. Besides, I was determined to be miserable, not to give my mother a heart attack."

"I remember you that night," he said, catching her completely by surprise.

Dinah sorted through her memories of the ball, trying to recall Cord being there. An image finally came to mind of him with the quietest girl in their class. "Oh, my God, that's right. You *were* there. It was Mitzi Franklin's grand rebellion. Frankly, I didn't think she had it in her."

Mitzi had been a shy, bespectacled girl that everyone pretty much ignored, Dinah included. Her arrival at the dance on Cord's arm had definitely stirred a fuss.

"I suspect you'd have been surprised about a lot of things about Mitzi," Cord said. "Most people didn't give her much credit for charm or personality. The boys dismissed her because she wasn't stunning and didn't sleep with them. The girls were afraid they'd be tainted by being seen with someone they deemed ordinary."

Dinah heard the censure in his voice. She knew she couldn't deny what he was saying. Her friends had been cruel. "Okay, tell me. What did we all miss?"

"That Mitzi had had a tough life. That she was shy and quiet because she stuttered until she was sixteen and had worked with a speech therapist for years. That she won a scholarship to Duke."

"I knew about the scholarship," Dinah said in her own defense. "It was the talk of the school. Everyone was astounded that she, of all people, would win a scholarship to Duke."

"But did you know it was for music? The girl is a helluva singer."

Dinah couldn't have been more stunned if he'd said it was for stripping. "You're kidding."

"Not kidding. She's playing jazz clubs in New York, Chicago and Los Angeles now. I've caught her act a few times and I have a stash of her CDs at home. Remind me and I'll play them for you sometime."

"You've kept in touch with Mitzi?" She didn't like how that made her feel not only a bit jealous, but small and shallow. Out of some ridiculous teenaged social prejudice, she'd apparently missed out on knowing someone interesting and talented enough to fascinate Cord.

"Sure, we've kept in touch. We had a lot in common. We were both outsiders."

Dinah had never thought of Cord as an outsider, except in the way he'd insisted on being. She'd always thought his isolation had been a deliberate choice, not the result of being shunned. Given the way kids were, maybe one thing had spawned the other.

"We weren't very nice to you, were we?" she asked.

"You weren't," he admitted, then gave her a roguish grin. "A lot of other girls made up for it. The bad-boy, outsider thing seems to be a magnet for some women."

"Still?"

"Hard to call myself an outsider, when I've got a company doing business with some of the oldest, most revered names in Charleston society. Even your mama finds me perfectly respectable these days."

"I suspect my mother's like every other female on earth. She's fascinated with that aura of danger you exude. She certainly made the safe choice when she married my father." She couldn't help wondering if it was a decision her mother had come to regret. Was that what was causing the tension between her parents? Now that both Dinah and Tommy Lee were grown, were they finding that there was nothing left to hold them together?

Cord's expression suddenly turned serious. "What about you, Dinah? You're the danger junkie. Do I appeal to you?"

More than she cared to admit, Dinah thought. The times they'd been together had revealed depths she'd never imagined. He was solid and kind in a totally unexpected way. That he'd championed a girl like Mitzi said a lot about his character. Oddly, that made him the most dangerous sort of man for someone who'd come home searching for solidity and strength and tenderness. She was beginning to see that she'd never given him nearly enough credit.

She was even beginning to see his betrayal as a desperate but well-meaning attempt to protect his brother from making a mistake. Maybe back then he hadn't been wise enough to understand the folly in interfering in his brother's life, but surely he'd learned from that mistake.

She gave him an impudent look. "You appeal to me enough to get out on the dance floor with you one more time," she told him lightly. "Then we probably should get home. I imagine you need a lot of rest to keep up with my mother's demands."

He laughed. "I can handle your mother on a couple of hours of sleep. You're the tricky one."

"How so?"

"I understand your mother. She's a perfectionist and she knows her own mind. You're a little unpredictable.

Something tells me if I keep hanging around you, I'm going to be up to my eyeballs in trouble."

"You're afraid of me?" Dinah asked, surprisingly pleased by that idea. No one had ever accused her of being too much of a handful before, not as a woman, anyway. As a reporter, she'd run across more than her share of skittish subjects who were afraid of the questions she might ask. She'd also encountered a lot of competitors who'd feared being beaten by her cutthroat ambition and talent. This, though, was new. She smiled at Cord. "I think I like that."

"Of course you do," he teased. "You're a woman who likes to control things." He met her gaze. "But one thing you need to know about me, Dinah. I'm not one bit like my brother. I am not going to let you have your way, not all the time, anyway."

The little shudder that washed over her at his words was not entirely unpleasant. In fact, it was downright loaded with anticipation.

Cord stood on the front steps of Dinah's house and looked down into her eyes. The combination of a little wine and some energetic dancing had made her unmistakably sleepy and just a little off her game. She looked so damned kissable that it was taking every bit of willpower he possessed not to devour that tempting mouth of hers. A kiss was also what she was clearly expecting. He figured she was long overdue for a little unpredictability from him.

"Good night," he said softly, his gaze locked with hers. "Sleep well."

A spark of indignation flickered for just an instant in her eyes. "Good night? Just like that?"

He hid his amusement. The tactic had worked like a charm. "Isn't that usually what people say when one person's going inside and the other's going home? I thought I had that part of the dating thing nailed down."

"What about a kiss?" she demanded.

That was definitely the wine talking, Cord concluded. "I kissed you before we went out," he reminded her. "Though I'm happy to oblige, as I recall you gave me a very firm lecture at the time. Now you want me to do it again?"

"No, I do not want you to do it again," she said, immediately contradicting herself once more.

He shook his head sorrowfully. "Is it any wonder men don't understand women? They keep changing the rules."

"Forget the damn rules," she muttered.

Before he knew what she had in mind, she grabbed his shirt and yanked his head down. Her mouth covered his and her tongue dove inside on his gasp of surprise. The kiss was hot and edged with just a hint of desperation. It made Cord's blood shoot straight from his brain to another part of his anatomy.

Just as his head started to swim from the lack of oxygen, she released him just as unexpectedly.

"*That's* how you say good night," she declared emphatically, then swept past him and went inside, slamming the door behind her. She was obviously very pleased with herself.

Grinning at her display of pure sass, Cord leaned on the doorbell. She threw open the door, and Cord picked her up, hauled her against his chest and kissed her until they were both gasping for air. Satisfied, he set her back on her feet. She looked thoroughly dazed and not half as sure of herself.

"I like my way better," he said, then walked away.

Damn, but this was turning out to be fun.

As soon as Cord got home, he called Dinah on her cell phone so he wouldn't wake the rest of the family.

"Sweet dreams," he said for the second time that night.

"You confuse me," she responded, sounding genuinely bewildered.

"Same here."

"Really?"

"Yes, Dinah," he said patiently. "Just when I think I have you all figured out, you go and do something surprising."

"Such as?" she asked. "I need to know. Maybe I shouldn't do it anymore."

Cord laughed. "Oh no. I'm not telling. I like your kind of surprises."

"You must be talking about the kiss," she concluded.

"Definitely memorable," he agreed. "But that's not it."

"Then what? I didn't do anything else."

"Sure you did."

"What?"

"You let me get away with coming back for more. Next time, I'll have to see what else I can get away with. Something tells me kissing's just a warm-up for us."

"I don't think so."

"Why not?"

"I'm not ready to start anything with you or anybody else," she said, her tone suddenly stone-cold sober.

"You were ready to marry my brother," he reminded her.

"That was different."

"You're going to have to explain that one to me. You don't think marriage is more serious than a little fooling around just for fun?"

She fell silent then.

"Dinah? Is this about the man you claim doesn't exist? Are you feeling guilty for some reason?"

"No," she said with evident sorrow. "There's no reason to feel guilty. Not anymore."

"What does that mean?" he asked, troubled by her somber tone and the odd logic that marrying Bobby was somehow less of a betrayal than sleeping with him would be. And why would she be considering either if there was a man out there somewhere who meant something to her?

She sighed deeply, but ignored the question. "Good night, Cord. Thanks for taking me dancing."

He could tell that was all she intended to say on the subject, though he couldn't begin to imagine why she was so reticent. Was she sparing his feelings? Or her own? Something told him he needed to get to the bottom of that, quite possibly for both their sakes.

The question of the mysterious man in Dinah's life was still on Cord's mind in the morning. He knew she was lying to him. What he couldn't figure out was why she'd bothered. It wasn't as if there was any reason to keep a secret about the past. They didn't owe each other a lot of detailed explanations about their prior love lives. Not yet, anyway. Maybe the time for full disclosure would never come.

He had to admit he was more attracted to her than ever even though they would never get seriously involved. He didn't do serious, not even for Dinah Davis. Everyone in South Carolina Low Country knew that. Dinah had her ground rules. He had his. From what he'd seen with his own mama and daddy, there was no such thing as happily-ever-after and marriage was the kiss of death to any kind of fun.

Besides, he had always attracted wealthy women who were drawn to him for his dangerous reputation but weren't interested in anything more. He'd achieved a lot, but in certain circles it would never be quite enough.

Still, he'd never been able to get past the fantasy of someday fitting in. He'd always thought that if and when he decided he wanted marriage, he would be able to marry someone with class, someone like Dinah, who'd always been out of reach. Since the odds of finding such a woman were a million to one, he'd learned to get by on his own.

Oddly, Dinah seemed more available to him now. He couldn't help feeling that the woman who'd become identified around the globe with courageous reporting was as vulnerable and fragile as a wounded bird. It made him feel surprisingly protective.

But he couldn't help her if he didn't know why she'd come home and what or who it was she'd left behind. Before he could do any research on that topic, though, he had to get his brother safely out of town.

He was in the kitchen, half dressed and drinking his second cup of coffee when Bobby wandered in. He looked like a man who'd had a rough night.

"What happened to you?" Cord asked. "Did the party go on till all hours?"

"No, the party ended at a perfectly respectable eleven o'clock. I spent the rest of the night battling with Rianna over the wedding."

"What now?" Cord asked, though he'd heard just about every variation on the subject he cared to hear. Still, it was evident Bobby needed to get this latest round off his chest.

"She wants to turn it into some sort of elaborate ceremony fit for a queen or something," Bobby said with dismay. "It's gotten completely out of hand. I told her to shave down the guest list, forget about the doves and hire something smaller than a symphony orchestra. She told me I didn't love her or I'd understand how important this is to her."

"Uh-huh," Cord said dutifully, barely tuned in to the familiar recitation.

"I do love her," Bobby declared, "but I sure as hell don't understand why she's got her heart set on something that's going to cost thousands and thousands of dollars. We could build a damn mansion for what she wants to spend on her dress and the cake alone. Hell, what's wrong with buying a couple of boxes of Duncan Hines cake mix? I asked her that and she dumped a glass of water over my head."

Cord regarded him with amusement. "Did you eventually resolve the impasse?"

Bobby nodded, his expression miserable. "In a way."

"What does that means?"

"She called off the wedding."

Cord's heart thumped unsteadily. He knew his dismay was not entirely pure. "She'll calm down," he assured Bobby.

"I don't think so. I'm not even sure I want her to. If we're this far apart on the wedding, how would we ever make our marriage work?"

"From what I hear, one thing has nothing to do with

the other," Cord told him. "Right now you're messing with a little girl's dream. She's probably been planning this wedding since she was eight."

"That's what she said," Bobby admitted.

"Then let her have it. Indulge her. You'll live in a smaller house to start with. You won't hire a nanny for the first kid. Besides, the company's doing better every year. You'll make up the money in no time."

"I don't think that's the point. I think we want different things."

Cord shook his head. "You want different *weddings*. There's a difference. Come on, Bobby. This is just a bump in the road. Go back over there and make things right before you go back to Atlanta. Don't let this turn into a big deal you can't fix."

"I thought you were on the fence about Rianna," Bobby said, regarding Cord with a perplexed expression. "Why are you suddenly so anxious for us to patch things up?"

Cord tap-danced his way through an answer. "Because even I can see that she makes you happy. She's crazy about you. Don't turn your back on that over a couple of doves flying around pooping on the wedding guests."

Bobby chuckled, just as Cord had hoped he would.

"You are so crude," Bobby accused.

"Maybe so, but I'm right and you know it. Now, go. Tell her she can have the doves and all the rest of it."

"Hold on. I came over here to figure out what's going on with you," Bobby protested. "So far all we've done is talk about my problems."

Cord grinned. "No time for that now. Besides, I don't have any problems worth discussing. I have to get to work." He grabbed his shirt off the back of a chair and headed for the door. "We'll talk later in the week."

"You're not off the hook," Bobby called after him.

Cord merely waved in response.

Instead of heading straight for Covington Plantation, though, he turned toward town. He'd concluded overnight that his best source for information on Dinah's state of mind would be her best friend.

Because it was early, he found a place to park right in front of Images and went inside. He'd already devised what he considered to be a brilliant ploy for being there.

"Cord," Maggie said with surprise when she found him wandering around looking at the art. "What on earth brings you by here, especially at this hour of the morning? I don't even have the OPEN sign out yet."

He hesitated. "Is it okay for me to be here, then? I had a few minutes to spare this morning and I thought I'd check out what you have. We're going to need some art for Covington once we finish up the work out there."

"Of course, it's okay. You're always welcome as long as I'm around."

Despite the welcome, she seemed skeptical, probably because his excuse was so pitiful. To give credence to the bald-faced lie, he made a thorough tour of the place, asking about everything and everyone except the one person on his mind.

Eventually Maggie regarded him with amusement. "You're not fooling me with this casual act, Cord."

He gave her a rueful look. "I'm not?"

"Please. You haven't set foot in here in all the weeks since you and I went out on that date. Only one thing could possibly bring you in here now."

"I came to look at the art," he insisted.

Maggie rolled her eyes. "You and I both know that Dorothy Davis is not about to let you pick what paintings will hang on the walls out at Covington Plantation. You're here about Dinah."

Since she was on a roll, he figured he'd give her enough lead to finish what she'd started. "Oh? What makes you think that?"

"I heard the two of you had dinner at Murrells Inlet a few days ago. I also heard you were out dancing just last night," Maggie said.

"Damn, that grapevine sure is quick," he commented.

"Always has been, especially when the news is spicy enough." She regarded him with curiosity. "How did you pull off the dancing thing?"

"Caught her at a weak moment," he said, then added, "She seems to be having a lot of those. Any idea what's up?"

Maggie hesitated, obviously torn between her loyalty to Dinah and the sincere concern she surely must have heard in his voice. "I honestly don't know," she said at last. "The truth is she seems to be avoiding me. I've only seen her a couple of times." She gave him a look filled with irony. "One of those was when she offered to help me land you."

Cord nearly choked. "What? She thought you and I…?"

"Oh, yes. She'd heard about our big date, about how much money I spent to win you in that auction. She figured she'd help me move things along."

There was a bitter edge to her tone, Cord didn't entirely understand. He studied her intently. "Did I miss something here? Was that date about more than help-ing out a good cause?"

"Not for you," she said wryly. "Which pretty much means it wasn't for me, either."

Her admission caught him completely off-guard. He'd completely missed the fact that she might have been hoping for more than a nice evening. He stared at her with real regret. "I had no idea. I'm sorry, Maggie."

"I know," she said. "Which is why it didn't hurt that much. Let's not belabor it now, please. It's humiliating enough as it is. We should be focusing on Dinah, since we both care about her." Her gaze narrowed. "You do care about her, right? You're not just intent on having one of your usual flings?"

"I'm not sure I'm ready to pin a label on it," Cord said defensively. "But I do want to help her. She's messed up, Maggie. She's not herself. I know some of it's because of where she was and what she's seen. I recognize all the post-traumatic stress symptoms, be-cause I've been there, but there's something else. A man, maybe. Has she said anything?"

"Not a word. Maybe it's about her job, though. She says she's glad to be home, but I think she's thoroughly unsettled without her work to go back to."

Cord stared at her in shock. "Hold it! Are you tell-ing me she's not going back, that this isn't just some extended vacation?"

"To be honest, I'm not sure if she quit or if she was fired. She wouldn't really say. She just said she was thinking about staying here, but she didn't want me to say a word to anyone." She met his gaze. "If it were any-one but you asking, I wouldn't have said a word, but I think maybe you're the only one she'll let help her."

"What makes you think that? It's not as if she and I are old friends."

"Maybe not, but at least she's spending time with you. Her mom says she's hiding out in her room at home and she's certainly not confiding in me."

"She's only been with me because I've tricked her into it," he admitted. "It's not as if she's ecstatic at the prospect of seeing me. I ask too many questions. Unfortunately, she's not answering most of them."

"Keep asking," Maggie encouraged. "You need to get to the bottom of the whole job thing. She loved her work, Cord. That was her identity. She worked damn hard to get on top and I can't imagine her giving it up easily. If it really is over, it's no wonder she's feeling lost. It would explain why she'd turn to your brother."

"Desperation," Cord said grimly. Knowing that made him even more certain that he'd done the right thing by keeping them apart. If Bobby had known Dinah was waiting in the wings when he'd had that fight with Rianna last night, there was no telling what would have happened. They might have gravitated together for all the wrong reasons.

"Exactly. Desperation," Maggie confirmed. "It's the only explanation I can come up with, but now that she knows about Bobby's engagement, I think she's given up that particular daydream. It never made a lick of sense in the first place. Why on earth would she choose Bobby when she could have…" Her words faltered and color bloomed in her cheeks.

Cord got the message. He didn't intend to go there, at least not with Dinah's best friend. "But you really don't have any idea why she'd take such a drastic leap and quit her job? Or why the network might fire one of their top correspondents?"

"No idea at all. She certainly didn't give me any clues about what happened. Maybe you should ask her."

"Maybe I will."

But even if he figured out precisely how to phrase his questions, he doubted he'd get answers that made any sense.

12

Dinah waited until after nine in the morning before wandering downstairs in search of breakfast. She'd been hoping to avoid her parents, her mother in particular. Unfortunately, Dorothy was still seated at the dining room table, the portable phone in one hand, a pen in the other. She was scribbling notes in her datebook. She barely glanced up long enough to take note of Dinah's arrival.

Dinah considered bolting to the relative safety of the kitchen, but before she could, her mother hung up and set the phone aside.

"There you are," she said cheerfully. "You and Cord must have been out very late, if you're just now coming down for breakfast."

"It wasn't that late," Dinah said. "Is there more coffee?"

"Of course. Would you like eggs? Toast? I'll tell Maybelle."

"No need to tell Maybelle anything," the housekeeper said, walking into the room with a tray. "I heard voices in here." She gave Dinah a scolding look. "About time you wandered down for breakfast. I fixed you half a grapefruit, an English muffin and a scrambled egg. Take it or leave it."

Dinah grinned at the imperious tone. "It's exactly what I wanted, Maybelle."

"Right answer," Maybelle said approvingly, as she poured Dinah a cup of her potent coffee. When Dinah's mother held out her cup, Maybelle merely took it from her. "You've had enough. I'll bring you decaf."

Dinah stared after her with amusement as she left the room. "Is there anyone else on earth who gets away with telling you what to do?" she asked her mother.

"No one else would dare try," her mother said, her expression filled with affection. "But I honestly don't know what I would do without that woman. I should insist she retire, but selfishly I can't bear the thought of her not being underfoot. She helps me clarify things."

What an odd thing to say, Dinah thought. Her mother always seemed so confident, so self-assured about everything. She regarded her mother curiously. "What sort of things do you ever need to have clarified?"

"Everything. Years ago she made me see that marrying your father was the right thing to do." She gave Dinah a rueful look. "I wasn't convinced, you see. I knew he adored me, but I wanted something, I don't know, more exciting, I suppose. I was a lot like you at that age. I wasn't at all ready to settle down."

"You were?" Dinah tried to imagine her mother being anything other than a wife and hostess and driving force behind a dozen or more charities. That's what she'd been bred to do, what she'd tried to teach Dinah. "I can't imagine you in any other role."

"I thought I could change the world," her mother said. "I'm not sure if I had a clue how to accomplish that, but I did know there had to be more to life than living comfortably in this little corner of it."

"What stopped you?"

Her mother looked vaguely disconcerted by the question, as if she somehow hadn't realized that it was bound to be the next one Dinah—or any reasonable person—would ask.

"You don't know?" her mother asked, her brow furrowed in a way that would have appalled her if she'd happened to catch herself in the mirror.

"Know what?" Dinah responded, baffled by the odd expression on her mother's face.

"Somehow I always assumed you must have figured it out."

"Figured what out?" Dinah asked impatiently. She was suddenly filled with dread. Whatever it was her mother thought she already knew wasn't going to be good.

"I got pregnant," her mother said simply.

The words hung in the air for an eternity. Coming from anyone else—Maggie, an acquaintance, *anyone*— Dinah would have known exactly what to say, but her mother? Added to the admission that she'd had an entirely different dream for her life, the pregnancy was too much. It had obviously changed everything for her mother.

"With me," Dinah said flatly, drawing the obvious conclusion. "*I* changed your life. You married Dad because of me."

"Please don't look so wounded, Dinah. You were the catalyst, yes, but I married your father because it was the right thing to do, even in that day and age when people were becoming more tolerant about unwed mothers and even abortion," her mother said. "People here weren't more tolerant."

"You could have gone away," Dinah said, but even as she spoke she realized it would have been impossible. For all her mother's talk about wanting something more, she was at heart a traditional Southern woman who must have craved the approval of her family.

"I suppose I could have," her mother admitted. "But I couldn't do that to your father. He had a right to know about you, to know you. He's a good, decent man. We've had a good life together."

"But you didn't love him." Dinah had to force the hard-to-swallow words out. Discovering that she was even remotely responsible for a marriage that might not otherwise have been was difficult to absorb.

"I did love him," her mother corrected. "I just wasn't in love with him."

"And now?" Dinah asked, terrified that one more part of her world, one more thing she'd always counted on to remain exactly the same was about to crumble under her feet.

"I suppose you could say we're both content," her mother said.

Dinah wanted to put her head down on the table and weep. She looked at the sadness in her mother's eyes and saw a truth that went way beyond her mother's words. If she had foolishly grasped at the straw of marrying Bobby, this was what she would have had to look forward to, being resigned to contentment. Cord had been right. She would have chafed at it sooner or later, just as it appeared her mother was doing now, whether she was ready to acknowledge it openly or not.

"I'm so sorry, Mother."

"Don't be," her mother said. "I should never have said anything. Even grown children shouldn't be burdened with their parents' problems."

"You obviously needed to talk about it. I'm glad you felt you could tell me," she said, uttering the lie with what she hoped was sufficient conviction to allay her mother's guilt. "Does Dad know how unhappy you are?"

"We certainly haven't talked about it," she said dryly. "That kind of conversation would send him fleeing to some trumped-up business meeting in a matter of seconds. He knows that something's changed between us, but I suspect he doesn't know what to do about it. Frankly, neither do I. I think it's been easier just to drift along as we have been, living separate lives in many ways. We both carry on with the illusion that things are just fine."

That explained why her father didn't get involved with any of her mother's projects, Dinah concluded. But if they couldn't share each other's business, what was left for them to share? Were they even sharing a bedroom? The very question made Dinah squirm uncomfortably. The truth was, she had no idea. Her room had always been far from theirs. In the old house, she and Tommy Lee had occupied rooms in a separate wing. Here in town, their rooms were on the third floor, while their parents had a suite of rooms on the second.

"Mother, is having me here a problem?" she asked worriedly. Were the tensions magnified by her being underfoot?

"Don't be absurd," her mother said fiercely. "This is your home, Dinah. Where else would you be?"

"I could stay with Maggie for a while, I'm sure. Or even Tommy Lee and Laurie."

"Absolutely not. Your father and I want you here, for as long as you can stay. We may disagree about many things these days, but never about that."

But that clearly couldn't last forever, Dinah realized with a sinking sensation in the pit of her stomach. A part of her wanted to lash out at both her parents for allowing her view of their marriage to be turned on its head, for disrupting the comfortable world she'd retreated to. A more generous part of her was filled with compassion for her mother, who'd never had a real chance to discover who she might become.

Impulsively, Dinah stood up and went around the table to give her mother a hug. "I think you're the bravest woman I've ever met."

Her mother looked up, tears spilling over and down her cheeks. That, too, was a shock. Dinah had never seen her mother shed a tear before.

"You have no idea what that means to me, especially coming from you, but I'm not at all brave, Dinah. In fact, I've spent my whole life simply doing what was expected. I suppose that's what I'll go right on doing."

"You don't have to," Dinah told her. "If you're unhappy, Mother, do something about it. Don't drift along another day wasting even one more of the precious few minutes we're given on this earth."

Her mother gave her a pointed look. "That advice could apply to you, as well. Haven't you been drifting ever since you came home? The only time I see you looking the least bit alive is when you're with Cordell."

Dinah had known that sooner or later they were bound to get back to Cord. She simply hadn't expected her mother to read the situation so clearly.

"I don't want to spend too much time with Cord," she said.

"Why? Because he scares you?" her mother asked perceptively. "That's a good thing, don't you think?"

"Cord doesn't scare me," Dinah insisted.

Her mother's lips twitched with undisguised amusement. "Oh, really?"

"Of course not."

"Then you'll be seeing him again soon?"

"No," she said flatly. "I wouldn't have seen him last night, if the two of you hadn't tricked me into it."

"And the evening was a disaster, then?" her mother asked innocently. "You didn't have fun?"

"It was…" She searched for an innocuous word. "Pleasant."

"You spent an evening out with Cordell and that's the best you can come up with?" her mother said with undisguised disbelief. "The man is seriously hot. Even I'm not too old to appreciate that."

A laugh bubbled up before Dinah could stop it. "Mother!"

"Well, he is," her mother said unrepentantly. "And you see it, too, which is why you've been so intent on avoiding him."

"Maybe I just don't think there's any point in starting something that won't go anywhere," Dinah retorted.

"And why won't it go anywhere?" her mother asked reasonably. "Because you're leaving?"

"Yes," Dinah said at once, seizing on the obvious, most believable excuse.

Her mother's gaze narrowed. "When?"

"When what?"

"When are you leaving?"

"I'm not exactly sure," she admitted.

"Then let me offer you a piece of advice I failed to heed. *Carpe diem.* In case you don't know, it means seize the day. It's pretty much the same advice you gave me not five minutes ago."

"I know what it means. I just don't know why you'd tell me to do such a thing."

"Because I see something in your eyes when you're with Cord that I haven't felt in years."

"What?"

"Passion, darling. Don't take it lightly. Love, honor, respect, decency, all of those things are solid and enduring, but the greatest gift any of us can be given is passion, whether it's for a person or a job. I don't see it when you talk about your work anymore, but I do see it when you're with Cordell. Grab on to it with everything you've got."

Dinah didn't want to acknowledge in any way the possibility that her mother might be right. Instead, she asked, "What about you, Mother? What are you passionate about?"

Her mother's expression faltered at the question. "My projects, I suppose."

"Is that enough?" Dinah asked.

"I've made it enough," her mother said quietly.

But Dinah could tell from the emptiness in her voice that it wasn't nearly enough. And that made her heart ache. Maybe they were two of a kind, after all.

Dorothy sat at the dining room table long after Dinah had disappeared upstairs. She had a million and one calls left to make, but she couldn't seem to work up the enthusiasm. It seemed as if she'd made the exact same calls to the exact same people for way too many years now. She was the go-to woman, the one everyone in town expected to pull off fund-raising miracles.

Over time, she'd assembled list upon list of the best caterers, the best donors, the best hotel ballrooms, the best florists. She could call any of them on a moment's notice and put together an event that would dazzle. Was her legacy going to be that she knew how to get people to part with their money?

Ironically there was no one on any of those lists who she considered to be a friend, at least not one to whom she would divulge the things that were troubling her. Perhaps that was why she'd said too much when Dinah had given her an opening just now. She was searching for some meaning to her life and she wasn't finding it on her own. She'd hoped that maybe her daughter could shed some light on it.

Certainly there was an important place in the world for what she did. Arts organizations, children's charities, the homeless, historic preservation projects all needed more money than cities, states or the federal government could provide. And as much as they needed the dollars, they also needed the attention that a successful event could muster. It helped to draw in new volunteers for the shelters, docents for the museums, new audiences for the arts.

It wasn't as if she'd wasted her life. It was just that lately she was feeling more and more incomplete, as if there was something more she should be doing to fulfill herself and not just the charity coffers.

She wondered if Marshall felt a vague dissatisfaction, as well, if that explained his increasingly short temper, his more frequent absences from the dinner table. Was it even possible he was having an affair, one it was more difficult to carry on with Dinah now living at the house?

She was distractedly tapping her pen on the table when Maybelle breezed into the dining room, her face full of disapproval.

"Why'd you go and dump all your problems on that girl's shoulders?" Maybelle demanded indignantly. "Don't you think she has enough on her mind?"

Dorothy stared at the housekeeper with dismay. "I never meant to add to her problems. It just sort of bubbled out."

"You sure about that? Maybe you were sitting in here feeling sorry for yourself and saw a way to get some sympathy."

Dorothy accepted most of Maybelle's scoldings as her due, but not this one. "I most certainly did not. Besides, maybe it's good for her to finally know the truth."

"That you and her daddy got married because she was on the way? That's exactly what every woman wants to find out when there's not a thing in the world she can do about it," Maybelle chided. "I think I saw that on *Oprah* one day or maybe it was *Dr. Phil*."

Dorothy winced. "Okay, okay, you've made your point. It was too much information. Still, for the first time in years, I actually felt as if I was connecting with my daughter."

Maybelle gave her a hard, unrelenting look. "Instead of resenting her, you mean?"

"I never resented Dinah," she snapped, then was overcome by shame. She scowled at Maybelle. "You see too damn much, you know that, don't you?"

Maybelle gave her hand a squeeze. "I know you love

that girl, but I know you were speaking the truth earlier when you said you were like her once. I was there, remember? You had a lot of fire in you, same as she does. I suppose it's only natural for you to feel bad that she was able to do things you used to think about doing."

"I would never have gone off to war," Dorothy said. "She's braver than I ever was."

"But you would have left home, instead of sticking close by to go to college. You were a dutiful child. You did what your daddy wanted."

"And then I tried to turn right around and make Dinah do the same thing," she recalled. "Thank God, she didn't listen. She's become a remarkable woman." She gave Maybelle a helpless look. "Why doesn't she seem to understand that anymore?"

"Something tells me that heart of hers is broken," Maybelle said.

"You think the change in her is about a man?"

"That or about all those awful things she's seen, things you and I can't even imagine. If you see the trouble in her eyes same as me, isn't it time you asked her?"

"I've been asking, but she won't say a word. She never did like it when I pressed her to talk about something before she was ready."

"Sometimes a mother has to do things whether her child's ready or not," Maybelle said. "I know you've been hoping that young man can get her to open up, but isn't getting to the bottom of this your job?"

Dorothy gave her a rueful look. "Yes, ma'am," she said dutifully. "You're my conscience, Maybelle. You always have been."

"You've got a good enough conscience of your own.

You just need a little practice getting in touch with it. About time, too. I won't be around forever."

"Yes, you will," Dorothy told her adamantly. "I'm counting on it."

"You got a say about a lot of things in this world," Maybelle told her. "But not about that. That one's up to the Lord."

"Of course it is," Dorothy agreed. "Why do you think I'm on my knees every single night praying to Him just for that one thing?"

"Maybe you need to do some praying on a few other things while you're at it," Maybelle chided. "Get some help for that child and maybe a sense of direction for yourself. And while you're at it, a prayer or two for your son wouldn't be amiss."

Dorothy studied Maybelle with a narrowed gaze. "Is there something going on with Tommy Lee?"

"Nothing that hasn't been right under your nose for a good long time now. He's never going to fit into that niche his daddy has all carved out for him. Pray on that."

Dorothy had always admired Maybelle's unshakeable faith, but she also believed that people had a duty to find their own way. Maybe the truth was that everyone needed to combine the two approaches.

"You say your prayers, Maybelle," she said. "I'll get to work on a plan."

"You and your plans," the housekeeper said with a shake of her head. "When you going to get it through your head that the Lord's up there having Himself a laughing fit every time He sees you trying to set everything down on paper in a nice, orderly list?"

"Lists give me comfort," Dorothy replied stubbornly.

"How many lists you got there in front of you?" Maybelle asked. "A dozen? Maybe more?"

"I suppose."

"I thought so. Now you look me in the eye and tell me you feel the least bit comfortable this morning."

Despite herself, Dorothy chuckled. "Okay, maybe you have a point."

"Well, of course I do," Maybelle said smugly. "Now clear this stuff off my table. I've got furniture polishing to do this morning and you're holding me up."

Before she could go, Dorothy reached for her hand. "Maybelle," she said urgently. "This is going to work out, isn't it?"

"I don't read tea leaves," Maybelle said. "But I do know this. Things tend to work out exactly the way they're supposed to." She met Dorothy's gaze. "Sometimes you just have to show a little patience."

But that was exactly the problem, Dorothy thought wearily. She'd been waiting for decades for something dramatic to happen to change her life and her patience was starting to wear a little thin.

Cord suspected that Dinah thought she'd been doing a pretty decent job of avoiding him. He'd been so busy for the past few days that he hadn't had ten seconds to pester her. Still, he'd been mulling over everything that Maggie had told him. He knew he was going to have to push Dinah harder if he was going to get her to finally tell him the truth.

He'd asked her mother less than an hour ago if she'd made any progress on that front. She admitted she hadn't. Apparently she was as reluctant to press the issue as he had been up till now.

Armed with grim determination, he went looking for Dinah in the most obvious place—at home. Maybelle gave him a glass of iced tea and pointed him in the direction of the pool.

"If she spends much more time in there, she's going to shrivel up like a prune," she predicted direly. "Do something."

"I intend to," Cord assured her.

He exited through a pair of French doors and found Dinah exactly as described, submerged up to her neck in the pool. All that clear, cool water looked refreshing on such a steamy afternoon, but it was plain she was making a career out of lolling around in it. The tips of her fingers were, indeed, shriveled.

"Looks inviting," he said, hunkering down on the edge and trailing his hand through the water till his finger skimmed her shoulder.

Dinah gave an involuntary shudder. "Mother's not home, if that's why you're here," she said, not meeting his gaze.

"I know. I left her driving the plumbing contractor crazy. She can't decide on the fixtures for the public rest rooms at Covington. Personally, I figure a urinal's a urinal, but she seems to have something else in mind."

That earned him a quick smile that didn't quite reach her eyes. "I hope you charged the board enough for this project."

"Believe me, we calculated in the nuisance factor."

"So, if you're not here to see Mother, why are you here?"

"I thought maybe you and I could talk."

Her expression immediately turned wary. "About?"

"Why an internationally-known foreign correspondent is lazing away the afternoon in her family's back-yard pool as if she doesn't have a care in the world?"

"I'm on vacation."

"Really? I heard you quit," he said bluntly.

Temper flashed in her eyes, but she didn't rush to deny it. "So what if I did?" she retorted instead.

"Why would you quit a job you loved, one you'd made a success of?"

"I don't see how that's any of your concern."

"Technically, I suppose you're right, but if you and I are going to get something started, then I think I have a right to know whether you're going to bolt at the first sign of trouble the way you apparently bolted off your job."

Her mouth opened, then snapped shut again.

Cord waited.

She sighed eventually. "There are so many things wrong with that sentence, I don't know where to begin."

"Doesn't matter. Just start."

"You and I are not starting anything."

"I think we are. I imagine I could prove it, too."

"How?"

He leaned down, tucked a hand under her chin and kissed her, lightly at first, then with the kind of passion he hadn't felt in years. Then he rocked back on his heels. "There you go," he said, giving her a look that dared her to contradict him. "Same spontaneous combustion every time we try it. Anything that predictable has to mean something."

She blinked hard, then swallowed. "I don't bolt from trouble," she said. "The truth is everyone thought it would be for the best if I came home."

"Everyone?"

"My producer, okay? And the network. I was the only one who wasn't entirely convinced."

"Then why didn't you fight it?"

"I tried. Then, I don't know, it just didn't seem worth fighting about it anymore."

"Because of the panic attacks?" he guessed.

"They certainly didn't help," she admitted.

"So you thought it would be easier just to come home and jump headfirst into a nice, safe relationship with my brother?"

"If I did, so what? It was my decision to make."

"Was it really? Or were you pushed into it?"

"Okay, I was pushed into coming home, but the whole thing about Bobby was my idea. We had a deal, but you know that. We've discussed it ad nauseum."

"Wasn't there any other alternative?" he asked. "Another assignment that would have been less stressful?"

"I didn't want another assignment. Everyone would have looked at it as if it were a demotion. I thought it was time to settle down."

"No, you wanted something safe," he corrected. "But you don't need safe, Dinah. You've spent your entire adult life avoiding safe."

"Maybe I don't need more of the same." Her gaze narrowed. "And in case you're wondering, I most certainly don't need you."

"That remains to be seen," Cord said mildly. "Let's get back to my original question. Why are you here, even now that you know Bobby is no longer an option? Why haven't you formulated some new plan and rushed off to put it into action?"

"I'm working on it," she claimed, avoiding his gaze. "Meantime, I'm enjoying being home."

"And you're going to be content to spend your days up to your neck in chlorinated water and sipping iced tea with fading debutantes, maybe following in your mama's footsteps and chairing a fund-raiser from time to time?"

"Yes," she said emphatically.

"Liar. Tell me what really happened to send you scurrying home. I'm not talking about your boss pushing you. I'm asking *why* he pushed you. What sent you off the deep end, Dinah?"

She glowered at him, her lips clamped shut.

He kept right on pushing, despite her defiant silence. "Did you miss a story? Wander in front of a stray bullet? What?"

"Nothing happened," she insisted, her voice escalating. "It was time for a change and I made one. You don't have to like it, Cordell. You don't have to understand it. It's my decision, period. And if I want to hang out in this pool till hell freezes over, that's my call, too!"

Cord sighed. He could tell he'd pushed her back to the wall and he wouldn't get anything more out of her, not today. But at least she was on notice that he wasn't going to let her get away with hiding out from the past and from him for too much longer.

13

Dinah was beginning to wonder if she could get on the *Dr. Phil Show*. Surely he'd be interested in interviewing a brilliant television news reporter who'd braved war zones and now suddenly found it nearly impossible to leave her own house for much more than a trip to buy chocolate. If she hadn't rediscovered her old addiction to Godiva, she might not have even done that. Her expedition to find Bobby seemed to have been the last burst of her old energy that she could summon. She had nothing left with which to battle wits with Cord, who still seemed determined to make her recovery his mission in life.

Thankfully, her room still provided a nice, safe little cocoon where not even Cordell could pester her with uncomfortable questions. She was fairly sure even he wasn't brash enough to risk her mother's wrath if she were to catch him upstairs. The pool clearly was no longer a safe haven. Certainly she should be allowed to sink into a damn depression if she wanted to even if it was totally uncharacteristic of her.

Cord, however, didn't seem inclined to let her get away with it for a single second. In fact, she could hear him arguing with Maybelle downstairs. Hopefully she was standing her ground and telling him exactly what Dinah had instructed her to say. Maybelle could be pretty formidable when she wanted to be.

Apparently she wasn't successful today, Dinah concluded when she heard the thump of distinctly male footsteps coming her way. Apparently her faith in the housekeeper and in Cord's fear of her mother had been misplaced. Unless she hid in a closet, he was going to march right into her room and find her still dressed in the oversize T-shirt she went to sleep wearing. Since it was almost noon, her attire was going to be hard to explain.

When the door opened without so much as a knock, she worked up the energy to scowl at him.

"Didn't Maybelle tell you I didn't want to be disturbed?" she inquired irritably as she gathered the thick comforter around her. Thank goodness for air-conditioning or she'd roast to death while she tried to get Cord out of her face and out of her room.

"She did," he said agreeably.

"But, of course, you didn't listen."

He raised an eyebrow. "Did you think I would? Surely you know me better than that, sugar."

"What about my mother? You know she wouldn't approve of you being up here."

He regarded her with pity. "Come on, Dinah. You know your mama doesn't scare me."

"She should. She scares the daylights out of me when she's on a rampage."

"Only when you're not feeling up to your spunky self, I suspect," Cord said. "Now do you want to know why I'm here or not?"

"I imagine you think you're going to cheer me up," she said.

He grinned. "Exactly. Now get some clothes on and let's hit the road."

"I don't think so."

He shrugged, obviously not impressed by her refusal. "Okay, then," he said. "I'll just join you."

She stared at him in alarm as he kicked off his shoes and reached for the snap on his jeans. "What the hell do you think you're doing?"

"You don't want me crawling into that bed with my clothes on, do you? Your mama surely would be angry if I put these old work boots on her fine Egyptian cotton sheets."

"What do you know about Egyptian cotton?" Dinah asked, distracted for a moment from the far more important issue of why Cord thought for one instant she would let him join her in her own bed. The queen-size mattress was big, but not big enough for the two of them. The perverse attraction she'd been feeling toward him was unnerving and she didn't need to tempt fate. Apparently her hormones hadn't died along with the rest of her.

"Enough to recognize it when I see it and when I feel it against my bare backside," he said audaciously.

"You keep your backside off this bed," Dinah ordered, scrambling up while still clutching the comforter. "And keep your clothes on."

He stood there with his zipper halfway down. "You sure about that?"

"Absolutely."

"Then you're coming with me?"

She weighed that against the alternative, which was

clearly going to be a seduction right here under her mother's roof. If she couldn't muster the energy to go out for lunch, she could hardly fight off the unexpected attraction she'd developed for Cord, especially not if he was even close to bare-assed and in her bed.

"Where?" she inquired warily.

"Does it really matter?"

"It might."

"The sun's out. There's a breeze stirring. I've got the convertible outside with the top down. I thought we'd take a ride over to the beach, wander around a little, sniff in some of that salt air, maybe stop for a burger and fries. What do you say?"

"Shouldn't you be working?"

"It's Sunday. I may not make it to church, but even I take Sunday off. Come to think of it, I'm a little surprised you didn't go off to church with your mama and daddy."

"They stopped pushing me to do that after the first couple of times I turned them down." She studied him curiously. "If you thought I'd be at church, why did you come by?"

"Took a chance," he said lightly.

Dinah didn't believe him, even though the lie had tripped right off his tongue. Spinning a good story was second nature to Cord. Lord knows, he'd done a good job when he'd told Bobby all about her supposed fling with another man. As close as she and Bobby had been, he'd believed his big brother. The rift might have been permanent, if she hadn't found out quickly enough and proved Cord had made the whole thing up to keep the two of them apart.

She glowered at him now. "My mother called you, didn't she? You're doing her a favor."

"This has nothing to do with your mother. I'm here because I thought we could spend a little time by the ocean. I find it soothing."

Dinah had always found the beach to be soothing, too. She told herself that was why she eventually caved in and said yes. Maybe the change of scenery would do what nothing else had. Maybe it would calm her and ease her soul.

"I'll be down in ten minutes," she told Cord.

He gave her a disappointed look. "Darn, I thought maybe you were going to let me hang around and get an eyeful."

"You wish," she said, trying to hide the smile tugging at the corners of her mouth. The man was outrageous, but he was beginning to grow on her. Of course, she didn't trust him, but that hardly mattered because all they were doing was hanging out together.

And her mother was definitely right about one thing. When she was with Cord, she actually did feel alive. The effect he had on her was rather remarkable. She was beginning to wonder if he would agree to a wicked, no-strings fling. Something told her it would be memorable.

And maybe that memory would finally be powerful enough to wipe out all the other devastating memories she couldn't seem to shake.

As they got closer to the sea, Cord noticed that Dinah visibly relaxed. The tension in her shoulders eased and a smile actually touched her lips from time to time. With her dark glasses covering her eyes, he couldn't see if the usual turmoil was still evident there, but he was beginning to think he'd had a fine idea when Dorothy

Davis had called to plead with him to get Dinah out of the house.

He watched as Dinah leaned forward, clearly anticipating the moment when she would be able to catch her first glimpse of the water. When she did, she sighed with obvious pleasure.

"We used to come out here every single summer for a month," she told him. "Mother and Tommy Lee and me. Daddy would come when he could, usually on weekends and for maybe a week in the middle. Tommy Lee and I thought we'd died and gone to heaven because we were allowed to run around barefoot and wear our swimsuits all day long." She gave him a sad look. "Life was so much simpler then."

"It usually is when you're a kid," Cord responded. "My best memories are of summertime. Of course, Bobby and I were lucky if we got to the beach even once, but we were allowed to spend all day away from home, riding our bikes, and steering clear of our father. In the morning, our mother would give us each a peanut-butter-and-jelly sandwich and a dollar for something to drink." He grinned. "We always split one drink and got a couple of Popsicles or a candy bar with the rest of the money."

"What did you do all day?"

"Found some other kids and played baseball or just rode our bikes to the Battery and sat by the water. Once in a while we'd run into a kid from school who lived nearby and he'd invite us home for lunch. Actually, he'd invite Bobby, but Bobby would always say he couldn't go without me. You should have seen the horrified look on the mother's face when her kid showed up with us in tow. I'd have turned around and left, but not Bobby. He just assumed we truly were welcome and breezed right on in. Next thing you'd know, sure enough, he'd won over the mother. I envied him that ability to make people look past his upbringing."

"You could have done the same thing," Dinah said. "Goodness knows, you don't lack for charm now."

Cord chuckled. "It comes in handy from time to time," he acknowledged. "Back then, though, it was a matter of pride. I wanted to be accepted for me, not because I knew how to kiss up to somebody."

"Was it hard?" Dinah asked. "I mean knowing that somebody had smoothed the way for you to be in our school, that some benefactor had paid the bills?"

"I hated it," he said succinctly. "But at least I wasn't fool enough to turn my back on it. I had just enough sense to see that it was an opportunity I had to grab or I'd wind up losing way more than I gained."

"Is that why you took every opportunity to remind the rest of us we were a bunch of privileged snobs?"

"Indeed," he said. "I wanted all of you to know that I could have the same education you had, but I didn't have to be you. I was determined to be my own man."

"Did you ever figure out who'd paid the bills?" she asked.

Cord shrugged. "Never seemed to matter, though once I was older, I wanted to thank him. I tried to get the school's administrator to tell me, but that old biddy was as tight-lipped then as she had been when I was causing trouble in her classrooms. Told me to be grateful and maybe pass along the kindness when I had the chance."

"That must have been frustrating." She studied him intently. "Is there anything you regret about staying on the outside?"

Cord gave the question thoughtful consideration. "I suppose if I'm being totally honest, I'd have to say it was lonely." He grinned. "At least until a few of the girls decided to live dangerously and start going out with me."

"I imagine you loved that, not just the social life, but knowing you were driving their mamas and daddies crazy," Dinah guessed.

"Absolutely. What's the fun of doing something wicked, if it's not going to stir things up?"

"Is that still your philosophy?"

Cord glanced over at her. "Pretty much."

She lifted her gaze to his and for the first time he could recall since she'd come back, there was something bold and full of life flashing in her eyes. It caught him by surprise and set his blood humming.

"Want to do something wicked with me?" she asked, her gaze unblinking.

Cord couldn't seem to tear his gaze away. "What are you suggesting, Dinah?"

"The beach is pretty private around here," she said, her expression all innocence, despite the heavy innuendo in her tone.

An image of steamy sex on a beach blanket immediately formed in his head and nearly had him swallowing his tongue. He needed to be absolutely certain, though, that he knew what she was suggesting. He couldn't afford to get this one wrong. Heck, he even supposed he needed to know for sure if *she* understood what she was suggesting.

"What did you have in mind?" he asked. "And, please, be explicit, sugar."

"You don't want to use your imagination?" she asked, opening the car door and heading off across the dunes after casting one, last tantalizing look over her shoulder.

Cord's imagination had gotten him in way too much trouble over the years. He wasn't taking any chances this time. He grabbed a blanket and cooler from the back seat of the car and set off after her.

Once he crested the dune, he began to find a very provocative trail of footprints and clothing. A sandal here, a scarf there. When he spotted the shorts and halter top, he dropped everything he was carrying and started stripping off his own clothes.

"Please tell me she had a bikini on under there," he murmured as he got down to his own swimsuit. It was the noblest moment of his life. He knew if he walked into the ocean and found Dinah stark naked, he was going to turn the entire Atlantic into a steambath. He was already hard and aching. He needed her to be wearing…something.

He splashed out in the water, grateful that it was still cold enough to bring his temperature down to a simmer. She popped up beside him, her shoulders completely bare, the water teasing at her chest which, thank heaven, was still submerged.

"You certainly took your time getting here," she said, moving closer, that diabolical glint back in her eyes.

"Something tells me I had on more clothes than you did," he said in a strangled voice.

She grinned. "You certainly do now."

Cord thought desperately. Nobility was not what it was cracked up to be. He would have backed up a step, but his feet were surprisingly firmly planted even in the shifting sand.

"What are you up to?" he asked warily.

An expression of pure mischief spread across her

face. "Cordell Beaufort, don't tell me that reputation of yours is bogus. Surely you recognize when a woman is coming on to you."

"Oh, I recognize the signs, no question about that," he said. "But since it's you we're talking about, I'm thinking maybe an explanation is in order."

She stared at him with evident surprise. "You want to discuss this?"

"Not really," he admitted candidly. "But I think we should."

"Kiss me and then we'll talk," she offered.

"If I kiss you, believe me, it won't be followed up with talking," Cord warned her.

She shrugged. "Okay, then. Kiss me, anyway."

"Dinah!" he protested, just as she closed the distance between them and plastered herself to his body like a barnacle attaching to a seashell. Desire shot through him with the force of a cannon. Dinah wasn't wearing so much as a scrap of clothing, and his swimsuit could hardly save him from the effect of all that bare skin next to his.

Before he could say a word, before he could even form a coherent thought, her mouth was on his, hot and greedy and demanding. She clearly wasn't going to take no for an answer.

Maybe she needed this, Cord reassured himself. He sure as hell needed it. He'd been needing Dinah, wanting Dinah as far back as he could remember. He knew she couldn't say the same, but did that really matter right here and right now? People made love for all sorts of reasons—lust, neediness, a way to forget. Would it be so terrible to take what she was offering without examining all the motives behind it, his or hers?

She framed his face in her hands and looked into his eyes before he could find an answer to any of that.

"Please," she whispered. "Please make love to me. Don't say no, Cordell. Whatever's going on in that head of yours can wait. It's not important."

Cord knew it was important, but in that instant, he also knew that he couldn't deny her anything. The desperation in her eyes, the desire, the heat of her surrounding him, it was all impossible to resist.

His gaze still locked with hers, he tugged down his swimsuit, lifted her slightly and plunged into her, joining them. There was an instant of stunned surprise in her eyes and then she began to move, taking what she wanted, her head thrown back, water streaming from her hair. She looked like a sea nymph, glorious in her passion, even more glorious when a powerful release shuddered through her.

When she would have moved away, Cord held her in place. "Not just yet, darlin'. That one was for you. Now let's do it one more time for the two of us."

The water slicked over them as his body found its rhythm. It was an extra sensation that he'd never experienced before, not even during some long and very provocative showers. Maybe it had something to do with the way the waves stirred around them so that her breasts played a tantalizing game of hide and seek. He cupped her bottom, tilting her hard against him, then plunged inside one last time, finally shattering the unbearable tension for both of them.

Dinah went limp in his arms, her cheek resting against his shoulder. "That was…amazing," she said, her voice still breathless.

"Definitely right up near the top of the Beaufort scale."

She glanced up at him. "The Beaufort scale?"

"Richter wasted time measuring seismic shifts in the earth. My scale measures another sort of earthquake entirely."

A grin tugged at her lips, even as she gave him a light punch. "You're irredeemable."

"Could be," he agreed. "But right at this moment, I'd have to guess you're glad about that."

She met his gaze. "Yes, I am, but smugness is not an attractive trait, Cordell."

"Duly noted."

With her legs still wrapped around his waist and her hands linked behind his neck, she looked in his eyes. "Do you know what I'd like right now?"

If it wasn't more sex, Cord thought he might very well cry. "What's that?"

"That burger you promised me. I'm starving. It's the first time in days I've felt like eating."

"Making love will do that to a person," he agreed, hiding his disappointment. "Brings back all sorts of appetites. Of course, if you expect to go someplace for lunch, you are going to have to let go of me, get out of the water and put some clothes on."

"You're not nearly as adventurous as you're cracked up to be," she accused.

He looked her in the eye. "You think I'm stodgy?"

She nodded, her lips twitching as she fought a smile.

"Really?" He sighed dramatically. "Then I suppose I'll just have to prove you wrong." He headed for shore with Dinah still clinging to him. When he would have carried her right on to the car, she started laughing.

"Okay, okay, put me down, you fool. I need to get my clothes."

"Then that was a test?" he asked, halting in his tracks, but still holding her in his arms.

"Of course it was."

"Oh, sugar, you should know better than to test a man like me. If there's a fork in the road and one way heads toward wicked, that's the path I'll take." Still holding her, he bent down and snagged her panties, then the scanty halter top she'd worn. "What are these worth to you?"

"You're holding my clothes for ransom?"

He grinned. "Pretty much. And just so you know, I hear voices."

"You do not," she said, suddenly looking just a little bit worried.

"If you don't believe me, listen."

She fell silent. Within seconds the unmistakable laughter of what was more than likely a carload of teenagers drifted toward them.

"Oh, my God," she said, snatching at her clothes.

"Oh, no, you don't. You have to pay up first."

"You haven't said what you wanted," she said, beginning to look a little frantic. Her cheeks had turned a bright shade of pink that couldn't entirely be attributed to the sun.

"Come home with me tonight," he said. "Stay with me."

Her gaze faltered. "I don't know, Cord."

"We just made love in public, twice as a matter of fact. Is it so much to ask that we try it in a nice, comfortable bed?"

"It's not the idea of sex with you that worries me," she admitted, her brow furrowed.

"Then what? And just so you know, the car's engine just cut off."

Alarm flared in her eyes. "It's the implication," she said in a rush. "This could get complicated, especially if we let this start to mean something."

"It *does* mean something," Cord replied quietly. "At least to me." He pushed the clothes into her hand. "Put these on and we'll finish this conversation over lunch. You can bring up the whole trust thing and tell me again how I ruined any chance of you ever trusting me when I told Bobby that lie to keep the two of you apart. That was ten years ago, Dinah. I like to think I'm a different man now."

A tiny flicker of guilt nagged at him even as he spoke. He could dismiss that old lie from now till doomsday and Dinah might even be willing to forgive him, but if she found out he was lying to his brother again right now—at least by omission—it would be all over.

He grabbed his own jeans and hiked them up just in the nick of time as a crowd of half a dozen teens came tearing over the dunes. They barely spared a glance for Cord and Dinah in their exuberant race to the water.

It was just as well, he concluded, because Dinah still looked as if she were a little dazed. Cord almost relented and took back his request, but something told him if he gave in too easily, they might never get back to this point. Dinah's guard would go up and all the progress they'd made would vanish as if it had never happened. In fact, it might be worse because knowing how incredible they were together had clearly scared her.

To be truthful, it terrified him, too, but he didn't want to turn back. And he'd find some way to make up for his silence about her return. He'd spin it in a way that would keep both of them from being furious with him.

"Dinah?"

She looked up at him blankly.

"You ready?"

She blinked as if coming out of a trance. "Sure."

"You want something to drink before we go? There's soda and beer in the cooler."

"No, I'll wait till we get to the restaurant."

"Okay, then, let's get moving. The place I have in mind is bound to be packed."

Her expression brightened slightly at that. "Good."

He regarded her with amusement. "We're still going to talk about you coming home with me tonight."

"As long as you feed me first, you can talk about whatever you want to talk about," she said.

"That's the spirit."

She gave him a sassy look as she passed him on her way to the car. "Doesn't mean I'm going to listen."

Cord stared after her. The woman was filled with so many contradictions, it might take a lifetime to unravel them all. He sure as hell was willing to give it a try, though.

14

Dinah was already regretting her impulsive, totally uncharacteristic behavior at the beach. She'd suddenly
been overcome with the desire to do something outrageous, something that would wipe away all the pain and
horrible memories she couldn't otherwise erase. She'd
known with purely feminine instinct that Cord would
never turn her down.

In the heat of the moment, so to speak, it had
seemed exactly right to take advantage of his bad-boy
reputation. For a few minutes she'd been carried away
on a sea of sensation so overwhelming that nothing
else had mattered. In that instant there had been only
Cordell and her, alone in the world, the sun on their
shoulders, the cool water splashing gently over them,
their bodies perfectly attuned. It had been instinctive,
mind-blowing sex at its most primal level. It was the
kind of thing she'd always imagined only happened
when two people came together in a desperate need to
feel totally alive.

And wasn't that what it had been about for her?
She'd seen too much death, suffered too much loss.
She'd needed to be reminded, if only for a moment, that

she wasn't dead, that the woman who had grabbed onto life with both hands and chose to live still existed even though a part of her had died right alongside Peter. She needed to figure out who that woman now was. Maybe making love to Cord would snap her out of her inertia.

Yet second thoughts were now raging in her mind almost as wildly as passion had earlier. She'd wanted a moment out of time, just one moment, but Cord evidently wanted more. As wonderful as she'd felt for that fleeting moment, Dinah wasn't sure she had anything more to give him. And even if she found it was possible, would she want to? This man had betrayed her and his brother once. Why would she allow herself anything more than a casual fling with him?

"For a woman who insisted she was starving for a hamburger, you haven't made even a dent in that one," Cord chided, breaking into her troubled thoughts. "Is there something wrong with it?"

"No, it's great," she said, taking a dutiful bite. It was charcoal broiled, juicy and topped with a thick slice of cheddar cheese, ripe summer tomato, onion, mayonnaise and ketchup. As burgers went, it was sublime, but it might as well have been sawdust.

Cord rolled his eyes, clearly not believing her act. "How about some steamed shrimp?"

"No, thanks. This is plenty."

"Ice cream?"

She gave him the kind of horrified look she would have expected from her mother, who was of the clean-your-plate era. "Before I finish my meal?"

He laughed. "You're a grown-up now. You can have dessert first. I'm thinking a huge hot fudge marshmallow sundae we can share. How about it?"

"You are definitely talking my language," she admitted. She eyed the burger with regret. "It seems a shame, though, to waste food like this."

He held out his hand. "If it will help allay your guilt, I'll finish it," he said a little too eagerly to be perceived as a martyr. "You order the sundae."

"I'm impressed with the nobility of your sacrifice," she said dryly.

"You should be. I'll have to add a couple of miles to my run in the morning."

"You run?" For some reason, she was surprised by that. She'd always envisioned him spending every spare second lazing around in that well-used hammock of his. That he had the discipline to run destroyed another leftover judgment she'd made about him.

"Every day."

"I used to," Dinah told him. She hadn't been out in months, not since the day Peter had died. All the running they'd done together hadn't done him a damn bit of good, so she hadn't seen the point in continuing the exercise.

But it might have been what saved your life, a voice in her head nagged now as it had been for months. She sighed. Running hadn't saved her life. Peter had, when he'd given her the chance to slip away.

When she looked up, Cord was studying her curiously. "If you stayed over at my place tonight, you could come with me in the morning."

Her lips twitched, despite herself. "And that's supposed to entice me? Running's hard. I hated every second of it."

"But it clears your head," he said. "Keeps you in shape. Releases all those good endorphins."

She frowned at that. "Is there something wrong with my shape?"

"Truth be told, you're still too skinny," he taunted.

"I didn't hear you complaining back on the beach," she reminded him.

"No reason to complain then. I had more important things on my mind."

"Your mind was disengaged from the minute you hit the water," she retorted.

Cord laughed. "I suppose that's true enough." His expression sobered. "So what about it, Dinah? Will you come back to my place tonight? I'm not asking for a lifetime commitment, if that's what's worrying you. I'd just like to hold you in my arms for one night."

"And one night will do it for you?" she asked, amused.

He grinned. "Depends on whether you snore or steal all the covers."

She weighed all the reasons it would be a perfectly awful idea against the one powerful reason for saying yes…that it would guarantee her the kind of exhaustion that might lead to a dreamless sleep, something she hadn't had in what seemed like forever.

"Yes," she said at last, impulse overruling her head for the second time that day. She met his gaze and gave him a long, lazy grin that had a justifiable wariness stirring in his eyes. "But you're gonna have to be the one to explain it to my mother."

His eyes danced with amusement at the challenge. "You sure you want me to do that, sugar?"

"I think it will be absolutely fascinating to see what you come up with," she said. "If you can turn it into some G-rated explanation, you will earn my undying respect."

"G-rated, huh?"

"That's the rule."

Dinah stared in disbelief as Cord pulled out his cell phone and punched in a single number. "You have her on speed dial?" she asked incredulously.

"This is your mother we're talking about. She's the ruler of all things out at Covington," he explained. His expression brightened as the phone was apparently answered. "Hey, Mrs. Davis, how are you?"

Dinah felt her stomach tighten as she waited to see if Cord would stick to the rules or say something absolutely outrageous to her mother that Dinah would never be able to live down.

"Your daughter asked me to give you a call and let you know that she's going to be spending the night at a friend's. She didn't want you to worry." He grinned at whatever her mother said. "Yes, ma'am, I surely will tell her that. You enjoy the rest of your day, okay?"

When he'd hung up, Dinah frowned at him. "What did she want you to tell me?"

"To be sure to use protection."

Dinah choked on her sip of diet cola. "She did not!"

"Sugar, your mama is an enlightened woman. I don't think you give her half enough credit."

Dinah knew that was probably true enough. She switched gears. "You broke the rules."

"Me? Did you hear one thing come out of my mouth that a six-year-old wouldn't say if he was going to have a sleepover at a playmate's?"

"What about that whole protection thing?"

"I didn't say that. Your mama did. I can't be held accountable for her having the intuition to figure out what you and I are up to." His gaze narrowed. "You're not intending to back out now, are you?"

Dinah shook her head. How could she, when she'd laughed more and felt more alive in the past couple of hours than she had in months? "I must be crazy," she said, half to herself. She met Cord's gaze. "But, no, I'm not backing out."

Dorothy hung up the phone, a smile on her lips. Thank goodness her daughter was finally showing some sense. A decade ago Cordell might not have been the man she would have chosen for Dinah, but times had changed. People changed.

Not only had Cord proved himself to be respectable and hard-working, but recently he'd shown himself to be caring where Dinah was concerned. And goodness knows he'd apparently dedicated himself to dragging her out of this depressed state she was obviously in. If he accomplished that and nothing else, Dorothy owed him her gratitude.

"Was that Dinah?" her husband asked when she joined him.

"No, it was Cord. He was calling on Dinah's behalf, though. I think they're becoming something of an item," she said with undisguised pleasure.

Marshall lowered the Sunday sports section and stared at her over the rim of his reading glasses. "Are you telling me that our daughter is getting mixed up with Cordell Beaufort?"

She heard the unmistakable disdain in his voice and responded with a touch of defiance. "Yes."

"And you're encouraging it?"

His censure grated. She frowned at him. "I most certainly am. Neither you or I have been able to do a thing to shake Dinah out of this lethargy she's been in. If Cord can do that, then he has my blessing."

"I don't understand you, Dorothy," Marshall declared with unmistakable disappointment in his tone. He raised the paper, putting an abrupt end to the discussion.

"There's nothing new about that," she retorted under her breath.

Apparently Marshall heard her, because he tossed the paper aside with a scowl. "What the devil is that supposed to mean?"

She decided that for once she would see the argument through to its conclusion. Placating him, trying to smooth things over every time they talked hadn't worked. Maybe a rousing good argument would.

"It means that you haven't understood me for years," she said. "In fact it's been decades since you even tried. If I were a less secure woman, I'd have to wonder if you weren't having an affair."

To her surprise a wounded expression crossed his face. He slowly removed his glasses and stared at her with the deep blue eyes that had once been her undoing. Now she merely returned his gaze with an unblinking stare of her own and waited to see if he'd confirm her half-formed suspicion. She convinced herself it would be a relief to know the truth.

"Are you mad at me simply because I don't see what you see in Cord Beaufort?" he asked. "Or are you fishing around to see if I'll admit to something?"

She regarded him with impatience. "Neither, Marshall. The truth is I'm not mad at you at all. I'm just sad."

He looked totally confused. "About what? Dinah?"

"No, you idiot. About us."

"Us! What's wrong with us? You know damn well I'm not having an affair."

If he'd been so dismissive of her fears and asked such a ridiculous question a few weeks ago, she would have walked out of the room in frustration, but watching Dinah struggle with her own demons had shown her that there was nothing to be gained by waiting for things to change. It was up to her to make something happen.

"I don't know any such thing, as a matter of fact. At least that would explain why we're simply coexisting, Marshall. You go your way. I go mine. I want something more out of marriage, don't you?"

His face suddenly registered a combination of dismay and fear. "You want a divorce?" he asked, his voice flat. "Is that what this is about? After all these years, you want to end our marriage?"

She actually thought about the question before responding. A divorce would certainly shake them out of this awful limbo. But how many of her friends had seized on that option and found themselves no happier than they were before? And if she were being totally honest, she felt genuinely bereft at the thought of losing Marshall. That, in itself, was a shock.

"No," she told him slowly. "I want to fix our marriage, if at all possible. I'm not ready to give up on it yet. But things have to change, Marshall. We have to put some effort into this relationship. Are you willing to do that?"

He looked thoroughly baffled by her question. "I have no idea what you think we need to be doing that we're not doing already."

She didn't find it all that hard to believe that he was

clueless. She didn't know exactly what she expected either. And that was precisely the problem. It was impossible and unfair to ask a man to change if she couldn't even tell him how she wanted him to change. Maybe that's why it had taken her so long to get around to having this conversation. She'd never known what to ask for.

"Am I the wife you wanted me to be?" she asked instead.

"Of course you are," he said at once. "I love you, Dorothy. You're an amazing woman. You juggle a hundred balls in the air and you do it with such finesse it leaves me in awe."

She stared at him in amazement. "You've never said anything like that before. I didn't think you even paid attention to anything I was doing."

"Of course I pay attention and I say it all the time," he contradicted, then paused, his expression turning thoughtful. "But perhaps not to you."

"Then who on earth do you say it to?"

"I brag about you to my colleagues."

"Really?" she said, oddly touched. "I always thought you were simply happy that I had enough to keep me occupied and out of your hair."

"Nonsense!" He peered at her intently. "Is that what you think is missing, a few compliments?"

She smiled at his wistful expression. "If only it were that simple, but we're making a start right now, Marshall. We're talking, really communicating, for the first time in years."

"We talk all the time," he protested with a faintly baffled expression still plastered on his face.

"Not about anything important. We talk about what

time we're expected at some dinner party or what happened at the bank. We never talk about what we're thinking and feeling or what we want. Do you realize you're getting close to retirement age and we've never discussed what you'd like to do or if you even intend to retire?"

"To be honest, I haven't given it any thought," he said. "I've been too busy."

"Maybe you need to start thinking about it," she said, then held up her hand when it was clear he intended to debate the point. "I'm not saying you need to plan your retirement tomorrow, just think about the future. Maybe we both do."

His gaze held hers. "I may not know a lot about what I want for the future," he said. "But there is one thing I do know with absolute certainty."

"What's that?"

"I want you by my side. I'll do whatever it is you want me to do or that you think we need to do together to make that happen."

Tears stung her eyes. "What if we can't figure it out?" she asked, voicing her greatest fear.

"We will," he said confidently. "Between us, thank heaven, we still have two great minds. If we put them together, I think we can do anything."

She wished she were as certain. She couldn't even figure out a place to begin.

"How about this?" Marshall said, taking the initiative in a way that stunned her. "From now on we set aside one night a week for the two of us. It'll be our date night. No dinner parties, no galas, just us."

She grinned at him, touched by the effort he was willing to make. It told her more than anything else might have that she'd gotten through to him. "Are you sure we won't bore each other to tears?"

"Not if we throw ourselves into it."

"I suppose we could take turns planning the evenings," she said thoughtfully. "That way there'd be a little something surprising about every date."

He gave her a wonderfully wicked look, one she hadn't seen in years and years. It made her regret not forcing this issue a long time ago, instead of drifting along in silent misery.

"Just be sure you take your vitamins, Dorothy, because I intend to give you a run for your money."

"And you think you still have it in you?" she challenged, amused by the sudden pep in his voice.

"I suppose we'll see about that. Which night shall we set? And who's going to plan the first date?"

"Let me check my datebook," she said, starting to rise.

"No," he said so firmly that she sat right back down. "If we're going to do this, it has to be a priority. Whatever's on either of our calendars can be changed to accommodate us. Pick a night."

She grinned. "Given that glint in your eye, it ought to be on the weekend. You're going to need your rest the next day," she teased. "But as a practical matter, it probably shouldn't be Saturday. We're bound to start running into conflicts with various events that neither of us can possibly cancel."

"I agree. We'd be doomed before we start. So, Friday then?" he asked. "Is that the deal?"

She saw a long list of potential problems with Friday, but none of them were worth losing out on this chance to get some life back into her marriage. "Definitely Friday," she said. "And since you seem to be the one with all the ideas, why don't you plan the first one, Marshall? Just keep in mind, I expect to be dazzled."

"You always did have impossibly high standards," he scolded. "But I promise you this, it will be an evening you won't forget." He winked at her. "Perhaps since you have such good things to say about the way Cord's handling Dinah, I'll ask him for advice."

"Perhaps you ought to keep your own counsel," Dorothy replied, then added dryly, "If you and I try to mimic Cord and Dinah, we're likely to throw our backs out."

Someone who obviously had a death wish was trying to drag Dinah out of bed.

"Go away," she muttered. She cracked one eye open and noted that it was still dark. "It's not even daylight."

"It will be in a few minutes," Cord said, grabbing hold of the covers and yanking them away.

"Unless you intend to crawl back into this bed and make love to me, you are a dead man," Dinah said, burying her face in the pillow.

"A fascinating offer, but last night you agreed to go running with me this morning."

"I lied."

"Too bad. I believed you and I am not leaving this house without you." He smacked her lightly on the bottom. "Move it, sugar."

"I don't have running shoes here."

"We'll stop by your house and get them."

Her eyes snapped open at the absurdity of the suggestion. "You want to arrive at my house at this ungodly hour and go inside, where my parents will most likely be waiting to cross-examine us about our relationship?" Even the thought of it made her shudder.

"I doubt your parents are even up yet," Cord said. "Stop making excuses, unless of course you don't think you can keep up with me."

Dinah debated rising to the challenge, but it required too much effort. "I can't keep up with you. I'll slow you down, so you'll hardly get any workout at all."

Cord laughed. "Nice try, but I think I can cut back a little just this once."

"You said you needed to work off all that food you ate yesterday," she reminded him.

"I think we got a good enough start on that during the night," he said, amusement playing over his face.

Dinah was beginning to get the idea that she wasn't going to win this debate, no matter what she said. She rolled over on her back, hoping the sight of her would give him some ideas about another form of exercise they could engage in. As he'd just noted, it had worked several times before during the night.

"My eyes are covered," he said. "That's not going to work."

"How do you know what I'm up to, if you're not looking?"

"I've figured out the devious nature of your mind," he said, snagging an ankle and pulling her toward the foot of the bed.

"I think I hate you," she said as her feet hit the floor.

"Okay."

"I know I hate running."

"That's okay, too. You don't have to love it. You just have to do it."

"But I've been getting exercise. I've been swimming," she protested.

"No," he corrected. "You've been hanging around in

the pool. If you've swum a single·lap, I'd be shocked. I can always ask Maybelle or your mother, in case I've gotten it wrong, though."

Dinah gave up. "Okay, okay, I'm getting up," she said sullenly. "But I won't thank you for this."

"Never expected it. Do you want something to drink or eat before we hit the road?"

"Just coffee," she said.

"No caffeine," he responded.

"Who died and made you my trainer?" As soon as the words left her mouth, an image of Peter slammed into her consciousness. They'd had debates just like this so many times she'd lost count. Before she could stop it, a sob bubbled up from somewhere deep inside where she'd kept it buried. It was followed by another and then another. She drew her knees up to her chest and let them come.

Cord stared at her in shock for a heartbeat, then dropped down beside her and pulled her close. He didn't say a word, just held her until the crying finally stopped. He handed her a tissue.

She blew her nose and he handed her another one. She mopped ineffectively at the tears streaming down her cheeks. "I suppose you're wondering what that was all about."

His gaze was filled with sympathy. "Only if you're ready to tell me. My instincts are already telling me it's not because you hate running."

"It's not about running," she said. "It's…" She tried to form the words, but they simply wouldn't come. It seemed wrong to be talking about Peter when she was sitting here naked with another man. "I can't," she said eventually. She met Cord's distressed gaze. "I will, I promise. Just not now, okay?"

"Whatever you say," he said easily. He stood up, then leaned down and pressed a kiss to her forehead. "Get dressed. I'll get you some water. Otherwise you'll be dehydrated before we even hit the streets."

"You still expect me to run?" she asked. "All those tears and you can't even muster up an ounce of pity for me?"

"You don't want my pity," he chided. "And, yes, we're still going to run. Something tells me it's more important than ever."

She sighed heavily. "Why couldn't you have turned out to be the lazy, no-account man I always thought you were?"

"Because then having me around wouldn't be doing you a lick of good," he retorted. "You'll thank me one of these days."

She frowned at him. "I hope you're not counting on that."

He laughed. "Where you're concerned, Dinah, I'm counting on a lot of things these days. You haven't let me down yet."

Dinah thought of all the people she'd let down over the past few months, most of all herself. She regarded Cord with disbelief. "Do you really mean that?"

"Of course I do."

His words weren't quite enough to restore her self-esteem in one fell swoop, but it was a start. For the very first time in longer than she could remember, she felt hopeful. Not healed, perhaps. Definitely not ready to tackle a marathon. But hopeful.

Maybe she would thank him one of these days, after all.

15

Dinah couldn't seem to run fast enough to get away from the memories haunting her. Once she and Cord had set out, she matched him stride for stride. Okay, perhaps he'd slowed down to accommodate her, but he certainly hadn't given her much of a break. She was panting and sweat was pouring down her face by the time he finally called a halt.

"Not bad for your first day out," he said.

She scowled at him. "First day implies there will be others."

He grinned. "Did you think this was it?"

"I was hoping," she admitted.

"How are your legs? Other than gorgeous, I mean. Do they ache?"

"Not really."

"Do a few more stretches, just to be safe."

"And then we get to go home?" she asked, unable to keep the plaintive note out of her voice.

"Then we go home."

"Thank God. I can hardly wait to step into a shower."

"With me?" he inquired.

"To be truthful, you weren't part of the equation. Don't you have to go to work?"

"I can be late if you'll make it worth risking a lecture from your mother. I have a meeting with her at nine."

"And you will be precisely on time," Dinah said emphatically. "Something tells me she's going to have more than enough questions for you as it is. Sorry, Cordell, the shower's out. Drop me at my folks' place."

"And here I thought we'd finally jump-started that adventurous spirit of yours," he said sadly.

"We all need an occasional reality check," Dinah reminded him. "You need to go to work and I need to…" Her voice trailed off when she realized that she actually had nothing to do. Despite the changes she'd made in the past twenty-four hours, one critical thing hadn't changed at all. She still hadn't found a new purpose for her life.

"You could spend some time with Maggie," Cord suggested, in an apparent attempt to be helpful. "You've been neglecting her since you got back."

"How do you know that?"

"She mentioned it."

"Really? You've seen Maggie?" She didn't like the streak of pure jealousy that immediately knifed through her. Or maybe what she really didn't like was the idea of the two of them closeted somewhere talking about her.

"A few days ago."

"Oh?"

Amusement danced in his eyes as he framed her face and kissed her thoroughly. "Maggie and I are friends, sugar, nothing more. You don't have anything to worry about."

"I wasn't worried," she said defensively. "You can see anyone you want to see."

"And that's you," he assured her. "So, will you at least think about spending some time with your best friend? The last thing I'd want to do is come between you, especially when the reason is something so ridiculous."

She promptly concluded it must have been one heck of a conversation. Very thorough, in fact. "You're talking about the auction," she said dully.

"Yes. We had a good time. We raised a little money. End of story."

"And Maggie understands that?"

"She most certainly does. You can stop worrying. We talked about it. We're cool. You're the one who seems determined to misread the whole situation."

"It just got complicated," Dinah said. "If she really, really cares about you…"

"She doesn't," Cord insisted. "Maybe there was a touch of infatuation, but that's all it was. And it was one-sided."

"I still hate to think that I might be hurting her."

"Then talk to her. You staying away is what's really hurting her. Seems to me you could use all the friends you can get. This isn't the time to be turning away from one of them."

"I suppose you're right." She frowned at him. "She's going to know right away that I've slept with you. She could always read me like a book."

"You ashamed of that?"

"No, of course not," she said emphatically. "I just hate to think I'll be rubbing it in her face. She might not be as over you as it's convenient for you to believe."

"She's over me," he repeated. "How about this? Since she can't have me, we'll make it our mission to find the second-best man in Charleston for Maggie."

Dinah chuckled despite herself. "You really do have a high opinion of yourself, don't you?"

"If I don't, who will?" he challenged. "You need to follow my example and show this town what Dinah Davis is made of. You've already done one outrageous thing by getting mixed up with the likes of me. Now find yourself a new adventure, something that challenges you. Going off to cover a war isn't the only thing you can do that'll make a difference in this world."

"I'll take it under advisement," she said because it was what Cord expected.

There was only one problem with that suggestion, Dinah thought. She honestly didn't know what she was made of anymore or if she even cared about making a difference. Had Peter dying made a difference, except to his friends? Was the world one bit better or safer because he'd sacrificed his life? If it was, she couldn't see it.

Despite his best efforts to hurry, Cord was fifteen minutes late for his meeting with Dinah's mother. Dorothy was sitting in the kitchen at the plantation, tapping her foot impatiently, and scowling at the clock.

"Don't blame the clock," Cord said when he walked in. "I got a late start."

"Obviously."

"Blame your daughter. She could distract a man from getting out of the way of a bulldozer."

Mrs. Davis smiled at that. "Then your date went well?"

"Well enough," he said neutrally. "And if you're looking for details, you've come to the wrong person. I don't kiss and tell."

"Sounds fascinating. I most definitely will have to have a talk with Dinah." Her expression suddenly sobered. "Do you think she's any better, Cord? Do you have any idea what's weighing on her?"

He thought of her inexplicable crying jag. "To be honest, no. She's not better. And I have no idea what to do to make her better. Whatever happened has torn her up. She's not the same confident woman she once was. Every now and then when she's sparring with me, I catch a glimpse of her old spirit, but most of the time it's as if she's, I don't know, defeated."

"That's exactly it," Dorothy Davis said. "It's as if there's not a speck of hope or anticipation left in her. What could have done that?"

"My guess is that it's something so awful we can't even imagine it. Maybe I should call that boss of hers over in Afghanistan. I imagine he could shed some light on it," Cord said, immediately warming to the idea. It was past time to get to the bottom of this and if Dinah wouldn't tell any of them, maybe someone else would.

"Don't be so quick to do that. She'd be furious," her mother warned.

"That might be a risk worth taking," Cord replied.

"Not yet," she insisted.

"Okay, then, I'll hold off a little longer, if you think that's best, but not forever."

"If it comes to that, let me make the call," her mother volunteered. "She might get angry with me, but she won't be able to shut me out of her life the way she could you."

"I'm not worried," Cord said. "I'd rather have her fighting mad at me and back to her old self, than shut off from most of the world. I think I talked her into spending some time with Maggie today."

"Really? That's wonderful. She's been refusing to take her calls or anyone else's, for that matter. All she does is hang out in the pool or watch those talk shows for hours on end. Maybe between you and Maggie, Dinah will start to find her way out of this depression she's been in."

Cord wondered guiltily if Bobby could have gotten through to her better than anyone else, but he quickly dismissed the idea. He might not know much about relationships, but even he knew that desperation and neediness weren't the basis for anything lasting.

He regarded Dorothy intently. "Can I assume that I have your blessing where Dinah's concerned?"

Her expression brightened. "Does that mean what I think it means? Do you want to marry her, Cordell?"

Cord swallowed hard. Marriage? Was that what he was thinking? "One step at a time," he corrected. "How about we think of this as a courtship?"

She laughed. "You pin whatever label on it that allows you to sleep at night, Cordell, but I think the handwriting's already on the wall."

He frowned at her with mock ferocity. "Better not be on one of *these* walls."

Maggie had a formidable scowl on her face when Dinah met her for lunch downtown. She'd deliberately chosen a public place for their get-together. She figured they needed neutral turf to discuss the whole Cord situation. She still wasn't convinced that her recent involvement with him wasn't going to cause a permanent rift between them.

"If I didn't know for a fact that you haven't been seeing anyone in town besides Cord, I would be very angry with you," Maggie said.

Dinah winced. So that was it? Maggie was ticked off about being shut out of Dinah's life. Truthfully, she could hardly blame her. "I know I should have called again before now," she said apologetically. She picked up the glass of sweet tea Maggie had ordered for both of them and took a long drink while getting her thoughts together.

"Or at least taken one of my calls," Maggie said. "Why have you been avoiding me?" she asked bluntly. "Is it because of Cord?"

Oddly, Maggie's directness was comforting. It gave Dinah permission to open up in a way she hadn't dared to before.

"That's certainly part of it," Dinah admitted, then sighed. "But it's more than that, Maggie. In case you haven't noticed, I'm a total mess."

Maggie didn't seem dumbstruck by the admission. "I got that when I first saw you. What I don't get is why won't you let me help."

Dinah wasn't sure she had a logical explanation to offer, so she merely told the truth. "I think this is something I have to figure out on my own."

"You're not shutting Cord out," Maggie reminded her. "And he doesn't know you half as well as I do."

"Only because he refuses to be shut out," Dinah said. "I haven't had the strength to fight him."

"Is that why you're sleeping with him, because it's the path of least resistance?" Maggie inquired tartly just as the waiter came to take their orders.

Dinah chuckled as color flooded the man's cheeks. "Maybe we should order before we get into that," she said dryly.

When the obviously relieved waiter had taken their orders and left, she faced Maggie. Ignoring the implied criticism behind Maggie's question, she remarked, "I just knew you'd guess right off about the sex."

"That's because despite the shadows that are still in your eyes, you're glowing. You've fallen for him, haven't you?"

"Fallen for Cord? No." She struggled for an explanation that made sense and wasn't demeaning. "He's what I need right now."

Maggie's temper stirred. It was flashing in her eyes, which Dinah had recognized long ago as a dangerous sign.

"And then when he's served his purpose, you'll go off and leave him?" Maggie demanded.

"It's not going to be like that," Dinah protested, though she couldn't honestly swear that it wouldn't be exactly like that.

"Then what will it be like?"

"You know Cord. He doesn't take anything seriously, either. This is a fling, Maggie, for both of us."

"Then you're either blind or stupid," Maggie retorted. "Cord's in love with you. He always has been. He stayed out of the picture back when Bobby was involved, but his feelings have always been there. I think that's the real reason he made up that crazy lie to split the two of you up, though he claimed he was trying to do his brother a favor. That's why he never took another woman seriously. On some level, he's always known he wouldn't settle for anyone besides you."

"That's crazy," Dinah said, honestly stunned by what Maggie was suggesting. "I'm like some sort of project for him right now. He'll get tired of me. I'll join that long list of women he's left."

"You keep telling yourself that," Maggie said. "Maybe it'll help you sleep at night when you take off and the rest of us are left to clean up your mess, just the way it was when you dumped Bobby." She met Dinah's gaze with an unflinching look. "You know I love you as if you were my own sister, but sometimes you are totally self-absorbed and selfish."

The accusation stung so badly, Dinah couldn't speak. It was just as well that the waiter chose that moment to return with their salads. He set them down and scurried away, as if he feared hearing something else that was way too personal.

"What?" Maggie prodded when they were alone again. "Nothing to say to that?"

"I don't know what to say."

"The truth hurts, doesn't it?"

"Yeah, it does," Dinah admitted. "That's actually how you see me?"

"That's how you are," Maggie said flatly. "All that single-minded drive that got your career into high gear is hell on the people around you."

"You included?"

"Me included," Maggie admitted. "You don't let anyone in, Dinah. Have you told one single person what's really going on with you?"

"Not entirely," she admitted. "You know more than most, as a matter of fact. That should give you some satisfaction."

"Oh yeah, I'm pleased as punch," Maggie said sarcastically. "Why haven't you shared the whole story, at least with those of us who love you? What are you afraid of, that we'll think less of you? Don't you know we would do anything in the world to help? Don't you know there's nothing you could have done or could do that we won't understand and forgive?"

Maggie could say that now, because she didn't know what she was talking about. If she knew about Peter, that Dinah had let him die in her place, if Maggie knew that she'd messed up at her job because she could no longer focus, would she still feel the same way? Dinah doubted it. She certainly couldn't forgive herself for any of it.

"It's my problem," Dinah said stubbornly.

"And that makes it ours," Maggie insisted just as stubbornly. "Maybe you've lost touch with friendship, but that's the way it works. When you shut us out, it puts a wall up between us. Maybe you don't mean it that way, but it tells us you don't think we're smart enough or caring enough to understand."

"It's not that at all," Dinah said, genuinely dismayed.

"When you were trying to decide whether to go up north to college, didn't I give you good advice?"

"Of course."

"And when you couldn't decide between the red sequined dress and the pastel pink for prom, didn't I tell you to go with the red? And wasn't every guy in the room drooling?"

Dinah laughed. "Oh, Maggie, I'm so sorry. Obviously I should be confiding in you. The red dress was a master stroke," she joked, then regarded her friend seriously. "But this isn't about a dress. It's about my life."

Maggie shook her head, her expression filled with

sorrow. "If you gave me half a chance, you might discover that I even have a few good ideas about that."

"To be honest, you probably have better ones than I do," Dinah said.

"Then tell me."

"I can't," Dinah said apologetically. "I wish I could, but I can't say the words, Maggie. I've tried. I'm afraid if I say it out loud, I'll start sobbing and never, ever stop."

Maggie immediately looked stricken as the depths of Dinah's distress finally sank in. "It's that bad?"

Dinah nodded. "Worse than anything you could possibly imagine."

"Okay, then," Maggie said briskly, pushing aside her uneaten salad and leaning forward, her elbows on the table in a way that would have had both their very proper mothers cringing. "Here's the deal, Dinah. I'm not going to press you to talk to me, but I am going to insist you see someone who can listen objectively to whatever it is and tell you how to cope. I may be way out of my depth, but I do know one thing. Hiding out the way you have been and hoping it will all get better or will simply go away isn't working. You said it yourself. You're a mess. First you wanted to marry a man you know you don't love. And now you've gotten involved with a man you once claimed to despise. Personally I can totally understand that, seeing it's Cordell we're talking about, but if you were in your right mind, you'd never reach out to him."

Dinah knew Maggie's intentions were the very best, but they were getting way too serious. "You're going to insist, huh?" she teased. "You and what army?"

Maggie didn't smile in response. "I won't need an

army. If I have to, I will have Cord throw you over his shoulder and haul you off to the appointment," she assured Dinah. "And if you don't think I will, just test me."

Something in her friend's unwavering voice and unflinching gaze told Dinah she would do exactly as she said. "I'll think about it," she promised.

"Not good enough. I'm calling you tonight to see if you've made an appointment. If you haven't, I'm making one for you and that's that."

"I don't need you to take charge of my life," Dinah grumbled.

"Somebody has to," Maggie retorted. "You're certainly not doing it yourself."

Dinah wanted to lash out at her presumption, but she couldn't. Unfortunately, Maggie had the situation pegged exactly right. And if she and Cord ever did team up on Dinah, there was little doubt that Dinah would wind up doing exactly what they expected.

"I'll make the appointment," she promised dutifully.

"By tonight?"

"Yes, Maggie. By tonight."

"And not for some time in November, either. Make it for tomorrow."

"I'll take the first appointment available," Dinah told her.

"Fine," Maggie agreed. "As long as it's for tomorrow."

"I think I was happier when I was avoiding you," Dinah lamented.

"No, you weren't. You were just living in a fool's paradise."

Despite herself, Dinah laughed, though there was an

edge of hysteria to it. If where she'd been living was any sort of paradise at all, she hoped she'd never catch a glimpse of hell.

Cord finally had a chance to stop by his office during his lunch break and was greeted with a sour look from his receptionist and a handful of messages, some dated days earlier.

"Nice of you to drop in," Pam said. "I vaguely remember a time when Covington Plantation was not where you spent every single second of your day."

"You can always reach me on my cell phone," he responded.

"Oh, really? Where is it right now?"

Cord reached into his pocket, but the phone wasn't there. He checked for the case he occasionally attached to his belt. Nothing.

"I must have left it somewhere," he muttered.

"You left it somewhere last week, to be precise. I've been trying to catch up with you since Friday."

"How come? What's so important?"

She handed him another little pile of messages. "All from Tommy Lee Davis," she said. "He wants to see you ASAP."

"Really? Did he say why?"

"Just that it was important and that you weren't to say a word about it to anyone."

"Why the secrecy?"

She frowned at him. "Do you actually think he bothered to explain that to me? He was ticked enough that I couldn't seem to track you down."

Cord couldn't begin to imagine why Dinah's brother was so anxious to see him. Nor did he have time to waste with another meeting, but something told him he needed to make the time for this one.

"See if you can reach him and see if now's a good time," he said. "I assume you have his cell phone number."

"And it probably works, too," she said sarcastically.

Cord let the comment pass and went into his office to try to straighten out the mess his desk had become. Pam tended to pile things on it haphazardly when she was annoyed with him. Important files were mixed in with stacks of junk mail and letters he needed to sign were buried under all of it.

He was trying to make some sort of order out of it when she stuck her head in the door. "Tommy Lee's on his way."

"Send him on in when he gets here," Cord told her.

"Can't," she said. "I'll be at lunch. I'll put the phone on the answering machine while I'm out. Keep your ears open for the door."

"Yes, ma'am," he said, amused despite her best efforts to let her displeasure be known.

"It's a good thing I like your brother," she said. "Otherwise you couldn't pay me enough to work here."

He laughed. "Duly noted."

Pam had been gone for barely ten minutes when Tommy Lee came in. Compared to Cord, the man was a veritable fashion plate in his Armani. Oddly enough, despite his blueblood background, the attire didn't seem to suit him. He looked as if he'd give just about anything to strip off the tie and open his collar.

Cord didn't know Tommy Lee well. He was younger than Dinah, so he and Cord hadn't crossed paths in school. They'd bumped into each other from time to time at social functions in recent years, but Tommy Lee had always struck Cord as a man whose life hadn't gone quite the way he'd expected.

Cord waved him toward a chair. "What's up?"

"This is between us, right?" Tommy Lee asked, his expression filled with concern.

"Sure. Who would I tell?"

Tommy Lee gave him a wry look. "You're pretty tight with my mother and from what I hear, you're even tighter with my sister."

"Fair enough," Cord said. "I won't tell either of them about this visit."

Tommy Lee nodded. "You're doing a good job out at Covington Plantation. My mother took me on a tour a few weeks back."

"Thanks."

"And I've been hearing a lot of good things about the projects you and Bobby have going over in Atlanta."

Cord regarded him impatiently. "Could you get to the point? I need to get back out to Covington."

"I want a job," Tommy Lee blurted.

If he'd announced a desire to appear on *American Idol,* Cord couldn't have been any more shocked. "Why? You're the heir-apparent to an entire banking empire."

Tommy Lee squirmed uncomfortably. "I hate banking. I love all this restoration stuff my mother gets mixed up in. And, to tell you the truth, I'd rather be building something and working with tools than pushing papers all day long."

Cord realized Tommy Lee was totally serious. "What's your father going to have to say about this sudden career change?"

"He'll blow a gasket when he hears about it," Tommy Lee said candidly, then shrugged. "Then I suspect he'll be relieved. He was dreading turning the bank over to me. He knows I'm no damn good at it. In fact, if I weren't family, he'd probably fire me. The one who's really going to be stunned is my mother. She'll think I'm throwing away my heritage."

Cord saw the distress in his eyes over that. "I think you're wrong," he told Tommy Lee. "I think she'll see it as exchanging one part of your heritage for another. You did get some of your genes from her, after all."

Tommy Lee's expression brightened at once. "Maybe she will see it that way. So, what about it? Any room at Beaufort Construction for me?"

"Do you want to buy into the company or do you just want a job?"

"A job," Tommy Lee said eagerly. "I know I need to pay my dues. I don't want to buy my way in. If it works out and I can make a real contribution, we could talk about the rest down the road."

"Do you have any skills in construction?" Cord asked.

"Enough not to embarrass myself or make you regret hiring me."

Cord liked what he was hearing, a combination of humility and eagerness. He tended to hire with his gut. The fact that Tommy Lee was a Davis was both a blessing and a curse, but he figured the positives outweighed the negatives. He stood up and held out his hand. "You're on. I can use another carpenter. We're behind schedule. When can you start?"

"Give me a couple of weeks," Tommy Lee said, clasping his hand in a strong grip. "I'll speak to my father today, but it may take that long for me to mop up the collateral damage."

"You need any help with your mother, send her to me," Cord offered. "But I think she'll surprise you."

In fact, as far as he could tell, most of the Davises were just full of surprises these days.

16

After Tommy Lee left his office, Cord's thoughts drifted back to Dinah's crying jag that morning and to her mother's opinion that they should delay taking the drastic action of calling her boss. He wished he were as certain as she was that they weren't making a mistake by waiting. Dorothy hadn't seen her daughter facedown in the mud at his house the night of the storm. Nor had she witnessed Dinah sobbing so hard it seemed as if she'd never stop. It was his opinion that time wasn't doing a thing to heal Dinah's wounds. If anything, she was worse than that very first night she'd turned up at his place full of sass and vinegar looking for Bobby.

He was about to violate his agreement with Mrs. Davis and call the network, when it occurred to him that Maggie might have had better luck with Dinah than he'd had. He'd call her, find out if they'd gotten together and once he had her take on things, then he'd decide what needed to be done.

As soon as Maggie heard his voice, she laughed. "Took you longer than I expected, Cordell. You must be slipping."

"Meaning?"

"I'm guessing you want to know how things went with Dinah. Or am I mistaken? Did you call to see if I was busy tonight?" she asked, her tone filled with irony.

Cord sighed. Maybe this had been a bad idea, after all. Now that he had her on the phone, though, he intended to plunge ahead. "No, it's about Dinah. I'm sorry if I'm putting you in an uncomfortable situation, Maggie. I really am. I wouldn't do it, if it weren't important."

"I know that, you idiot," she chided. "I was teasing. You have not broken my heart, so stop getting all weird every time you talk to me. We're bound to run into each other and it'll be thoroughly uncomfortable if I have to watch every word out of my mouth."

"Sorry."

"Stop apologizing, dammit! I haven't heard so many *sorry*s out of one man's mouth since—well, I won't say who—had a little difficulty in the romance department one night, if you know what I mean."

Cord laughed. "I'm a little tense."

"After seeing Dinah, I can't say that I blame you. She's in trouble, Cord. More than either of us imagined."

"Trust me, my imagination has already run pretty wild on this score. Did she tell you what it's about?"

"No. She flatly refused to get into it. I got the impression she's terrified that once she talks about whatever it is, we're all going to lose respect for her."

"That's absurd."

"I didn't say it was rational," Maggie told him. "I just think she's expecting all of us to be as hard on her as she's being on herself. I did convince her to make an appointment with a counselor of some kind. I gave her the name of someone I know, but whether she goes to him or someone else, I made her promise to schedule an appointment for tomorrow."

"And she actually agreed to that?" Cord asked, surprised. In his experience, Dinah was not the sort of woman who'd be inclined to ask for help from any direction, no matter how desperate the circumstances. "If she won't take advice from people she trusts, what makes you think she'll consider taking it from a stranger, even a trained professional?"

"I added a little incentive," Maggie said smugly. "I'm certain it will do the trick."

"Which was?"

"The image of you throwing her over your shoulder and carting her in yourself, if she didn't do it on her own."

He bit back a smile. He had to admire Maggie's gumption, to say nothing of the depth of her friendship. "And she bought that?"

"To tell you the truth, I think she likes the idea of you as a caveman type, but I don't think she'll risk doing anything to see if you'll pull it with her, especially in public."

"Just what I've been longing to hear," Cord said wryly.

"Are you going to see her tonight?" Maggie asked.

"We don't have plans. Why?"

"Because one of us needs to make sure she made the appointment."

"I'll head on over there," Cord said at once. His intention of getting any work done this afternoon had been pretty much doomed from the minute he'd left the plantation, anyway.

"She's going to think we're all ganging up on her," Maggie warned. "It could backfire."

"Then there's always the caveman thing," Cord said,

resigned to being the bad guy, if need be. "Thanks, Maggie. She may not be happy with either one of us, but if it snaps her out of this state she's been in, that's all that matters."

"I agree, but don't push her too hard, Cord," Maggie said, worry threading through her voice. "For her to be so withdrawn and willing to let things happen, rather than taking charge of her own life, I suspect she's more fragile than either of us imagined."

Cord agreed. "Hey, I know a little bit about finesse," he claimed.

"And a whole lot about charm," she added. "Use it."

"That's a promise." He wanted Dinah whole again. He wanted that flash and sparkle back in her eyes, the temper in her voice, the grit and determination in her attitude. Even if that meant she'd leave him in the end, pushing her to get help was the only choice he had.

Maybelle greeted Cord at the front door with a sour expression. "You, again."

He grinned. "Not happy to see me, Maybelle?"

"Just getting tired of answering the door when I've got other things I could be doing. You going to be showing up all the time, you might start coming round to the back and save me some time."

"I'm going to assume you don't mean to suggest that I'm not good enough to cross the front door threshold," he said.

She didn't seem to appreciate his attempt at levity. "Got nothing to do with that. It's got to do with me not being as young as I once was."

"Then I'll take that into account," he promised. "Where's Dinah? Out by the pool?"

She shook her head. "In her room, watching the television again. She's been up there most all afternoon. Seeing her like this is worrisome."

"I know."

"Then do something about it. You want to go up there, it's fine by me," Maybelle said, then gave him a fierce look meant to intimidate. "Just mind your manners, you hear me?"

"Yes, ma'am."

"That girl's not been herself since she came home," Maybelle said, her brow furrowed with genuine concern. "I'm trusting you to do something about that and not just add to the problem."

"I'm doing my best."

"See that you do."

Cord took the stairs two at a time, aware that the housekeeper's watchful gaze was on him. At the top he gave her a jaunty salute that almost put a smile on her lips.

When he got to the third floor, he rapped on Dinah's door, though he doubted she could hear him over the sound of the television blaring the argument between a mother-in-law and her son's wife over who had more right to the man's attention. Cord heard enough before he walked in to know he was on the daughter-in-law's side.

"Somebody ought to tell that old biddy to butt out," he said as he sat gingerly on the edge of the bed beside Dinah.

She didn't seem all that surprised to see him. In fact, she never even glanced away from the TV. He decided to up the ante by stretching out beside her.

"Someone just did," she commented, seemingly

more fascinated by that than she was by the fact that he was lying right there thigh-to-thigh with her.

"Do you suppose we could turn that off or is it more scintillating than my company?" he inquired, trying to keep his tone light.

She did look at him then and turned the sound down, but not off. "Did you come over here prepared to be scintillating, Cordell?" she inquired with evident fascination. "Right here in my mother's house?"

He gave her his most wicked grin. "Now that truly would be my pleasure, sugar, but actually I came to talk."

She groaned. "Not you, too. Did you and Maggie compare notes and decide I needed a booster pep talk?"

"Something like that," he admitted, seeing little point in denying it. He didn't want her to get all sidetracked by conspiracy theories.

She turned the sound on the TV back up. "Then go away."

"Not until you tell me what happened in Afghanistan," he said, removing the remote from her hand and clicking the TV off entirely.

She frowned. "I thought the deal was that I had to talk to some shrink or something."

"I'm giving you one last chance to talk to me first."

"I don't want to talk to you. To be perfectly honest, I don't want to talk to anyone, but Maggie kept pushing, so I agreed to see a professional. I can tell you now what he'll say. He'll tell me that it's going to take time. At a hundred dollars an hour, I figure that's a waste of money, but if it will shut the two of you up, I'll do it."

"Did you make an appointment?"

"Not yet."

"Office hours will end soon. It's already past four."

She shrugged. "Then I'll call in the morning."

Cord backed down from that fight for the moment. "How about I tell you what I think happened over there? You can correct me if I get it wrong."

"Whatever," she said without inflection, her gaze averted.

He took that for a yes. "Okay, here's the way I see it. You were a little too close to the action. Someone died, probably right in front of you. Maybe even someone you knew," he said, watching her face closely for any sign that he was getting close to the truth. Her face remained perfectly blank, but there was a tiny flicker in her eyes. Anguish, if he wasn't mistaken. He kept pushing. "You didn't do anything. You couldn't. That started you off on the panic attacks. It made you second-guess everything you were doing."

He looked into her eyes, but once more she averted her gaze. He tucked a finger under her chin and made her face him. "How am I doing so far?"

Her lips stayed stubbornly clamped together, but there was even more turmoil in her eyes.

"You were used to being the best in the business, but all of a sudden you were off your game. Your bosses wouldn't cut you any slack. They wanted you at full speed or not at all. Before they could fire you, you quit."

She swallowed hard and a tear leaked out and trailed down her cheek. Cord had to fight the longing to wrap his arms around her. He kept pushing.

"Why'd you quit, Dinah? Did they really back you into a corner? Or were you the one who decided you couldn't cut it anymore? Now I may not know much about the network news business, but the way I see it, you were too valuable for them to suddenly toss you out on your behind. My guess is they tried to get you to take a leave of absence or another assignment, just something you could handle till you got your head straight, but your pride kicked in. You saw anything less than being on the front lines as a humiliation, right?"

She blinked hard, but the tears kept coming. "Why are you doing this?" she asked, her voice choked.

"Because you need to face it," he said. "You got scared that you couldn't cut it anymore, so you ran. And now you don't know what to do with yourself. You've lost confidence. That would be one sorry thing for most people, but for a woman like you, a woman who's always known her own mind, fought to get what she wanted, it's a downright shame."

Now there was real fire flashing in her eyes, thank God.

"I am still a better reporter than ninety percent of the people over there," she shouted at him. "You don't know anything about it, Cordell. You don't know what it takes to do that job."

"No," he agreed. "But you do. Can you still cut it, Dinah?"

"Yes," she said emphatically.

"Then why are you here? Come on, Dinah. Just say it. Why are you here, instead of over there doing what you do best?"

Her fragile hold on her temper snapped. "Because I'm terrified, dammit! There, I said it. Does that make you happy?"

Cord did wrap his arms around her then. "No, it doesn't make me happy. It breaks my heart." He leaned away and smiled at her. "But it's the first step on the road back, Dinah. I'd stake my life on that."

She gave him a startled look. "You want me to go back?"

Cord struggled to get the next part right. "No," he said, wiping a stray curl away from her damp cheek. "The last thing I want for my sake is you leaving here to go anywhere at all. But I want you to know that you can go back, that you're strong enough to do it, if that's what you choose to do. Journalism mattered to you. Nobody should lose something that matters to them that much just because they're scared."

She gave him a sad look. "I don't know how not to be scared anymore." She waved an arm around the room. "This isn't where I belong. I know that. Hiding out isn't who I am. I just don't know how to stop."

"Face whatever happened," he said. "Once and for all, face it. Until you've done that, you'll never be able to put it behind you. That means looking all the ugliness straight in the eye without blinking. No more hiding from it. No more keeping it bottled up inside. The more you talk about it, the less powerful its hold on you. Right now you've got it built up in your head like this huge, awful black monster that can swallow you up. I can't chase it away—Lord knows, I would if I could—but you can."

He reached for the phone beside the bed and handed it to her along with a slip of paper with the number Maggie had given him. "Call now and make that appointment."

She looked as if she might argue, but finally she took the phone from his hand and dialed. Her voice was steady and emphatic when she said she needed an appointment for the next day.

Her gaze locked with Cord's. "Yes, it's an emergency," she said quietly.

"What time?" he asked when she'd hung up.

"Noon."

"Want me to take you?"

Her chin rose a notch. "Thank you for offering, but no. I need to do this on my own. If it's supposed to be my first step back, I can't very well have you carrying me."

The return of her independent streak was cause for celebration, but for reasons he didn't want to explore right now, Cord didn't feel one bit like celebrating. In fact, he had to wonder if he hadn't just sent Dinah straight down the path that would eventually rip them apart.

Once Cord had gone, Dinah retreated to the familiar sanctity and comfort of the pool. She had a lot of thinking to do before tomorrow's appointment. She needed to figure out if he was right about why she'd taken the drastic action of quitting her job, instead of taking either a leave of absence or one of the many other assignments Ray and the network had dangled in front of her.

Was it pride and the fear of failing even at some nothing little assignment that had made her insist on a clean break? The fact that she'd been packed and out of that hellhole the instant her replacement's plane had touched down suggested her hurry had been all about desperation and not about some sudden longing to get home to Bobby and her family. Bobby had simply been the excuse she'd used, the safety net. She wasn't any more in love with him now than she had been a decade ago. Discovering that he was engaged had been inconvenient, nothing more.

God, she really was as selfish and self-absorbed as Maggie had accused her of being. She would have married a man just to solve her own problem without a moment's thought about what it might do to his life. Or, eventually, to her own.

Unfortunately now she was stuck with her impulsive decision. She did not regret coming home for one single minute, but the truth was she had no idea what she was going to do now that her backup plan was in disarray. Cord and Maggie were right about one thing. It was past time to do some heavy-duty soul-searching and formulate a new plan, instead of drifting along waiting for some epiphany to show her the way. The last take-charge thing she'd done was drive to Atlanta to look for Bobby.

Except for seducing Cord, she reminded herself with an unwilling twitch of her lips. She had made that happen. Apparently her old spirit wasn't entirely dead. Maybe there was hope for her, after all.

Of course, there was no need to get started before she had to, which was noon tomorrow. Until then she could stay right where she was in the pool, her skin puckering.

When her mother arrived home, she took one look at her daughter and went back inside. When she returned, she was carrying a pitcher of vodka and tonic, a cut glass dish filled with slices of lime, and two very tall glasses.

"We need to talk," she said as she set the tray of drinks on a table shaded by a giant umbrella. When Dinah didn't move, she added, "Now, please."

Dinah recognized a command when she heard one, even if it was coated with sugary politeness. She climbed out of the pool, rubbed her shriveled-up body dry, then sat down opposite her mother and took a sip of the drink her mother had set before her. It was strong enough to make her choke.

"Trying to loosen my tongue?" she asked wryly.

"Precisely," her mother said without the slightest hint of regret. "Your father and I have been so relieved to have you home and safe, I've kept silent up till now, but I can no longer ignore the fact that you're getting thinner and thinner with each passing day. There's no sparkle in your eyes. I think you need to see a doctor."

Dinah felt her gut tighten. "I'm not sick."

"Sick at heart, then," her mother said. "See a psychologist."

Dinah took a deep breath, then admitted, "You're not the first to suggest that today. I already have an appointment scheduled for tomorrow."

"Really?" Her mother's expression filled with heart-felt relief. "Thank goodness."

Dinah's eyes stung with tears at her mother's reaction. "I'm sorry. I had no idea how worried you've been."

"Don't be sorry. All that matters is that you're going to get help. It's plain to all of us that whatever happened has been eating away at you."

Dinah couldn't deny the truth of that. She'd been trying for months to bury the memory of Peter's death, to deny that it had taken something important out of her, but all of her efforts had been in vain.

Cord had come so close to putting the story together. When had he developed the knack for seeing into her head? And what did it mean that he cared enough to do so?

None of that really mattered right now, though. All that mattered was banishing the memories that had haunted her from that fateful day. The only problem was, she had no idea what to do to change her approach.

The solution Cord and Maggie were offering—talking about it incessantly—wasn't her way. Davises didn't whine. They were cool and unemotional. They accepted life's knocks and moved on. They triumphed. Just look at what her mother had made of her life.

The fact that Dinah couldn't seem to get past what had happened to her, the fact that she still awakened in the middle of the night in a cold sweat with her heart pounding wildly filled her with a sense of complete failure. How on earth could she share that with anyone?

But even as those dire thoughts filled her head, she remembered anew that one person had already guessed most of it. And when she'd looked into his eyes, she hadn't seen disgust or disdain. She'd seen concern.

No, she corrected, recalling what Maggie had told her at lunch. She'd actually seen the love Maggie had been talking about. If Cord could still have feelings for her after everything he'd guessed about her dark secret, then wasn't it time she was brave enough to start to love herself again?

As much as she hated the thought of going to see a psychologist, she knew now that she had no choice. Maybe this person that Maggie had found for her and that Cord had forced her to call was the answer to Dinah's unspoken prayers.

Dinah reached for her mother's hand and gave it a reassuring squeeze. "I love you, Mother."

A pleased smile spread across her mother's face and Dinah realized how rarely she'd ever spoken those words to either of her parents, how rarely she'd expressed them to anyone. It had always been safer to keep silent, to avoid any hint of vulnerability.

Now that she knew the truth about her mother's pregnancy forcing the marriage, Dinah had to wonder if she hadn't subliminally known all along that she hadn't been the blessing they'd longed for, but rather an inconvenience that had rushed them to wed. Maybe she'd kept her emotional distance because she'd feared that her love for her parents wouldn't be returned in full measure.

"Everything's going to work out for the best, Dinah. I truly believe that," her mother said.

"I think I'm beginning to believe it, too," Dinah said, her heart lighter than it had been for months. She held out her glass. "Pour me another drink, Mother."

Her mother chuckled. "Happily. The first one worked like a charm. Who knows what secrets I might be able to pry out of you after two?"

"Ah, just in time, I see," Tommy Lee said, coming around the side of the house. "Can I have one of those, too?"

To Dinah's surprise, her mother gave him a sharp look. "You seem a little too eager. I'm beginning to worry about that."

"I'm not drinking too much," Tommy Lee said defensively. "In fact, I'm here to celebrate. I'll get myself a glass and bring out more vodka and tonic."

As soon as he'd gone inside, Dinah exchanged a look with her mother. "You're worried about him, too, aren't you?"

Her mother nodded. "He's not happy. He hasn't been for a long time."

"Is it Laurie?" Dinah asked.

She shook her head. "I don't think so. In fact, they seem more in love with each other than ever."

Dinah reached over and touched her hand. "Perhaps he'll explain when he comes back out."

A few minutes later, Tommy Lee poured himself a stiff drink, then sat on the edge of a chaise lounge facing their mother. "I wanted you to be the first to know that I'm leaving the bank," he said quietly.

Dinah gasped, even as her mother sat up perfectly straight with fire in her eyes.

"Is this your father's doing?" her mother demanded.

"No, it's my idea," Tommy Lee assured her. "He doesn't even know about it yet."

"But why on earth would you quit? And to do what?" Dorothy asked.

Dinah watched Tommy Lee's face and saw a flash of pure excitement in his eyes. It was wonderful to witness.

"Actually I'm going to work with Cord and Bobby," he said. "Cord hired me this afternoon."

Dinah exchanged a stunned look with her mother. She had no idea what to say to any of this. The fact that Cord hadn't mentioned a word of it also grated.

"Are you going to be a partner?" her mother asked Bobby.

"Nope. I'm starting at the bottom. I intend to do this right. There's a lot I don't know."

Dorothy gave her son a befuddled look. "But why?"

"Because I love working with my hands. I love all the restoration projects you've been involved in through the years. This is my chance to see if I can make a career of it."

Dinah noticed that their mother didn't look convinced. She decided to throw in her two cents to be supportive. "I think it's a wonderful idea, Tommy Lee. Do this while you're young. The bank will always be there, if you change your mind."

He shook his head. "I'll never go back to the bank and I'm sure Dad wouldn't have me, if I was willing. No, I'm cutting the ties with this decision."

"This is your father's doing, isn't it?" Dorothy asked again, even more heat in her voice. "I've sensed something going on between the two of you lately. He's forcing you into this. I'll talk to him."

"No, Mother," Tommy Lee said emphatically. "This is my decision. It's what I want." He regarded her worriedly. "And I want to be the one to tell Dad, too. Don't get involved, okay? I don't want this to become a bone of contention between the two of you."

"Are you sure?" Dorothy asked, her worry apparent.

Dinah studied her brother. "Can't you see how happy he is, Mother? I can."

Tommy Lee winked at her. "Thank you."

Dorothy still didn't look convinced. "I'm behind you a hundred percent, of course," she told him. "But if you change your mind…"

"I'm not going to change my mind." He set aside his drink, which was mostly untouched. "I guess I'd better go break this to Dad."

Dinah grinned at him. "Without even finishing your drink?"

"Tempting as it would be, I don't want to show up in his office half-drunk. If he's ever going to have any respect for me, he needs to know I made this decision while I was stone-cold sober." He leaned down and kissed his mother's brow. "Love you. Turns out I'm a lot more like you than either of us realized. I'm glad I faced that before it was too late and I'd wasted my whole life doing something I hated."

Dinah noticed that her mother's worried gaze followed him as he left. "I'll tell you the same thing you told me earlier. It's going to be okay."

Her mother gave her a weary smile. "I hate to say it, but you're not all that convincing."

"Hey, I'm doing the best I can," Dinah told her.

"And I suppose that's all any of us can do," her mother responded. "I just hope in your brother's case, it's enough given what he's throwing away for this impulsive decision of his."

Dinah gave her mother's hand a pat. "I don't think it's impulsive at all. I think it's been a long time coming. He wants this, Mother. I could see it in his eyes. He's truly excited. Be happy for him. Be proud of him for figuring out what he really wants and going after it. Isn't that the most any of us can ask for, that we spend our lives doing what we love?"

Her mother nodded. "But I'm still going to speak to your father about this. I know he had a hand in it. He's put way too much pressure on that boy."

Dinah regarded her with concern. "Don't you and Dad already have enough going on between you? Tommy Lee's not a boy, Mother. He's a grown man who knows his own mind. Let him handle Dad."

Her mother's gaze faltered at that, but her chin set stubbornly. "It doesn't matter. Tommy Lee is our son. I won't let him be pushed aside."

Dinah saw she wasn't going to win. Besides, she had her own battles to worry about. Tomorrow's appointment with the shrink was going to be here a whole lot sooner than she'd like.

17

Dinah was on her fourth trip up in the elevator of the small office building where psychologist Warren Blake had his offices. She'd ridden right back down three times. Hopefully this time she'd be able to make herself actually exit the stupid thing. It was going to be embarrassing if she started running into the same people on one of these trips.

This time at least she was alone in the car. She punched the button for the seventh floor, then stood at the back of the elevator in a corner as it whooshed up way too quickly. The doors opened onto a now familiar carpeted corridor. She sucked in a deep breath and tentatively stepped out, holding the elevator door so it couldn't close behind her.

"If I go back down one more time, it just proves that I really do need to be on that shrink's couch," she muttered. For a woman who once had been intrepid enough to face bullets or land mines, this office visit shouldn't be such a ridiculous ordeal, she thought, hoping that the self-derision would motivate her to walk down that hallway.

With a great deal of effort, she made herself release

the death grip she had on the door. She winced as it closed, taking away her option to retreat.

For an instant, she truly regretted not accepting Cord's offer to come with her. It would have been nice to have him here to goad her into doing what she needed to do. Then she could have spent a few days resenting him, but at least she would be inside the office and not cowering here in the hallway, proving to herself what a ridiculous ninny she'd become.

She glanced at the number on the office door across from her, then counted down three doors to a suite that had to be Dr. Blake's. It wasn't so far, she encouraged herself. She could walk down there and stand outside until she got her bearings. She could still change her mind.

But when she was facing the heavy oak door with its discreet sign, Warren Blake, PhD, it suddenly swung open and a man with an open, friendly face and twinkling brown eyes stood there gazing back at her.

"Dinah Davis?"

Caught and unable to speak, she nodded.

"I thought so. I recognize you from TV. I'm Warren Blake." To her surprise, he came into the hallway and let the door close. "You running late or running scared?"

She grinned despite the tension churning in her stomach. "Scared," she admitted.

He shrugged. "Happens all the time. We could go downstairs for coffee, if you'd feel more comfortable."

Relief washed over her. "Really?"

"Really," he confirmed, then warned, "Don't get too excited, though. You still have to spend fifty-five minutes with me, hopefully telling me what brought you here. You told my service it was an emergency."

"Not like an appendicitis attack," she said, feeling foolish.

"Good thing. That's definitely not my specialty." His compassionate gaze settled on her face. "What's it going to be? In here or downstairs?"

"Downstairs this time, if you don't mind."

"Fine by me."

He walked off toward the elevator without waiting to see if she was following. He obviously assumed she would, even though it had seriously crossed her mind to bolt for the staircase. That stubborn pride of hers, which was occasionally good for something, kept her from doing it. She refused to have one more person thinking she was a terrified wimp.

The coffee shop off the lobby was packed with the lunch hour rush, but Dr. Blake managed to snag a table that was just being vacated. "You stay here," he instructed Dinah. "I'll get the coffee. Anything to eat?"

"No, thanks, but you go ahead. This is probably your lunch hour."

"Don't worry about it. I'll be right back."

When he returned, he set her coffee in front of her, then settled back with a disgustingly healthy bottle of water.

"You know until I saw you with that, I thought you might be a perfectly normal person," she said wryly. "Now I know you're a health nut, like everyone else these days."

He laughed. "I can drink coffee if it will put you at ease."

Dinah shook her head. "Something tells me there's not enough coffee in the universe to put me at ease." She met his gaze. "How do we do this? I mean without the whole couch thing?"

"You've been watching too much TV. We hardly ever ask clients to sprawl out on a couch unless that's the way they feel most relaxed. As for what we do now, you talk. I listen."

"Could we start with the weather?" she quipped.

"We could, but it would be a waste of your money. It's Charleston in summer. What is there to say once you get past hot and humid?"

Since the weather was out, Dinah asked, "How do you know Maggie? That's the friend who recommended you, in case I didn't mention that to your service."

He chuckled. "Nice try, but I get to ask the questions. You fill in the blanks."

She clung to her cup and took a drink. It was still so hot, it burned her tongue. "Maybe you should ask one then. I don't seem to know where to start. I've never done this before."

"Done what? Had someone poke around in your head?" he asked, his amusement plain.

She nodded.

"It's not an invasive procedure, Dinah. You don't need to be scared of it. All that needs to happen is for you to trust me enough to talk to me. I won't tell anyone what we've discussed. Your secrets are safe." He leaned forward, his expression suddenly intense. "But I'm not psychic. I might be able to tell if you lie to me or skirt the truth, but I can't get at the truth unless you reveal it. You ready to give it a try?"

Was she? Not really, but there was little question that she was going to be badgered to death by everyone if she didn't make an honest effort to give this a chance.

"Okay," she said at last, still clinging to the cup so tightly it was a wonder it didn't break.

"Then why don't I start? Anytime I'm getting off-track, you stop me and point me in the direction you'd prefer to go, okay?"

Relieved by the suggestion, she seized it. "Sure."

"You've spent a lot of your career reporting in war zones, is that right?"

She nodded.

"Must have been pretty brutal."

"At times."

"Did you get used to it?"

She regarded him with shock. "No. Who could ever get used to it?"

"But you found a way to cope," he guessed.

"I suppose."

"Tell me how."

She gave the question some thought. "The same way all reporters or soldiers or cops do, I suppose. We resorted to irreverent humor. We sort of clung together and formed really deep bonds. Somehow we managed to create this little island of sanity in the midst of the chaos. It was an illusion, of course, but it worked."

"Did you work with the same people most of the time?"

She thought she saw where he was going, straight at the bottom line, as a matter of fact. "Yes," she said, her tension already building as he moved toward the inevitable question.

"Anyone you were especially close to?"

A lump formed in her throat and tears promptly welled up in her eyes. "Yes."

He regarded her with a patient, reassuring expression. "Am I getting too close, Dinah? Is this what's so painful?"

She nodded.

"Would you rather not talk about it here?"

She was suddenly overwhelmed by a helpless feeling. Maybe this was the best place. Surely she wouldn't fall apart right here, not with all those years of training under her mother's tutelage about the proper way for a Southern lady to behave in public. Maybe she could control her reactions, just say the words and then let Dr. Blake guide her through the anguish. Maybe it could all be very clinical and cool.

Moreover, maybe she needed to just blurt it out while she had the nerve. If they left this table, this café, by the time they reached his office, she might have stuffed everything back down again until she felt safe and in control.

"It's okay. We can do this here," she said at last. "I was very close to my cameraman." She tried to say his name and couldn't. "He was an amazing man, a brilliant photographer."

"*Was?*" Dr. Blake repeated, his tone gentle.

She forced herself to meet his gaze, forced herself to get that one devastating word past the huge boulder in her throat. "He died," she said softly, feeling her composure crumble. "He died."

Tears trickled down her cheeks, then came in a torrent. Dr. Blake handed her a fistful of napkins, his expression revealing not the slightest hint of embarrassment at sitting here with a woman who was quietly crying. Maybe he was used to people coming unglued in public places. Maybe everyone in here was used to the psychologist and his unstable patients occupying this very table. The thought crept in and made Dinah smile, even though she was on the verge of filling the whole room with a foot of water from her seemingly unstoppable tears.

"Was he the cameraman whose death was reported on all the newscasts a few months back? He was killed by a car bomb?"

She nodded.

"And you were there?"

"Yes," she whispered.

"Have you talked about this with anyone?" Dr. Blake asked.

She shook her head.

"Why not?"

She shrugged. He was speaking so calmly and with so much compassion, she wanted to respond the same way. She summoned her reporter's objectivity, leapt behind the wall she'd always tried to keep between herself and her subjects.

"At first everyone over there tiptoed around what happened to avoid upsetting me," she said. "Then when I was finally ready to talk about what had happened, no one wanted to hear."

"Really? Not even your friends?"

"You have to understand," she said earnestly, trying to defend the people who'd all but willed her to keep silent. "Over there we all have to do what we can to keep the very fragile grip we have on things. If something like this could happen to one of us, it could happen to any of us. Talking about it reminds people of that, so after the first shock wears off, we pretty much stuff it down and forget about it."

"But, of course, no one really forgets," he suggested.

"No, not really."

"So how long did you stay there keeping your friend's death all bottled up inside?"

"About six months."

"And then what happened?"

"I came home."

"By choice?"

"In a way. I was no longer as effective as I had been. My bosses were worried about me. They wanted me to take a leave of absence or another assignment till I was more myself." She swallowed hard. "I didn't take it well, when they told me that. I guess I thought they should cut me some more slack, at least at first. Then, when I was forced to admit they were right, that I'd lost my edge in the field, I quit."

"So you'd lost your friend and then, in essence, you lost your job?"

She forced a grin. "Yep, that pretty much sums it up. Pretty pathetic, huh? Local success story comes home a failure."

For the first time he regarded her with a trace of impatience. "You think of yourself as a failure? For what? Caring about your friend's death? Caring that your life has changed dramatically? Do you know that two of the biggest stresses anyone can face—*anyone*, Dinah—are the loss of someone important and the loss of a job? And do you know a third? Moving. So, here you are back home in Charleston without the career that apparently defined you, at least in your own mind, without someone who mattered to you, and far away from the world you'd been living in for how long?"

"Ten years."

"Well, gee," he said, his tone wry, "I don't see anything there that you could possibly be depressed or upset about, do you? I'm surprised as heck you're not out dancing and whooping it up every night."

He'd just made her sound almost...normal. Dinah regarded him with amazement. "I'm not crazy?"

He laughed. "Not unless you persist in beating yourself up over this."

"Then I'm cured?" she asked happily.

His expression sobered instantly. "Sorry. It's not that easy, I'm afraid. You and I are just getting started."

Her momentary joy dimmed. "Really? But I thought—"

"You thought I could just snap my fingers or wave a magic wand and you'd start to feel better, right?"

"But I do feel better," she insisted.

"But do you have the slightest clue about what comes next?" Dr. Blake asked. "Is your grief for your friend manageable? You haven't even told me his name, Dinah. Or how he died. I know because I remember the incident, but you didn't say the words. Doesn't that tell you something? You made it as impersonal as you possibly could, but this man wasn't some almost anonymous colleague. For you to be this sad, he must have mattered deeply to you. You need to get all of that out in the open. We haven't even ripped the scab off the wound, much less cleaned it out so it could heal."

Dinah knew he was right, but she'd wanted so badly for there to be some quick fix. She'd wanted that magic wand he'd talked about.

"Same time tomorrow?" he suggested. "But in my office, okay?"

"You really think I'm going to come unglued, don't you?"

He gave her a look filled with understanding and compassion. "If you're lucky."

* * *

Dorothy was still upset about Tommy Lee's decision to leave banking and go to work for Cord. If that was his dream, fine, but she knew in her gut that he'd come to it because Marshall had pushed him too hard. She'd heard all her husband's barely concealed innuendoes about Tommy Lee's lack of skills. If he said such things to her, what had he been saying to their son?

Even though she'd promised Tommy Lee she would stay out of it, she headed to the bank right after her monthly garden club luncheon. She'd intended to have this conversation with Marshall last night, but he'd been late coming home, probably because he'd guessed she was going to be furious with him.

Inside the bank, she marched straight past his secretary with little more than a cursory greeting, then walked into Marshall's office. He was in the middle of a meeting with one of the bank's vice presidents, but after one look at her face, he told the man they'd finish up later.

Dorothy acknowledged Grayson Pickett as he left, then took the seat he'd vacated.

"I assume you want to discuss Tommy Lee's absurd decision to go to work for Cordell," Marshall said, seizing the initiative.

Dorothy was familiar with the tactic. It was meant to take the wind out of her sails, but today she had quite a lot to say and she intended to spit out every word.

"A decision which you no doubt pushed him into making," she retorted.

"Me?" he said incredulously. "You can't seriously blame this on me. I've done everything I could to see that Tommy Lee knew what was expected of him here.

Running this bank is a huge responsibility. Tommy Lee's never been interested in buckling down to get it right."

"Which I'm sure you've been pleased to tell him at least once a day," she snapped. What had ever made her believe she could work things out with this cold, disapproving man? Right this second, she wanted to smack him for hurting their son.

He frowned at her. "What did you expect me to do? Let him slide along because he's my son? As it is if he'd been anyone else, I would have fired him years ago."

"Then I'm sure you're delighted with this turn of events," she said.

"No, I am not delighted," Marshall snapped. "I would have preferred it, if he'd shown even a modicum of interest in assuming his rightful heritage. You asked me not long ago if I'd given any thought to retirement. Now do you get why I haven't been able to do that? After four generations, the only thing I can do now is to sell out to one of the huge, impersonal banking conglomerates. This place will no longer be in Davis hands. How the hell do you think that makes me feel?"

"Maybe you should spend more time worrying about how your son feels," she said. "Obviously he knows he's let you down. I'm sure he must feel like a failure."

"Well, how would you describe him? After every advantage we've given him, he's going to work in construction."

She regarded him with dismay. She was no happier about that than he clearly was. "Isn't there something you can do? Can't you give him another chance?"

"It's not a matter of giving him another chance, Dorothy," he said wearily. "This was his decision. Maybe

I pushed him. I can't say. But the truth is, he wasn't happy here. Not from the very beginning. As much as it pains me to say it, I think this is for the best. Maybe he'll find what he's looking for working with Cord." He gave her a sad smile. "There's a lot more of you in him, than there is of me."

Wasn't that what Tommy Lee and Dinah had both said? She hadn't wanted to look at it in quite that way. Had she wanted another excuse to be mad at Marshall? Maybe instead of being furious with her husband, though, she should be proud of her son. Tommy Lee had felt pressured to get out of banking, but perhaps he'd found the one thing for which he was better suited. Perhaps they should both be rejoicing in that and not making the decision about the two of them and their failures at all.

She sighed and regarded Marshall apologetically. "I'm sorry I came in here ready to blame everything on you."

He smiled. "Believe me, you haven't said anything I didn't say to myself last night after Tommy Lee told me what he intended to do. You and I had a lot of dreams for our kids, but in the end they've had to find the dreams they wanted and we've had to learn to let them."

"Do you think we failed them?"

"Not if they find what they're looking for," he consoled her. "I want to believe they'll both come out all right in the end."

She stood up and walked around his desk and slid into his lap. "I guess that leaves us to figure out what we want," she said, her hand on his cheek.

His grin was as mischievous as it had been when they'd first met. "I know what I want," he said.

"Tell me."

He shook his head. "Not till date night," he said. "This isn't the place. Besides, it'll do you good to let the anticipation build a little."

"What are we doing?"

"You'll see."

She laughed. "You're not even going to tell me that? How will I know how to dress?"

"I'll give you just enough notice," he promised. "I don't want you to waste a lot of time stewing over the right thing to wear. This is all about us learning to be impulsive again, okay?"

Dorothy couldn't recall the last time she'd thought of her husband and impulsiveness in the same sentence. She touched her lips to his. She was certainly ready, though, to give it a try. If their marriage was ever going to be more than an obligation again, they needed to put a spark back into it, the same kind of spark she'd seen in Tommy Lee's eyes when he'd told her about his decision. For the first time since he'd made his stunning announcement, she let herself be truly happy for him.

And gazing into Marshall's eyes, she allowed herself to feel the first faint stirring of hope.

Cord had ruined half a dozen pieces of wood meant for the detailed chair rail in the plantation dining room. He couldn't seem to get Dinah off his mind. He was kicking himself for not insisting on going with her to see the psychologist, not into the room of course, just to the reception area, so she'd have some moral support. Sometimes she needed somebody to override this independent streak of hers, whether she realized it or not.

And who knew if this guy Maggie had recommended was any good? Dinah could come out of the session a basket case, in no condition to get behind the wheel of a car. He should have been there for her, made sure she had a shoulder to cry on if she needed it.

He looked at the six-foot length of pine he'd just run through the saw and muttered a colorful expletive. For an expert using a mistake-proof saw, he'd made a mess of things yet again.

"Nice talk," Dinah said, coming up behind him. She slipped an arm through his and glanced at the ruined wood. "Does my mother know you're this sloppy?"

"No, thank God." He studied her. "Have you been crying? Your eyes are red."

She grinned. "Thanks for noticing. I thought I'd performed miracles with my makeup before driving out here."

"Did that shrink make you cry?" he inquired, fighting the desire to go pummel the man even though he knew perfectly well tears were probably inevitable if the shrink was doing his job right.

To his astonishment, Dinah turned slightly and wrapped her arms around his waist. She wearily rested her head against his chest. "You going to beat him up, if he did?" she murmured.

"Only if you want me to," he said, feeling completely out of his depth. "Are you okay?"

"Not exactly."

"Want to talk about it?"

She shook her head. "I've done all the talking I can bear for one day."

"Then what can I do?" he asked in frustration.

She looked up at him, tears pooling in her eyes again.

"Take me home with you. I don't want to be alone, Cordell."

He tossed aside his protective goggles at once. "Let's go."

She pulled back and stared up at him. "You'll walk right out of here, just like that?" she asked with surprise.

"You need me, you're the priority," he said flatly.

"You're amazing. I expected a whole litany of excuses."

He grinned down at her. "Did you now? Was this a test? You gonna back out now that you've got my hopes all built for a lazy afternoon in my hammock?"

She ran her hands up under his T-shirt. "Not a chance, especially if you'll lose the shirt."

He stripped it over his head. "Done. Now what?" he asked, his lips twitching.

She stood on tiptoe and whispered in his ear. Cord felt every drop of blood in his body pool directly in the lower part of his anatomy.

"I'm accommodating, sugar, but this place is crawling with workmen. I don't know about you, but I'm not much of an exhibitionist."

"You did a pretty darn good imitation of one over at the beach," she reminded him with a wicked gleam in her eyes. "But I suppose I can wait till we get to your place."

He winked at her. "You ever get naked in a hammock?"

"Not that I recall," she said primly. "But I surely am looking forward to it."

"Me, too, sugar. Me, too."

Dinah had instinctively gone looking for Cord after her session with Dr. Blake. The fact that Cord had been willing to drop everything in the blink of an eye just because she'd asked meant more to her than he could ever understand.

Every day it seemed she discovered one more example of just how rock-solid and dependable the onetime bad boy had become. Not that he'd turned into a saint. He was just far more complex and fascinating than she'd expected. Danger and reliability weren't half as incompatible as she'd always thought they were.

Right now, this afternoon, though, she was hoping for a little of Cord's trademark wickedness.

He'd barely pulled his truck to a stop in front of his place and come around to open her door, when she leaped into his arms, wrapped her legs around his waist and kissed him until his breath was coming in ragged gasps.

Eventually he pulled back and regarded her with vaguely dazed eyes. "You hungry, sugar?"

"You have no idea," she said, diving back in for another stomach-dipping, roller-coaster ride of a kiss.

She put one hand on his chest so she could feel the thundering of his heart. This was it. This was life pumping through him, she rejoiced.

She could feel the maddening heat and fullness of his arousal pressing against her. She wanted all of that heat inside her, coaxing her back to life, making her blood pump and her pulse race. She wanted the oblivion of mind-numbing sensation, sensation that rolled through her in waves, that made every nerve sing.

"Love me, Cord. Please, love me."

He headed for his hammock and rolled into it, settling her astride him and meeting her gaze with a lazy, self-satisfied smile that she'd come to identify with him years ago when he'd driven her half crazy with a desire she'd never wanted to acknowledge. She'd fought the attraction, choosing Bobby, not just because he was reliable, but because he was safe. He would never consume her like this, never make her want like this. Apparently she'd known subconsciously that she would be able to leave Bobby while she wouldn't be able to walk away so easily from his brother. Cord had given her the perfect excuse to hate him when he'd betrayed her by lying about her to his brother. She thought she understood now just why he'd done it. She also believed he'd never do anything to hurt her so badly again.

She looked into Cord's eyes and guessed that he'd seen all along the combustion that would happen if they ever got together. He'd stayed in the background and waited, risking the possibility that she might never come back, might never discover what they could be together.

She ran her hands over Cord's powerful chest, let her fingers tangle in the dark hair, felt again the jump of his pulse. He'd deliberately linked his hands behind his head, leaving whatever was to happen up to her. He seemed to sense intuitively that she needed the control.

Oddly, now that she had it, she was happy to give back, rather than take. She slowly, carefully slid open the zipper of his jeans and took him in her hands. That startled him.

"Nice to know I can still surprise you," she whispered as she ran her tongue over the tip of his arousal.

"Darlin', don't you know you take my breath away just by walking into a room?" he asked, his voice husky, his breath hitching to emphasize the point. "This might just about kill me."

"We wouldn't want that," she teased, pulling away.

"I'll risk it," he said fervently.

Dinah leaned back down and claimed him, feeling his body jolt and set the hammock in motion. When she couldn't stand it a moment longer, she slipped off her panties and lowered herself onto him, taking him inside and then waiting, letting the sweet tension build. Cord's eyes were closed. His muscles tensed as he waited, ceding the control as if he knew how desperately she needed it.

The hammock didn't allow for the wild ride she'd intended, so she settled for something lazy and slow, something that allowed her to savor each sensation as something separate and distinct before, at last, they blurred together into something that sent them both into a shuddering, magnificent release.

When her pulse finally quieted, Cord stroked a hand over her backside, then lifted her and settled her next to him, her head resting on his shoulder.

"You know what you've done, don't you?" he said, his voice threaded with amusement.

"What?"

"You've taken a perfectly good hammock and ruined it for me," he said, though he didn't sound especially distraught about it.

Dinah looked at him suspiciously. "Ruined it how?"

"Up till today, I've always been able to come out here with a beer, lay back and let my mind wander, while I wait for a breeze to stir through these big old trees."

"You won't be able to do that anymore?"

"Not a chance. From today on, I'll be thinking about this." He grinned. "I've got to tell you, there is nothing restful about the images that are going to come to mind."

"Then I suppose you'll have to call me whenever you intend to come out here, so we can do something about all those wild ideas I've planted in your head." She met his gaze. "I like the thought of driving you a little crazy."

"You're good at it, that's for sure," he admitted.

She studied him seriously. "Do you mind?"

"Mind what? You coming by to ravish me?"

She grinned at his interpretation. "Yes, that."

"I may mind in fifty or sixty years," he said, that lazy, smug look firmly in place. "I'll let you know."

Dinah laughed. "You do that," she said, but underneath the laughter she felt a tiny little shiver of panic at the implication in his words, the unspoken promise of an enduring love. That alarm told her as nothing else might have that she was a long way from being able to let herself risk loving someone again.

18

Long after Dinah had fallen asleep in his arms, Cord lay awake in bed thinking about the unmistakable flicker of fear in her eyes when he'd casually tossed out a comment suggesting they'd be together a few decades from now. He'd let it pass at the time, but it made him wonder just how she saw things between them.

Throughout his adult life, he'd never been interested in much more than the occasional fling, but it was different with Dinah. There was no question that he was in love with her, probably had been all of his life. He'd fought it because of Bobby, ignored it because it didn't make a lick of sense, but now that it seemed possible, he knew it was going to break his heart if she went off and left him.

Which meant he had to figure out some way to make her want to stay. It wouldn't be enough just to persuade her and he surely didn't want her to do it because she had no other options, the way she'd been willing to settle for his brother. No, she had to want to stay in Charleston with him, because it was what was right for her. He wasn't smug enough to think that mind-altering sex was going to do it.

And there was also that nagging little matter of trust.

If she discovered that he'd stood squarely between her and Bobby once again, she was going to be furious and whatever they were building now could blow right up in his face. He needed to figure out a way to keep her and his brother from ever finding out the role he'd played in keeping them separated.

First things first, though. He had to get her to want to stay. He thought about what had taken her away from Charleston in the first place. Ambition, in a word. A career. He couldn't offer her a war zone, but he could surely point her in the direction of a job.

But did he dare? Especially now that she was seeing that shrink and struggling with whatever demons she'd brought home with her? No, he concluded reluctantly, now was not the time. She had to work through her problems first. Once she had, she might be receptive to a gentle nudge or two.

He turned his head and gazed at her, still not quite believing that she was here with him. Her cheeks were flushed, her hair a tangle of curls, but she looked at peace for a change.

Almost as if his thoughts had touched her, she stirred restlessly, moaning a little. Her hand, resting against his chest, clenched.

"No," she murmured, a tear leaking out and running down her cheek. "No!"

Cord brushed away the tear. "Sssh!" he soothed. "Everything's okay. You're right here with me. You're safe, Dinah. I'll keep you safe."

His words must have reached her, because she sighed and snuggled closer. Her hand relaxed.

"What happened to you?" he whispered, his heart aching.

More important, what was it going to take to make her whole again?

Dinah was starting to like Warren Blake more and more with each visit. He pushed, but only so far. He seemed to know instinctively when she was getting close to the breaking point. And no matter how well or how badly a session went, he regarded her with approval, never with disdain or disappointment. Oddly, that reaction from a virtual stranger reassured her. Perhaps no one else in her life, especially those who loved her, would be disappointed when they learned the truth about what had sent her fleeing from Afghanistan.

"Are you married?" she asked Warren out of the blue as her third session in a week drew to a close on Friday.

He gave her a chiding look. "I thought we'd agreed that I get to ask the questions."

"We're off the clock now, doc. I'm on my way out."

His gaze narrowed then. "Are you asking for yourself? A lot of people tend to develop an attachment to their psychologist. It's normal, since the things we're dealing with are so intense."

It sounded very practiced, as if he'd had to deliver the same gentle rebuke a hundred times before. Dinah smiled. "I'm not asking for myself."

He looked thoroughly flustered by that. "Oh."

"I was thinking about Maggie," she admitted. "But then you already know her, so I'd probably be wasting my time pushing you in her direction. I mean you're both adults who are capable of getting together if you're interested, right? You don't need me interfering."

He laughed. "We don't. In fact, knowing Maggie's stubborn independence, I have to wonder if she would appreciate you meddling in her love life."

"Actually she doesn't get a say," Dinah said, turning aside the scolding. "She was happy enough to meddle in mine."

"I see." He assumed his perfectly bland, shrink face again. "How do you feel about that?"

Amused, Dinah tapped her watch. "Time's up. Gotta run before you charge me for another hour." She stood up and started for the door. She had her hand on the knob, when she realized he was studying her with a long, thoughtful look.

"Actually I held the next hour open, in case you wanted to keep going today," he said quietly.

She regarded him with surprise. "Why?"

"Because we keep dancing right up to the real break-through and just when we get close, you go dashing out the door. I'm beginning to think you've got the timing down pat."

"In my business, timing is critical," Dinah said, unable to keep the defensive note from her voice, because he was exactly right. "If a piece was slotted for three minutes, it had better be three minutes down to the second."

"I'm not talking about your business now," he said coolly. "I think you know that. So, what's it going to be, Dinah? Are you staying so we can make some real progress? Or are you going to run away to avoid the same thing?"

She certainly wanted to run. There was something

unrelenting in the psychologist's eyes today, as if he'd tired of her evasions, not for his sake, but for hers. She really wasn't sure she wanted to do this, not just today, but ever.

She hesitated, debating with herself. Then her pride kicked in and she stepped back into the room. "I'll stay."

"Good." He waited until she finally sat back down before suggesting bluntly, "Tell me some more about Peter."

It was the first time he'd brought Peter's name up on his own and hearing it casually mentioned startled her even though she'd known when she made the decision to stay that this was the conversation they were going to have.

"He was one of the greatest cameramen I've ever known," she said neutrally. "He'd won every major award." She sounded like a biographer rather than his lover.

"What was he like as a man?"

That answer took longer, not because she couldn't find the right adjectives to describe him, but because remembering his best traits made her unbearably sad. "Warm, irreverent, dependable."

"Until he went and died on you," Warren said.

Dinah flashed him a look of pure hatred. "Yes, until he died," she snapped. "But he didn't let me down, if that's what you're implying. Far from it."

"Then you tell me. How did it happen, Dinah?"

She saw the scene again in her mind—their capture that night, the driver walking away and leaving them with an impossible choice to make, Peter insisting that she let him cover her escape. But that's where the images stopped, in the back of the car, with Peter still very much alive. She wouldn't allow the reel to play on. She couldn't. She didn't want to see it or hear it or experience it again, much less describe it to a man who was, after all, a virtual stranger.

"Dinah?" he coaxed. "Don't stop now. Tell me what happened."

When she continued to remain silent, he asked, "Were you there?"

She nodded, feeling numb.

"Tell me," he encouraged. "Take your time and describe what happened."

"I can't," she whispered.

"You can," he said, his tone unrelenting. "You must. No evasions this time, Dinah. It's time to let it out. You're safe here. It's over. You survived."

She remembered dimly hearing Cord's whisper in the night. "You're safe," he'd said. And she had relaxed. She had believed it.

Yet now she felt as terrified as she had on that deserted highway. There was nothing safe about remembering or talking about that night. The only safety was in stuffing it down deep inside where she wouldn't have to face the guilt that came with knowing she'd survived and Peter hadn't.

Even she could see the illogic of that. She knew Peter was dead. She knew she'd lived.

Even so, panic welled up and overwhelmed her. Her heart began to race. She broke out in a cold sweat. Her breath snagged in her throat. She glanced around the room wildly, needing air, certain that all of the oxygen had been sucked right out of her.

Realizing the windows were sealed and overcome by

a choking fear, she bolted for the door, then down the seven flights of stairs, not pausing until she was outside, gasping in air, leaning against the wall of the building, her heart still pounding in an out-of-control rhythm.

The door opened again and Warren Blake appeared beside her, his eyes filled with kindness and regret. He put a hand on her shoulder and waited until she finally began to relax, the panic slowly releasing its grip on her.

"How often do you have these panic attacks?" he asked.

She leaned back against the wall of the building, her eyes closed. "Not so much lately," she said eventually. "They only come when I...you know."

"Start to think about what happened," he guessed.

She nodded. "Or when something happens that reminds me," she said, recalling the clap of thunder that had sent her diving into the dirt at Cord's at the beginning of the summer.

His gaze narrowed. "Something like what?"

"Thunder," she said, then realized how telling that probably was, after all.

"Any loud noise?" he asked.

"Yes."

"Did Peter die in a car-bomb explosion?"

Hearing the words spoken so calmly, so matter-of-factly filled her with an odd sense of relief. It was only three little words—car-bomb explosion—she thought with amazement. Why hadn't she been able to make herself utter them?

Because with those words came images too horrifying to express, she realized, as they began to creep in. Images of the charred metal of the car, the rising smoke, and then, worst of all, Peter's shattered body.

"Oh, God," she whispered with a barely muffled sob. She covered her eyes as if that could keep away the fresh pictures that were winding through her head in a horrifying, never-ending loop.

Each image was more appalling than the one before. And with each she let out another sob, and then another, until she was bent over, clutching her stomach, the tears streaming down her face.

Warren Blake remained beside her, steady as a rock, his hand on her shoulder reassuring, as she cried her heart out. For Peter. For herself. For a world gone mad with hatred.

For once, Dinah didn't try to stop the tears from flowing. She let them come, feeling the cleansing that came with them, the letting go of the anguish that had been eating her alive, that had kept her from moving on.

These tears felt different from all the others she'd shed. Was it because she was finally able to acknowledge why she was crying and for whom? Were these the first honest tears she'd shed?

Slowly, the sobs eased and the tears dried up, all on their own, she realized with surprise. It seemed there wasn't an endless supply of them after all. How astonishing!

When she stood up at last, Warren handed her a box of tissues. The gesture made her lips twitch with an unexpected smile.

"Are you always prepared for anything?"

"Pretty much, but I saw this coming," he said. "You did good, Dinah."

She frowned at the praise. "Do you get some sort of

weird thrill out of watching a woman unravel before your eyes?"

"No, what thrills me is seeing someone finally face their demons." He reached in his pocket and pulled out his cell phone. "You're in no condition to drive right now and you need someone with you. Who would you like me to call?"

Her mother would be soothing. Maggie would be comforting. But it was Cord's name she instinctively gave him. She needed to feel his arms around her, though if she kept bombarding him with her neediness, he was going to wind up losing his job.

"I'll call," she said, accepting the phone and dialing. "It's me," she said when Cord answered. "Can you come get me?"

"Where are you?" he asked at once, not even hesitating.

She gave him the address for the office building. "I'll be in the café off the lobby."

"Twenty minutes, sugar. Will you be okay till then?" he asked, his voice threaded with worry. "Maggie's closer."

"No," she said. "I'll wait for you. I want you, Cord."

"You've got me. I'm on my way."

She held tight to his words as she handed the phone back to Warren. "He's on his way."

"I'll come in and wait with you," he said.

"You don't need to do that," she insisted.

"Yes, I do."

She frowned at his determination. "Do you think I'm going to fall apart again?"

His brows rose. "Do you?"

"I hadn't planned on it."

"Well, then, neither will I," he retorted mildly.

Inside, he bought two cups of coffee and set one in front of her. Dinah clung to it, just to have something to do with her hands. Now that the whole scene was over, she was swamped with embarrassment.

"There's nothing for you to be embarrassed about," Warren said.

She scowled at him. "Are you reading my mind now?"

"No need to," he said. "I know how this stuff works. People have a breakthrough and instead of dancing in the streets, they get all twisted up and uncomfortable about creating a scene."

"How do you stand it?" she asked, genuinely curious.

"Stand it?" he repeated with amazement. "It's what I live for. What just happened with you means you're finally on the road to recovery. You're getting in touch with your emotions again, instead of blocking them out. How could I not be happy about that?"

"You are in a very weird profession," Dinah said, then felt compelled to add politely, "If you don't mind me saying so."

He laughed. "You're not the first. Your friend Maggie equates what I do with some form of black magic or something. She doesn't have any use for it."

"She sent me to you," Dinah reminded him. "In my book that says she respects you."

He seemed startled by the assessment. "You think so?"

"For a man who makes a career of reading between the lines, you seem oddly clueless about Maggie," she said, studying him speculatively. "I think she just loves yanking your chain. You must make it easy for her."

His expression turned thoughtful. "I probably do. Maybe I'll ask her out one of these days so I can investigate your theory, see if there's convincing data there to support it."

Dinah grinned. "Sounds like a plan to me. Just don't make it a case study, doc. Try thinking of it as a date." She looked up just then and saw Cord's truck angling into a no-parking space in front of the building.

"There's my ride. I'd better get out there before he goes toe-to-toe with a cop over his illegal parking." She met Warren's gaze. "Thank you for today. Same time Monday?"

He glanced in Cord's direction, then shook his head. "I think you deserve a long weekend off. I'll see you again on Tuesday."

Dinah brightened as if she'd been given a pass to skip school. "Really?"

He winked. "Enjoy yourself. You did good work today."

A warm glow washed over her at his praise. Who'd ever have thought that she'd be complimented for getting in touch with her own emotions when she'd always been trained to keep her feelings at bay.

She walked toward the door and got there just as Cord yanked it open, his expression filled with worry. The instant he spotted her, he opened his arms and gathered her close.

"You okay?" he asked.

"None the worse for wear," she said, breathing in the musky, masculine scent of him and the faint aroma of sawdust. It was a scent she was beginning to crave.

"Let's go home."

"Yours or mine?"

She chuckled at the uncertainty in his gaze. "I think mine, for a change. Something tells me Mother and Dad need to have their world shaken up a bit."

"And you think you showing up with me in tow will do that?" he asked, an edge in his voice.

"No, I think them figuring out you're upstairs in my bed will do that," she corrected, then grinned. "You game?"

Cord laughed. "As long as you're the one who intends to fend off Maybelle and her rolling pin when she spots me sneaking up the stairs."

"That's a deal," she promised him.

What had ever made her think that life in Charleston was destined to be dull? In some ways she'd taken more risks here in the past few weeks than she had in years. And maybe these were the risks that really mattered.

"What the hell is that?" Cord asked, snapping awake to the sound of a powerful engine right outside the window.

Dinah was sitting upright in bed beside him looking every bit as startled and confused as he was. "It sounds like a motorcycle," she said. "But who would be riding a motorcycle in this house? Surely this isn't one more part of Tommy Lee's rebellion." She frowned at Cord. "We need to talk about that, by the way, but not right now. The motorcycle thing is more pressing."

"One way to find out who's on it," Cord said, crawling out of bed and padding bare-assed over to the window to peek outside. As soon as he caught a glimpse of the candy-apple-red Harley and its driver, he burst out laughing.

"What?" Dinah demanded, coming over to join him.

"Will you look at that?" Cord said, just as Dorothy Davis exited the front door in a pair of jeans, boots and a black T-shirt with the logo of some rock band splashed across the front in a psychedelic tie-dyed pattern. In his opinion, she looked carefree and damn good for her age. He could imagine Dinah looking just like that in another twenty or thirty years.

"Mother," Dinah said, her mouth gaping.

"And unless I miss my guess, that's your daddy on the motorcycle," Cord said, watching as the man helped Dorothy climb on behind him, then handed her a helmet.

"Have they lost their minds?" Dinah muttered, vanishing from his side.

By the time Cord turned away from the outrageous, unexpected scene outside, Dinah was pulling on her robe and heading out the bedroom door. He shouted for her to stop, but she was evidently on a mission.

He debated following her, but concluded his sudden appearance in the driveway half-dressed would put a damper on whatever impulsive craziness was going on with the Davises. In his opinion, they were old enough to make their own decisions. Dinah, he suspected, did not see it that way.

In less than a minute, he heard the motorcycle roar off and guessed that Dinah hadn't gotten outside in time to confront her parents. In his opinion, that was just as well.

He settled back against the pillows and waited for her return.

It didn't take long for Dinah to reappear, her expression filled with indignation. "They didn't stop. They acted like they didn't even hear me."

"How could they? That engine was pretty loud."

"Oh, they heard me. My mother looked straight at me and grinned like some schoolgirl," she said, flopping down on the bed beside him, only to stand up and start to pace. "What on earth are they thinking?"

"That it's a great day for a ride?" Cord ventured, only to draw a scowl.

"It's a great day for a drive in the country in the car," she retorted. "Or even in a convertible. But a motorcycle? Come on, Cordell. They'll kill themselves."

"Maybe they've done this before," he suggested. "Maybe they're experienced."

"Oh, don't be ridiculous," Dinah said with a dismissive wave of her hand. "My father on a motorcycle? Mr. Uptight and Professional? I've never seen the man when he hasn't been wearing a suit."

Cord chuckled, then smothered it when Dinah glared at him. "I'm sure he's gotten out of his suits from time to time."

"Not in my lifetime," she insisted.

He resisted pointing out that Marshall Davis had evidently gotten undressed with his wife on at least two occasions since Dinah and Tommy Lee did exist.

"You've been gone for ten years," he reminded her quietly. "Things change."

Dinah sat down on the edge of the bed looking thoroughly lost and confused. "Could they possibly have changed that much?"

"I guess you'll just have to ask them when they come back," he said.

"*If* they come back," she said direly.

He beckoned to her, intent on improving her mood. "Come here."

"Why?" she asked suspiciously.

"So I can make you forget all about your parents and whatever it is they're up to."

She looked for an instant as if she were going to argue, but then she stripped off her robe and headed his way. "It's a good thing you have this amazing talent for making me forget things," she said. "But you're going to have to work really, really hard to pull it off this time."

"I'll do my best," he said modestly.

Something told him if he was going to spend a lifetime trying to get Dinah's mind to shut down, he was going to need some potent vitamins.

19

It had been so many years since Dorothy had done anything as outrageous as climbing onto the back of a motorcycle that she couldn't even remember the occasion. Nor was she convinced that her proper, Southern gentleman husband had been involved.

Marshall had always been all about doing the right thing, which was just one reason she'd never really believed him capable of cheating on her. He'd had his life planned out from the time he was old enough to understand that banking was the family business. She sometimes imagined him sitting behind his father's desk at the age of two learning how to sort little piles of money.

This evening, as he headed onto a country road shaded by live oaks draped in Spanish moss, she clung to him and rested her head against his back. It was far too noisy to ask all the questions running through her head, which meant all she could do was enjoy the totally unexpected ride.

If Marshall had been half as surprising and inventive as this back in their youth, maybe she never would have had her doubts about marrying him when they'd first been pushed together by their respective parents.

Maybe they never would have settled into the dull routine of their lives if she'd known he was capable of this adventurous streak.

Of course, the blame was partially hers. She'd never asked anything more of him than what he'd offered, which was a quiet devotion.

She smiled thinking about Marshall's mysterious call earlier in the afternoon. All he'd told her was to be ready at five and to dig in the closet for something casual that absolutely did not have a designer label on it.

"I'm talking jeans and sneakers," he said adamantly. "Okay?"

"Have you lost your mind?" She wasn't even sure she owned such clothes anymore. Thank heavens, though, Dinah's closet was full of such outfits. Apparently it was close to being a uniform in her daughter's line of work.

To her surprise, Marshall had laughed. "No, coming to my senses, as a matter of fact. If you don't have what I'm talking about, go to one of the superstores. I'm sure they'll have whatever you need."

"I imagine Dinah does, as well," she admitted. "I'll borrow something from her. Amazingly enough, we're the same size."

"Why is that a surprise? You're as slender as you were the day we met. But whatever you do, don't tell Dinah why you're stealing her wardrobe. She'll never let us hear the end of it."

"See you at five."

She'd hung up feeling the first faint stirring of anticipation that she'd felt in decades. Sneaking into Dinah's closet and finding something to wear had only added to the spirit of adventure. When, only a few minutes later, she'd heard Dinah and Cord slipping into that very same bedroom, she'd relished the narrow escape.

Now, out here on this shaded, winding road, she wouldn't say it was nervous anticipation that had her stomach feeling all fluttery. It was more like plain old nerves. Riding a motorcycle was scary business at their age, but she had to admit it was as exhilarating as the sheer unexpectedness of it.

She hung on for dear life and gave herself up to sensation—the hard muscles in her husband's back, the throb of the engine between her thighs, the wind rushing past, the familiar scent of Old Spice, which Marshall had refused to trade for any of the more trendy, designer aftershaves men wore these days.

If this was his idea of a surprising first date to put some life back into their marriage, he had succeeded admirably. She was going to have to work hard to top it. Hang gliding, perhaps? Flying lessons? Up until today, she'd been thinking dance lessons, but now that seemed far too tame for two people who were still young enough to live on the edge a little. She refused to let the image of broken bones deter them.

With her mind drifting, Dorothy hadn't been paying much attention to where they were going. When Marshall turned off the highway and onto the road to Covington Plantation, she was startled. Why here, of all places? He'd never shown a lick of interest in it before.

But maybe that was the point, she concluded, feeling a smile steal over her face. She was grinning from ear to ear when he skidded to a reckless stop in front of the gracious old house. He cut the engine and they both sat there, he with his gaze on the house, she trying to adapt to the sudden silence. It was the first time it had been this quiet here in months. The workmen had obviously gone for the day.

Marshall finally climbed off the Harley and turned to help her off. He met her gaze, his eyes filled with a glint of uncertainty.

"How do you like the date so far?" he asked.

"It's not what I was expecting," she said.

His gaze narrowed. His brow creased with worry. "Do you mean that in a good way?"

She stood on tiptoe and kissed him until the uncertainty disappeared from his eyes and the furrow in his brow eased. She'd never before known her husband to be anything but totally self-confident. Seeing the hint of vulnerability, knowing how hard he was trying to please her gave her even greater hope for the future.

"I mean it in the very best way," she assured him. "I hate to tell you since we're in the middle of nowhere, but I'm actually starved. I skipped lunch, since I figured we'd be going someplace for dinner."

He laughed. "Do you honestly think I'd let you starve to death? Assuming Cordell followed my instructions, everything's under control."

It was yet another startling twist to this evening that seemed to be filled with them. "You spoke to Cord? I thought you didn't approve of him."

He shrugged. "I realized I don't know him well enough to be judgmental. Since you seem rather fond of him, I called this morning to tell him what I had in mind. He said he'd handle it on this end. I must admit I was impressed by how quickly he caught on and how willing he was to help."

Butterflies danced in Dorothy's stomach. "What on

earth have you dreamed up, Marshall? I can't imagine what you've done."

"Come with me," he said. "Around back, I believe."

Dorothy took his outstretched hand and walked with him around the side of the house. There, on the veranda that overlooked the gardens, was an elegantly-set table with flowers and candles, Nearby sat a bottle of champagne chilling on ice.

"I wanted to go with lobster, since that's what we had on our wedding night, but I was afraid if we got held up it would spoil," he said apologetically. "There should be a cooler around here with all the other dishes, though."

Dorothy stared at him in amazement. "You remember what we ate on our wedding night?"

"Of course I do," he said. "It was the most important night of my life."

Her eyes suddenly swam with tears. "How have I missed it all these years?" she murmured with genuine regret.

"Missed what?" he asked, rubbing away the trail of tears with the pad of his thumb.

"That you're such a romantic?"

"I think we stopped looking at each other in that way years ago," he said. "I realize now that it happens unless people make the effort to keep the romance alive."

Dorothy wrapped her arms around her husband's waist and laid her cheek on his chest. "But we're not going to let that happen ever again, are we? Promise me that, Marshall."

"We won't if I can help it."

She lifted her gaze to meet his. "I do love you, Marshall. I think all this is what I missed. I thought I'd never have another chance at it."

He gave her a sad look. "Were you ever tempted to find it with someone else?"

She thought of the mild flirtations that had kept her alive through the years, but that's all they'd been. Her loyalty to her husband had kept her from acting on them.

"Tempted," she admitted candidly. "But you're my husband, Marshall. That means everything to me. What about you?"

"No one ever measured up to you," he told her. "They couldn't."

"Why did we let things drift along for so many years?" she asked him. "Why didn't we fight for this?"

"Maybe it just wasn't time," he said. "But we'll get it back, Dorothy. One date at a time."

"You've set a pretty high standard," she lamented. "What on earth will I be able to do to top it?"

"All you've ever needed to do to keep the magic alive for me is to be by my side."

"You deserve more," she said at once. "And I promise I'll think of something. Meantime, let's see what sort of food has been left here for us."

In the cooler there was a Caesar salad, a chilled potato soup, cold roasted chicken and strawberries with a huge bowl of whipped cream. Dorothy grinned when she saw them.

"Did we actually eat the strawberries on our wedding night or did we put the whipped cream to a better use?" she inquired, a teasing note in her voice.

Her husband gave her a wicked grin. "Surely you remember that much," he replied. "I certainly found it memorable."

She regarded him with genuine affection. "It's coming back to me."

Over the years she'd forgotten that there had been very good times. Not everything had been about her resentment over the unexpected pregnancy or being trapped into a marriage she wasn't ready for. In fact before she'd found out she was carrying Dinah, she and Marshall had been wonderful friends and lovers.

She met her husband's gaze. "Why did you decide to come here for dinner? I was so sure you'd opt for one of Charleston's fine restaurants, the way we usually do for special occasions."

His expression sobered. "Too ordinary for a night like this. Besides, I know how much this place means to you. I also know I haven't shown nearly enough interest in the things that matter to you. I wanted you to understand that I intend to change that, starting tonight."

"Thank you," she said, touched.

"Will you give me a tour later?"

"I'm not sure if we have any working lights in the place," she said.

He gestured toward the candles on the table. "We can tour by candlelight. It can be the start of a tradition for this place, an annual candlelight tour."

She grinned. "Don't those usually happen at Christmas?"

"We'll make this a private tour," he suggested. "Surely there will be some perks for the woman who made all this happen."

"If there aren't any planned, I'll definitely see to it," she said, reaching across the table and linking her hand with his.

"Of course you will. You've always done anything you set your mind to."

"I didn't make a good marriage for us," she lamented.

"You can't take the blame for that. It belongs to both of us," he said. "And from this moment on, we're not looking back. We're looking forward. Agreed?"

She looked into his brilliant eyes and saw the possibilities. "Agreed," she whispered softly. Tonight wasn't a panacea, but it was a magnificent start.

"What on earth do you suppose my parents were thinking?" Dinah fretted as she and Cord sat in the kitchen eating the fried chicken, collard greens and cornbread that Maybelle had left for them. Everything was considerably colder than it had been intended to be, because it had taken them a long time to slip out of her bed once they'd known for certain they were alone in the house.

"That they wanted to do something outrageous," Cord said.

"But why? My parents aren't the type to do outrageous things."

"Maybe they are. How well do children ever really know their parents? Few of us ever see them as people. We put them into the parent niche and expect them to stay there, for better or worse."

She regarded him curiously. "In your case it was for the worse, wasn't it?"

His gaze shut down. "Bobby and I did okay."

"But it must have been so awful to have kids like me treating you as if you weren't good enough to associate with us and then to have a lousy support system at home, too," she said. "I'm sorry."

"I've been all grown up for a long time now. I survived. I don't need you deciding to pity me at this late date."

She was about to apologize for that, too, but she realized he wouldn't appreciate it. Better to let the subject drop. However miserable Cord's childhood had been, he hadn't let it hold him back.

In the silence that fell, she went back to thinking about her parents. "Where do you suppose they went? I can't imagine they're having dinner in some biker bar, though, come to think of it my mother was certainly dressed for it. I have the strangest feeling those clothes she had on came out of my closet with the possible exception of the T-shirt. I have no clue where that came from."

She glanced at Cord and thought she detected a vaguely guilty expression on his face. "You know something, don't you?" she accused.

He grinned. "Just a little," he admitted.

"Spill it now."

He shook his head. "I'm not sure I should."

"Did anyone specifically ask you to keep it a secret?"

"No."

"Then you won't be breaking any confidences by telling me," she concluded triumphantly. "Spill it."

He leaned back in his chair and gave her a long, considering look. "What are you going to do with the information if I give it to you?"

"Well, assuming their lives aren't in imminent danger, I'm not going to do anything."

"Then this is nothing more than curiosity?" he asked, amusement dancing in his eyes.

"Curiosity, concern, whatever. Tell me." She frowned

as another thought occurred to her. "And while you're at it, tell me why you know about this and I don't."

"I know because your father needed my help."

Now there was a stunning twist. Dinah couldn't imagine her father turning to Cord for assistance with anything. "Did he want you to build something?" she asked, mystified.

Cord laughed. "No, nothing like that. He wanted to surprise your mother."

"I'd say the motorcycle would do that," Dinah said wryly.

"Only part of the package," Cord assured her. "And to be honest, he didn't mention that part to me."

"Then what did he tell you?"

"He wanted to have dinner set up for her on the veranda at Covington Plantation. I took care of getting everything in place before I left there to pick you up."

"He planned a special meal just for the two of them?" Dinah asked, completely stunned at the magnificence of the gesture. It was perfect. She couldn't think of a thing that would please her mother more. Amazingly, she'd never thought of her father having a romantic bone in his body, but it was apparent now that he did.

Cord nodded. "Did it up right, too. Candles, flowers, champagne. He had a cooler filled with food sent over from the same restaurant they went to on their wedding night."

Dinah set down her fork and stared at Cord in amazement. "But why? It's not their anniversary."

Cord's lips twitched. "Some folks think it's acceptable to do impulsive, romantic things any old time," he said. "Take us, for instance. We seem to be making a habit of coming home to your place or mine and climbing into bed in the middle of the afternoon."

Dinah winced. "I'm going to get you fired for that one of these days, aren't I?"

"I'm not worried," he said. "I am curious, though. How long do you expect to keep up that particular tradition?"

She studied his expression, but she couldn't read anything into it. "What are you asking?"

"Just wondering when you're going to get bored and go wandering off in search of more excitement," he said in such a casual tone that there was no mistaking that the question was anything but casual.

Dinah knew she had to phrase her response very carefully. They'd never been about permanence. Surely Cord understood that. He wasn't any more interested in commitment than she was. And once she'd accepted that the quick fix of marrying Bobby was no longer an option, she'd somehow assumed that she'd eventually get her act together and move on. The progress she'd made today with Warren had reassured her that it wouldn't be too much longer before she'd be able to take off and resume her old life, or at least some variation of it.

"You've gone awful quiet all of a sudden," Cord said. "Should I read anything into that?"

"I don't know what to say."

"In other words, you are gonna pack up and leave once the shrink pronounces you cured of whatever's been on your mind," he concluded flatly, his eyes suddenly dull.

"Journalism is my career," she said, knowing that

she'd hurt him somehow, but unable to be anything less than honest.

"Last I heard we had a few television stations right here in Charleston," he commented. "I'm pretty sure those folks who cover the news around here and tell us about the rain showers on the way aren't doing it from halfway around the world."

"I cover wars," she said fiercely, trying to make him understand.

"Which came damn close to destroying you," he retorted, real heat in his voice. "And that's what you want to go back to doing? Putting your life and your sanity on the line?"

"It's what I do," she said, helpless to explain it in any other way.

Cord nodded, his face devoid of expression. "Then I guess that says it all." He tossed aside his napkin and stood up. "Good night, Dinah."

She chased after him and caught his elbow. "Cord, don't be angry with me."

He met her gaze. "I'm not angry," he told her.

"Disappointed, then," she said. "You should be glad. If it weren't for you, I might never be ready to go back. You helped me a lot."

He leveled an icy look into her eyes that made her wince.

"Does my heart good to know that sleeping with me was real useful," he said, his voice dripping sarcasm. "I'll be sure to put that on my resume with the next woman who comes along. Maybe even add it to my business cards: Cord Beaufort, Cures What Ails You. Has a real nice ring to it, don't you think?"

He brushed past her and walked out of the house,

leaving the door standing wide open behind him. She
might have felt better if he'd slammed it. There would
have been some passion in that. Instead, she had the
feeling that he was just giving up and walking away
without a backward glance.

Well, what the hell did you expect? The question immediately popped into her head and reverberated there,
awaiting an answer she didn't seem to have. What had
she expected?

She realized then that, despite all the evidence she'd
seen to the contrary, some part of her had continued to
think of Cord as the same insubstantial, no-account
guy who could be easily dismissed when the time came.
She hadn't given one single thought to how her actions
might affect him. She'd simply been grateful for the
time and attention and the sex that he'd willingly shared
with her.

Not until she'd watched him walk out that door had
she realized how much she was going to lose if he
walked out of her life for good. Or if she walked out of
his.

Suddenly desperate to make sense of it, she instinctively picked up the phone and called Maggie.

"Can you come over?" she asked without preamble.
"Or could I come there?"

"You had a fight with Cord," Maggie guessed at
once.

"How on earth did you know that?" Dinah asked.

"It was bound to happen."

"Why was it bound to happen?"

"Because you're you and Cord is, well, Cord."

"Which makes absolutely no sense," Dinah retorted.

"I have a bottle of Pinot Grigio open. Maybe by the

time we finish it, I can make you understand," Maggie said.

"I'll be there in ten minutes."

"Make it five. I have a date on his way, so I don't have all night and this conversation could take a while."

Instantly guilty, Dinah said, "Maybe I should wait till tomorrow. I don't want to intrude on your date."

"You won't," Maggie said with a laugh. "Believe me, I am kicking you out the instant he shows up. It's taken him too darn long to getting to asking me out."

"You're going out with Warren Blake," Dinah guessed. "I knew it. I knew he wanted to ask you out."

"You're wasting time. Get over here now," Maggie said, ignoring Dinah's guesswork.

"I'm on my way."

If Dinah had been startled by the news of Maggie's big date, she was even more stunned when she walked in and found Cord sitting on Maggie's sofa.

"You!" she said, her temper stirring. "You didn't waste any time finding someone new, did you?"

He scowled at her. "What the hell are you talking about?"

Maggie rolled her eyes. "Heaven save me from people who don't communicate," she muttered. "Okay, here's the deal. I have a date rolling up here in about fifteen minutes." She glowered at Dinah. "It is not Cordell. However, you two obviously need to talk, so I am going to wait for my date outside. Do not leave this room until you've settled things. Lock the door on your way out."

"There's nothing more for us to say to each other," Cord said, already on his feet. "Dinah's made up her mind to go back overseas."

Maggie gave him a shove in the middle of his chest that had him sitting right back down. Dinah was impressed by her gumption, if not wildly enthusiastic about her friend's determination to force this confrontation.

"Then convince her to stay," Maggie told him. She whirled on Dinah. "And you listen for a change, instead of just announcing the way things are going to be. I expect a full report from both of you first thing in the morning and I'd better like what I hear."

Dinah grinned despite the awkwardness of the situation. "Who died and left you in charge?"

"Since you both came over here for advice, I assume you wanted to hear it," Maggie said. "Talk. That's my advice. Good night."

She was gone before either of them could recover enough to argue.

Dinah slanted a look in Cord's direction. His mulish expression had eased. In fact, it almost looked as if he was fighting a grin.

"She's something, isn't she?" Dinah said.

"Pushy," Cord said succinctly, then met her gaze. "She has a point. I probably shouldn't have gotten all bent out of shape just because you were being honest back at your place. I think I already knew what you were going to say. I just wasn't ready to hear it, after all."

"And I'm sorry if I made it seem that you're not important to me, because you are," she said, leaning forward to meet his gaze. "You do matter to me, Cord. I don't think I realized how much until you walked out. That's why I called Maggie."

"Might have made more sense to call me," he commented.

"I didn't say I was up to being rational yet."

"So, now what?" he asked.

"Can we do the one day at a time thing?" she asked wistfully. "I wish I could offer you something concrete about what the future holds, Cordell, but I honestly don't have a clue."

"Then you're not slamming the door on staying here?" he asked, his gaze searching hers.

She thought about how readily she'd dismissed that possibility earlier, but she wasn't nearly as confident of her opinion now that she'd discovered just how much Cord mattered. Evidently she was going to have to figure him into the equation.

"I'll leave it open for now," she said at last.

"That's all I'm asking."

But they both knew he was asking for much more. Even without the words, he was asking for a commitment Dinah wasn't sure she would ever be able to give him. She just knew she owed it to both of them to think about a future with him very much in it.

20

The next morning Cord was besieged with anxious subcontractors and the almost impossible task of trying to coordinate their schedules when Maggie showed up at Covington. He was hardly overjoyed to see her. While he and Dinah had come to an understanding of sorts the night before, it still wasn't an optimum solution from his point of view. He doubted he could work up much enthusiasm for Maggie's benefit.

"Don't you give me that go-away-I'm-busy look," she warned. "I'm in no mood for it. I was busy last night, but it didn't stop you or Dinah from coming over to my place so I could solve your problems."

"Point taken," he agreed reluctantly. "So, what brings you by here? I know you didn't just happen to be in the neighborhood."

"As if you didn't know," she said, rolling her eyes. "I came for answers. I told you I would."

"So you did. Sorry, though. I'm fresh out."

"The two of you didn't work things out?" she asked, her disappointment plain.

"We're not furious with each other anymore," he

said, putting the best possible spin on things. "Is that good enough to satisfy you?"

"No, it's not even close to good enough," she said flatly. "What is wrong with you?"

"Me?" he replied indignantly. "I'm not the problem. Dinah's the one who's all set to bail."

Maggie wandered over to the refrigerator, found herself a can of soda, popped the top and took a sip, her expression thoughtful. When she turned back, she asked, "Have you told her not to go?"

"In so many words, yes," he said.

She frowned at him. "What does that mean? In so many words? Sounds to me like you danced around it to save your pride."

"Possible," Cord admitted.

"Oh, for heaven's sake," she said impatiently, "just ask the woman to marry you and put us all out of our misery."

Cord's heart began to pound. He was pretty sure the mention of the M-word was the cause. "What?" he asked, praying he'd somehow misunderstood. The last thing he needed was Maggie pushing him and Dinah down the aisle before they were ready.

"You heard me," Maggie said, clearly not intending to cut him any slack. "It's going to take a marriage proposal to keep Dinah here. You love her. She loves you. I don't see the problem."

"Who said I loved her?" he demanded, then sighed at her unblinking stare. "Okay, I love her. Always have. But just like before, I don't know what the hell to do about it."

"For starters, you tell her," Maggie said with exaggerated patience. "You use the actual words, I-LOVE-YOU. Get it?"

It was as if she were trying to explain something to a two-year-old, an attitude Cord might have resented if he weren't hanging on every word. He waved her on. "Keep going."

"She's a reporter, not a mind reader. She works with evidence and facts, not conjecture." She shrugged. "Or so they say."

Cord grinned. "I thought every time we crawled into bed, the evidence was pretty clear."

Maggie groaned. "What is it with men and sex? They want us to believe that it and love are two entirely separate things, something that goes entirely against the grain with women. Then when we reluctantly take them at their word, they go and change the rules and we're supposed to guess when that happens."

"Another valid point," he conceded grudgingly. "You're just full of them this morning. Does dating a shrink make you all-wise?"

"It has nothing to do with Warren. I've always been wise, which is one of the reasons you came to see me last night," she suggested. "You admire my clear thinking."

"Actually I came for a sympathetic shoulder to cry on," he said.

She frowned at that. "Nonsense!"

He laughed. "I could have sworn that was it. The shoulder, nothing else."

"Then all the rest is just a bonus. You can thank me later." She looked him over intently. "You know, if you really wanted to stack the odds in your favor, you wouldn't leave things to chance."

"Meaning what?"

"There are all those Charleston TV stations you

talked about last night. Surely you know someone at one of them," she said casually. "Just an idea."

Before he could contemplate anything Maggie was gone, probably to complete the second half of her morning's mission. He didn't envy Dinah one bit.

As he tried to solve the half-dozen scheduling issues with his subs, Maggie's suggestion remained in the back of his mind. He had had quite a few contacts with one of the stations in town and it just so happened to be an affiliate of Dinah's old network. In fact one of the reporters there had been itching to do a feature on the work at Covington. Normally agreeing to that would be up to Mrs. Davis, but Cord thought he could get away with dropping by to see the man and offering him an exclusive. If Mrs. Davis had a fit, he could always tell her the real reason he'd done it…to get Dinah through the doors of a television studio again without her realizing what he was up to.

Unfortunately, subtlety wasn't his strong suit and that's what the situation required. He was smart enough to recognize that if Dinah ever realized that he was trying to manipulate things behind the scenes, his plan would blow right up in his face. Oh, well, he'd just add it to the potentially explosive items stacked between them, including his meddling between her and Bobby.

After all, what was life without a few risks, he concluded. That was certainly a philosophy Dinah could appreciate.

"How was your date with Warren?" Dinah asked the minute Maggie arrived at the house. She was hoping to forestall all the questions Maggie obviously had about Dinah's efforts at detente with Cord.

"Challenging," Maggie responded. "He kept asking me how things made me feel. I felt like I was on the couch in his office, instead of sitting beside him on the one in his living room."

Dinah grinned. "Yeah, I imagine the whole shrink thing doesn't translate all that well into everyday conversation."

Maggie shrugged. "Of course, it does tend to make him very attentive. I've never had a man actually listen to what I'm saying the way Warren does. Unfortunately, just when I'd start thinking it was kind of sexy, I had this odd vision of a bill for his time turning up in tomorrow's mail. It took the edge off the romance."

"Did you try turning the tables on him and asking him questions?" Dinah asked.

"Oh, yes. It made him damned uncomfortable." Maggie chuckled. "Come to think of it, that was the best part of the evening, seeing Mr. Calm, Cool and Collected get all rattled. In fact, that was so much fun, I kissed him to see what effect that would have."

Dinah grinned. "And?"

"Good kiss," Maggie assessed. "Right up there with the best, all slow and soft and sweet. You know, the kind that you want to go on forever, instead of the kind that makes you want to jump straight into the sack." Her cheeks turned pink. "Of course, he was pretty good at those kind, too."

"You didn't!"

"Didn't what?" Maggie asked, looking flustered. "Go to bed with him? No, I did not, though it wouldn't be any of your business if I had."

"I don't know. I feel kind of responsible," Dinah said, regarding her friend thoughtfully. "I did give the man a nudge in your direction. I'd hate to think you completely overwhelmed him on the first date."

Maggie laughed. "Trust me, Warren was not overwhelmed. Once he got the hang of things, he held his own quite nicely."

"Really? How fascinating. Another date in the works?"

"Tonight, as a matter of fact." Maggie frowned at her. "And while all that sharing was perfectly lovely, now it's your turn. I want your take on the whole Cord situation."

"We resolved things," Dinah said carefully, even though she knew that Maggie would never be satisfied with such a bland response.

"Resolved things how? So you're comfortable with them?"

"Well, yes."

"And Cord?"

"I guess he's okay. He agreed we'd just keep things light and casual for now."

"You guess he's okay," Maggie muttered. "What is wrong with you? Are you or are you not in love with him?"

"I can't be," Dinah said.

Maggie gave her a look that would have intimidated anyone who hadn't known her since grade school as Dinah had. "And precisely why is that?" she demanded.

"Because he's here and my life isn't," Dinah said succinctly.

"Let me get this straight," Maggie said in a way that suggested she understood everything perfectly, but didn't like what she was hearing. "You could have settled down here with Bobby, whom you haven't seen in ten years and with whom you have no idea if you could ever really feel anything more than friendship, but you can't make the same commitment to Cord, who obviously makes your toes curl. Do I have that right?"

"Pretty much," Dinah said, realizing the admission made her sound idiotic.

"Gee, that must have made Cord's heart go pitter-pat. I'm not entirely surprised he walked out on you."

"But we worked it out," Dinah protested.

"No, you didn't. I don't hear any hint of compromise. You got your way. That is not working it out, Dinah. That's you being selfish, again." She shook her head. "I wish to hell I'd told him to give up on you and find someone who appreciates him."

"I do appreciate him," Dinah said defensively. "And why are you in the middle of this, anyway?" she added resentfully.

"Because you put me there. Now tell me just how you show this appreciation you claim to feel," Maggie demanded, her tone scathing. "If you really appreciated him, you wouldn't treat him like this, not knowing that the man's been crazy about you forever. You'd end it here and now before he really gets hurt."

Dinah saw her point, but she knew she couldn't do that. It would kill her to cut Cord out of her life right now. She needed him and the lifeline he'd tossed to her.

But if all he represented was a lifeline, then why was she still clinging to it so hard, now that she finally had her head above water?

When the phone rang, she was relieved to have the momentary distraction, until she heard Cord's voice.

"You free later today?" he asked.

"I can be. Why?"

"I thought maybe we could take a drive down to St. Helena Island, take a walk on the beach and have dinner there. You haven't had a good Gullah meal since you've been back, have you?"

Her mouth watered at the prospect of the spicy food with its African-American roots, but thinking about what Maggie had been saying not two minutes before, she hesitated. "Cord, I don't know. Maybe that's not such a good idea."

"Why not?"

"With everything so up in the air, maybe it would be best if we didn't spend so much time together."

"I'm confused. I thought we settled that last night. We're taking this one day at a time, right? I'm talking about supper tonight, Dinah, not breakfast, lunch and dinner for the rest of our lives." When she didn't respond immediately, he sighed. "I get it. Maggie's there."

"Exactly."

"What's she been telling you?"

"I really couldn't say."

"Well, if it has something to do with you giving me space till you figure out what you want, forget it. I'm not worried, Dinah. You shouldn't be either. I'm a grown man. I know the score. I might not much like it, but I can live with it."

She heard the certainty in his voice, but when she glanced up, there was no mistaking the genuine concern in Maggie's eyes. "Maybe another night," she equivocated.

"Has to be tonight," Cord countered. "The rest of my week's a mess."

Dinah closed her eyes so she wouldn't have to see

the disapproval on Maggie's face. "Okay, sure," she said, giving in. "What time?"

"Will four o'clock suit you?"

"I'll be ready." She hung up the phone slowly, then turned to her friend. "Go ahead, say it. I have the will-power of a gnat."

To her surprise, Maggie grinned. "Actually you have the willpower and stubbornness of a mule, which should tell you something."

"What?" Dinah asked blankly.

"If you can't make yourself stay away from Cord for one single evening, maybe you ought to think about spending every evening with him for the rest of your life. There are worse things than spending your life with a man who makes your toes curl."

Dinah felt shock steal over her. "You think I should marry him?"

Maggie held up her hands. "Not for me to say. I'm just suggesting you add up the evidence and see where it takes you."

"What evidence?"

"I think I'll let you figure that out. You're pretty good at researching the things that matter to you." She shrugged. "At least you used to be. Lately, I'm not so sure."

Dinah frowned. "Is that some sort of crack about me staying away from journalism?"

"I'm sure you can figure that out, too," Maggie said, then added cheerfully, "And now that my work here is done, I have a life of my own that could use a little at-tention. I'm going to buy something sexy." She re-garded Dinah innocently. "Want to come?"

Dinah considered saying a prim and proper no, but

why should she? Rendering Cord speechless had proven to have a number of perfectly fascinating benefits.

"Black lace or red?" she inquired as she grabbed her purse.

"Red," Maggie said at once. "Just be sure you know how to resuscitate the man."

"What about you?" Dinah asked curiously.

"Me, I'm going for something demure and white," Maggie said. "I think I need to work up to things slowly with Warren."

"I don't know. The shock factor could work in your favor," Dinah said. "While he's getting his tongue untangled, you could move in for the kill."

Maggie laughed and linked her arm through Dinah's. "We really need to work on your idea of romance. I think it could use just the teensiest bit of tweaking."

"More than likely," she admitted.

Maybe her own mother could give her some advice. Dorothy still wasn't home from her hot-and-heavy date the night before. Dinah would have panicked when she'd discovered the empty place at the breakfast table earlier if Maybelle hadn't reported that her mother and father had taken an unexpected trip. Given the gleam in Maybelle's eyes, she was every bit as aware as Dinah was that it was definitely not a sudden business trip.

Once Cord had Dinah in the car, which had been no easy task thanks to Maggie's presence when he'd called to arrange things, he bypassed the interstate and headed downtown instead.

"Where are you going?" she asked, regarding him

suspiciously. "I thought we were going down to Beaufort, then out to St. Helena Island."

"We are. I just have to make a stop first. It won't take long."

She studied him with a frown. "You're up to something. What is it?"

"What makes you say that?"

"Because it doesn't make any sense that you'd make such a big deal about going to have Gullah food, then make a stop along the way. Why didn't you take care of whatever business you have before you picked me up?"

"Because this is on the way," he said mildly. "Why are you making such a big deal out of adding five minutes to the drive?"

"Because I don't trust you," she said.

"I thought we were long past the days when you considered me untrustworthy," he scolded.

"Not entirely."

"Have you always gotten sexually involved with men you don't trust?"

"Never before," she admitted. "I seem to have made an exception for you and right this second I'm regretting it. Why won't you give me a straight answer?"

Cord laughed. "My answers have been perfectly straightforward. If you're overreacting, it must have something to do with low blood sugar. Don't you have any chocolate in that purse of yours?"

"I ran out. In fact, I ate it the last time you exasperated me."

"I'll stop at a market so you can stock up," he offered.

She merely scowled back at him, clearly not placated.

"I still think you're up to something," she declared.

Cord sighed. She might be right, but he didn't think now was the time to tell her exactly what his intentions were. She was liable to leap from the moving car. It would be a whole lot smarter to get her that chocolate first. Maybe she'd mellow out before they reached his destination.

He pulled into a gas station that had a market. "Sit tight," he ordered. "I'll be back."

He returned in less than five minutes and upended a bag filled with candy bars in her lap. "That ought to hold you."

She tore the wrapper off of a Hershey bar and broke off a chunk, then sighed with pleasure.

"Feeling better?" he inquired with undisguised amusement.

"Marginally. Talk to me again when I've finished."

At least the candy silenced her until he turned into the parking lot of one of Charleston's major television stations. Then she literally froze beside him.

"Why are we here?" she demanded, her voice like ice.

"I need to drop off some papers with the news director. They're putting together a piece on Covington Plantation. Your mother asked me to see that they had whatever they needed."

"And you need to do this on Saturday?"

"It's for a feature on the Sunday news. That's always a slow news day, right?"

She scowled. "I suppose."

As it turned out, every word of what he was saying was true. He'd had a chance to speak to Mrs. Davis and get her approval even before he'd called Dinah. Even though he was on the side of the angels on this one, he could see that Dinah wasn't buying it for a second.

Still, he intended to play this out. Maybe he could manage to entice her to walk into the building with him. Maybe not, but he needed to try.

He stepped out of the car and walked around to open her door. "You coming?" he asked, when she didn't budge.

"To help you carry a few pieces of paper inside?" she asked, her tone scathing. "I'm sure you can manage."

Cord tried another tactic. "It's hot out here. You'll roast if you sit in the car."

"I'll be fine. You won't be in there more than a couple of minutes, right?"

"Unless the news director has questions," he agreed. "He might. Then I could be tied up for a lot longer. At least wait for me in the lobby where it's air-conditioned."

"If you thought it was going to take forever, why did you insist on picking me up?" she asked with evident frustration. "Give me a break, Cord. This is some plot you and my mother hatched to get me to go inside and take a look around. It wouldn't surprise me a bit if you alerted the news director that I would be coming with you."

He had done exactly that, but even so he kept his expression neutral. "Why would I do that?"

"Because you all think there's something wrong with me not working in my chosen profession. I'm not the first person to get tired of a job."

"No," he said agreeably. "But you might be the first person who lived and breathed her job one day, then wanted no part of it the next. I'm not asking you to walk in there with me today and go to work there tomorrow. I'm asking you to come with me, take a look around, say hello to a couple of people with whom you might have a lot in common. That's it." He shrugged. "If you don't want to do it, that's fine, too. I'll be back out as soon as I wrap up this meeting."

"I don't want to do it," she said flatly.

"Okay," he said, resigned. He'd tried and failed. That didn't mean he wouldn't try again.

"But I will," she said, surprising him. "Just to prove to you that I'm not a coward."

Cord leaned down and kissed her hard. "Never thought you were," he said gently.

"Yes, you did," she retorted. "But that's okay. I suppose I haven't given you any reason to think otherwise. It's just a building and a few people. No big deal."

"Exactly."

Even so, her steps dragged as they got closer to the entrance. Cord realized that she really was terrified to step across the threshold. Maybe he was being a jerk for forcing her to do this. There was every chance in the world it could backfire. She could sink right back into that depression that had held her in its grip when she'd first arrived home. Or she could rediscover her love of television news and be on the next plane overseas, rather than seeing the value of the contribution she could make right here.

"Second thoughts?" he asked mildly.

She met his gaze and her chin rose a notch. "No," she said firmly. "Not a one." She swallowed hard. "But if I suddenly bolt for the door, I hope you won't be too embarrassed."

"You could never embarrass me," he assured her.

"Unless you decided to have your way with me on the anchor desk and the cameras caught us and broadcast it all over Charleston."

Dinah chuckled, her tension obviously easing. "Now you've gone and made it interesting."

She breezed past him and went inside.

21

Dinah's momentary flash of self-confidence waned about two seconds after she and Cord walked into the television station lobby. By the time they were escorted to the newsroom, her palms were sweating and her heart was racing. She felt as if she were on the verge of another full-fledged panic attack, something she'd been all but convinced was behind her. She hadn't had one since her breakthrough session with Warren the week before.

Overwhelmed by the oppressive sense of dread washing over her, she came to a halt the instant they stepped into the brightly lit newsroom with its maze of desks and computers and clutter. A few years ago walking into a room that was a beehive of activity in preparation for the evening newscast would have been second nature to her. Even on weekends, newsrooms were busy. The stir of excitement, the ringing phones, the shouted exchanges between reporters, producers and the news director would have kicked her adrenaline right into gear. Now all it stirred was an ever deepening sense of panic and dread. She wasn't ready to go back to this, not by a long shot.

Cord stopped beside her and regarded her with concern. "You okay?"

Dinah forced a smile. "Sure," she said, barely managing to squeak out the brazen lie.

"Rick's office is right over there," the perky young intern who'd been sent to escort them said. "I'll let him know you're here. He'll be with you as soon as he's free. You can wait here." She gestured toward a couple of empty chairs in front of computers that had the station logo flashing as a screensaver.

"Thanks," Cord said.

The young girl looked at Dinah curiously. Then her expression brightened. "Oh my gosh, I recognize you. You're Dinah Davis. You're a legend around here. But didn't I hear a few months back that you…" Her voice trailed off in embarrassment. "Sorry."

"It's okay," Dinah reassured her, her curiosity piqued. "What did you hear?"

The girl looked as if she'd rather go on *Fear Factor* and eat snails than give Dinah an honest answer. She finally swallowed hard and said, "Well, that you'd been fired. That you were all washed up. Is that why you're here?" she asked disingenuously. "Are you here to talk to Rick about a job?"

Dinah immediately felt sick to her stomach. So that's what the rumor mill was saying about her sudden disappearance from the network. Sadly, it was too darn close to the truth. She might have made the decision to go, but only because she'd been backed into a corner.

"No," she said quietly. "I'm not here about a job. Mr. Beaufort's the one who's here to see Rick. I'm just tagging along."

"Oh," the girl said, obviously flustered. "Sorry. I

don't care what happened. It would be a real coup to get someone like you here. I'll bet there are a million things you could teach us. You were…" She blushed furiously and corrected herself, "You *are,* like, an idol to a lot of us."

Sure, Dinah thought. She could teach them a lot, like how to drive a career straight off a cliff. She managed to smile. "Thanks. That's very sweet."

The intern finally looked as if she realized that she'd said too much on a very touchy subject. Backing away, she murmured again, "I'll let Rick know you're waiting."

Suddenly Dinah's knees felt weak. She sank down on one of the empty chairs. She realized her hands were shaking, as well. His expression filled with compassion, Cord hunkered down in front of her and took her hands in his, chafing them between his to get the circulation going.

"The first time's always the scariest," he said quietly.

"I don't know what you're talking about," she said stiffly. Her pride wouldn't let her admit the truth about her dismay even now, even to this man who'd been so supportive whenever she'd needed him to be. For a woman who'd faced death too damn often, how could a benign little newsroom in Charleston throw her for such a loop? It was absurd.

Because Cord knew her so well, he grinned, clearly not intending to let her get away with such a blatant lie. "Sure you do. Remember way back to the first time you fell off a bike? Remember how terrified you were to get back on? Or even the first time you had to walk back into a classroom after you'd stood up in front and had the teacher rip apart a report you'd worked on?"

Oddly enough, she did. What surprised Dinah was that Cord understood that kind of emotion. She'd always assumed his ego was powerful enough to withstand anything. "Did you ever feel like that?" she asked.

"All the time," he admitted. "I knew a lot of people at school were expecting me to fail, maybe even hoping I would. If someone like you messed up, it was no big deal. When I did, I knew that there was going to be someone who'd say I didn't deserve to be there. Every single day something happened that made me want to take off and never come back."

"But you never did," she said, remembering. "You had perfect attendance. You even got an award for it the year you graduated. Bobby was so proud of you." Now that she knew more of the story, she was more in awe of that record than she had been at the time, but Bobby had evidently understood even then what it had taken Cord just to show up day after day and struggle to rise above all the contradictory expectations.

"Because he knew how hard it was for me," Cord confirmed. "I wasn't the brightest kid in that school, but I'll bet I worked the hardest. I was determined not to blow that opportunity and if I had to face down every kid in the school every single day, it was a small price to pay."

"That must have taken amazing courage," she said, her admiration for him growing.

"Not courage, just plain old grit and determination," he said. "I didn't want to let down whoever had taken a chance on me. I wanted them to know they'd done the right thing."

"Grit and determination are the same as courage," Dinah said. "I think that's what kept me going on all those tough assignments, grit and the determination not to fail." She sighed wearily. "But in the end, I did."

"No, you didn't," Cord insisted. He looked away for an instant, then drew in a deep breath and met her gaze. "I never in a million years thought I'd ever say this, but you'll only fail if you want to go back and don't."

Totally unprepared for his words, she stared at him with shock. "You want me to leave and go back?"

"No," he said fiercely. "It's the last thing I want. But I do want you to do whatever you need to do to make peace with things. If that means going back over there, for however long it takes, then I'll support your decision a hundred percent."

She looked deep into his eyes. "If I did go—and I'm not saying I want to or that I will—would you wait for me to come back?" She wasn't sure why it was so important to her to know the answer to that, but it was. "I know I don't have any right to ask such a thing."

He touched a hand to her cheek. "Sugar, I don't have any choice. You're a part of me, no matter where you are. Don't you get that by now?"

Dinah felt her heart swell. That he would say such a thing, that he would give her that freedom once more proved what a remarkable man Cord had become. If only the future would lay itself out for her with such unwavering clarity.

The morning after the visit to the TV station, Cord could have kicked himself from Charleston to Atlanta for virtually pushing Dinah back onto the network fast track. Not that he'd had much choice in the matter. He'd seen that when he'd looked into her haunted eyes. He'd known instinctively that he had to encourage her to do whatever it took to wipe away the last traces of fear and put the sparkle back. Until she was whole, she couldn't possibly give him all he wanted from her.

Whatever had sent her fleeing back to Charleston had taken away something important. He wished she would share all that with him, but maybe he didn't need to know. Maybe the only thing that really mattered was that she get it back.

By the time they finally spent a few minutes with news director Rick Morgan, Cord already considered the visit to the station to have been a costly mistake. Instead of enticing Dinah to stay, it had paved the way right back toward her old job. Not that she'd said a single word during that meeting with Rick or later over dinner about going back to the network, but Cord saw the handwriting on the wall. Eventually she was going to see it, too.

"How did your trip to the television station pan out?" Dorothy Davis asked him, catching him by surprise with her sudden appearance.

Cord looked up from yet another printout of final cost projections and met her concerned gaze. "It backfired," he said succinctly. "I have a feeling Dinah's going to try to get her job back at the network."

"Oh, Cord, you can't be serious," Mrs. Davis said, clearly dismayed. "How on earth did that happen? I thought this was a way to show her that she could stay right here and still be a top-notch reporter."

"That was the plan," Cord agreed. "But there was a look in her eyes." He hesitated. "I'm not sure I can explain it. I just knew that if I didn't encourage her to go back if that's what she feels she needs to do, we'd both wind up regretting it."

"And you think she will go back?"

"I'm almost certain of it," Cord admitted. "I'm sorry. I really made a mess of things."

To his amazement, Mrs. Davis crossed the room and gave him a fierce hug. "Don't you dare say that. What more could I want for Dinah than a man who loves her enough to let her go?" She gave him a thoughtful look. "And it's not the first time, is it? You stayed away for your brother's sake once, too, didn't you?"

Cord shrugged, uncomfortable with her insight.

"You must love her very much," she concluded.

"Either that or I'm a fool," he said.

"It's never foolish to love someone unselfishly," she scolded. "I think I'm discovering that for myself for the first time."

He regarded her with amusement. "Then you and Mr. Davis had a good time on your date the other night?"

She actually blushed. "We had an amazing time."

"You almost gave Dinah heart failure," he noted. "The motorcycle was a bit unorthodox for you and her father. She was sure you were both riding off to certain death."

"Well, she'll just have to get over that. That Harley was magnificent. Did Marshall tell you he bought it?"

Cord laughed at the excited gleam in her eyes. "Is that so? Is he getting you one, as well?"

She shook her head. "That would defeat the purpose, don't you think?"

"Which purpose is that?" Cord asked innocently, fighting to contain a smile.

"Me hanging onto my husband for dear life," she said. "It's quite exciting. Perhaps Marshall will loan it to you and Dinah some evening when we're not using it."

"You plan on using it a lot?"

"Every chance we get."

"It's going to cause quite a stir next time you arrive at a charity ball," he observed.

She laughed, suddenly looking years younger. "That might be one of the nights we loan it to you. Some of those old stick-in-the-muds would probably keel right over dead if we rode up on a motorcycle and we can't have that, at least not until we get the charities into their wills."

"You know what, Mrs. Davis. I hope that Dinah and I get the chance and have the good sense to shake things up when we're your age."

"Something tells me you will," she said, giving his hand a pat. "I believe I know my daughter reasonably well. Dinah's smart enough not to let a man like you get away."

Cord wished he were half as certain, but her encouragement did push him to give Dinah a call and make plans for her to join him at his place. If she was eventually going to leave, then he didn't want a single night to pass without her being in his arms.

"If you're going to keep luring me out here, I'm going to have to leave an extra toothbrush and some clothes," Dinah told Cord that night. "I can't keep wandering around the house in one of your shirts and going home in the morning in the same clothes I wore the night before. Maybelle is giving me very disapproving looks."

"And your folks? What kind of looks are they giving you?"

Dinah frowned, worry creasing her brow. "They're not home. I'm still trying to figure out if they're getting out of the house at the crack of dawn these days or if they're sneaking around and staying in hotel rooms."

"Would you disapprove if they were?"

"Disapprove? Why on earth would I? It's just odd, that's all. I could have sworn when I first got home that they were on the brink of a divorce."

"I don't think you need to worry about that now," Cord said.

Dinah scowled at the comment. "What do you know that I don't?"

"Nothing really. I spend a lot of time with your mother. She seems awfully happy lately."

"Yes, she does, doesn't she?" Dinah said. "What on earth do you suppose changed?"

"My guess is that motorcycle played a big part in it." He gave Dinah a speculative look. "She offered to loan it to us, you know."

"She did?" A horrifying thought occurred to her. "Wait a second. Did my father actually buy it?"

"That's what she told me."

Dinah shook her head, more bemused than ever. "I thought he must have borrowed it or rented it. What's next? A plane?"

"You never know."

"Oh, bite your tongue. I was kidding."

"Hey, they're just living life to the fullest," Cord countered. "There's nothing wrong with that."

"They're taking crazy risks," Dinah retorted.

Cord's expression sobered. "And you don't get that?"

She returned his gaze for the longest time, then sighed. "Yes, I suppose I do."

"Now then, we've spent enough time talking about your folks. Come with me," he said. "It's a clear night and I believe I detected a breeze earlier. I have a yen to spend an hour or two out there in that hammock looking at the stars."

Dinah grinned at him. "Nothing risky about that."

"Oh, I think I can find a way to make it downright dangerous, sugar."

She laughed as he scooped her up and headed for the door. "Yes, I imagine you can," she told him, her face nestled in the crook of his neck. "You have a real talent for it, in fact."

Cord had just set a plate of scrambled eggs down in front of Dinah when the kitchen door burst open. To his shock, Rianna charged in. When the woman got herself all worked up, he could almost see what Bobby saw in her. Normally she was way too accommodating for his taste.

"Cordell, whatever it is you're up to, it has to stop," Rianna declared, her hands perched on her full hips, her eyes flashing fire. Only when she caught sight of Dinah did she falter a bit. "Sorry. I didn't realize you had company."

Cord debated the wisdom of introducing the two women, but before he could decide whether rudeness or discretion made the most sense, Dinah held out her hand.

"I'm Dinah."

"Rianna," Bobby's fiancée announced. "Don't I know you from somewhere? You look awfully familiar."

The scene was spinning out of control right in front

of Cord's eyes. If Rianna figured out who Dinah was and spilled the beans to Bobby, his life was going straight to hell. He had to get Rianna out of here before she put any of this together.

He latched onto her arm and spun her around, aiming her straight back out the door. "Let's not bore Dinah with whatever's on your mind," he said hurriedly. "It's a family matter. We can settle it outside."

Reminded of her purpose in coming, Rianna didn't argue. When they were beside her car, she regarded him with a perplexed expression. "I swear I know that woman."

"I doubt it. It's been years since she lived around here," he said. "Now why did you come busting into my house this morning?"

"It's about your brother. Why are you keeping him over in Atlanta? We have a million and one decisions to make. I cannot possibly put this wedding together on my own. You have to do something, Cord."

He refused to be drawn into her need for drama. "I hear phones are real helpful under circumstances like these."

"I can't show him a flower arrangement on the phone," she snapped.

Cord bit back a grin. "Sweetheart, let me give you a piece of advice about my brother. Bobby doesn't give a damn about the flowers or the food or the invitations. The only thing he cares about is marrying you."

"But it's his wedding, too," she protested. "I want his input."

"Really? From what I hear, every time he's given it, you two have wound up close to calling the whole thing off," Cord reminded her. "Aren't you more likely to have the wedding of your dreams if he's not around to question every little detail?"

She frowned at that, her expression turning thoughtful. "Okay," she said slowly. "I see your point."

"Of course you do. And hasn't Bobby told you to do whatever you want?"

"Yes."

"Then do it."

She studied him worriedly. "Then this isn't some ploy of yours to keep us apart because you don't think we ought to get married?"

"Absolutely not," Cord assured her fervently. "Nothing will please me more than seeing the two of you standing in front of a minister saying your vows."

She didn't look as if she believed him entirely. "Really?"

"I'm telling you the honest truth," he insisted, thinking about how much was at stake for him. He wanted that wedding to take place almost as much as Rianna did. Unfortunately her unexpected arrival this morning might have already put it all at risk. "Could you do one little thing for me, Rianna?"

"I suppose."

"Don't mention to Bobby that you found a woman here when you came busting in this morning. I'll never hear the end of it. In return, I won't tell him you tried interfering in his work."

She considered his proposal for an awfully long time before finally acquiescing. "That seems reasonable."

"Thank you."

"But when the wedding gets closer, you are going to let him move back here, right?"

"That's a promise," Cord said. "All this stuff going on over in Atlanta should be wrapped up soon.".

"I'll hold you to that," she said as she climbed into her car.

Cord stood in the driveway and watched until she was out of sight, then turned and went back inside. Dinah was sitting exactly where he'd left her, the eggs in front of her untouched.

"Bobby's fiancée, I assume," she said, her voice tight.

Cord nodded.

"Why didn't you want her to know who I am?"

He wrestled with an answer that wouldn't get her dander up. "You know it will only complicate things if she tells Bobby you're not only home, but sleeping with me. It's liable to shake up their relationship. Bobby's likely to come back here and break my jaw." He grinned. "You wouldn't want that on your conscience, would you?"

She gave him a wry look. "I'm not entirely sure about that. Something tells me you've been playing fast and loose with a lot of things to get your way. Maybe Bobby should punch you. And maybe I was wrong to take your word that Bobby wouldn't care that I'm back. Cord, what have you been up to? Please tell me you didn't deliberately set out to keep me and Bobby apart."

He couldn't let her start down that path. Cord pulled her out of the chair and into his arms. "Are you telling me you're not satisfied with the way things have been going between us? Are you still thinking about my brother?"

"But—"

Cord kissed her until she began to relax and throw herself into the kiss. The temper in her eyes turned to a different sort of heat.

"Take me back upstairs," she suggested. "But one of these days, you and I are going to have to have a serious conversation about all of this. If I find out—"

Cord touched a finger to her lips. "Hush, sugar. All this talk is spoiling the mood and I don't have a lot of time. Sooner or later, I do have to get some work done."

All of the unasked questions died then and she gave him a provocative smile that made his pulse scramble. "I vote for later."

"That's most certainly the vote that counts," he said at once, scooping her into his arms and heading for the stairs, grateful for the narrow escape. It was a warning, though. He needed to get this whole thing out in the open with her and with Bobby before one or the other of them put the pieces together. For now, though, he grinned at Dinah. "I expect you to write me a note explaining my absence so I'll have something I can give to your mother."

Dinah laughed. "Trust me, you do not want me writing you an excuse to show my mother. Any truthful thing I'm likely to say would give her a heart attack."

"You think what we're doing is that scandalous?"

Her smile spread. "I surely am hoping, Cordell."

22

Dinah hadn't been able to shake Cord's comment a few days earlier about her going back to Afghanistan. Was that what it was going to take to finally put the past and Peter behind her? Her sessions with Warren had taken her so far, but not far enough. What Cord said made sense, that she needed to go back to the place where she'd lost everything and reclaim her sense of her own strengths.

As a practical matter, though, could she even do it? Assuming the network and Ray agreed, was she well enough to handle the stress? Only one person she could think of might have the answer to that.

As soon as her session with Warren began, she asked him. "Here's a hypothetical for you. If I did decide to go back to my old job, would I be okay?"

"What do you think?" he replied.

She frowned at him. "Do you know how annoying it is when you do that?"

"So I'm told, but that is the bottom line, Dinah." He regarded her with an unblinking gaze. "It doesn't matter what I think. The only thing that counts is what you think."

"It's still an irritating question," she said stubbornly. "Maggie thinks so, too."

He laughed. "She's mentioned it. In her case, I'm trying to break the habit. You're another story, though. You're a patient, or a client, if you prefer. I need to use the techniques that work with you." He gave her a penetrating look. "So, have you avoided the question long enough now? Are you ready to give me a straight answer or would you like to tap-dance around it by questioning my methods for a while longer?"

Dinah faltered for a second. "I actually think I've forgotten the original question."

"Blocked it out, maybe, not forgotten it," Warren said. "Do you think you're ready to go back to an overseas assignment, especially in Afghanistan? Do think you can take the pressure? The memories? You still haven't told your family or friends about Peter's death, have you?"

She shook her head. Who would she tell and what would be the point? It would only upset everyone, knowing that she'd been through something so devastating. They would be hurt when they realized that she'd deliberatcly minimized it months ago when they'd first asked her about the incident. Worse, there was nothing they could do to change any of it. They'd feel as powerless as she'd felt all these months. Why put them through that?

"Your silence should tell you something," Warren said.

"That I still haven't put it behind me," she concluded without prompting.

"Exactly."

"But maybe this isn't the right place to do that. I

mean talking about it is one thing, but that's not going to help me put it in the past. Maybe I need to do that there, where it happened. Isn't that the only way I can really face it?"

"Possibly."

She regarded him with frustration. "Can't you ever just give me some kind of direct guidance?"

He shrugged. "These aren't my decisions to make. They're yours. I can only help you find your way."

"Well, do it, then," she snapped irritably. The old Dinah had been capable of making life and death decisions in a heartbeat. Now she pondered everything for an eternity and decided on nothing. She hated her indecisiveness regarding her life, what to do about Cord, everything.

As she wrestled with self-disgust Warren simply sat there and waited, completely unintimidated by her sharp retort. Obviously he was used to patients who balked at doing the hard work themselves.

She finally gave him a helpless look. "Why can't I decide anything? I used to be so good at it."

"What was the last important decision you made?" he asked.

"To move back to Charleston."

He nodded. "And before that?"

She thought back to that awful, fateful night with Peter. "To get out of the car and run," she said slowly, stunned as the implication sank in. "And look what happened," she murmured to herself. "Peter died and I lived."

"Would anything have changed if you'd stayed with him?" Warren prodded gently.

There was only one thing that Dinah could think of. "I would have died with him."

"Quite likely. Is that what he wanted?"

She shook her head as tears streamed down her face. "No, he wanted me to run. He wanted me to live."

"Then you really don't have to go on feeling guilty, do you?"

Unable to speak, Dinah shook her head. Relief began to slip in and replace the guilt, and that was enough to show her the way toward forgiving herself. "Peter wanted me to live. He wanted to give me a chance that he knew we both couldn't have," she said again, smiling through the tears. "It was his last gift to me, wasn't it?"

"I would say so."

"Then I should stop squandering it," she said, feeling stronger and more in control than she had in months. It was time to start seizing every moment of this blessed second chance.

"You should," Warren concurred, nodding in approval. "So, what does that mean to you?"

"That I should go back to work and finish the job we started over there," she said decisively. She suffered a twinge of regret when she thought about leaving Cord behind, but he'd told her he would wait.

She'd simply have to make sure it wasn't for too long. The man wasn't really known for his patience. She smiled, thinking of just how many times he'd demonstrated that.

Then, again, if Maggie was right, he'd been waiting for Dinah for years now. How long would he be willing to wait if the reward was having her come back to him a whole person in command of her life?

Filled with a new sense of purpose, Dinah went straight home and called Ray.

"Hmm, the voice sounds vaguely familiar, but it's been a long time," he teased. "Who is this?"

"You can't have forgotten me that fast," Dinah said.

"No, you're definitely one of the unforgettable ones," he agreed. "How are you, Dinah? You sound good."

"I'm very good," she said. "I've finally pulled myself together, Ray. For the first time since Peter died, I'm almost back to my old self."

"That's great. I'm happy for you."

She drew in a deep breath before she explained the real reason for the call. She already knew what his reaction was going to be and she dreaded it. She also knew he would accede to her wishes in the end, but not without one of his trademark lectures about what was best for her. She had to make him understand that her mind was made up.

"I want to come back," she said at last. "Can you make it happen?"

His silence seemed to go on for an eternity. "Are you sure this is what you want to do, Dinah? You know how I feel about it. I'd like to see you staying right where you are, or at least someplace you'll be safe. Nothing's changed here. Every day is a life or death challenge."

"I need to go back to work," she said. "And I need to do it there. I need to prove something to you, to the network and, maybe most of all, to myself."

"You don't have to prove anything to anyone," he said with a familiar touch of impatience. "You made your mark, Dinah."

"I did," she conceded. "But at the end, I messed up. It took a lot away from my reputation in the business. I want to go back to being the best."

"And then what?"

She thought about her reply for a long time before answering. "And then when the time is right, I'll come back home," she said at last. "On top. I need to leave on top, Ray. It's important to me."

"I don't like it," he said, his voice laced with worry. "But I understand what you're saying."

"Then you'll put in a good word for me?"

"Yes," he said with undisguised reluctance. "I'll see what I can do."

"Do you think the network will go for it?"

"I'll be honest with you. It would be easier if you'd taken the leave of absence they offered, but they'll go for it. You were their superstar over here. If you come back in top form, they'll be thrilled. You are in top form, right?"

"Never better," she assured him, knowing she might be stretching the truth just a little. She wouldn't be absolutely certain of her state of mind until she'd tested it over there, but she was ready to give the assignment her all.

"Then I'll see what I can do and get back to you," he promised. "So, what happened to that backup plan of yours? I thought maybe you'd fight for the guy, steal him away from his fiancée."

Rather than feeling the once-familiar letdown over her failure to wind up with Bobby, she thought of Cord. "Actually I found something even better. I'll tell you all about him when I see you."

"If there's someone special in your life, why the hell are you coming back here?" Ray asked incredulously.

"Because I need to."

"But it's not forever, right?" he asked. "That is what

you're telling me. You're not going to get back over here and turn into that driven, single-minded woman who let ambition overrule her common sense?"

"No," she said slowly. "This isn't about ambition, Ray. It's just about regaining my self-respect. It's probably best not to tell the network that, but I owe it to you to be honest. It's not forever. A few months, a year at the outside. Can you live with that?"

"How about I ask them for a six-month commitment? Then we can all decide where to go from there? That ought to be the kind of win-win situation they can live with."

Only six months, Dinah thought, oddly dismayed. Her old contract, the one she'd walked away from, had been for three years with built-in extensions the network had always been eager to exercise. The short-term deal Ray was suggesting was proof that she really was going to have to prove herself all over again to everyone. But given the circumstances, it was a fair deal. And it would get her back to Cord that much more quickly if things worked out the way she expected them to.

"Six months sounds good," she said at last.

"Then I'll make some calls and get back to you later," Ray promised, then cautioned, "Don't set your hopes too high. There's always a chance they won't go for it, Dinah. The new VP for news is a tough guy who's trying to make his own mark and you burned some serious bridges on the way out."

"But your word will count for a lot. If you want me back, they'll listen," she said, needing to believe that.

"Up to a point," he agreed, then hesitated. "I know this one will hurt, Dinah, but if they want to see you in person, see for themselves that you're ready to work again, are you willing to fly up to New York?"

As Ray had obviously anticipated, Dinah chafed at the implication that her past performance wasn't recommendation enough. Maybe she should have called her old agent, after all, and let him handle this negotiation, but she hadn't seen the need for it. Besides, she'd burned that bridge too, when she'd quit so unceremoniously. She bit back her instinctive huffy retort and said only, "I'll do whatever I need to do, Ray. I'm anxious for this to work."

"Okay, then. We'll make it happen," he said more confidently.

"Thank you."

"Don't thank me. Who the hell would thank someone for helping them put their life on the line?"

He hung up on her before she could respond.

Cord regarded Dinah with dismay as he listened to her end of a conversation she was having on her cell phone. She'd been nervous all evening, evidently waiting for this call. Now he understood why. There was no question about what was going on. She was taking off on him. She was going back to work, back to that hellhole, just as he'd feared.

When she finally disconnected the call, she hesitated for a long time before meeting his gaze. "You heard?"

He nodded. "You're going back," he said flatly.

"Please try to understand," she said, her pleading gaze locked with his. "You said it yourself, this is something I need to do."

It made him sick when he thought about it, but he

resigned himself to the inevitability of it. "When will you go?"

"Two weeks," she told him. "They need to make some decisions, figure out who to move around, assign me a new photographer. It'll take that long to work out the details."

"I see."

She crossed the room and slipped onto his lap, then rested her hand against his cheek. "Please don't be furious with me, Cordell. This isn't about me not being happy with you."

"I know that and I'm not furious," he said, trying to pin a label on what he was feeling. "I guess I'm disappointed, but I told you I would support whatever you decided, so I can hardly take it back now."

"It's not forever," she told him. "That's the deal. It's just for six months with one possible extension. That's it."

"So, we're talking a year at the outside?"

She nodded.

"What if it gets your adrenaline pumping the way it used to?"

She looked everywhere but directly into his eyes. "I don't know," she said at last. "I don't think that's going to happen, but I can't promise it won't."

Cord bit back the desire to curse a blue streak at her naivete. The stupid job had consumed her for ten years. It had become her life. They both knew it would turn out that way again. He had lost…again.

Worse, he had no one to blame but himself this time. He'd actually been stupid enough to encourage this folly.

Still, he forced one of his trademark wicked grins.

"Then I guess we'd better make these next two weeks count." He intended to store up enough memories for a lifetime.

Time slipped away far too quickly, and Cord's level of frustration grew. As intimate as he and Dinah had become, he still had this nagging feeling that there was more to her decision to go back than she'd ever shared with him. Maybe if he understood what it was, he could make peace with her decision, but every time he'd broached the subject, she'd shut down on him. He had to wonder if all those sessions with Warren had really gotten to the bottom of things, after all.

Normally he was not a patient man. He was used to spotting problems and solving them quickly and decisively. There was one way he could do that with Dinah. All he had to do was pick up the phone and call her bosses. Hell, he might even be able to get answers on the Internet by tracking what had happened in Afghanistan around the time Dinah had come running home. Much as he wanted the answers to come from her, he was prepared to do it the hard way if he had to and risk her wrath in the bargain. At least there would be no secrets between them when she left.

Before he could act on his decision, though, Cord heard the outer door of his office slam, heard Bobby's terse greeting to their secretary, then saw his own door being wrenched open and slammed against the wall as Bobby strode in. Judging from the glint in his brother's eyes, Rianna hadn't kept her end of the bargain. Cord braced himself for the inevitable scene. If Dinah leaving was his worst nightmare, the one about to begin came in a close second.

"You and Dinah!" Bobby shouted, clearly infuriated, though there was unmistakable hurt behind his tone. "That's why I was exiled in Atlanta for weeks on end, so you could get it on with Dinah Davis?"

Cord leveled a look at this brother. He wouldn't lie to him and make it all worse. "Yes. How did you find out?"

"Does it really matter?"

"No, I suppose not, but my guess is that Rianna blabbed. I knew when she walked away after finding Dinah at the house with me that she was incapable of keeping a secret," he muttered.

"Forget about Rianna's role in this. The point is that you should have told me yourself," Bobby said. "You should have called me up weeks ago and told me Dinah was back in town."

"Probably so," Cord admitted.

"Then why the hell didn't you?"

"I decided it was a bad idea."

"Why? You know how I feel about her."

Cord raised an eyebrow at that. "Really?"

"Oh, for heaven's sake, Cord, Dinah and I will always be friends."

"And if she wanted more than that?"

Bobby's already grim expression turned downright explosive. "What the devil do you mean by that?"

"Dinah came back here specifically to see you," Cord admitted reluctantly. "She was all caught up in some ridiculous nostalgia thing. It wasn't healthy, Bobby. Not for either of you."

"Who were you to decide that? Didn't you think I had a right to know?" Bobby asked incredulously. "Dammit, Cord, what gave you the right to keep us apart? I thought you learned your lesson that last time you tried to come between us. You know how much I loved her."

"That was a long time ago," Cord said defensively. "I'm your brother. I was looking out for you back then and I'm doing the same thing now."

"Oh, really?" Bobby said skeptically. "As if I believe that."

"Okay, if you want the unvarnished truth, here it is. Maybe I was looking out for myself," Cord conceded. "Dinah turned up at the house one night and to tell you the truth, I think I went a little nuts. The woman always did twist me in knots. That night was no exception."

His straight answer promptly deflated Bobby's outrage. He sank into a chair and stared at Cord. "She came to see me and you just decided you had to have her for yourself."

"It wasn't like that, at least not entirely. In case you've forgotten, you have a fiancée. I assume you're in love with her."

Bobby regarded him incredulously. "You kept quiet and kept me away to protect Rianna? Please, Cord. The noble act doesn't suit you. This is all about you."

"Not entirely," he insisted. "I was thinking about your engagement."

"And the rest? I'm assuming it was more than your usual need to get some forbidden female into the sack, because if it wasn't, Cordell, I will personally skin you alive."

It was now or never. He had to admit the truth and let the chips fall where they may. There was no other choice.

"I'm in love with her," Cord said quietly, then gave his brother a wry grin. "Ain't that a kick in the pants?"

Bobby blinked hard. The last of his temper dissipated. "It is a surprise, I'll give you that." He studied Cord intently. "Are you sure?"

Cord laughed at his brother's doubtful expression. "As sure as a man like me with no experience in that particular arena can be."

"Well, I'll be damned."

"Since we're getting all the cards on the table, you ought to know that she came home because of that stupid backup plan the two of you agreed to years ago. She didn't just want to see you, Bobby. She wanted to marry you."

Bobby's mouth gaped. "Then she really did come home for me? That wasn't just some crazy idea you got in your head?"

Cord shook his head. "It was all about you."

"Well, I'll be damned," Bobby said again.

"How do you feel about that?" Cord asked, feeling surprisingly uncasy.

Bobby's expression turned thoughtful. "Honored, I guess."

"And? Would you have dumped Rianna and married Dinah?"

"Hell, no," Bobby said without hesitation. "Dinah was like this dream for me. I loved her, no question about it, but the handwriting was on the wall for the two of us years ago when she turned down my proposal. I knew that no matter what happened, she'd never love me the way I loved her."

Cord breathed a sigh of relief. "Good to know."

"I could have told you sooner if you'd asked me," Bobby pointed out.

"I didn't know how much the answer mattered until you walked in here just now."

Bobby's gaze narrowed. "What would you have done if I'd said I still wanted her?"

"I'd have done the right thing," Cord said. "I'd have walked away."

Bobby shook his head. "Who are you trying to kid, Cordell? No, you wouldn't. You never did like to share. This time you'd have fought me tooth and nail to keep her. I'm not blind or dumb, I know that stunt you pulled years ago wasn't entirely altruistic. You wanted her for yourself even then, but you couldn't make yourself admit it to me, to Dinah or, more than likely, even to yourself."

Cord grinned, accepting the truth of his brother's words. He'd had his fill of being noble about Dinah the last time around. "Yeah, I guess you're right. I would have fought you for her this time. Keeping the two of you as far apart as possible seemed like a good way to prevent her from coming between us."

Bobby gave him a long, considering look. "Does she feel the same way about you?"

"We're working on it," Cord admitted. "Her life's a little mixed up right now. In fact, she just announced last night that she's going back to Afghanistan for a while. Says it's something she has to do."

"And you're okay with that?" Bobby asked, obviously shocked. "You've got her now and you're letting her go?"

"To tell you the truth, I hate it, but what are my choices? It's been plain since she got here that her head's all messed up. If this is what it takes to finally make her feel good about herself again, then how can I stand in her way?"

Bobby shook his head. "The self-sacrificing crap

doesn't suit you, Cordell. Lord knows, I don't want you to make the same mistake I did by just standing by and watching her walk away. Fight for her. Make her want to stay." His expression turned thoughtful. "Maybe I should talk to her."

"Forget it," Cord said fiercely. "I do not want my baby brother interfering in my love life. I can work this out with Dinah just fine on my own."

"Yeah, I can see that," Bobby said scathingly. "You're about to watch her jet back into a war zone." He gave Cord a disgusted look. "And people say you got the brains in the family."

"What would you suggest I do?"

"Ask her to marry you," Bobby said at once. "And if you can't talk her into doing it before she leaves, then get the damn commitment in writing and set a date. If her mama's got a wedding all planned, that ought to guarantee Dinah will come back to you right on schedule. Mrs. Davis will see to that, if she has to fly over there and haul her back."

The idea held some appeal, but Cord knew he couldn't do it. Dinah had to come home when—and if—she wanted to, not because she had an obligation to show up for a ceremony. It would never work otherwise.

"Sorry. Not a good idea," he told Bobby. "But thanks for the advice."

"I think you're making a mistake," Bobby said.

"Won't be the first time," Cord retorted blithely.

Unfortunately, though, it might be the only mistake that had ever truly mattered.

23

Dinah was packing when she heard a male voice downstairs, then footsteps heading her way. Assuming it was Cord, she kept right on packing.

"If you aren't a sight for sore eyes," Bobby said from the doorway of her room.

Dinah whirled around, a smile spreading across her face. "Bobby!"

She flew into his outstretched arms. "Oh my gosh, it is so good to see you," she said, holding on tight.

She studied his once-familiar face and saw the new maturity in the lines around his eyes, the softer line of his jaw. He hadn't aged as well as his older brother, but he was a handsome devil just the same. And, oh, how she'd missed him. She hugged him harder.

"Even better to see you," he said. "I just found out you've been hanging around Charleston for weeks now."

"You didn't know? I thought Cord was going to let you know I was back. I assumed when you never called it was because of your engagement."

"Does it really matter now?" he inquired lightly.

"I think it does," she said stiffly.

"Even though you've spent all these weeks making a fool of yourself over my brother?"

She tried to work up the proper indignation over Cord's latest betrayal, but it simply didn't matter anymore. She was with the man she was meant to be with. She let the surge of anger go and grinned at Bobby. "Is that the way he tells it?"

"Is that the way it is?" he countered.

"Pretty much." She met his gaze and was happy to discover that there wasn't the slightest spark of attraction. There was just the warm comfort of being with an old and dear friend. It was nothing at all like what she felt with Cord.

"I love him," she admitted candidly.

"Then why the hell are you packing?" he asked.

"I have to go back to work."

"Have to or want to?" he demanded, sitting on the edge of her bed and regarding her with an unflinching look that insisted on an honest answer.

She faltered a second under his unyielding gaze. "Have to," she insisted. "A lot happened when I was there before and I need to face it and put it behind me once and for all."

"You can't do that here?"

"Actually I have done a lot of that here," she said. "Unless you'd seen me when I first got here, you can't possibly have any idea how much better I am. But I have to go back to take the final step."

"And what about my brother?"

"I won't be any good to him unless I do this," she said, hoping Bobby could understand. She wasn't entirely sure Cord did. He said all the right words, but the hurt was in his eyes every time she looked at him. It killed her. It reminded her that she'd once done the same thing to his brother. Cord knew from experience that she wasn't all that reliable when it came to coming home for a man.

"I do love him, Bobby. I want to come back here and be with him."

"That's something, I suppose. But I swear if it was me, you'd never walk out that door. I wouldn't take a chance on losing you."

She gave him a sad look. "But you did just that when I left ten years ago."

"I know and I regretted it. That's why it's a whole lot easier for me to see what a mistake it is. A job's just a job, Dinah. It's love that matters in this world. It's the only thing that matters. I hate to see you and my brother throwing it away."

"We're not throwing it away," she argued. "We're putting it on hold for just a little while."

"And what if it turns out to be forever?" he asked. "You won't be the first person to die over there, Dinah."

She knew better than he could possibly imagine how true that was. "I have to believe it won't turn out that way," she said simply.

"And what if you're wrong? Is it okay with you that Cord will be back here living with a broken heart because the only woman he ever loved is gone and he never had the chance to love her the way she deserved to be loved?"

Dinah thought about that long after Bobby had gone. Was it okay with her? Look how she'd felt after Peter had died. Had it been worth it knowing that he'd died doing something he loved? Had it been okay that she'd had to go on alone? Aside from the fact that he'd died practically in front of her eyes, no, none of it had been okay. If she'd had a choice, would she have wanted Peter to spend the rest of his life doing the kind of camerawork at which he excelled, knowing that he was at risk of dying every day?

It was a hard question, especially knowing how things had turned out. But, yes, she conceded reluctantly, she would have encouraged him to continue, because it was what he loved. And that was the unselfish gift Cord was giving to her.

She understood on some level how selfish it was for her to go. Goodness knows, Maggie had had enough to say lately on Dinah's tendency toward selfishness. She was leaving Cord here, knowing that every day would be filled with anguish and uncertainty and, perhaps in the end, nothing but heartache. All so she could prove something to herself, something she'd already proved a thousand times in the past. She'd been the best and brightest, the most courageous. She was worthy to be a Davis, even if she hadn't done things the traditional way. She didn't have to prove it over and over for it to go on being true.

Maybe the real courage—the real maturity—was in moving on, doing what was best for her *and* for the man she loved.

As the truth of that sank in, she began taking clothes out of her suitcase and tossing them right back into drawers. When everything was back where it belonged, when she'd called Ray and told him her decision, then listened to the genuine relief in his voice as he'd given her his blessing, she borrowed her father's new motorcycle, spent a few minutes getting the hang of handling it in the driveway, and then headed for Covington Plantation.

She had a question on her mind, maybe the most important one she'd ever asked. And for once she was the one in a hurry for an answer.

Cord was working on a scaffolding at Covington Plantation. He'd never been fond of heights, but he'd learned to scramble around on the roof as surefooted as a mountain goat and, when it was required, he could spend hours on a scaffolding like this one scraping off paint or replacing rotting boards.

It was peaceful high up off the ground and there was a breeze stirring. He could barely hear the distant sound of hammers on the other side of the house, the faint strains of a radio from inside.

The mindless task of scraping paint gave him time to think, which on a day like today wasn't the best thing in the world. The only thoughts spinning through his head had to do with Dinah leaving and, worst of all, maybe never coming back. He told himself he had to face it, but it made his stomach churn. The thought of never seeing her again, never making love to her or having babies with her left him with an aching heart. He'd sure as hell never expected to care this much about anyone, especially an uppity woman like Dinah, who'd always struck him as being way out of his league.

The roar of a motorcycle broke into his troubled thoughts. He looked into the distance and caught just a glimpse of the candy-apple-red Harley coming up the winding driveway. The damn thing was going way too fast for the condition of that bumpy roadway.

Certain it had to be Marshall Davis with a death wish or maybe even Dorothy in some maddening attempt to recapture her youth, he was about to lower the scaffolding to the ground to ream out whichever one it was when one of the ropes holding the scaffolding broke. Taken by surprise as the boards tilted precariously, Cord tried to catch onto one of the remaining ropes, but he was too late. It slid right through his hand.

Next thing he knew, he was plummeting straight toward the ground in a dive that promised to hurt like hell when he landed. Just before he hit the ground, he realized that the woman who'd arrived on the Harley was Dinah. He caught one glimpse of her stunned gaze, slammed onto the hard ground and lost consciousness.

Every damn bone in his body felt like it was broken. Cord swam back toward consciousness, dimly aware of Dinah's gut-wrenching sobs and the gentle, probing touch of her fingers, light against his pounding head.

"Don't die on me, Cordell Beaufort. Don't you dare die on me," she said, her voice thick with emotion and anguish. "Oh, God, I can't do this again. I can't lose you."

Cord recognized that there was something significant in her words, but he was too out of it to put his finger on it. He just knew she needed him to stay awake, needed him to reassure her.

"You can't get rid of me that easily," he managed to murmur, fighting the waves of pain washing through him.

Just before the world turned dark again, he felt her tears on his cheeks and heard her shouting for help. He wanted to reassure her that he wasn't dying. He wanted to console her, but the effort was beyond him.

"Hold on," she kept whispering in his ear. "I'm right here, Cord. Hold onto me. Don't leave me."

"Won't," he whispered, the one word a desperate struggle.

This time when he blacked out, he couldn't seem to fight his way back.

The waiting room was filled with anxious men from the crew out at Covington. They'd all come running at Dinah's shouts and taken charge. Someone had called the paramedics. Someone else had tracked down Bobby. They'd even called Dinah's mother. She was sitting beside Dinah right now, her complexion pale, her hand tight around Dinah's.

"He's going to be just fine," she assured Dinah. "Cord's tough."

"He certainly has a hard enough head," Bobby commented from his place on Dinah's other side.

"He was wearing a hard hat," Dinah said. "But I think it fell off before he hit the ground. He landed right at my feet. I heard something snap, looked up and he was tumbling through the air."

A sob bubbled up in her throat at the memory. "I tried to catch him, but I wasn't fast enough."

"And he would have broken half your bones, if you had," Bobby said.

"But it would have been a softer landing than him hitting the ground," she lamented. Once again she had failed someone she loved. It was the only way to look at it.

Maggie and Warren came rushing into the waiting room. Maggie regarded Bobby with surprise, then turned to Dinah. "You okay?"

"I'm not the one who fell off a scaffolding," she said.

Warren regarded her with understanding. "Want to

take a walk?" he asked. "We can bring back some coffee for everyone."

Grateful for his discretion, Dinah nodded at once. "Yes. That's a great idea."

Maggie regarded her with worry. "Need any extra help?"

Warren gave a subtle shake of his head. "We can manage. Right, Dinah?"

As soon as they were in the hallway, she stopped and leaned against the wall. "I don't think I can bear it if he dies," she told Warren.

"Have the doctors said anything about him dying?"

"They haven't said anything, period, not even to Bobby. The nurses keep promising to have news from the doctors soon, but no one's come to talk to us."

"Isn't it more important that they help Cord?" he asked reasonably.

"Yes, of course, but the waiting's so hard."

"Harder for you than the others?" he suggested.

"Of course not. Everyone in that waiting room cares about him."

"Of course they do, but they haven't had another man they love die right in front of their eyes, have they? You've been having flashbacks ever since Cord fell, haven't you? His fall and Peter's death have gotten all twisted together in your head, haven't they?"

She nodded.

"It's not the same, Dinah." He tucked a finger under her chin and forced her to face him. "And you're not to blame. You're not some sort of curse to the men you love."

She gave him a startled look. "How did you know that's what I was thinking?"

"That's why you pay me the big bucks, to figure out

what's going on in your head, sometimes even before you do."

She sighed. "I rode out there to tell him I wasn't going back to Afghanistan, that I was going to stay here with him."

Warren smiled. "Best news I've heard in a long time. I imagine he'd think so, too."

"What if…?" Her voice trailed off.

"You will get to tell him," he said confidently.

"You can't be sure of that," she retorted.

"Sure? Maybe not, but I do believe in the power of prayer and positive thinking. Now let's get that coffee and go back into the waiting area, so we'll be there when the doctors finally do come."

She slanted a look at him. "I don't suppose you have any pull around this place, do you?"

"What kind of pull?"

"Can't you go back in there and find out what's going on? Or better yet, take me."

Warren gave her hand a squeeze. "Go get the coffee. Meantime, I'll see if I can track down somebody who can give us news. Cord doesn't need you to be underfoot while they're trying to patch him up. He needs you out here thinking good thoughts."

Dinah wanted to snap that it was going to take more than that to heal his injuries. She'd said a million prayers on that short walk toward Peter, but they hadn't done a lick of good. They hadn't brought him back, hadn't made him whole. Like Humpty-Dumpty, some things were just too broken to be put back together again.

Her breath caught on another sob, so she forced herself to do as Warren had asked and go to the cafeteria for coffee. Doing something helped her to hold it together.

But when she got back to the waiting area just as the doctor was describing the extent of Cord's injuries, she heard the words *fractured skull* and then *touch-and-go*. She promptly dropped the tray of coffees she was carrying. It hit the floor with a clatter that brought all heads turning in her direction.

Bobby got to her first. "Don't you dare fall apart on me now," he told her emphatically. "Cord needs you to be strong."

Rianna appeared and slipped her hand into Bobby's, but the look she turned on Dinah was filled with compassion. There wasn't even the faintest whiff of jealousy. "Bobby's right. Cord needs you. He loves you. I could see it in his eyes the day I came to the house."

Bobby's gaze searched Dinah's face. "You ready to go in there? They want us to take turns sitting with him and talking to him. Just a few minutes at a time. Something tells me, it's your voice Cord would want to hear when he's coming around."

"But you're his brother," Dinah protested.

"I'll get my chance," Bobby assured her. "Go in there and tell him you love him. Tell him you're sticking around." His gaze met hers. "You are, aren't you?"

Dinah nodded.

"That ought to pull him out of this, knowing what he has to look forward to," Bobby told her. He squeezed her hand. "You ready? I'll walk back with you."

Dinah sought out Warren, who was sitting with her mother and with Maggie. He gave her an encouraging nod. She turned back to Bobby.

"Let's go," she said, drawing on every last ounce of courage she possessed.

"He's alive, Dinah. That's what we need to hold onto," Bobby said. "It's up to the doctors and us to keep him that way."

"Heap on a little pressure, why don't you?" she retorted uneasily.

"You don't have to do it alone, Dinah. You saw that roomful of people back there. And I'm right here beside you. We'll do it together."

She nodded slowly, feeling some of her distress ease. Having backup really did made a difference.

Cord heard Dinah's voice in his dreams. She told him over and over that she was staying in Charleston, staying with him. He kept trying to fight his way through the fog in his head to tell her they were going to have a great life together, but he couldn't seem to get all the way back.

And though he had no sense of time passing, he knew on some level that it had, because she kept growing more and more frantic as if she feared he was slipping away.

He felt her holding his hand, felt the dampness of her tears and ached for the pain he was putting her through. He had to get back to her, had to take away the anxiety.

"Dinah," he whispered, his voice raspy.

He sensed her moving, getting to her feet, leaning over him as if she couldn't quite believe that she'd heard his voice. He tried to whisper her name again, but it was beyond him. Instead, he just squeezed her hand.

"Oh, Cord," she whispered, her voice breaking. "You are coming back. Let me get the doctor."

"No."

She looked into his eyes, which he was having to fight to keep open.

"Just you. Need to look at you."

"I'm right here," she said, a smile on her lips.

"Never left?"

She shook her head. "Not for a minute."

"Leaving town?"

She touched a finger to his lips. "Sssh! No, I'm not leaving. Not ever."

Even in his semiconscious state he could see that her complexion was pale and her eyes were haunted. He'd obviously scared her. Was that why she was staying?

"Because of me?"

"Because of us," she corrected. "Now rest. I want to let the doctor know you're coming back to us. I've got to tell you, Cordell, it was a revelation to all of us that that head of yours wasn't as hard as we'd always believed."

"No jokes," he murmured. "Hurts to laugh."

Since it hurt to do anything, Cord decided to go back to sleep.

Later he was awakened by Dinah's cries, a whimper at first, then more of those gut-wrenching sobs that had brought him back to consciousness out at Covington the day of the accident. He forced himself awake and saw that she was asleep in the chair beside the bed, her head resting on the edge of the mattress.

Moving gingerly, he managed to reach out to stroke her hair, murmuring soothing words and coaxing her awake with reassurances. It took some effort, but he swung his legs over the side of the bed and pulled her into his arms.

When her eyes finally blinked open, she sucked in a deep, shuddering breath and swiped impatiently at the tears on her cheeks.

"You're awake," she said happily.

"You were crying."

"Sorry."

"Don't you dare apologize," he said. "Tell me about the dream. It didn't have anything to do with me, did it? And it's not the first time you've had it."

She shook her head.

"Tell me."

The story he'd been waiting weeks to hear finally spilled out in fits and starts in his hospital room. The nightmare she had lived—hearing a car bomb explode, finding the man she'd loved blown to bits beside a road in Afghanistan, blaming herself for all those long months because she'd lived and Peter hadn't—was even worse than Cord could have imagined.

"I was ready to die. I *wanted* to die," she told him. "But I didn't. I got another form of death sentence. I had to go on living with the memory."

"So for all these months you've been dealing with the trauma of seeing him die coupled with survivor's guilt," Cord said. "I'm so sorry. If I had put it all together long before now I could have been more help."

She regarded him with a wry expression. "How could you, when I refused to let you in? I'm sorry about that. I just couldn't talk about it. It made it all too real. But when I saw you lying on the ground out at Covington…" She shuddered. "I came unglued all over again. I thought I'd lost you, too."

"You're never going to lose me."

She met his gaze. "I've told you this before, but I'm

not sure if you heard me or understood what I was saying. I decided not to go back."

A whoop of pure joy was beyond him, which was probably just as well. Besides, he needed to know why she'd made the choice. "Because I fell?" he asked warily, knowing if that was it, he'd have to find the strength once more to encourage her to go as she'd planned.

"Well, it's true that if you're going to take these idiotic chances, someone needs to be around to look out for you, but no, that's not why I'm staying. I'm staying because I love you. I was coming to tell you when you fell. In fact, I thought you'd get the message when I showed up on the motorcycle."

The relief that flooded through him nearly overwhelmed him. Still he felt compelled to ask, "You're sure about this?"

"As sure as I need to be. I can't change the past. And you're my future, Cordell. I'm not entirely sure who I am anymore, but I do know that I don't need to be the intrepid woman who wasn't afraid to go anywhere ever again."

Even though she seemed to have made peace with her decision, Cord wasn't entirely convinced. He found the words to say a few things she needed to hear.

"Sugar, I want you to hear what I'm telling you. You don't need to be that woman because you are Dinah Davis, of the South Carolina Davises. You *are* strong. You're talented. There are lots of different kinds of reporting. If you don't want to put your life in danger again, so what? That seems damn sensible to me. There's injustice and corruption to be exposed anywhere, even right here in Charleston, I imagine."

He tucked a finger under her chin. "You're also the

woman I love, and that makes you the most important woman on this earth to one man." He searched her face. "Or maybe you don't consider me to be that much of a catch."

"Any woman would be lucky to have you, Cordell, but you know that."

"I only care about one woman. Do you want me, Dinah? You say you're not going back to Afghanistan, but are you ready to stay here in South Carolina and make a home and babies with me and maybe spend your spare time chasing crooks and criminals for a local TV station? Maybe dressing me up in a monkey suit and dragging me to a charity gala from time to time to keep your mama happy?"

Her expression brightened. "Is that a proposal, Cordell Beaufort?"

"Yes, indeed it is, sugar. I'm no Bobby, but I think I'm offering a mighty fine backup plan. What do you think?"

"I think you're crazy as a loon to want me in my current state of mind and to propose when I must look like a train wreck, but I accept. And just so you know, you're not a last resort, Cord. This is the smartest decision I ever made."

"It's for damned sure the best one I ever made," he said. "Now if you don't mind, I'm going to kiss you and crawl back into bed before I pass out cold." He grinned. "But fair warning, sugar…give me a day or two and I'm dragging you into this bed with me. This old hospital can use a little scandalous behavior to shake things up. You with me?"

"Always."

There it was, he thought as he drifted back to sleep. The conviction and certainty was finally back in Dinah's voice. And damned if he hadn't helped put it there.

Epilogue

Cord paced the back of the chapel, sweat beading on his brow. Where the devil was she? Had this whole wedding thing been too good to be true? Dinah was already twenty minutes late and nowhere in sight. Even Dorothy Davis was beginning to look just the teensiest bit nervous, though she murmured reassurances with her usual aplomb.

"She'll be here any minute," she promised Cord.

"Of course she will," Marshall said gruffly. "Though I have to say this isn't a bit like her."

"Stop it!" his wife ordered in a hushed voice. "Don't get Cord any more nervous than he already is."

"At least she never stood me up at the altar," Bobby murmured under his breath.

Cord knew the crack was meant to lighten the tension, but he scowled at his brother. "Would you just shut your mouth?"

Bobby grinned. "Hey, you're the one who insisted on marrying an unpredictable woman. I know where my wife is. She's inside sitting in the front row."

"Okay, everybody, hush," Maggie ordered. "Dinah will be here. She is not about to miss her own wedding."

"Then where the hell is she?" Cord muttered.

Just then he heard the roar of a motorcycle tearing through the Saturday afternoon downtown traffic. "Dear God in heaven," he said as the candy-apple-red motorcycle whipped around a corner with Tommy Lee driving and Dinah clinging to her brother for dear life.

"Sorry," she said, leaping off the back as it skidded to a halt in front of Cord. "I was covering a story outside of town and my car broke down. Thank heaven, I caught up with Tommy Lee as he was about to leave the house."

"And you couldn't have gone to pick her up in a car?" Dorothy asked her son indignantly. "What were you thinking?"

Tommy Lee shrugged. "It was an emergency and Laurie had already left for the church in my car. Dinah flatly refused to ride in my pickup. Can't say that I blame her. I was hauling lumber back from Savannah for the floors out at Covington. It's a mess."

"Actually the motorcycle was kind of a thrill," Dinah claimed, grinning at Cord. "I think we should get one, unless Mother and Daddy will agree to loan us theirs from time to time."

"Are we going to stand around out here all day and argue the merits of owning a motorcycle?" Cord grumbled. "I was hoping to get married sometime today."

Dinah pressed a soothing kiss to his cheek. "Me, too," she assured him. "Give me ten minutes."

Her mother regarded her with dismay. "You can't possibly be ready in ten minutes. This is your wedding, Dinah. You're not going out for burgers and fries."

"Stop fussing, Mother. Between you and Maggie,

you'll have me whipped into shape in no time. You're both magicians when it comes to hair and makeup."

Cord gave her a resigned look. "Is this the way it's always going to be? You're going to be chasing after some big story and nearly miss all the important occasions in our life?"

"I promise I'll be on time for the birth of our children," she teased. "Will that do?"

Cord finally felt the tension in his shoulders ease. "I suppose it'll have to. I'll go inside and tell the guests the ceremony will be in a half hour."

"I'll do that," Bobby said, giving his shoulder a squeeze. "Maybe you should have a drink."

Cord's gaze followed Dinah as she headed for the choir room where her wedding dress was waiting. "I don't need a drink," he told his brother. "I have everything I need now."

"You scared Cord half to death," Dinah's mother scolded as she lowered the wedding gown carefully over Dinah's head.

"It was good for him," Maggie claimed. "He was getting entirely too complacent."

Dinah ignored both of them and stared at herself in the mirror with a sense of shock. After years of wearing mostly black, she was stunned by the image of herself in sleek white satin. The gown was the simplest one she'd been able to find, a slim sheath that pooled at her feet with just the barest hint of a train. Even so, for the first time in her life, she felt more like a woman than a tough-as-nails journalist. A Southern woman, she thought as her mother handed her the bouquet of lily-of-the-valley and white roses with its trailing ribbons.

"You're breathtaking," her mother said with a satisfied sigh.

"Absolutely glowing," Maggie confirmed.

Dinah winked at her friend. "Want to hold the bouquet so you can get the feel of it? I'm tossing it straight to you."

"Don't you dare," Maggie said. "I'm not ready to get married."

"Neither was I," Dinah told her. "Things have a way of happening when you least expect them."

"Not to me," Maggie insisted.

"What about Warren?"

"Bad idea," Maggie said succinctly.

Dinah regarded her with dismay. "But I thought things were going so well. What happened?"

"I guess once he dug deep enough into my psyche, he didn't like what he found," Maggie said with a shrug. "No big deal. There are plenty of fish in the sea."

Dinah thought of the gorgeous, impudent man she'd met weeks ago when she'd gone searching for Bobby in Atlanta. Cord or Bobby would certainly be able to track him down for her. What was his name? Josh something? Parker, that was it. Josh Parker.

Pleased with her plan, she gave Maggie's hand a squeeze. "You don't need plenty of men. One will do. And I think I know just the one."

"Would you stop matchmaking on your wedding day?" Maggie grumbled. "Concentrate on marrying Cord and living happily-ever-after."

"Haven't you heard? I excel at multitasking," Dinah responded. She reached for her mother's hand. "I learned from a master."

"Then let's go get you married," her mother said. "After that, you can multitask to your heart's content."

But minutes later at the front of the church, Dinah gazed into Cord's eyes and promptly forgot everything except this man and the vows he was saying with such solemn sincerity. In that instant, she knew she'd never, ever need another backup plan. All she'd ever need was Cordell Beaufort.

And maybe a cherry-red motorcycle.

* * * * *

*Please turn the page for a sneak peek at
the second book in Sherryl's*
LOW COUNTRY TRILOGY,
*FLIRTING WITH DISASTER,
on sale in December 2005
from MIRA Books!*

As interventions went, this one pretty much sucked. Not that Maggie knew a whole lot about interventions, having never been addicted to much of anything with the possible exception of making truly lousy choices in men. She was fairly certain, though, that having only three people sitting before her with anxious expressions—one of them the very man responsible for her current state of mind—was not the way this sort of thing ought to work.

Then again, Warren Blake, Ph.D., should know. He'd probably done hundreds of interventions for his alcohol- or drug-addicted clients. Hell, maybe he'd even done a few for women he'd dumped, like Maggie. Maybe that's how he'd built up his practice, the louse.

"Magnolia Forsythe, are you listening to a word we're saying?" Dinah Davis Beaufort demanded impatiently, a worried frown etched on her otherwise perfect face.

Maggie regarded her best friend—her *former* best friend, she decided in that instant—with a scowl. "No." She didn't want to hear anything these three had to say. Every one of them had played a role in sending her into this depression. She doubted they had any expertise that would drag her out of it.

"I told you she was going to hate this," Cordell Beaufort said.

Of everyone there, Cord looked the most relaxed, the most normal, Maggie concluded. In fact, he had the audacity to give her a wink. Since he was yet another one of the reasons she was in this dark state of mind, she ignored the wink and concentrated on identifying all the escape routes from this room. Not that a woman should have to leave her own damn living room to get any peace. She ought to be able to kick the well-meaning intruders out, but she'd tried that and not a one of them had budged. Perhaps she ought to consider telling them whatever they wanted to hear so they'd go away.

"I don't care if she does hate it," Dinah said, her expression grim. "We have to convince her to stop moping around in this house. It's not healthy. She needs to get out and do something. This project of ours is perfect. If she doesn't want to help us with that, then she at least ought to remember that she has a business to run. She has a life to live."

"What life is that?" Maggie inquired with faint curiosity. "The one I had before Warren here decided I wasn't his type and dumped me two weeks before our wedding? Or the humiliating one I have now, facing all my friends and trying to explain? Or perhaps you're referring to my pitiful and unsuccessful attempt to seduce Cord before you waltzed back into town and claimed him for yourself?"

Of all of them, only Warren had the grace to look chagrined. "Maggie, you know it would never have worked with us," he explained with great patience. "I'm just the one who had the courage to say it."

"Well, you picked a damn fine time to figure it out,"

she said. "What kind of psychologist are you that you couldn't recognize something like our complete in- compatibility a year before the wedding or even six months before the wedding?"

Warren regarded her with an unblinking gaze. "We were only engaged for a few weeks, Maggie. You were the one who was in a rush to get married."

"I was in love with you!" she practically shouted, ir- ritated by his determination to be logical when she was an emotional wreck. "Why would I want to waste time on a long engagement?"

Warren's patient expression never wavered. It was one of the thing she'd grown to hate about him. He wouldn't fight with her.

"Maggie, as much as I would love to think that you fell head over heels in love with me in a heartbeat, we both know the rush was all about keeping up with Dinah and Cord. The minute they got married, you started getting panicky. We'd already stopped seeing each other after just a few mostly disastrous dates, but you decided we should give it another chance."

"I was being open-minded," she countered. "Isn't that what the sensible women you so admire do?"

Cord tried unsuccessfully to swallow a chuckle. Warren and Dinah frowned at him.

"I have to say, I think Warren is right," Dinah chimed in. "I think you latched on to Warren as if he were the last life-raft in the ocean."

"Oh, what do you know?" Maggie retorted. "You and Cord are so into each other, you barely know any- one else is around."

"We're here, aren't we?" Dinah asked calmly. "We know you're in trouble and we want to help."

"Who invited you?" Maggie responded sourly. "I don't need the three of you sitting here with these gloom-and-doom expressions on your faces trying to plan out my life. Hell, Dinah, you're the one who talked Warren into going out with me in the first place. Considering how things turned out, I should hate you for that."

In fact, she was pretty darn irritated about it. If it hadn't been for Dinah's meddling, Maggie would never in a million years have fallen—even half-heartedly—for a man like Warren Blake. He was rock-steady and dependable, quite a contrast to the men she'd always been attracted to in the past. Men like Cord Beaufort, as a matter of fact. Dark, dangerous and sexy.

If she were being totally honest, she'd have to admit that she'd known all along she was settling for someone safe with Warren. He might not rock her world, but he'd never hurt her either. At least that's how her muddled thinking had rationalized the relationship. As it turned out, she'd been wrong about that. He had hurt her, but mostly it was her pride he'd devastated, not her heart. If a man like Warren couldn't truly love her, who would?

That's what she'd been pondering inside her Charleston carriage house for a few weeks now. If she wasn't interesting enough, sexy enough, or lovable enough for Warren, then she might as well resign herself to spinsterhood. He was her last chance. Her safe bet. Sort of the way Bobby Beaufort, Cord's brother, had been Dinah's backup plan.

Even as Maggie was struck by that notion, she realized she should have seen the handwriting on the wall.

Wasn't she the one who'd told Dinah that *safe* was never going to be enough? If it wasn't good enough for Dinah, why had Maggie ever thought it would work for her?

"Mind if I say something?" Cord asked, his gaze filled with surprising compassion.

Maggie shrugged. "Suit yourself."

"Here's the way I see it," Cord said.

He spoke in that slow, lazy drawl that had once sent goose bumps down Maggie's spine till she'd realized he'd never want anyone except Dinah.

"Nothing's stopping you from sitting in this house of yours all the livelong day, if that's what you want to do," Cord said. "Your art and antique gallery can pretty much run itself, thanks to those competent employees you've hired. And if it doesn't, so what? You've got a nice little trust fund from your daddy. You don't need to do a thing."

Maggie bristled. She'd never liked thinking of herself as the kind of spoiled little rich girl who didn't need to work for a living. She'd poured her heart and soul into making a go of Images, just to prove she was her own person. She'd never treated it like a hobby. She'd taken pride in the success of the high-end shop that catered as much to Charleston's wealthiest citizens as it did to the tourists who came through the historic district every day. As for her employees, she didn't know where Cord had gotten the crazy idea they were competent. She'd be lucky if they didn't run the place into bankruptcy.

If Cord was aware of her growing indignation, he ignored it. "Maggie's a smart woman. I think we should let her decided for herself how she wants to spend her days," Cord continued mildly, aiming his words at

Dinah and Warren and leaving Maggie to draw her own conclusions. "She can go back to work running her business, if that's what matters to her. She can come on out and help us with this project we've been telling her about and make a real difference in someone's life. Or she can sit right here and feel sorry for herself. It's her choice. I think once we clear out and give her some space, she'll make the right one."

Maggie saw the trap at once. If she did what she wanted to do and hung around here wallowing in self-pity and Häagen-Dazs ice cream, they'd worry, but they'd let her do it and they wouldn't think any the less of her because they loved her. But in her heart, she'd see herself for the ridiculously self-indulgent idiot she was being. She'd lost a man. So what? Warren wasn't the first and undoubtedly he wouldn't be the last, despite her current vow to avoid all males from here to eternity.

"Tell me again about this stupid project," she said grudgingly.

Cord, bless his devious little heart, bit back a grin. "We're going to be building a house for someone who needs one. The church got the idea, a benefactor donated the land, and the preacher asked me to put together a volunteer crew. Dinah and her mama are in charge of raising money for whatever building supplies we can't get donated."

"What do you expect me to do?" Maggie asked suspiciously.

"What you're told," Dinah said with a glint of amusement in her eyes. "Same as me. It'll be a refreshing change for us. At least that's what Cord says.

We'll be hammering and painting right alongside everyone else."

Maggie turned her gaze on Warren. "And you?"

"That's up to you," he replied. "I said I'd help, but I'll stay away if you want me to."

Maggie wasn't sure Warren had any essential skills for building a house, so sending him away might not be much of a loss, but why bother? Maybe it was time to show all of Charleston that she wasn't devastated by her broken engagement. It was past time she held her head up high and behaved like the strong woman she'd always considered herself to be.

"Do whatever you want to do," she said indifferently.

"Then you'll help?" Dinah asked.

"I'll help," Maggie agreed. "If I don't, who knows what sort of place you'll build. Everyone knows I'm the one with taste in this crowd."

"We're building a three-bedroom bungalow with the basic necessities for a single mom with three kids," Cord warned. "Not a mansion."

"You're building a house," Maggie retorted emphatically. "I'll turn it into a home."

But just as she said the words, Maggie spotted the satisfied glint in Dinah's eyes and wondered if she wasn't making the second worst mistake she'd made all day. The first had been opening the door to these three.

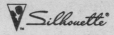

USA TODAY Bestselling Author

LAURIE BRETON

When Faith questions her cousin's suicide, no one
in the fading mill town of Serenity, Maine, wants to
face the truth. As a web of drugs, violence and deceit
closes in on her, Faith has to rely on a man she can
barely trust to help her outwit a faceless enemy.

LETHAL LIES

*Available the first week of March 2005
wherever paperbacks are sold!*

www.MIRABooks.com

MLB2151

SHERRYL WOODS

32048 DESTINY UNLEASHED	___ $6.50 U.S.	___ $7.99 CAN.
66955 ALONG CAME TROUBLE	___ $6.50 U.S.	___ $7.99 CAN.
66901 ASK ANYONE	___ $6.50 U.S.	___ $7.99 CAN.
66815 ABOUT THAT MAN	___ $6.50 U.S.	___ $7.99 CAN.
66722 FLAMINGO DINER	___ $6.50 U.S.	___ $7.99 CAN.
66600 ANGEL MINE	___ $5.99 U.S.	___ $6.99 CAN.
66542 AFTER TEX	___ $5.99 U.S.	___ $6.99 CAN.

(limited quantities available)

TOTAL AMOUNT	$ _____
POSTAGE & HANDLING	$ _____
($1.00 FOR 1 BOOK, 50¢ for each additional)	
APPLICABLE TAXES*	$ _____
TOTAL PAYABLE	$ _____

(check or money order—please do not send cash)

MIRA®

www.MIRABooks.com

MSHW0305BL